CW00431344

Shattered Pieces can Still Shine

- Georgie's story

By Gloria Eveleigh

CHAPTER 1

1950

Daddy Days

"Mummy, what time will Daddy get home?""Three-and-a-half-year-old Georgie was so absorbed in looking at the colourful pictures in her favourite picture storybook about a dancer, that she hadn't lifted her eyes as she'd spoken, so her mummy's harsh words shocked her to involuntary tears.

"Bother! Now look what you've made me do. I'm already behind in getting our tea ready on time!"

Georgie, as young as she was, had watched how hard Mummy worked to make ends meet. They didn't have meat every day. Mummy said it was too expensive. But when Daddy was there, Mummy liked to make especially tasty meals and would always use the more expensive ingredients.

Mummy's tone prompted the little girl to look up just as the lid of the meat pie landed half on and half off its meaty base. She saw the angry look and the brightening pink cheeks that signalled the reaction her innocent question had triggered.

"You made me jump, Georgie!"

Georgie, who had inherited the same thick, blonde, wavy hair as her mummy, Florrie, became immediately distraught as she sat there on the flagstone kitchen floor, tears running down her crumpled face and dripping onto the picture of the little girl who had grown up to become a dancer. Georgie dreamed of becoming a dancer too, but this was the last thing on her mind as she let her hurt emotions flow freely.

"Oh, no don't cry, Baby. I'm so sorry. I didn't mean to let out my frustration on you."

As Mummy bent down and encompassed her in a floury hug and a thick mop of blonde hair, Georgie leaned into the ample bosom and drank in the comfort it gave even though it threatened her ability to breathe.

"Now what did you ask me, Babe?"

Georgie sniffed up the tears and tried again.

"I just wondered what time Daddy will arrive. I looked on the calendar and saw that it's Tuesday, so I know it's a 'Daddy Day'."

"You're a clever girl, Georgie, being able to read a calendar, and not even at school yet," said Mummy, simultaneously wiping her daughter's tears away with the corner of her bright, flower-patterned apron.

The little girl beamed. In truth, Georgie spent most of her time alone with her mummy.

"Sometimes I think I'm chatting to another grown-up when I chat with you, Babe," Mummy often told her, and Georgie felt ten feet tall every time she heard it.

"But what about telling the time?" Mummy asked with a twinkle in her soft, hazel eyes.

Georgie jumped up from the floor and bounced excitedly on the spot.

"Test me, Mummy. Please test me!"

"Okay, Babe. What is the time when the big hand points straight up and the little hand points to the number seven?"

Georgie sensed her mummy's eyes on her as she searched her young mind for the correct answer.

"Yesss!" she said, punching the air and smiling from ear to ear.
"Don't tell me you know the answer already? I can see by that sparkle in those big hazel eyes of yours that you feel pleased with yourself," said Mummy, grinning as widely as her little daughter.

"Seven o'clock. It's seven o'clock, Mummy."

Mother and daughter spontaneously clapped and cheered.

"Well done! Well, at seven o'clock you can go out into the sunshine and watch for Daddy at the garden gate. Then as soon as you see him coming up the lane on his bicycle, shout to let me know and I can put this pie in the oven so it will be ready the moment he gets in. Then you can run to meet him."

Georgie loved it that Mummy never worried about her being outside alone. Their white-walled, slate-roofed cottage was perched on a gently rolling fell at the edge of the sprawling village of Ousby in Cumberland. Mummy said that this was a safe place, even though their nearest neighbour was a half mile away down the narrow lane that led to the compact village store-cum-post office. Very few people passed by the cottage, and Georgie had heard Mummy telling her daddy, Alfie, that she was glad because it prevented tongues wagging when he arrived on Tuesday evening and didn't leave until Thursday. Georgie couldn't really work out what Mummy meant by that but she could see it pleased her daddy so that was fine with her.

"Okay, Mummy. How long is it till seven o'clock, please?"

"Just fifteen minutes so you'd better get watching that living room clock."

Georgie kept her eye on the clock, stepping from one foot to the other as the big hand moved slowly towards the twelve. At seven o'clock sharp, she ran to the front door and, leaving it wide open, she rushed down the narrow garden path to the wooden gate. She stepped up on to the bottom rung, from where she'd have a clear view all the way down the lane. As

she waited, she tried to distract herself by listening to the buzzing of the several bees happily collecting nectar from the blue flowers on the Ceanothus bushes that marked the perimeter of the garden. Mummy had taught her the name and she remembered it. She didn't take her eyes off the lane. Georgie knew that her daddy had a long cycle ride from where he built council houses in Penrith, nine miles away, and she also knew that by the time he reached the bottom of, what they affectionately called Half-Mile Lane, he'd be more than happy to get off his bike and walk the slope with his little daughter riding on his saddle.

"I can see him, Mummy" pierced the air like a foghorn at sea, followed by excited screeches as Georgie jumped off the gate, opened it wide and ran down the slope at an ever-increasing speed towards her beloved daddy.

"Daddy, Daddy," accompanied the violent waving of her small but sturdy arms as she got nearer. By now, Daddy, a broad but tall twenty-eight-year-old man, had dismounted and was climbing the slope towards Georgie, guiding his bike beside him with one hand and returning Georgie's waves with the other.

"Ey up, Georgie. Slow down. Tha'll fall if tha runs any faster!"

But Georgie kept running until she landed in her daddy's one-armed hug, almost causing him to lose his balance.

"Daddy, Daddy, you're home," she screeched between trying to catch her breath.

Bending at the knees to reach down to his shorter-than-average daughter, her daddy hugged and kissed her before lifting her with ease onto the saddle of his bicycle.

"Hold on t' handlebar now, Bairn. I don't want thee falling off and getting hurt or yer mam might make us go without us tea," the big man grinned.

Georgie giggled as her daddy pretended to huff and puff all the way up the slope until they reached the open front door and the delicious smell of hot meat pie.

"Wherst that woman o'mine?" he shouted playfully whilst lifting Georgie gently to the ground just in time to catch the excited Mummy who seemed to fly out of the open door and into his open arms.

Georgie loved this bit of the proceedings when her mummy and daddy held each other close, kissing between their repeated words of 'I love thee' and 'I've missed thee'. It's when she saw Mummy at her happiest and when she herself felt at her most secure.

This weekly scene had been repeated ever since Georgie could remember and it always heralded two days of fun and glorious happiness for this excited little girl. She sometimes noticed Mummy looked a bit edgy during those two days but thought that this was because she was thinking about the five days that would follow without Daddy when, like Georgie, she would miss him.

After their tea, Mummy filled the kitchen sink with warm water before she stood Georgie on the table and undressed her. While Mummy popped upstairs to the airing cupboard on the small landing of the two-up, two-down cottage, Daddy lifted Georgie over to the wooden draining board, tickling her under her arms as they went and then placing the giggling child down with her feet dangling in the deep stone sink. By then, Mummy had returned with a soft towel and face flannel, and Georgie's cotton nightdress.

"Here, catch this," she'd shout playfully.

"I'm not a goalie, our Lass," as Daddy pretended to miss it, only securing it after a pretend juggle.

This weekly ritual was something that never failed to warm Georgie's little heart.
"Bubbles now, Daddy."

"Hmmm. So, what's tha payment for this bubble-blowing, Young Georgie?"

Her answer was always the same.

"I'll go straight to bed and stay fast asleep till the morning."

At this point Daddy always turned to face Mummy.

5

"Mammy, what does tha think? Is that a good enough deal for me to demonstrate my expert bubble-blowing skill?"

"Most definitely," replied Mummy without hesitation, at which point she would join Daddy at the sink to each rub their hands vigorously on the wet soap, make an O shape with their fingers and gently blow. Georgie's eyes opened wide as she waited for the magic, and then clapped her hands together to burst the resulting rainbow spheres. The 'ooos' and 'ahhhhs' and 'hoorays' became loud and boisterous enough to frighten away any nearby foxes and badgers that may have been quietly passing through the dusk-covered, tree-lined back garden.

After all the fun and laughter, and once dried and tucked under her bedclothes with teddy cuddled close, Georgie would always fall quickly into a peaceful and contented sleep. The fact that Mummy and Daddy would soon be sleeping in their big, soft double bed right next door to her small front bedroom added to her sense of security.

The night wasn't always so peaceful for Florrie. She often woke to the flailing arms, laboured breaths and trembling wet body of her bedpartner, realising that yet again Alfie was in the throes of a nightmare. He'd been diagnosed with Battle Fatigue from his war experiences, and it wasn't unusual for Florrie to hear his screams in the middle of the night. At first, he would not recognise where he was, and Florrie would patiently hold him close until his trembling subsided, and he gradually returned to himself.

"There, there, Darling. It's alright. I'm here," she would whisper in his ear as she attempted to sooth him as she would a distressed baby, gently stroking his brown hair and face. She never minded comforting her beloved Alfie, no matter how much sleep loss this caused her. She knew that his wife, Mavis, had little energy left for her husband after an exhausting day looking after their three young children. She also knew that Alfie had only married Mavis after coming home from the war to find she had, unbeknown to him, been in the family way when he left her on his eighteenth birthday in 1941. It was a shocking homecoming for a twenty-two-year-old man to find he had a four-year old child, and Florrie knew he'd felt obliged to marry Mavis for the sake of that child.

If the truth be known, Florrie had never stopped loving Alfie since they'd been boyfriend and girlfriend at school when they were only thirteen. She had just moved up to Ousby from South London so that her mother could

take up a teaching role at the local school. Florrie didn't really mind being the 'other woman' either. How could she when Alfie had given her the most beautiful child she could ever have hoped for? Georgie was her raison d'être, her source of true happiness. The two days a week that they were able to spend with Alfie were, in many ways, a bonus for Florrie. Her only fear was that he would wake Georgie in the night with his screams and frighten the child.

Crash! Florrie and Alfie woke with a start.

The morning sun shone through their window even though it was only six o'clock.

"What on earth was that?" Alfie asked to the vacant side of the bed. Florrie was already halfway downstairs, having peeked into Georgie's empty bedroom on the way.

"Sorry, Mummy. I tried not to wake you, but I lost my balance as I was standing on the chair to reach the jam," came Georgie's distressed little voice.

Georgie had heard Mummy running downstairs and into the kitchen. She had peaked from behind the larder door and watched as Mummy noticed the loaf of bread, packet of margarine, plate and knife sitting on the table. She realised Mummy couldn't seem to fathom where her voice was coming from until she looked in Georgie's direction and her confusion seemed to disappear.

"Oh, Georgie, are you hurt?"

"No, but the jar of jam is, Mummy," said the little girl as she hobbled out of the pantry.

"What on earth are you doing up at this hour of the morning? And why are you hobbling? Oh no, you have hurt yourself, haven't you? Georgie, what were you doing?"

"I'm sorry. It's just that I woke up and the sun was shining, and I was so excited about going out with you and Daddy today that I thought I'd get up and make the sandwiches to save time."

7

Georgie rubbed her swollen knee as she waited to see if Mummy was going to be cross about the jam or more worried about her injury. She saw the scowl change to concern and was relieved when she found herself in a big hug as Mummy lifted her onto the draining board to get a closer look at the swelling.

"Nothing a little arnica cream won't cure, Baby, but it could have been much worse if you'd cut yourself on the broken jar of jam. I know you were only trying to help but one of these days, your impatience will get you into real trouble."

"Sorry, Mummy. But what time are we going out? Will we go to the river like last week? Most of all, I'd like to go to the seaside. I've never seen the seaside. But I don't mind going for a picnic in the fells, especially if we see the big cows again, and if we go on the swings and slide in the park ..."

"Slow down, slow down. If you fidget any more, you'll end up falling off the draining board and getting a worse injury," said Mummy as she picked her wriggling daughter up and placed her gently on the flagstones.

By now, Daddy had joined them and was carefully clearing up the mix of broken glass and sticky jam from the pantry floor. He had followed Mummy downstairs and, seeing that Georgie was not badly hurt, and her mam was busy attending to their little daughter, he had got on with attending to the mess in his usual practical way.

Coming out of the pantry with a dustpan full of sticky glass, Daddy looked directly at Georgie.

"Why aren't yer dressed yit, Young Lady? Me pal, Gerald from work, is picking us up at ten o'clock in his car. He owes me a favour, so I asked him if he'd be able to give us a lift to Penrith to catch train to Ullswater Lake, but he said Ullswater is the same distance from here as Penrith is, so he's driving us straight there."

"Hooray!" Georgie yelled as she bounced out of the kitchen door, only to return almost immediately with "Will I be able to paddle, Daddy?"

"Aye, Georgie. You can paddle from t' beach we're going to."

"Yippee!"

When Georgie returned for a second time, both Mummy and Daddy were still looking at the doorway. They laughed as her face re-appeared.

"Should I take my swimsuit, Mummy?"

"No. Just wear your shorts. You can paddle in those."

"Whoopee!"

Georgie knew her mummy and daddy were listening to her light footsteps as she ascended the stairs and entered her bedroom. She knew they would be shaking their heads and saying,

"Where does she get her energy from?"

She also guessed that Mummy would say to Daddy, "She gets it from you, Alfie – her impatience too."

She heard them both giggling and could picture Daddy tickling Mummy just as he often tickled Georgie, and Mummy trying to push him away just as Georgie always did. Georgie stood still listening for the inevitable silence and she smiled knowing for sure that her parents were kissing.

Gerald turned out to be a quietly spoken but jovial man, shorter than Alfie and originally from London. His unruly flock of red hair danced on his head as he kept the whole family laughing all the way to the beach at Ullswater where he dropped them off, waving from his open car window as he left to return home.

"I like Gerald, Mummy. Do you?" asked Georgie as the three made their way onto the beach and placed their belongings on a soft grassy bank.

"Hey cheeky, its Uncle Gerald to you. But yes, he's lovely, Georgie. His accent reminds me of my dad who used to make me laugh when I was a little girl like you, living in London."

"Oh, so tha likes Gerald, dost tha, Florrie?" said Alfie as he gave her a grinning wink.

Georgie noticed that her mummy's cheeks went pink as she laughingly pushed her daddy onto the grass to get her own back for the earlier tickle in the kitchen. Georgie jumped on top and quickly it became a tickling battle between all three until five minutes later they ended up slumped side by side, trying to get their breath and cool off from the scrummage.

The day continued in the same happy vein as all three paddled, ate their picnic, and lay soaking up the warm sunshine to the sound of gentle laughter from the few other groups on the narrow beach. At five o'clock, they walked to the train station licking ice cream cones from a little beach kiosk as they went. By the time the Penrith train arrived, Georgie had fallen asleep leaning against her mummy on the bench they'd occupied.

Alfie lifted his little daughter into his arms and carried her onto the train, where she remained fast asleep, and stayed that way until he lifted her from the taxi they'd got from Penrith to Ousby and placed her gently in her bed fully clothed.

"It's not worth waking t' bairn just to change her into her nightdress, Florrie. She'll be areet as she is. Anyway, all that sunshine has made me feel sexy so it will be good to have t' evening to ourselves."

Florrie didn't object.

Summer for Georgie slid by in a haze of fun and laughter. Now the nights were drawing in and the leaves on the trees were starting to change colour, so Georgie could no longer watch for her daddy coming home because it was dark. Instead, she had to content herself with listening for the creaking sound of the garden gate before she rushed to the front door, opened it before the key got anywhere near the lock, and jumped into Daddy's waiting arms, closely followed by Mummy. Tea was always a cooked meal and was ready and waiting, knowing that the nine-mile cycle ride for Daddy would have made for a very hungry man.

As all three sat around the kitchen table and tucked into their beef stew and dumplings, conversation flowed freely as usual.

"I'm worried about you, Alfie," said Mummy with a half-full mouth.

"Worried about what, Our Lass?"

"Cycling all that way in the dark. The evenings are quite cold now and it's a long way down those dark lanes after a hard day's work."

"Well, as it happens, you've no need to worry anymore, because me pal, Gerald, has offered me a lift to and from work when I'm here. He'll meet me outside t' village store each morning and drop me back here in t' evening."

"That's kind of him. Will you pay towards his petrol?"

Daddy shook his head.

"Nae, he won't let me. He says he's doing t' journey anyway, so it'll cost him no extra if I'm in t' car with him. I think he's glad of t' company, cos he lives on his own."

"Well, the least you can do is invite him in for supper. As you say, he's probably lonely, and it will be nice for him not to have to make the effort of cooking for himself on Tuesdays."

Georgie had been vigorously nodding throughout her mummy's suggestion and now she could no longer resist joining in the conversation, even though she knew that it was rude for children to do so.

"Please, Daddy, let Uncle Gerald come to supper. He's so funny and you know he makes all of us laugh."

"Well now, how can I resist the pleas of me two blonde-haired beauties? That's actually a good idea, Our Florrie. I'll see what he says."

So, the decision was made and from then on, every Tuesday evening Gerald came in for his supper. As soon as supper was finished and he had helped Mummy and Daddy with the washing up, he'd say his thank yous, hug Mummy and Georgie and kiss them on the cheek, shake hands with his pal, and then return to his car for the short drive to his home. Occasionally Mummy and Daddy managed to persuade him to stay for a game of Ludo before Georgie had to go to bed.

"Please stay, Uncle Gerald, Ludo is always more fun with four people playing."

"I think maybe there's an ulterior motive in this, Young Georgie. Maybe the possibility of a later bedtime than usual?" grinned Gerald.

Georgie's cheeks flushed as everyone laughed, but she soon joined in despite her embarrassment at being found out.

So, the weekly routine was set, and it brightened up the winter days when outings were no longer possible, except for visits to the swings down in the village, or short walks across the fells.

Georgie celebrated her fourth birthday in November, staring into the flames of the large, sparking bonfire and screeching with pleasure at the exploding colours of the fireworks Daddy let off in the garden. Uncle Gerald attended, adding to the little girl's laughter as he screeched alongside her. A scooter from Mummy and Daddy, and a pink tutu from Uncle Gerald, plastered a permanent smile on the four-year-old's face.
"Thank you, Uncle Gerald. I will wear my tutu to practise my dancing every single day 'cos I'm going to be a dancer in a theatre when I grow up, you know."

"Are you now, Georgie? Well, if that's your goal in life, I'm sure a determined young lady like yourself will definitely achieve it."

Georgie hugged Uncle Gerald for the third time since he gave her the present.

Then, one Monday morning not long after her birthday, Georgie woke up to the sound of retching. She leapt out of her bed and charged into the bathroom where Mummy had her head over the toilet.

"I'm here Mummy, I'm here," as she held her mummy's blonde hair out of the way.

"Thank you, Baby," came the words between the retches.
After a few minutes, Mummy pulled the chain and sat back on her haunches, wiping her mouth with a piece of toilet paper.

"Your face has gone white, Mummy. Shall I fetch you a glass of water while you get back in bed?"

12

"No, it's okay, Sweet Girl. I'm fine now so I'll come downstairs and have a piece of dry toast and a cup of tea. No need to worry yourself."

"No, you're ill. You must go to bed like you make me do when I'm ill."

"I'm not ill, Darling. I must have reacted to something I ate. See, I'm fine now."

Georgie was unconvinced but she accepted the reassurance, especially as the colour was gradually coming back into Mummy's cheeks. However, the small child insisted on supporting her mummy's arm as they slowly made their way downstairs.

"Thank you, Georgie. You are a very caring little girl and I'm dead proud of you."

Georgie beamed as she pulled the kitchen chair out for Mummy to sit on. But the next morning the same thing happened. This time Georgie went as ashen as Mummy.

"Maybe you need a doctor, Mummy?" she suggested as she held the blonde hair out of the way.

"No, I feel better already, Baby. It's honestly nothing to worry about."

It played on Georgie's mind all morning, until Mummy took some strips of gummed coloured paper out of her sewing drawer.

"The bacon pudding is steaming away over the saucepan and the vegetables are prepared ready for supper, so let's make some paper chains to decorate the house for Christmas."

Immediately, the bouncy Georgie returned. She loved the bright colours of the paper strips.

"What do we do with the coloured strips, Mummy? When's Christmas? Will we be able to hang the paper chains up as soon as they are finished?"

"Whooha, slow down, Child. Christmas is still nearly four weeks away and you know we don't hang up the decorations until one week before

the big day, when we also put the Christmas tree up and have our own Christmas day with Daddy."

"Oh yes. I remember last year. After we finished putting the decorations up, we visited Santa's Grotto at the village hall. Do you remember he gave me my picture book about the dancer?"

"How can I forget? You've kept on about being a dancer ever since."

"Yes, and I will be one day. Uncle Gerald believes in me, Mummy. He said he has no doubt that I will do it because I'm very deterred."

"I think the word is determined," Mummy giggled.

Georgie joined in with the giggling while she watched Mummy make a hoop with a strip of coloured paper and then thread a second strip through the hole and stick the ends together to make a second hoop.

"You don't need glue, Baby. You just lick the shiny bit at the end of each strip and stick it to the other end like I did."

A couple of hours later, the two were still sitting on the floor surrounded by several yards of paper chain when Georgie heard the creak of the front gate.

"Daddy's home," she screeched, jumping over the pile of decorations, and heading towards the front door. By then, she'd forgotten all about Mummy's sickness episodes and was completely focussed on showing Daddy and Uncle Gerald the result of their afternoon's hard work. Most of teatime was spent with Georgie explaining in detail how the paper chains were made. Uncle Gerald stayed for a game of Snakes and Ladders and the game went on so long and with so much laughter that Georgie didn't get to bed until much later than usual. As a result, she slept in the next morning, but Mummy looked all right and was smiling when Georgie got up, so she assumed that her mummy probably hadn't been sick and didn't worry for the rest of the day.

Over the next few days Mummy was up early and downstairs in the kitchen when Georgie woke up. She thought she heard retching but by the time she got downstairs, Mummy was wiping her mouth with a handkerchief, so Georgie couldn't really be sure.

14

Georgie now woke up earlier and earlier each morning to rush downstairs to tick another day off the calendar, followed by a ritual count out loud with Mummy of the number of days left till their special Christmas. Daddy joined in when he was there on Wednesday and Thursday mornings.

Then came the day they'd all been waiting for. They spent the morning buying the Christmas tree, and the afternoon decorating it and hanging the paperchains that Georgie and Mummy had made. At teatime, they sat around the kitchen table that Mummy had covered in a festive tablecloth with matching serviettes. Georgie looked at Daddy and, wide eyes, they watched as Mummy opened the oven. They both inhaled deep breaths as a large platter of crispy golden turkey surrounded by brown-edged roasties passed their expectant noses. They licked their lips with a slurping sound as this was joined by a dish of steaming, butter-covered sprouts and peas. They simultaneously made 'mmmm' sounds when the plate of tiny Yorkshire puddings, and a jug of thick gravy joined the other fragrant food before them. Soon the only sounds to be heard were the slapping of gravy-covered lips and the occasional 'yum'.

When the meal was finished, including Georgie's favourite jelly drowned in Libby's Milk, she looked on the welsh dresser expecting to see the usual three presents wrapped in colourful Christmas paper. There were none. Mummy and Daddy seeing the look on her face, grinned at each other. Then Daddy cleared his throat and moved his hand to cover Mummy's.

"Reight, Bairn, Mammy and I have got a special Christmas present this year – one yer can't yet see or play with. Can yer guess what it might be?"

Georgie crinkled her forehead into a question mark, loving the guessing game. After a short pause, her eyes began to shine as the corners of her mouth climbed upwards towards her rosy cheeks.

"I know, I know. Is it a visit to the seaside?"

"Hey, Baby, that is a really clever answer - but it's wrong."

After two more minutes of Georgie's crinkled forehead, Mummy nodded at Daddy to carry on.

"Georgie, the present is ..." pause for effect while Georgie's eyes opened wider, and her eyebrows made their way towards her hairline ... "a new baby brother or sister."

The blank expression on Georgie's face only lasted for a split second until it was replaced by a huge grin as she leapt over to her parents to give and receive cuddles as she gabbled excitedly.

"Really? You're joking me, right? Am I going to have a baby sister to play dancing with me? I can't believe it. This is the best Christmas present ever."

"I knew you'd be pleased, Baby Girl," grinned Mummy, watching Georgie attempt to pirouette around the kitchen. "But remember, it might be a baby boy. What then?"

"Then I will teach him to be my dance partner."

"Well, I think we should calm down now and have a quiet game of cards before you go to bed," said Mummy while Daddy nodded in agreement.

Georgie noticed a ghost of a scowl cross Mummy's face, but it was so quickly replaced with a smile that the little girl dismissed it.

CHAPTER 2

New Year 1951

Mother and Daughter Rebellion

"Alfie, are you pleased about this new baby?"

Florrie was snuggled in Alfie's lap as he spooned her under the warm bedclothes.

"Aye, Our Lass, of course I am."

"You don't sound too pleased."

"Don't be daft. I was just going off. If yer happy, then I am."

"You didn't look too pleased either. I could see how difficult you found it to appear happy when we were telling Georgie."

"Nowt of t' sort Florrie. Yer happy about it aren't yer?"

"I don't know."

"Look, Florrie, you're talking in riddles. Spit it out will thee, so we can both get some sleep."

"I'm feeling anxious."
Alfie turned on to his back with an impatient sigh.

"Anxious! Does tha always want to talk when we're about to go off? Now just tell us what's bothering thee so we can both get some sleep."

"I'm worried I won't be able to cope with another mouth to feed. I struggle as it is with just Georgie and me, let alone the extra I have to find when you're here."

"But tha does really well. Why don't yer go to sleep now, and everything'll feel fine in t' morning?"

"No, Alfie. This is something we need to talk about. It won't go away in the morning."

Florrie sat up and repositioned the pillow to support her back. Alfie grunted and stayed where he was.

"Calm down, Our Lass. Tha knows I give thee as much as I can. I work overtime five nights a week and sometimes Saturday, too. With Mavis and t' three bairns at home, it's already hard trying to make ends meet."

"And that's another thing. I can't do this on my own. It's not fair that you spend only one full day and two nights with us whilst you're with Mavis and the kids all the rest of the time. I'll need more support. A new baby is hard work."

"Ah, I knew tha'd get around to this. And how am I supposed to spend more time here? Mavis would get suspicious, reightt? The three bairns would get upset, too. My life would be hell."

"I think you've been having your cake and eating it for too long. You've got as much responsibility towards me and the two children as you have to your other family. You told me that you only married Mavis cos, unbeknown to you, she was in the family way when you went away to war, and you came home to find you had a four-year-old child. I get that - it was the honourable thing to do. But you also told me that you loved me. And let's face it, I'm definitely more sympathetic towards you when

18

you have your nightmares. What doesn't add up is that when we met again after all those years since school, you chose to stay with Mavis – the woman you didn't love – and then to make matters worse, you went on to father two more babies with her. How do you think that made me feel? Don't we mean anything to you?"

"Keep your voice down, Our Lass, or you'll wake t' bairn. Look, we're both aeriated. Let's talk about this in t' morning when we're calmer."

"How can we talk about it in the morning? It's Thursday tomorrow and you'll be up at the crack of dawn and rushing down the hill to meet Gerald for your lift to work."

Alfie turned away from Florrie, pulled the covers up to his chin and yawned deeply. Florrie sat still for a few minutes and then, taking her pillow with her, slid down under the covers with a sigh of resignation. But sleep evaded her as she thought through their conversation again and again until she found herself screwing up the corner of the sheet tighter and tighter as her body stiffened and began to tremble to the point of threatening to vibrate her clean off the edge of the bed onto the adjacent rug. When, a short time later, Alfie let out a snore, she was almost at screaming point.

'If I don't get out of this bed, I'm liable to strangle the man in his sleep,' she decided as she moved the covers quietly off herself and twisted into a sitting position, sliding her feet into her slippers as she did so. She stood up carefully, wary of the creaking floorboards and left the room like a burglar creeping away from a crime scene. For that's how it felt to Florrie. She now realised that the man she had loved for so long had been using her for all those years – and with her full consent. And now, that same man was turning his back on her fears for the future. She felt cheap and dirty for the first time in her life.

Two hours later, sitting on a kitchen chair with an empty pot of tea before her, and eyes swollen, red and sore, she heard a tiny creak and knew at once that Alfie was out of bed and would be coming down to find her.

"What are you doing sitting down here in t' middle of night, Our Lass?" looking decidedly nervous.

19

He turned up the gas flame under the kettle and helped himself to a mug from the hooks under the wall cupboard. Lifting the pot from the table, he added a couple of teaspoons full of tealeaves, and stood tapping the spoon on the work surface waiting for the kettle to boil. With every tap of the spoon, the wound-up spring within Florrie tightened and the trembling returned.

'Will he apologise and agree to move in with me? Will I have the courage to end this relationship if not? Will he continue to provide financial support if I do? Am I cutting off my nose to spite my face?' The thoughts were coming as thick and fast as Florrie's heart beats.

'Take deep breaths. Calm yourself down, woman,' she told herself.

The kettle boiled. Alfie picked it up and filled the teapot before he quietly replaced it on the stove. He stirred the tea, replaced its lid and cosy, and lifted it back over to the table with his mug. Sitting down opposite Florrie, he lifted the pot towards her with questioning eyebrows. Florrie shook her head and tried her best to look calm. Alfie filled his mug, blew on the tea to cool it down and took a long slow draught, savouring the taste in his mouth before finally swallowing.

"Okay, Lass. Tell me again exactly what it is tha wants from me."

Florrie tried to speak but it was as if she had been struck dumb as no words would come.

"Look, Florrie, I've got out of me bed to try to sort this out even though I've got work to go to today. Speak up and be done with it will yer."

Alfie's obvious aggravation didn't help Florrie at all. Her head was swimming, and her mouth was dry despite two mugs of tea. Alfie breathed out impatiently.

"Florrie is this some sort of a game yer playing? Cos if it is, it's not funny."

"No, it's not a game," she blurted.

"Then tell me," - avoiding eye contact.

"I want you to leave Mavis and move in with me."

And there it was, the giant sitting between them. Alfie's eyes flamed and his face and neck turned bright red.

"Just what makes yer think I'd leave me real family for thee?"

The bullet ricocheted straight into Florrie's heart leaving it as cold as stone.

"Do you know, Alfie, I really can't imagine what reasons I could possibly have for thinking such a thing. So, I suggest you go get ready for work, take your belongings and get out of here right now."

"I'm warning thee, Florrie, if I do that, it'll be the last time tha'll ever see me again. Nor will tha receive another penny from me."

"So, you would make the children, your children, suffer, would you?"

"That's reight. So, get used to the idea before tha decides what tha wants."

"Oh, believe me I already know what I want and it's not you. And if you care so little about the children, you can forget about ever seeing them again – and that includes the new babe."

"But Florrie ..."

"Out. Get out!"

"Alreight, alreight. Quieten down or tha'll wake t' village. I'll go."

With that, Alfie left the room and within ten minutes was coming downstairs dressed and with his spare set of clothes under his arm. He left, banging the front door behind him. Florrie was paralysed. The room seemed to close in on her.

'What have I done?'

Suddenly her senses were thrown into alert. She could hear a tiny sob from upstairs.

'Oh no! Georgie. Did she hear everything we said?'

Florrie rushed upstairs to find her daughter lying face down on a wet pillow.

Georgie felt herself being picked up by Mummy and put down on her knee. She felt her tears change direction as they traced a tiny stream down her cheeks and dripped into her lap.

"Oh, Baby. My beautiful girl. Don't cry. Please don't cry."

Georgie felt the comfort of Mummy's buxom figure as the cuddly woman pulled her in close, rocking her soothingly.

"Tell me Georgie. Tell Mummy."

"Daddy said he had to leave cos you don't want him anymore. Is that true? Did you make him go? Did you send my daddy away?"

Georgie felt Mummy's heart speed up and her body tense.

"Yes, I did."

Georgie immediately released herself from the hug and began to pound Mummy's chest, screaming as she did so.

"I hate you. I hate you. I want my daddy. Tell him to come back, Mummy. Tell my daddy to come back."

"I can't do that, Baby. I'm so sorry. I know you don't understand, but you'll have to trust me until you're a big enough girl for me to explain it all to you."

"No, no, no," Georgie continued, still hitting her mummy as hard as she could.

Mummy held Georgie's hands and gently forced them downwards to encapsulate them in a hug from which Georgie could not escape. Her screaming increased. It went on and on until eventually she ran out of steam and slumped into her mummy's cuddle totally exhausted.

"I hate you. I hate you," she murmured as her red, puffy eyes slowly closed and she slipped into a deep unconscious sleep.

Mummy must have carried Georgie into her big bed because, when she next opened her eyes to the bright midday sun shining into the bedroom, she found herself cuddled up close to Mummy who was purring away steadily with her eyes closed.

Georgie wondered for a split second where she was and why she was sleeping next to Mummy. Then, like a surge of volcanic lava, the memories of just a few hours ago engulfed her, taking her breath away with the intensity of her emotions. She looked at the sleeping face of the person that had caused her more hurt and grief than she could contain.

"I'll never forgive you for as long as I live," she whispered with a voice that she didn't recognise – a voice of pure venom, as she slid from between the sheets on to the bedside rug and back into her own bedroom.

A full hour later, Florrie's eyes fluttered open and scrunched up to protect them from the bright daylight. She never closed the curtains in her bedroom as there was no light to shut out or nosey neighbours to look in. She lay there, with both hands shading her eyes until she became used to the glare. Then, as it had hit Georgie, the memory of the earlier events hit her like a steam train. Her heart and stomach somersaulted simultaneously and dropped into a deep dark chasm of despair. Then she remembered that Georgie had been in bed with her, and fear lifted her from the chasm into panic. She took off from under the covers and flew into the front bedroom.

"Georgie?"

But the small bright room was empty, as were the two open drawers of the wooden chest.

23

"Georgie, where are you, Baby?" she called as she descended two stairs at a time and turned left to the end of the hallway and into the kitchen.

Nothing. No Georgie to be seen. Only the empty teapot and dirty mugs sitting on the kitchen table, reminding Florrie with a jolt that Alfie was gone, choosing to be with his wife and three children over her and Georgie. Her hand immediately flew to her stomach as she thought of the tiny child growing inside her – a child who would never know its father.

'Maybe that's not as bad as a child who has to bear the loss of a father who meant everything to her.'

The thought jolted the distraught Florrie back to the present. Rushing from the kitchen to the lounge to the back garden and back through the hallway into the front garden, confirmed what she feared most. Georgie was gone. Florrie opened the front gate and looked down the slope that led to the village store. Half Mile Lane was empty.

"Georgie," she screamed. "Georgie, where are you?"

It was then that Florrie realised she was still wearing her screwed up old dressing gown and slippers. She ran back into the cottage and upstairs, taking another hopeful look in Georgie's bedroom - just in case the child had been hiding to play a trick on her. Her hopes were dashed at the sight of the empty drawers and when she investigated the wardrobe to see if Georgie's duffle bag was there, she knew for certain what the empty space meant.

'How long before me did Georgie wake up? It could have been hours. She could have walked a long way by now. And what direction did she go in? If she went across country, she could be anywhere.'

These thoughts circled her mind as she threw on her clothes, rushed back downstairs, grabbed the front door key, and exited via the garden gate before she stopped dead.

'Left to open country or right to village store? Georgie wouldn't have wanted anyone to see her.'

Florrie turned to the left.

'No. Alfie always came from the bottom of the slope. She maybe wanted to find her daddy.'

Florrie turned to the right.

'But if she was still crying, she'd be too embarrassed to risk anyone seeing her.'

Florrie turned back to the left.

'Florrie, pull yourself together. This is a four-year-old child. She wouldn't be thinking like an adult. She's more likely to have chosen to go downhill because that's the way we always go.'

Decision finally made, the distraught mother started to jog down the slope towards the village store, scouring the surrounding rolling slopes as she went. Nobody was about as usual. She didn't stop until she was at the counter inside the village store where she came face to face with the kindly postmistress.

"Ey up, Florrie. What's up, Lass? Tha looks as red as raspberry jelly melting in the sun."

Just at that moment, Mr Braithwaite, the shopkeeper, and husband of the postmistress, appeared from the back parlour with a little girl in tow, duffle bag on her back and chocolate smears around her lips.

"I think mebbe this bairn belongs to you, Young Florrie," he said with a twinkle in his eyes.

Georgie, head bowed, stood glued to the spot. She sensed her mummy's relief and hoped she wouldn't embarrass her by weeping. She looked up in time to see Mummy swallow hard, and fully expected her to run over to where she herself was standing next to Mr Braithwaite. But this didn't happen. For an instant Mummy didn't move but stood where she was with a serious look on her face.

"Baby, I was so worried about you. Come now. Thank Mr Braithwaite for the chocolate," grinning at the jolly man, "and we'll be on our way back home."

25

Mummy's unexpected change of attitude shocked Georgie.

"No. I don't want to come home. I want to stay here," shouted Georgie rudely.

Mr Braithwaite and his wife looked momentarily taken aback before the kind man came to the rescue.

"Now, Young Georgie, 'tis no way to speak to yer mammy. It was such a treat having thee visit but yer can't stay here. Anyway, Mammy will need a reight hard push to get her back up that slope after such a fast run down it. Can tha not see how short o' breath she is?"

Georgie walked toward Florrie without looking up, passed her and made her way to the shop door.

"Georgie, where's your manners? Say thank you to Mr Braithwaite, please."

"Thank you, Mr Braithwaite," came the monotone answer as the child walked out of the shop without turning around, just catching Mummy's apology to the shopkeeper before the door closed itself behind her.

When the door opened again, it was Mr Braithwaite accompanying Mummy and saying,

"Think nowt of it, Florrie. I know how children can get 'emselves all in a tiz woz over something and nothing. I also knew yer would be down here soon enough to find her. Take t' bairn home. It'll all blow over in no time at all."

Georgie watched Mummy blow the man a kiss before she approached and grabbed Georgie's hand. The silence all the way up the slope to the cottage was a sign of things to come.

Mummy had no sooner turned the front door key in its lock than Georgie pushed the door open, stamped up the stairs, continued into her bedroom and slammed the door behind her. She half expected Mummy to follow her to smack her bottom for both running away and being rude to the shopkeeper. She held her breath in anticipation until it became clear by the sound of Mummy's footsteps into the kitchen that it wasn't going to happen.

Florrie's instinct had, indeed, been to run up after her daughter and punish her. But she had realised that it was herself wanting to give vent to her own stress from the worst day of her life, so she had held on to the stair post, taken a few deep breaths, and then forced herself to walk into the kitchen to put the kettle on the hob. She again felt the pain of Alfie's departure as she emptied and rinsed the teapot and filled the two dirty mugs with water to soak in the sink.

'A nice cuppa will make it better,' she convinced herself as she put two teaspoons full of tealeaves in the warmed teapot, stirred it, and put the cosy on in just the same way as she had always done. How she wished she had someone's shoulder to cry on. This was the first time she'd felt this way since her own parents had turned their backs on her when they had discovered she was pregnant with Georgie. They'd come on their weekly visit to the cottage that Florrie's gran had left to her in her will. Florrie had been so thrilled to be carrying Alfie's child that it had never occurred to her that her previously loving parents would be anything but happy for her. With scowling faces, they had looked at Florrie with disgust.

"Did it not occur to you to think of us before you started an affair with a married man and got yourself in the family way?"

Florrie had been struck dumb with shock. It had never once occurred to her that her own parents, who loved her, wouldn't have continued to be as loving and supportive as they'd always been.

"It never even entered your mind, did it?" her shaking mother had taunted. "What are your father and I supposed to do now? We'll never be able to show ourselves at Chapel again. Our neighbours will find out soon enough and then steer clear of us, gossiping among themselves behind our backs. You've ruined our lives as well as your own, Young Madam. Oh, the shame of it, Florrie. How could you?"

That had been the last time Florrie had seen her parents in almost five years. It was only when she had tried to let them know that Georgie had been born that she discovered they had moved back down south not long after that conversation. None of their neighbours had known their new address — at least, if they did, they hadn't let on. Florrie had felt

bereft for several months after that, but eventually the feeling had faded, and only now did it return as she sat there sipping her tea and feeling totally alone.

CHAPTER 3

Early 1951 continued

An Unexpected Shock

Rat-a-tat-tat.

Florrie jumped out of her reverie, nearly dropping her half full mug of cold tea.

"Florrie, are you there? It's me, Gerald."

Florrie ran to the front door and opened it wide.

"Oh, you poor love," said Gerald sympathetically as he entered the hallway, pushed the door closed with his foot and opened his arms invitingly.

The floodgates opened as Florrie accepted the unspoken invitation and leaned into the welcome hug, letting Gerald hold her until she felt the storm subsiding, and then allowing him to gently lead her back into the kitchen, deposit her on the kitchen chair and proceed to boil up another kettle of water. Ten minutes later, sitting opposite the kindly man, but still sobbing quietly, she held the steaming mug he had handed her, and

watched him sit down opposite her with an identical steaming mug in his hand. As Gerald started to speak, Florrie couldn't hold back the landslide of words that seemed to tumble, uncontrollably from her quivering lips.

"He chose her rather than me and Georgie, Gerald. All this time he's convinced me that it's me not Mavis that he loves, but when it came to the crunch, he chose her. And now here's me, pregnant with his child, and him saying he'll pay nothing to support us. And to top it all, Georgie hates me because she's too young to understand why I had to kick him out. She ran away, Gerald, she actually ran away."

The sobs again threatened to overcome Florrie, prompting Gerald to move his hand across the table to cover hers.

"Now, now, Florrie. Try to calm down if you can. Wipe your eyes and try taking a few deep breaths. You don't want to spoil that beautiful face of yours, do you?"

Florrie tried to grin under her deluge and then slowly managed to stem her tears.

"You say Georgie ran away? Do you know where she went? Do we need to go out and search for the child?" asked Gerald.

Florrie was calmer now and managed to tell Gerald how and where she had found Georgie.

"So, how did you know about me and Alfie?" she asked Gerald.

"He turned up at my place early this morning in a right temper. I eventually got out of him what had happened, and I knew you must have been really upset for it to have come to the point of kicking him out, so I got off early from work and came straight here to check on you."

"You're a good friend, Gerald. Thank you for caring."

"Of course I care. I'm fond of all of you. After all, there's not many other folks who laugh at my jokes."

Florrie grinned for the second time that morning as Gerald continued.

"And anyway, I can't bear the thought of you and Georgie being unhappy. I'll do whatever I can to make sure that you get the support you need, even that new little one not yet born. At least I can make you all laugh, can't I, and laughter makes everyone feel better."

"So, are you going to be my new daddy?"

Florrie and Gerald started in surprise, simultaneously turning towards the doorway to see Georgie with a belligerent look on her face. The two adults went slightly pink in the face.

"Georgie, that's not the sort of question to ask Uncle Gerald. Come and sit down. You must be starving, Baby. You've eaten nothing all day but some chocolate from Mr Braithwaite."

Georgie ignored her mummy completely, but instead continued to question Gerald.

"Do you know, Uncle Gerald, my mummy doesn't want my daddy anymore, so she sent him away?"

"Yes, I do know that Georgie, but it's much more complicated than that, far too difficult for you to understand, Darling. Your mummy loves you very much and she wouldn't do anything to hurt you if she could help it. She needs you to love her more than ever right now, especially with a little brother or sister on the way."

Florrie and Gerald saw Georgie's face contort as if trying to prevent the tears coming to her eyes. She bowed her head to hide her embarrassment. Florrie immediately moved around the table, knelt in front of her child, and lifted the small quivering chin. She received her little daughter with a huge sense of relief as Georgie flung herself into her mummy's arms, heaving with escaping sobs, which flowed straight into Florrie's heart, sealing that invisible mother–daughter connection that meant so much to her.

"There, there, Baby. No need to cry. Mummy will always love you. We'll be a real family, just you, me and the little one. We'll all take care of each other, Georgie. We can be happy together, just the three of us."

Georgie looked up into her mummy's eyes.

"But what about Uncle Gerald, Mummy? Can he be our daddy?"

Gerald laughed, breaking the awkward silence that ensued.

"We'll see about that, Young Georgie, but first things first," said Gerald. "You need to get some warm food inside you. Why don't you go upstairs and wash your face while Mummy makes you a nice meal?"

Florrie smiled as she watched Gerald begin to tickle Georgie, who couldn't help but giggle and squirm as she screeched jovially at him to stop.

"Will you stay and eat with us? Mummy, tell Uncle Gerald to stay. Please Mummy, please."

Florrie looked at him questioningly and he nodded in response.

"Okay, Baby. Now off you go and get washed while I prepare us some nice eggs and bacon with bread and marge."

So, breakfast turned out to be supper, and much to Florrie's relief, a fragile but happy peace reigned over the little group as they ate hungrily.

"Uncle Gerald," said Georgie from under her heavy eyelids at the end of the meal, "It's my bedtime now so you and Mummy have to wash me and do bubbles."

"No, Baby ... "began Florrie.

"It's okay, Florrie, I'm more than happy to oblige, if that's okay with you?" Gerald interrupted.

So, Florrie cleared the table and the three acted out the evening ritual that Alfie had always been part of, including Gerald tickling the nude little girl as he transferred her to the draining board. Florrie grinned as Georgie was quick to issue her directives each time that Gerald got it slightly wrong.

Florrie tucked her small daughter up for the night, feeling a returning sense of peace until she heard the words that came from beneath the covers.

"I still miss my real daddy, Mummy, but Uncle Gerald will get used to being my new daddy soon, won't he?"

Florrie's sadness returned in a flash, and she couldn't answer her sleepy child's question. But it didn't matter because as she struggled with her emotions, she heard the deep rhythmic purring coming from her daughter that meant Georgie was already fast asleep.

Downstairs, Florrie found Gerald at the sink, washing up the dirty dishes.

"You don't need to do that, Gerald," said Florrie, as she picked up the tea towel to dry up.

"My pleasure. At least young Georgie has gone to bed somewhat happier than she was earlier. It's good to know that I can still make both of you laugh."

"Yes, but now she's expecting you to take over Alfie's role, and I'm afraid she's going to be a very disappointed little girl when she realises that's not going to happen."

"It could happen."

Florrie rocked on her feet.

"W-what do you mean?"

"I mean, I could be Georgie's new daddy if you wanted."

Florrie's face coloured up.

"I've loved you ever since I first saw you," Gerald said quietly, "I know you don't love me but I'm a patient man and let's face it, you and those two little children will need both financial and practical support, as well as a good laugh from time to time."

"But ... but ..."

"Sorry, Florrie. Trust me to jump in with both feet. The story of my life," he grinned cautiously. "But I do love that little girl of yours, too. Just give

33

it some thought. I'll not push you. In fact, I'll not contact you again if that's what you want. Take your time, Florrie. The offer's there if you want it."

Washing up completed, the man dried his hands on the kitchen towel and made his way to the stair post where Florrie had hung his coat earlier. She watched as Gerald turned towards her with a nervous grin, but he said nothing more – just gave a quick salute and then quietly left. Florrie was dumbstruck and couldn't quite absorb Gerald's words. Then a click of the letterbox made her start and she saw a small piece of paper with an address written on it flutter onto the doormat. Like a sleepwalker, she picked it up, knowing that it was Gerald's address. She floated upstairs and automatically placed it in the drawer of her bedside cabinet. The only other thing in the drawer was a photograph of Alfie in his army uniform. She picked it up and turned it over to read the message that she knew was on the back beneath his army number:

'To the one I love most in all the world. Always and forever yours, Alfie xx'

Florrie's eyes remained dry as she thought how hollow those words now sounded. Replacing the photograph, she closed the drawer and made her way into the bathroom to run herself a comforting bath. She sprinkled pink bath salts into the swirling water and while she waited for it to fill, she peeked into Georgie's room, where the child hadn't moved from the position in which she'd fallen asleep.

Florrie lay in the bath, still feeling as if she was in some sort of parallel life, until it was almost cold. She still loved Alfie, she knew that for sure, but would she ever invite him back into her life? No – of that she was certain. She and Georgie deserved better than to be second choice to a woman Alfie had said he'd never loved. She put her hand on her slightly swollen abdomen, where she knew her second child was slowly growing and developing, and spoke out loud to the little unborn life.

"Don't worry, little one, Mummy's here. I'll always love you and take care of you for as long as you need me."

By the time she stepped out of the cool water, Florrie had made up her mind. If she had to marry Gerald to secure her children's future, then that's what she would do.

Florrie woke with a start on Friday morning. She had been dreaming that Alfie had decided to leave Mavis after all and had moved in with her. She had felt so gloriously happy in her dream world until there had been a knock at the door and Alfie had gone to answer it. Suddenly she heard raised angry voices and what sounded like a scuffle and a crash as the door slammed. That was the point at which she jumped and woke up.

'Who was at the door?' she wondered as she tried to make sense of her dream.

'Mavis come to get her husband back? No, it couldn't have been. Mavis wouldn't have had the strength to fight a man, and Alfie would never have fought a woman.'

'It must have been Gerald. He's the only other man who might knock at my door. But who fought with who?'

Florrie stopped herself analysing and threw her covers back to get out of bed.

'For goodness' sake, Woman,' she addressed herself not for the first time of late, 'it was only a dream.'

She went into Georgie's room and found her daughter still fast asleep.

'Not surprising really. Yesterday was very traumatic for her.'

By the time she had washed, dressed, and arrived downstairs; Florrie's thoughts were beginning to work overtime again.

'Maybe the dream was a warning not to make a decision about Gerald too soon. Maybe Alfie will change his mind and decide to come back to live with me and Georgie after all.'

The possibility of Alfie returning raised her hopes and triggered her to relive the feelings she'd had in her dream when Alfie was living with her. The sudden sound of Georgie getting out of bed brought Florrie back to reality and her focus changed to preparing breakfast. She thought no more about her situation until later in the day when she and Georgie

returned from doing the weekly shop in Mr Braithwaite's village store and the two were doing the housework together.

"I like helping you scrub the table, Mummy."

"Do you, Darling? You are very good at it, and you really do help Mummy get the housework done quickly."

Both continued scrubbing away together in silence for another five minutes.

"Will my new daddy come on the same days as my old daddy, Mummy?"

Mummy continued scrubbing but Georgie noticed her slow down a little and her face looked perplexed.

"What days will he come, Mummy?"

This time Mummy took a deep breath before responding.

"Uncle Gerald will just be coming to see us now and then, Baby."

"Oh, so he will surprise us. I love surprises, Mummy. I was very surprised when you and my first daddy told me about our new baby that's growing in your tummy. How big is the baby now, Mummy? When will she come out of your tummy?"

Georgie watched Mummy's facial expression change again. This time she looked relieved and stopped scrubbing as she peered across the wet table and into Georgie's face.

"The new baby - and remember it could be either a little boy or little girl - is not due until June, so it is still very small, but the weather should be warm and sunny then, so we'll be able to take him or her out for a walk in the pram."

"What pram, Mummy? Will I be able to push it when we go shopping? Will I be able to take her out of the pram and in to see Mr Braithwaite?"

"Slow down, Georgie," as she walked around the table and gave her excited child a big damp cuddle.

"Well, the pram is the one that I used for you when you were a tiny baby."

Georgie's eyes were two saucers.

"Where is it? Can I see it now?"

"Hmmm. I think you've forgotten that small word, Young Lady."

Georgie looked momentarily perplexed.

"Can I see the pram now, please?"

"You most definitely can, Baby. It's covered up in the garden shed. It will probably need a bit of cleaning up before June, so let's go and look right now."

With the bouncing Georgie beside her, Mummy took the shed key from the hook next to the back door and led her daughter into the garden, walking its length to the wooden shed. Once Mummy had uncovered the pram, Georgie was mesmerised.

"This is only big enough for a dolly. Was I really as small as a dolly?"

"You sure were. What if we take this indoors and clean it up? Then we can get all your baby clothes and cot and pram covers out of the loft so they can be washed clean and put in one of the drawers in your bedroom ready for the baby."

"Yippee! We need to take it indoors so that we can show Uncle Gerald when he comes on his surprise visit. Now he's my new daddy, will he be able to live with us to help look after the baby when she's born?"

Mummy looked stunned for a moment before she spoke.

"I don't know, Georgie. But there's no time to think about that now, we've got lots to do. If you're going to be my helper, then we'd best get on with it."

The rest of the day was spent cleaning up the pram until it was spotless.

That night in bed, Florrie was still wondering what she should do for the best.

'Do I wait in the hope of Alfie changing his mind? After all, he is Georgie's real daddy. It must be best for her to have him around rather than a stepfather, mustn't it? But he probably won't come back to me, so would it be best for me and Georgie to try to go it alone. She'll be going to school three months after the baby is born, so I'll be looking after just one child for a lot of the time. I looked after Georgie, so I'm sure I could do it. But then what about money? Gerald would provide that, and he says he loves Georgie already, so he'll probably feel the same about the new baby. What should I do? What should I do?'

Florrie eventually fell asleep still worrying and inevitably dreamed again. This time she was back in the kitchen with Alfie, and he kept repeating those words that had pierced her heart.

"You don't think I'd leave my real family for you, do you?"

As before, she awoke suddenly, but this time tears were rolling down her face and her heart felt as though it was going to burst. She knew how cruel Alfie could be, but she also knew what happy times they'd had. Exhaustion finally forced her back into a restless sleep for the remainder of the night, but by the morning she finally knew what she must do. Those words from Alfie had hurt her too much. She would write to Gerald and invite him to tea so they could talk over the future.

Before Georgie had awoken, the letter was written, and Florrie read it one last time before she placed it in the envelope and stuck it down ready to post.

Dear Gerald,

I have been thinking about what you said on Thursday evening, and I wondered if you would like to come for tea next Friday after work so we can discuss the matter further.

Yours Sincerely,

Florrie.

Later that morning, mother and daughter walked together to the village store.

"Georgie, while I'm buying today's dinner, will you take these pennies to the post office counter and ask the postmistress for a postage stamp please?"

The post office counter was situated at the side of the shop, completely separated from the grocery counter. Georgie loved feeling grown up and she was more than happy to oblige. She purchased the stamp and brought it to her mummy who was chatting to Mr Braithwaite about the choices available for dinner. Mummy finally decided on cheese and potato pie and bought the ingredients.

"Yum yum. I love cheese and potato pie, Mummy. It's my favourite," said Georgie

"You told me yesterday that sausage was your favourite."
"I know, but cheese is my favourite too."

Mummy and Mr Braithwaite laughed, and Georgie grinned as she left the shop with Mummy, waving goodbye as she went. Once outside, Mummy took a letter out of her bag, stuck on the stamp, and slipped it in the post box before Georgie could ask to do it.

"Oh, I wanted to do that, Mummy."

"Sorry, Babe. I wasn't thinking."

They then walked hand in hand back up half mile Lane. Georgie noticed that her mummy seemed deep in thought, so she chatted away happily to fill the void.

CHAPTER 4

Late February 1951

The die is cast

The week passed quickly for Mummy and Georgie. They had removed Georgie's old baby clothes from the loft, spent ages washing them gently between playing with the soap suds in the kitchen sink, hung them carefully on the washing line, and finally placed them neatly and lovingly into the bottom drawer of Georgie's bedroom chest. Throughout the whole procedure, Georgie had kept on with her questions.

"Mummy, when is Uncle Gerald coming to see us again?"

"I don't know, Baby."

"Mummy, will Uncle Gerald be coming today?"

"Not that I know of, Georgie."

"Mummy do you think Uncle Gerald will like being my new daddy?"

"Who said he'd be your new daddy, Baby? You've got such an imagination."

"Mummy, do you like Uncle Gerald as much as you did my real daddy?"

"Come and have your tea now, Baby."

On and on it went until the pressure was too much for Georgie's mummy. Georgie was excited when Mummy eventually gave in and told her that Gerald would be coming to tea on Friday. When Thursday came, Georgie realised she had only one more day to wait, and her tummy lurched with excitement. She still missed her real daddy a lot, and the feeling of loss seemed stuck in her little heart. She stopped mentioning him to Mummy as she saw the tears in Mummy's eyes whenever she did so, and had caught her sitting alone crying once or twice when she had come downstairs during the evening to ask for a drink of water. Georgie had tried to distract her mummy by asking about Friday's menu and discussing what part she could play in the preparations. She knew that at least this would bring a bit of excitement for them both.

Georgie wasn't quite so excited when on Thursday afternoon, Mummy said they must both wash their hair. She especially hated it when Mummy tried to detangle her long locks with a wide-toothed comb.

"It has to be done, Babe," she'd hear her Mummy say as she flinched and wriggled under every tug, trying to focus on the result of the lovely, shiny, blonde waves that she would see in the mirror once it had dried. Mummy then helped Georgie to decide on the dress she would wear the following evening, after which they moved into Mummy's bedroom to sort out which lipstick and perfume Mummy would wear for the event. Together they chose one of the two lipsticks she owned, placed her powder compact next to it on the dressing table, and then looked for the one bottle of scent she had. Georgie remembered Daddy giving it to Mummy one Christmas. It had stuck in her mind because of the bright midnight blue colour of the small bottle.

"Here it is," Mummy exclaimed, "Midnight in Paris."

She unscrewed the tiny gold-coloured top and held it out for her daughter to sniff after having done so herself.

"Mmmm that's lovely," they agreed in unison.

"I'm really looking forward to seeing Uncle Gerald again, Mummy. Are you?"

Mummy thought for a moment before she responded with a dreamy look in her eyes.

"Yes, Georgie, I really am."

The rest of Thursday went by quickly as mother and daughter sat at the kitchen table together drawing pictures of what they thought the new baby would look like.

"My picture is for Uncle Gerald, Mummy. After all, if he's going to be my new daddy, that means he'll be the baby's daddy too. So, it's good that he can have the picture to know what she, I mean she or he will look like."

Friday morning finally came, and Florrie woke up full of anticipation. She could feel butterflies in her stomach – or was it? She waited for a few minutes and felt it again.

'Oh, my goodness, my baby is moving for the first time. It now feels like a real little person. This must be a good omen for my future with Gerald.'

Rushing into Georgie's bedroom, she gently shook the sleeping child. She had to tell someone about the baby and since Georgie was the only other person in the house, it had to be her.

As Georgie opened her eyes drowsily, she saw her mummy moving impatiently from one foot to the other next to the bed.

"Georgie, Georgie, give me your hand. The baby is moving for the very first time and I want you to feel it."

Georgie was immediately wide awake and grinned as she held out her small hand for Mummy to guide onto her baby bump.

"You'll need to concentrate, Baby. It's like the tiny flutter of butterfly wings. There, there … did you feel it?"

Georgie couldn't feel it, but as she looked up at the expression of wonderment on Mummy's face, she felt a surge of emotion and tears formed in the corners of her wide eyes.

"I can almost feel my baby sister moving!" she exclaimed at which Mummy grabbed her and both jumped up and down, hugging.

Even in the excitement, Georgie heard her mummy reminding her for the umpteenth time that it could be a boy.

Later that morning, the excited pair almost skipped down to the village store to buy the ingredients for the big tea. Both had shiny, clean hair and were wearing clean dresses under their coats.

"Aye up, Lass. I've got some lovely pig's liver here for thee, fresh in this morning. With a bit o' bacon, it'll make a meal fit for a king," said Mr Braithwaite as they entered.

"We aren't cooking for a king, Mr Braithwaite. We're cooking for Uncle Gerald who's going to be my new daddy."

Georgie saw the shopkeeper twinkling at her mummy, who was looking hot and embarrassed.

"Should a be congratulating yer then, Florrie Lass?"

"Erm … well … I …"

"Nay don't worry yersen, Lass. Bairns have a quick imagination and a slow brake."

Georgie wondered why Mummy went pink and what Mr Braithwaite was on about, but she had little time to think about that as Mummy took her hand and almost dragged her out of the shop, waving goodbye as she did so. As Georgie looked back to wave, she noticed the wink that passed between the shopkeeper and post mistress behind her mummy's back.

The rest of the day seemed to drag by for Georgie. She helped Mummy tidy the house and sat with her to have a sandwich for lunch.
"Best you go upstairs now and have a little snooze, Baby. You're bound to be up late tonight with Uncle Gerald here."

"But I'm not tired, Mummy."

"You will be if you don't have a little snooze. I tell you what, if you go for a snooze in your room, I'll be just next door in mine, finishing off the last bit of tidying. Then if you're not asleep by the time I've done, you can forget the snooze. How's that?"

Georgie agreed and laid on top of her bedclothes with her dressing gown acting as a cover over the top of her.

Florrie, as good as her word, busied herself next door, putting fresh white sheets and pillowcases on her bed and tidying the top of her dressing table.

'Why am I changing the bedclothes?' Florrie asked herself, but then refused to dwell on it for fear of having to admit her reasons. Instead, she crept out of her bedroom and peeped into Georgie's room. The dressing gown-covered mound on the bed was rising and falling rhythmically so she continued downstairs, avoiding the few creaky treads. She busied herself preparing the liver and bacon and the vegetables, placing them in a large metal dish ready to put in the oven later. From then on, the afternoon seemed to pass slowly, and Florrie felt pleased when Georgie came bouncing down the stairs.

"How long is it before Uncle Gerald arrives, Mummy?"

"A little while yet," responded Mummy as she made up the fire in the lounge and then turned on the wireless for 'Listen with Mother', which was Georgie's favourite. While they listened, they sat on the rug in front of the fire playing 'Snap', the only card game that Georgie had managed to master. Then while Georgie sat at the wooden table in the kitchen, finishing her picture of the new baby for Uncle Gerald, Mummy put the tea in the oven and opened a tin of sliced peaches in syrup, which she poured into a cut glass bowl and covered with a clean tea towel ready for their afters later.

Georgie was glad when Mummy said they needed to get ready, and she happily walked up the stairs next to Mummy and entered the bathroom. Georgie and Mummy took turns to wash their faces and brush their hair before Mummy put on her bright red lipstick and pretended to put some on Georgie's lips too. Despite having done that, Georgie still felt that the time was passing too slowly.

"Get one of your story books, Georgie, and I'll listen to you reading while we wait for Uncle Gerald to arrive."

Georgie, as always, chose her favourite picture storybook that featured a dancer, and she was just about to turn to page three, when the sound of the door knocker made her and Mummy start.

Georgie immediately jumped up from the settee and ran to open the front door, where Uncle Gerald stood, wrapped up in a thick coat with a blue and yellow striped scarf wound tightly around his neck. Georgie felt so excited that she couldn't stop herself leaping up into Uncle Gerald's arms. She discovered too late that he was holding a bouquet of red roses in one hand, which he almost dropped. Georgie giggled as he laughed and gently returned her to the ground.

"Well, what a lovely welcome, Young Georgie."

"Please come in, Uncle Gerald, may I take your coat?" offered the little girl in a posh accent.

"Oh yes please, Kind Lady," Uncle Gerald played along with a slight bow.

Then Georgie whispered. "Mummy is wearing her best dress, and she looks so pretty. She's even got her red lipstick on."

Uncle Gerald nodded as he steadied Georgie who was now balancing on the second stair up trying to reach the stair post to hang his heavy coat on. Mission achieved, she bounced back down the stairs, took Uncle Gerald's hand, and led him into the lounge where Mummy was looking slightly pink. Georgie noticed that Mummy and Uncle Gerald were staring at each other, and it took Mummy a few seconds to speak.
"Hello Gerald. It's lovely to see you. I'm so glad you were able to come. Georgie has been so excited waiting for this evening to arrive."

"Not just me, Mummy - you too."

Georgie didn't understand why Mummy face became even pinker, as Uncle Gerald stepped forward to hand her the bouquet.

"You look more beautiful than ever tonight, Florrie."

"What about me Uncle Gerald?"

"Oh, you too, Young Georgie. Definitely you too."

"I've coloured you a picture and I was really careful and didn't get any crayon on my best dress."

"Well, what a clever girl you are. Where is the picture?"
"It's on the kitchen table. I'll go and get it for you," as she ran out of the lounge to retrieve her work of art.

When the tornado that was Georgie arrived back in the lounge, she noticed that Uncle Gerald was holding Mummy's hand and at that moment she thought how pretty her mummy looked with her eyes sparkling so brightly in the light from the fireplace.

"I'll just check on the meal while Georgie shows you her picture. Do sit down and make yourself comfortable, Gerald," said Mummy, sliding her hand from his.

Georgie enjoyed the meal her mummy had prepared and chatted away with Uncle Gerald throughout. She tried to stifle a yawn after they'd all played two games of Ludo together but couldn't quite manage it.

"It's bedtime for you, Baby. You look tired. Up you go and change into your nightdress, and I'll be up to tuck you in and kiss you goodnight in a few minutes."

"But I haven't had my wash and bubbles time."

"I think we can forgo that just this once, Baby."

"Can Uncle Gerald come up and kiss me goodnight too, please, Mummy?"

Georgie saw Mummy glance at Uncle Gerald who nodded with a smile.

"Okay then. Just call us when you're in bed. Don't forget to clean your teeth."
Georgie happily bounced upstairs.

Florrie turned around to smile at Gerald, who held eye contact, seeming to peer into the depth of her soul. It was she who finally spoke up and broke the spell.

"So how have you been since we last saw you?"

With brown eyes still fixed immovably on hazel ones, Gerald responded softly.

"I've been fine, thank you, Florrie. Just a little tense waiting and wondering if I would hear from you again after what I said when I was last here. My heart took off and flew when I received your letter and invitation. Am I assuming you have decided to accept my offer of taking over the role that Alfie so cruelly dismissed?"

"MUMMY, UNCLE GERALD, I'M IN BED," prevented Florrie's response.

They both stood up and made their way upstairs, Florrie in front, Gerald close behind. Ten minutes later after hugs and kisses from both, they left Georgie who had turned on her side and closed her eyes, still with a slight smile on her lips.

Downstairs, sitting side by side on the settee, a slight awkwardness came over Florrie and Gerald.

"Would you like a cup of tea, Gerald?"

"That would be lovely, Florrie," he responded, nervously pushing his unruly red hair back from his forehead.

She was almost relieved to leave the room, not really understanding where the awkwardness had come from after such a relaxed time before Georgie went to bed. She half-filled the big kettle from the tap in the sink

and placed it on the hob, lighting the gas with her battery lighter. After placing two cups and saucers on a small tray and adding a small jug of milk and bowl of sugar, Florrie returned to the lounge to wait for the kettle to boil. Gerald had an unusually serious expression on his face.

"Florrie, I need to know if you have decided whether or not our future is together. I can't stand the tension for a single moment longer. Even if you're going to disappoint me, it would still be better than not knowing."

Florrie looked into his pleading eyes as she leant forward and gently kissed him on his expectant mouth. He responded and the kiss lengthened as he drew her closer. Only the hiss of the boiling kettle brought them back to reality.

"Does that answer your question, dear Gerald?" she said as she rose from the settee and went to pour the bubbling water from the kettle into the small teapot. Gerald had not moved when Florrie returned with the full tray in hand. She placed it on the coffee table in front of the settee and sat down beside him to pour. It wasn't until she handed him his cup and saucer that he seemed to recover from his shock.

"Milk and sugar?" asked Florrie.

"Yes, please."

"Say when," as she poured milk from the miniature jug.

"When."

"How many sugars?"

"Two, please."

It was then that she realised she hadn't put a spoon in each saucer.

"Won't be a sec."

"Okay."
She fetched two teaspoons, twice scooped a spoonful of sugar into Gerald's cup, which had remained static in her absence and gently placed the spoon into his saucer. She poured a little milk into her own

cup, stirred, and looked back up into his eyes. She grinned. He mirrored her grin.

"Well, are you going to say anything, or will we spend the rest of this evening in silence?"

"Did that kiss mean what I think it did, My Beautiful Florrie?"

She giggled.

"Well, I'm not in the habit of kissing a man for the fun of it, although I must say it was very lovely and I enjoyed every second of it."

At that, Gerald carefully placed his cup and saucer back on the tray, slid onto one knee and took Florrie's free hand.

"Will you do me the honour of becoming my wife?"
Florrie's eyes glistened with unshed tears.

"I will, Gerald, I will.

CHAPTER 5

April 1951

New beginnings

The church bells rang as Georgie proudly watched her mummy from behind. They were walking down Half Mile Lane, with Mummy on the arm of the portly and jolly Mr Braithwaite, who had happily agreed to give her away in the absence of her father. It was a warm, sunny April day. Mummy wore a cream, tulle and lace, tea-length dress, a hand-me-down passed on to her by the generous and smiley postmistress. Georgie had watched mesmerized as Mrs Braithwaite had deftly pinned and sewed, until the dress not only disguised her mummy's baby bump, but was a perfectly fitting, full skirted dress with short sleeves and a round neck that made her mummy look stunning. The small spray that she held contained one stem of lily-of-the-valley set in fern leaves and bound with a cream satin bow and was only slightly larger than the identical one that Georgie carried. Mummy's thick blonde, wavy hair was pinned up and miraculously held in place with just a single hair grip disguised with a short sprig of lily-of-the-valley. Georgie occasionally glanced to check if it was still in place as she followed behind with a broad, proud smile on her face. She, herself, felt almost as pretty in her short, full skirted, pink lace dress that Mummy had made by hand. She flicked her blonde, free-hanging hair back, aware that the sun would be reflecting its shine, and

hoping that the pure joy she felt would be reflecting from her hazel eyes as much as she was sure it was reflecting from her mummy's.

Very few people were around to see the small procession making its way to St Luke's Church from which the sound of bells was joyfully emanating. But the little bridesmaid was content with knowing that if there had been, they'd not only have noticed the beauty of the bride and bridesmaid, but also the huge smiling moustache of the proud shopkeeper.

As Mummy and Georgie walked up the aisle towards the groom, the only other people present to witness the ceremony apart from Uncle Gerald and the vicar, were the Braithwaites, but the whole small group looked full of joy and anticipation. As Georgie watched Mummy and Uncle Gerald turn to face each other to make their vows, the small child fleetingly thought of her real daddy and wondered if her mummy was doing the same. But she immediately pushed that thought out of her mind, determined to focus only on the happy life that was ahead for her and Mummy. She noticed the tears in the eyes of the rounded shopkeeper and his wife, both of whom she had always felt a connection with and was sure they felt the same. She sensed that the connection would deepen over the course of time.

When the happy group arrived back at the cottage, the postmistress uncovered the plates that Georgie had seen her help Mummy to prepare earlier. Various cuts of cold meat and a mixed salad still looked perfectly fresh arranged around the large kitchen table on a crisp white tablecloth. Mummy and Uncle Gerald sat on one side of the table, with Georgie between them. Mr and Mrs Braithwaite and the vicar sat along the other side. Uncle Gerald uncorked the large bottle of Asti Spumante (a gift from Mr Braithwaite) and filled the variety of small glasses in front of each plate, allowing Georgie just half an inch in the bottom of her glass. Happy chat and laughter accompanied the simple meal, which finished with cheese and crackers. A refill of glasses signalled the time for Uncle Gerald's speech, which made everyone laugh even louder. He seemed to have a natural funny way with him whatever he did.

Then, seeing the postmistress wink at her, Georgie jumped up from her chair and bounced her way to the corner of the dresser. All eyes were on her.

"Mummy and Uncle Gerald, this is a surprise for you."

51

Georgie's mummy and her new husband, the vicar and Mr Braithwaite, raised their eyebrows and grinned. Georgie, watched as the postmistress lifted the lid from a white cardboard box which had been sitting on the far corner of the dresser hidden under a clean tea towel. Georgie slowly looked in turn at each person at the table causing eyebrows to raise even higher. She then placed her small hands into the box and again looked around for effect. Mummy giggled. Uncle Gerald's grin broadened.

"Come on, Lass. I can't stand tension," said Mr Braithwaite with the vicar nodding in agreement.

Georgie slowly lifted the content of the box and brought out a beautiful wedding cake. Everyone in the kitchen gasped and clapped. Georgie grinned proudly. Then Pattie did a small cough, and the group went quiet.

"This young lass made and decorated this beautiful cake fer her mammy and new daddy a few days ago," said the postmistress.

"You helped me, though," piped up the ever-truthful Georgie, triggering another round of applause and laughter.

Georgie carefully placed the cake on the table in front of the bride and groom, with the postmistress adding a large bread knife. It was a Victoria sponge, covered in white fondant icing and two little figures made and decorated with food colouring to resemble a bride and groom. A sprig of lily-of-the-valley adorned each corner, with a wide cream satin ribbon tied around the cake's sides to hold everything in place and finished with a bow. As Mummy and Uncle Gerald stood to cut the cake together, Georgie smiled from ear to ear and applauded all on her own when Mummy said that Georgie's cake had made this the happiest day of her life.

After the meal, everyone adjourned to the lounge where the joyful chat and laughter continued, helped along by the several glasses of sweet sherry they imbibed. Georgie was fascinated as she watched each person, including the vicar, become more and more relaxed as the evening proceeded, until their voices began to slur, and they swayed a little whenever they stood up to go to the bathroom. She eventually fell asleep on the rug with her head resting on a cushion from the sofa.

Later, Florrie looked lovingly at her sleeping daughter as she gently wrapped Georgie in a warm blanket, lifted her from the floor and handed her to Mr Braithwaite to carry down Half Mile Lane next to his wife. Georgie was to spend the night in their spare bedroom to give her and Gerald some time alone.

Gerald didn't consummate their relationship that night. He told Florrie that he did not want to risk hurting the new baby that was growing within her.

"Anyway, My Love, I can see you are tired after the big day, and we'll have plenty of time for that after the baby is born."

Florrie hid her feelings of horror and disappointment, but comforted herself with the fact that she was, indeed, very tired and Gerald was just being considerate of her condition. In truth, she had wondered if making love with Gerald would be the same as it had been with Alfie, the only other man she had ever given herself to. But with just over two months until the baby was due, she convinced herself that the time would fly, and she would enjoy the experience much more without her baby bump in the way. As it was, Gerald still held her close, told her how beautiful she was and cuddled her gently for the whole of that first night. She awoke next morning feeling safe and secure, not only for herself but also for Georgie and the new baby. She fleetingly wondered if Gerald was put off by the knowledge that the steadily growing foetus inside her did not belong to him. Maybe once the new baby was no longer within her, he would be keener to claim her for his own.

As the days and weeks went by, Florrie could not fault her new husband in any other way. He was attentive and supportive towards her and spent many hours playing and chatting with Georgie who was clearly becoming more and more fond of him.

Georgie continued to call her new daddy Uncle Gerald until one day in late June. She had watched him make Mummy, who was now very large, comfortable on the garden bench supported by several carefully placed

cushions. Mummy looked radiant as she sat in the sunshine and watched Uncle Gerald and Georgie play-fighting and tickling each other on the grass. Georgie was screeching with laughter as she sat on top of her play partner.

"Hooray. I'm the winner, Daddy. I beat you!"

She surprised herself and went silent for a split second before she continued tickling the squirming man beneath her. As she did so, she glanced over at Mummy and grinned, sensing that her mummy would be pleased to hear her referring to Uncle Gerald as Daddy. She was right. Mummy returned the grin with a look of contentment on her face. This pleased Georgie because she had overheard a conversation a couple of days ago between Mummy and Uncle Gerald and had sensed that Mummy had been worrying.

"Supposing the baby turns out to look just like Alfie, Gerald. Will that make you feel differently about living with me, especially if I have a little boy?"

Uncle Gerald had said that nothing would make him stop loving her and both of her children, whatever the baby looked like. Mummy had seemed to be relieved by this, but it had planted a seed of doubt in Georgie's mind, and she had wondered if the same was true for Mummy, who had certainly seemed more restless since then. At least Mummy now had a close friend in the postmistress in whom she'd be able to confide. Georgie loved the fact that the Braithwaites had now become close family friends and she was allowed to call them by their first names.

"Oh, just call us Pattie and Robert," the postmistress had said. "If you call us Aunty and Uncle, you'll just make us feel old."

Georgie began to smile as she recalled all the fun that they had enjoyed together every Saturday evening since the wedding. One week, Robert and Pattie would come to the cottage, the next week Mummy, Uncle Gerald and Georgie would walk down Half Mile Lane to the living quarters behind the village store. They would eat tea together and then play cards or a boxed game, chatting about anything and everything as they passed each pleasant evening. Georgie knew that Pattie was totally dependable, as a friend for both her mummy and her.

Then it happened, forcing Georgie straight out of her reverie.

54

"Arghhh!" came the gurgled scream from Mummy.

Georgie and Daddy instantly froze, and then quickly rushed over to Mummy who was white-faced and writhing on the bench.

"It's happening," she gasped, "The baby's on its way. That's the second contraction and it's really strong – much stronger than I had with Georgie."

Tears of pain rolled down Mummy's face and Georgie could see her holding her breath. At that moment, Georgie was glad that she had been with her mummy during the regular visits from Mattie, the midwife, over the past few months. The woman always appeared confident and knowledgeable to Georgie, and this had rubbed off on both her and Mummy.

Georgie remembered what Mummy had said to Mattie.

"Mattie, I keep thinking of Georgie's birth and it's making me feel a little nervous."

"Why's that, Lass?"

"The pain was so bad. It was probably no worse than for most first babies, but it really shocked me at the time. I suppose I'm a bit of a coward."

"Ey, Florrie, it's always easier for t' second baby so try not ter worry," said Mattie, who was small in height, but had a big personality.

Georgie and her mummy had liked Mattie from the start. She wore her long, shiny brown hair pinned up at the back in a French pleat which gave her the appearance of a no-nonsense person. However, on the few occasions when she had been running late after attending a long birth the evening before, she had turned up at the house on her old black bicycle with her hair sticking out in every direction, not having had time to brush it after grabbing a couple of hours sleep. Georgie would watch her out of the living room window as she opened her saddlebag, removed her hairbrush, and smoothed her wayward tresses back into place. On those occasions, Mattie's personality seemed to change to match her appearance.

"Ey up Florrie and Young Georgie."

"Hello, Mattie. I wanted to run something past you today," said Mummy. "Gerald and I having been discussing the birth and I would like both him and Georgie to be present. Would that be alright with you? I know it's unusual."

"You sure, Lass? I've seen many a husband keel over at t' first sight of blood. I've no objection but can you cope with Gerald ending up laying on t' floor beside you?"

Mattie began to giggle, and Georgie and her mummy found themselves joining in.

"Does that happen often, Mattie?" said Mummy.

"Often enough, Lass. Has Gerald got strong stomach?"

"I think so. He's very caring so he'll likely focus on me rather than what's going on down below."

"Are you sure t' bairn will cope, too?"

Georgie could keep quiet no longer.

"Mummy told me all about how babies are born, and I want to be with my daddy to see my baby sister born. I'm not worried about blood, Mattie. When I fall over and graze my knees, I never cry."

"I think it would make us closer as a family if we were all there when the baby takes its first breath," explained Mummy. "I know this is unheard of but, well I'll be giving birth in my own home, and as long as you are happy with the situation, I don't really care what anyone thinks about it."

"Sounds exciting to me," enthused Mattie. "I've always had a bit of t' rebel in me, so if we're going to do this, I'd better make sure young Georgie here knows the ropes."

So, from then on, Georgie had been Mattie's willing pupil and had made it her responsibility to pass on her knowledge to her new daddy.

56

"When time comes, Georgie, you just run down ter village store and ask them to ring me. I'll be on t' way within the flick of a lamb's tail," she had assured her.

Right now, Mummy, Daddy and Georgie were waiting to see how long it would be before the next contraction grabbed and squeezed Mummy's significantly bulging abdomen. As they waited, Mummy went through the short list that she knew off by heart, checking that everything was ready for this new child's entrance into the world. The clean baby clothes were still in one of the drawers in Georgie's bedroom. A second-hand Moses basket, a gift from Pattie that she had found in a charity shop in Penrith, sat waiting on top of two chairs pushed together next to Mummy's side of the bed.

Georgie remembered the happy hours she'd spent as Mummy taught her to sew a small mattress, pillowcases, and matching covers from one of the spare white sheets she had. Mummy had carefully written the word 'Baby' across one corner of each pillowcase and bought a skein of yellow silk embroidery thread for Georgie to follow each letter with tiny backstitches. Georgie had wanted Mummy to use some of the leftover pink lace from her bridesmaid dress to trim the pillowcases and sheets – so sure was she that the baby would be a little sister for her. But she had reluctantly accepted Mummy's decision to use the yellow embroidery instead.

Then it happened again.

Another gasp and gurgled scream came from Mummy, her face screwed up and ashen.

"This isn't right," she gasped between laboured breaths, "too quick … too soon."

Georgie now felt scared, and she couldn't stop the tears from forming and rolling down her face. She could also see that Daddy looked totally lost. She was glad when Mummy suddenly seemed to take charge.

"Georgie, darling, don't be scared. I'm sorry I frightened you. Everything will be fine. Everything is fine. The baby has started to come so I need you to stop crying and be the big girl you are. Run down to Robert and Pattie and ask them to ring the midwife. Okay? Can you do that for Mummy?"

Georgie nodded, wiped the tears with the back of her hand and ran straight into the kitchen, out through the front door and was a third of the way down Half Mile Lane before she took a breath. She reached the village store quicker than she had ever done before and rushed straight inside to find Robert serving a customer. Pattie was first to see her and knew immediately what was happening. As quick as lightening, she picked up the telephone receiver and dialled the midwife. She then emerged from behind the post office counter, grabbed Georgie's hand and the two puffed their way back up to the cottage. When they arrived, they found Mummy writhing about on the rug in front of the fireplace.

"Couldn't make it upstairs," she said between gasps as Georgie rushed to kneel at her mummy's side and take her hand. The lessons from Mattie had really sunk in and Georgie confidently began to play out what she'd learned. Pattie rushed upstairs to gather lots of towels and the recently purchased waterproof cover for the floor. Gerald stood by, still looking lost.

"Put t' kettle and some saucepans of water on ter boil, Gerald," bellowed Pattie as she took the stairs two at a time.

The assertiveness of her loud voice roused Daddy from his daze, and he immediately rushed into the kitchen, relieved that he now had orders to follow. Georgie stayed on the floor and confidently directed her mummy.

"Mummy listen to me. Take deep breaths and squeeze my hand."

The sound of Georgie's assertive voice seemed to calm her mummy and she obeyed her four-and-a-half-year-old daughter as if the child had suddenly become a young woman. She stopped writhing and focused on her breathing as Pattie gently slid the waterproof sheet and some clean towels beneath her friend's bottom, removing her underwear just in time to catch the flow as Florrie's waters broke.

When the midwife arrived, everything seemed to be in control. Georgie was still holding her mummy's hand and issuing her regular orders to breathe. Pattie was wiping the perspiration from Mummy's red, screwed-up face. Daddy was hovering in front of the hob in the kitchen willing the various containers of water to boil.

"Right, I can see yer already have everything organised here," said Mattie as she smilingly assessed the situation and made her way over to where Mummy was laying on the floor with the serious-faced Georgie hanging on to her hand as if the world depended upon it. Mummy was just going into another contraction, eyes screwed tightly shut but following her daughter's instructions.

"Breathe in 1-2-3. Breathe out 1-2-3 …"

"Aye, Georgie Lass, yer really are on top o' this, aren't yer?"

Georgie nodded without breaking her concentration.

"Breathe in 1-2-3. Breathe out 1-2-3 …"

"The hot water's boiling. What do you want me to do with it?" asked Daddy from the lounge doorway.

"Mix a brew, Lad. Yer got t' most important job of all."

The tension was broken, and everyone laughed with relief, even Mummy as she slowly came out the other side of her latest contraction. Only Georgie retained her straight face as she continued to monitor her mummy's wellbeing.

"Right Florrie, me love, let's see how far gone yer are," said Mattie.

Everyone looked away as Mattie carried out her intimate examination of her patient there on the floor in front of the fireplace, immediately exclaiming in surprise that Mummy was almost fully dilated. This made Mummy grin, as it did Pattie who was still on cold flannel duty, and Georgie who leaned over and kissed her mummy's warm, damp cheek. Only Daddy, who was just making his way into the lounge holding a large tray of cups, saucers, and full teapot, didn't laugh. In fact, the sight of Mattie removing her surgical gloved fingers from his wife's private parts, caused him to almost drop the tray in shock, which only added to the mirth of the others.

"My, this is certainly t' best birthday party I've been to," joked the midwife as she got to her feet, removing her surgical glove deftly with her left hand and dropping it into a large paper bag she'd brought with her for that purpose.

At that moment, Mummy launched into a groaning, straining, bellowing noise that neither Georgie nor Daddy had ever heard before. Georgie recovered quickly as she remembered Mattie's lessons and knew that this meant Mummy felt the need to start pushing the new little baby out of her body. That lesson had brought with it a short biology instruction about which orifice the baby would emerge from. At the time, Georgie's eyes had watered at the thought of how this could possibly be, knowing that, like every child of her age, she had explored her own small body and couldn't imagine how a real-life baby the size of her dolly could possibly squeeze itself through such a tiny exit. She had concluded in her logical childlike way that the baby must be very, very tiny when it came out.

Meanwhile, Daddy, who had been juggling the tray to prevent any breakages of china or spilling of tea from the teapot, again started at the noise, causing him to almost drop the tray as he placed it on the coffee table. Mattie found this hysterical and couldn't stop laughing, which again started the others off.

"What a day," she exclaimed. "Sorry, Gerald, but there's no time to drink tea right now. There's work to do."

The decidedly pale man picked the tray back up and was more than glad to make his way back into the kitchen, where he found himself having to lean over the empty sink in case his feeling of nausea came to fruition.

Ten minutes and several pushes later, the baby's head was born.

"Can I look, Mummy, Mattie?"

Mummy gently pushed her little daughter further down her body towards Mattie.

"Oh, Mummy, she's got lots of wet hair," shouted the excited Georgie, who then rushed out to the kitchen, grabbed her daddy's hand, and pulled him with all her might towards the lounge.

"Come and see the baby's head, Daddy. Quick or you'll miss it. Come on, come on."

60

Just as Georgie and Daddy arrived back in the lounge, they witnessed the baby's head twist upwards to reveal the sweetest little face imaginable.

"Come on Florrie Lass, one more big push should do it," instructed Mattie.

"Come on, Mummy, you can do it," reiterated the spellbound Georgie.

At the sight of the baby's face, Daddy seemed to come to his senses. He approached his wife, knelt beside her, and helped to lift her a little so that she could see the birth of her new child. Mummy pushed until her face was puce and then, as she took a deep breath, the baby's shoulders appeared, and it slid swiftly into the waiting hands of the midwife. Everyone held their breath as, with umbilical cord still attached, Mattie examined the little body to check its gender and Georgie mused over the fact that it was indeed the size of her dolly.

"It's a girl!"

Georgie cheered and clapped as everyone laughed with joy and the new baby let out its first cry.

"I told you it was going to be a little sister, didn't I? I told you and I am right. I can teach her how to dance. Can we make her a tiny dance dress from the pink lace left over from my bridesmaid dress, Mummy?"

Mummy, totally devoid of energy, had leaned back into Gerald's waiting arms as he leant down and kissed her gently on her dry lips.

"Well done, my clever Florrie. She's as beautiful as you and Georgie. I do love you all so much."

Mummy felt the tears drop from Gerald's moist eyes as she lay with the newborn in her arms and looked up into her husband's kind face, his red hair shining like a halo in the light from the lounge window.

'All will be well,' she silently thought as she drifted into a well-earned sleep

CHAPTER 6

April - June 1951

Baby blues

It was dark when Florrie finally opened her eyes. She was lying in bed next to Gerald, who was gently snoring. With a sudden rush of excitement, she remembered that she had a new tiny baby girl. She turned her head to the left and saw the sleeping baby, her little face shining like a miniature beacon in the moon's reflection, her rosebud lips fleetingly turning up at the edges as if she was having a happy dream. Her eyes were closed in peaceful slumber and her dark blonde hair still stuck in places to her perfectly formed head. Florrie tried to turn on her left side to get a better view of her sleeping angel. As she did so, she found that she was wearing her long nightdress and was duly padded up to prevent the bleeding that always followed a birth. Every joint in her body felt stiff, every muscle tight and sore. She guessed that Mattie must have cleaned her up while she was asleep, and that Gerald must have carried her upstairs and put her into bed. She had no memory of it. She tried again to turn onto her side. She had an urgent need to check that her tiny offspring had all her fingers and toes intact, as well as an urgent need to visit the bathroom. She achieved both of her aims without waking her husband. Once on her feet, she found that a little strength flowed back into her weak body, and she was even able to check on the sleeping

Georgie in the next room. She felt incredibly thirsty and was relieved to find a full glass of cool water on her bedside cabinet, which she downed in one before she got herself back into bed, had a last glance at the new little life beside her, and fell back into a deep refreshing sleep.

Meanwhile the worried Gerald was pretending to be asleep beside his wife. He hadn't told her that he had been given a week's notice from the building job in Penrith just a few days ago. It was all Alfie's fault. He hadn't spoken to Gerald since he'd discovered that his once best mate had stepped into his shoes just a few weeks after he had left Florrie. Gerald knew this must have really stung Alfie, who obviously still missed Florrie and Georgie, and had likely even thought about begging Florrie to take him back. But he also knew that Alfie was tight with his money and may even have decided that he couldn't afford to leave his wife and three children as well as finding more money to provide the extra financial support Florrie had demanded. Yes, Alfie was stuck between a rock and a hard place, which would have frustrated him enough without the fact that Florrie had so quickly replaced him with a man who would be taking over the fathering of his daughter and new baby. Alfie was the jealous type and Gerald knew it would irk him to think of Florrie in bed with another man, and his children having a new daddy. Gerald knew that Alfie had every reason for punishing him and will have thought and planned long and hard about the best way to do it. He was a proud man, Alfie, and would have seen Gerald as an insipid, freckle-faced 'Ginger' compared to him, the strong good-looking guy. Alfie would have resented Gerald's sense of humour too, and especially his ability to make people smile with his daft jokes. Yes, all things considered, Alfie was never going to take things lying down. And he didn't. The vindictive man lost Gerald his job, no doubt believing that Florrie would lose respect for a husband who couldn't be the breadwinner, and would quickly turn back to him, desperate for his return. Gerald reflected on how clever Alfie had been in his method of reprisal. He had used the well-known fact that rumours always spread like wildfire on a building site. The men loved to boast about the sexiness of their women which, laced with their lewd imaginations, would expand into imaginary adventures that would spread like wildfire. Alfie used that fact by making up a story about Gerald's past – dwelling on the fact that Gerald had avoided this subject ever since he had started working on the building site. Many a time, Alfie had asked him about it, but Gerald had invariably side-stepped and been clever enough to divert the conversation before Alfie had realised what was

happening. Gerald knew that this was a point of frustration for Alfie and wasn't surprised when he'd invented a ridiculous story about Gerald having been a dangerous womaniser down south where he used to live. He had, no doubt, told one or two of the guys the story 'in confidence' knowing that was the quickest way to trigger a rumour. In the end it got back to the boss who used it to sack him. The rumour had been that Gerald had slept with both the wife and daughter of the director of the finance company he'd worked for and had got both pregnant. Both babies, born within a week of each other, had red hair, a trait that was unseen in either the director's or his wife's sides of the family. Two and two had been put together and Gerald had been sacked. But Alfie's story didn't stop there. He had told his mates that the director then discovered Gerald had been guilty of virtually the same thing in his previous two companies and had eventually been cited by the police as a dangerous sexual predator after all three directors had made their allegations. The evidence was, after all, irrefutable. Six separate babies, all with Gerald's colouring. Clearly Alfie had been aware of what a laughable story he was making up, but he would have known that the men he worked with would swallow it hook line and sinker. He would also have known that they wouldn't be willing to risk the reputations they had built up for themselves concerning their sexy women, especially the middle-aged, pot-bellied boss who had somehow managed to catch himself a tall, glamorous beauty and was ever protective of her amongst his bawdy work force. Alfie's plan had worked like a dream, and the rumour had spread faster than a case of measles in a school classroom. The workers had begun to steer clear of the once-popular joker, leaving him confused at their sudden standoffish manner towards him. It wasn't till later that he found out why when the boss had called him into the office, told him the rumour, and given him a week's notice.

"But why would you believe such a ridiculous and far-fetched rumour?" Gerald had asked, completely confounded by his boss's words.

"It's not just the rumour. I've been told by head office to cut down on workers, so as you were the last man in, I'm afraid you have to be the first one out."

Gerald had tried to object, knowing that there was more work on that site than the current work force could manage, but his boss was adamant and turned tail, leaving him standing alone in the office.

Since then, Gerald had tried to act as if nothing was wrong. He didn't want Florrie to worry, so he had purposefully distracted himself a lot of the time by playing with Georgie who never failed to make him laugh, just as she had been doing the day before when Florrie had gone into labour. As he now lay in bed faking sleep, he had come up with a plan of his own. After all, there were plenty of other building sites in Penrith working hard to provide council dwellings for the men who had returned from the war and their families. He would collect his final wages next Friday and then pretend to go off to work each day as usual, spending the time job searching. He was sure to find something within the week, especially with his building experience.

Gerald must have drifted off to sleep because the next thing he knew was the sound of a baby crying. At first, he didn't know where he was and then he remembered the events of the previous day and turned over to face Florrie just as she picked up the tiny child and held it to her breast. The baby snuffled as she sought nourishment but once latched on, her thirsty sucking replaced the snuffling and all that could be heard was the satisfied slurping of tiny lips.

"Morning, Sleepy Head," said Florrie with a demure and peaceful expression on her lovely face.

Gerald still couldn't believe his luck at finding his perfect little family after living alone for so long. He leaned across to kiss Florrie on her right cheek and wondered at the softness of the baby's hair as his lips gently caressed the little head. He looked up to see Georgie standing in front of the Moses basket, eyes fixed lovingly on her new baby sister, listening intently to the small, contented noises that emanated from that little mouth.

Mattie had told Georgie all about how the baby would get milk by sucking at Mummy's nipples. She had wondered if milk would come from her own nipples should she have the flexibility to lean down and suck them. She'd tried squeezing them, but nothing had come out. She now felt a small pang of jealousy at the closeness of her new sister to her mummy. She wondered if Mummy would let her have a go at trying to suck some milk out of her nipples that were the source of nourishment for this tiny being. She determined to ask her when Daddy wasn't there. Instead, she sat on the edge of the bed and continued to observe the

idyllic scene until Mummy lifted the baby away from her nipple, supported the tiny girl in a sitting position and started to gently tap her little back.

"Why are you doing that, Mummy?"

"Watch and you'll soon find out, Babe."

Just as Georgie thought that nothing was going to happen, the loudest burp she could have imagined emanated from the tiny creature in front of her. Georgie's first reaction was to laugh out loud, as did her mummy and daddy, but this made the baby jump in surprise and begin to cry. The crying didn't last long because Mummy turned her around and held her to her other breast, where she immediately did a repeat performance and was soon slurping away happily until her little eyelids began to flutter and she became as if in a drugged state, allowing Mummy to lift her off to wind her again. The burp this time was not quite as loud and only caused the baby's head to jerk upwards slightly from the hand that was supporting it under the chin. Georgie was mesmerised as Mummy lay the baby on her lap and deftly changed the rather bulky nappy without her even stirring. Then Gerald jumped out of bed, cautiously lifted the sleeping bundle from his wife's arms and placed it into the Moses basket. Georgie lifted the little covers that she had helped her mummy to sew, and gently tucked her little sister in.

"Night night, Daisy," she whispered as she kissed the little lips and looked up feeling full of pride.

"Daisy?" came the simultaneous question from her mummy and daddy.

"Yes, I thought of it while I was falling asleep in bed last night. She is so pretty, just like a little daisy twinkling in the sunshine."

"Hmmm. Daisy. That's not a bad name at all," said Mummy.

"Then we're all agreed," chipped in Daddy, "Daisy it shall be."

Georgie grinned from ear to ear. She decided that this was the happiest day of her life, all four-and-a-half years of it. Mummy slid from under the covers and with the small wet bundle of nappy in one hand, she drew her eldest daughter into a one-armed hug with the other, hanging on just a little longer than normal. Georgie noticed this and snuggled closer to her mummy in response. Daddy also slid from under the bed clothes, and in

a surprise swoop, lifted Georgie up into his arms holding her like a baby, and followed Mummy downstairs amidst lots of giggles. He then disappeared upstairs, returning with the Moses basket, which he gently placed on the settee next to Mummy, before relieving her of the wet nappy and carrying it into the kitchen to its bucket of soapy soaking water. When he next appeared, it was with a bowl of warm water, a bar of soap and a face flannel, which he placed on Mummy's lap. He wiped her face gently with the squeezed-out wet flannel while she soaped and rubbed her hands together in the bowl. As young as she was, Georgie was touched by this loving act, until something struck her as funny, and she started to giggle all over again. Mummy and Daddy looked round, wondering what she was finding so funny. She said nothing but disappeared up to the bathroom and came bouncing down with a soft hand towel, which she gave to Mummy to dry her face and hands.

"Whoops, I thought I'd forgotten something," said Daddy, pushing his red hair back from his forehead as was his habit.

Georgie continued to giggle as she placed her little arms around his neck and kissed him full on his lips.

"Why, thank you Kind Daughter. I shall be forever in your debt," he responded, at the same time tickling his little girl under her arms, which he knew she couldn't take without laughing.

Gerald returned to 'work' the next day and Pattie popped in from time to time to do the odd bit of housework and food preparation. As time went on, Florrie gradually gained in strength, but rarely smiled, which Pattie noticed and questioned.

"I'm just tired," explained Florrie to her friend. "Waking up every night to give Daisy her feed is taking it out of me. Then, of course, Gerald must get up early for work, so I'm forced to get up to look after the children. I try to get a nap between feeds, but of course, I know Georgie must be feeling the lack of attention and I feel guilty if I don't spend time with her. What with that and the extra washing and ironing, I don't seem to be able to regain the energy that I always had so much of."

"Well, I can help yer there, Lass. I have to work behind t' post office counter, but you can send Georgie down to me. She'd love to help me

or Robert serving t' customers and it'll give you the chance to relax properly and catch up on yer sleep."

Georgie, who was listening to what Pattie was saying, looked overjoyed at the idea of serving the village store customers.

Every morning after breakfast, Georgie kissed her mummy and sister goodbye and skipped joyfully down Half Mile Lane to her new 'job'. She was as happy as a sandboy standing on the little stool that Pattie had placed behind the counter. Customers joined in the game as Georgie gave them her sweetest smile.

"How may I help you?" she asked just as Pattie and Robert had taught her.

The customers loved it and often gave her a penny as a thank you.

But even though this gave Mummy the respite she needed, Pattie and Georgie could both see that she was still not her normal self. Daddy also looked worried as Mummy became more and more lethargic, even to the point of ignoring Daisy's crying. Georgie was in the lounge with Mummy, Daddy, and baby Daisy when Daddy expressed his concern.

"I'm really worried about you, Florrie. You seem to have lost your zeal for life. In fact, it's so rare to see a smile on your face that the days seem dull compared to what they used to be. Georgie and I miss that bright smile. Please tell me what's wrong, Darling. Do you feel ill?"

"I don't feel ill, Gerald, more tired, so tired that I almost feel drugged. No matter how much sleep I get, it just doesn't seem to be enough. My energy seems to have left me, so much so that I almost dread Daisy crying because it means I must make the effort of picking her up and feeding her. I somehow feel resentful towards her for making me feel so low. And Georgie, I'm sorry Babe but I just don't seem to be able to summon up the energy to give you my attention anymore. In fact, I just feel too numb to love anyone or anything right now."

Georgie saw the tears sliding down Mummy's cheeks and did her best to stem her own tears of hurt at the news that Mummy couldn't love her right now. Daddy held Mummy gently as he sat beside her on the settee,

giving her time to give vent to her emotions. After a while her tears stopped, and he passed her his clean handkerchief to dry her cheeks and blow her nose.

"What can I do to help you, Florrie? Just say the word."

"I don't think anyone can do anything. I don't understand why, but I sort of feel a numb sadness all the time. In my head I know that I've got everything I need to make me happy – two beautiful children and a caring husband, and two lovely friends in Pattie and Robert who can't do enough to help me, bless them. But knowing doesn't seem to make any difference."

Mummy's words shocked Georgie deeply, and she found it even harder to stop herself from crying, especially as Mummy's tears had started flowing again. Then on top of everything, Daisy started to cry, which made Mummy cry even more. Daddy seemed to be at a loss and looked a bit panicky to Georgie, which made her feel scared. At that very moment there was a tap on the door and in walked Pattie. She stopped dead as she took in the scene. Daisy's crying was reaching a crescendo, Mummy was sobbing, Daddy looked panic stricken, and Georgie's face was white and shocked. As soon as Georgie saw Pattie, it triggered her into action. She rushed over to Daisy's Moses basket and gently picked up her little sister, instinctively holding her close and rocking her from side to side. Pattie observed the scene with a look of love and concern on her face.

"Reight, Gerald, you go and put t' kettle on for a brew while I sort matters out here. Florrie, you just wipe those beautiful eyes of yours, because no matter how yer feel at this moment, that little babby needs to be fed and yer t' only one who can do that."

Pattie's words seemed to bring Mummy to her senses, because she instantly responded to her friend and sorted herself out.

Georgie felt a sense of overwhelming relief as Pattie continued with her orders.

"Now Georgie, take Daisy over to yer mum and then run upstairs to get a clean nappy and t' baby's talcum powder, please."

Georgie instantly obeyed.

69

Soon peace was restored, and everyone sat drinking the tea that Daddy brought into the lounge on a tray as Daisy happily sucked away at her mother's breast. Once the baby had finished feeding and Pattie had instructed Daddy on how to change a nappy, she sat next to Mummy on the sofa with Georgie on her lap.

"Reight, Florrie, my lovely friend, let's talk about what's causing thee ter look so sad all time - and don't look so surprised – yes, I've noticed it too, as I'm sure has young Georgie here. You're usually such an energetic and happy person. You've always given Georgie so much love and attention and she's bound to be missing that. I know she'll be understanding that you're tired because of little Daisy, but she'll not be able to understand why you so seldom cuddle her anymore. It's not just tiredness, is it, young woman? So, spill t' beans. I think we all deserve an honest explanation."

Mummy looked slightly shell-shocked at her friend's forthright approach, but at the same time clearly recognised the truth in what she said.

"You're right of course, Pattie. I know I haven't been … I'm still not myself. I think I might have a touch of the baby blues. That's when you feel sad for no reason, Georgie. It often happens after having a baby but usually passes. It's not that I don't love you, Babe, I really, really do. It's just that the baby blues makes it difficult for a mummy to feel it and to show it."

Georgie accepted Mummy's outstretched hand that drew her in closer for a cuddle. Sliding from Pattie's lap, she put her small arms around her mummy's neck, returning the hug that she was so pleased to receive. Pattie smiled.

"Right, now that's out in t' open, what are we going to do about it?"

At that point, Daddy interrupted.

"I'm going to call the doctor and get him to come in to see you, Florrie. Maybe he can give you some pills and you'll start to feel better in no time at all."

"No, I'd rather you didn't do that, please. I think this is something that I'm going to have to deal with myself. I've never heard of any sort of magic pill that can make the baby blues go away."

"Okay, Darling. Well at least let me talk to the doctor about how you're feeling just in case he can suggest anything. I think maybe a small glass of brandy every evening might help you to relax, but I'd rather check with him first."

To Georgie's relief, Mummy agreed to Daddy speaking to the doctor, so a few minutes later, he walked around to the surgery. When he returned, he told Mummy, Pattie, and Georgie that the doctor had confirmed that there was little in the way of medication that would help, but he had agreed that a daily brandy couldn't hurt.

"It's worth a try, Lad. But do let me know if things get any worse," responded Pattie. "T' chances are that, as Florrie regains her strength, things will naturally right themselves."

So, every evening when Georgie was in bed and Daisy had gone down after a good feed, Georgie knew that Daddy would be going to the sideboard and taking out the bottle of brandy. As she lay in bed, she would visualise him carefully pouring a small amount into a sherry glass and passing it to Mummy. She pictured her mummy sipping the dark liquid as they chatted together about how the day had gone, and she prayed that the brandy would do its magic and make her mummy well again. So concerned was Georgie that she would often still be lying awake when she heard Mummy and Daddy coming upstairs to bed. She'd listen hard, hoping there'd be a clue as to how Mummy felt. After a few days, she overheard Mummy telling Daddy that she felt ready to face both the baby's night-time feed and the prospect of the following day. The impact of those positive words was so great on Georgie that she very soon fell asleep and even overslept the next morning.

Daddy had also insisted that he would be staying home to ease Mummy's workload until she felt better, which cheered Georgie up even more. Mummy told Daddy that she was grateful and relieved to have him around so that she could get some proper rest at last. It looked to Georgie like Mummy had turned a corner and that all would now be well again, especially when she heard Mummy telling Daddy that she was looking forward to the time when she'd be able to start enjoying three-week old Daisy again.

CHAPTER 7

Late July 1951

Deterioration.

"Look, Gerald. I just want to be on my own with the children. You've been off work for a good couple of weeks now, and it's not helping. Please go back to work. I can conquer these baby blues better without you continually hovering over me."

Mummy's voice sounded harsh to Georgie who was sitting on the settee stroking Daisy's soft cheeks and making smiley faces at her to teach her little sister to smile back at her. Even at her young age, Georgie was sensitive to tension and could hear that her mummy's patience was wearing thin. Initially Mummy was glad about Daddy's support, and the daily brandy had seemed to help, but now she seemed aggravated by him and even more edgy than she had been just after Daisy's birth. The atmosphere in the cottage was affecting both Georgie, who had lost her natural bounce and exuberance, and baby Daisy who was unsettled and irritable. Mummy's beautiful blonde hair now hung in greasy rats' tails and her clothes were stained. She just didn't appear to have the energy or inclination to look after herself anymore.

"But Florrie, it's clear that you can't conquer anything right now," said Daddy.

"You're unwell. You aren't even managing to look after yourself, let alone the girls. It's making Georgie unhappy, and Daisy does nothing but cry."

Georgie started at the increased pitch and volume of her mummy's voice.

"Don't you criticise me, Gerald, and how dare you comment on my children. Just remember you're not their real father, so just butt out!"

Daddy paled. Georgie turned tail and ran upstairs. Daisy began to cry. Georgie sat on the top step straining to hear the words that Daddy was calmly saying.

"I'm going to ring the doctor, Florrie."

Georgie quietly slid down a few steps so she could look beneath the bannister rail and into the sitting room just in time to see her mummy's face redden, before she began to scream like a banshee, curses emanating from her angry mouth in words that Georgie had never heard before and, by the look on Daddy's face, were also alien to him. Daddy turned his back on Mummy and walked calmly out of the sitting room towards Georgie. He climbed the few stairs and sat beside her, wiped the tears of fear from her face, took her by her trembling hand, and led her to the bottom of the staircase and out of the front door. The two shocked and silent figures walked down Half Mile Lane and entered the village store. Pattie and Robert asked no questions when they saw the expressions on Georgie's and Daddy's faces. It was no secret that they had noticed how much Florrie had deteriorated over the past few weeks. Instead, Pattie took Georgie's small hand from her daddy and led her through the door at the back of the shop into the living quarters.

"Can I use your 'phone to ring the doctor, please mate?" asked Gerald in a quiet voice.

Robert beckoned him behind the post office counter where the black telephone sat. Gerald nodded and without a word, proceeded to dial the doctor's surgery.

It was a sluggish Gerald who returned alone to the cottage wondering what he would find. On entering he was shocked to see Florrie cowering at the far end of the settee, wide eyes flaming, holding the screaming Daisy tightly in her arms.

"Keep away from me. Don't come any nearer!"

Gerald walked slowly towards his distraught wife in an attempt to calm her with his quiet, comforting voice.

"Hush now Darling. No need to be upset. Let me take Daisy and put her in her cot so you can get some rest."

Florrie seemed to be relaxing a little, so Gerald moved slowly closer.

"It's alright my beautiful Florrie, everything is going to be fine. Relax now. I'm here to make things better."

Gerald calmly reached out to take Daisy from his wife's arms, but before he could do so, he was almost knocked backwards by the force of Florrie's deep groan that seemed to come from the pit of her very being, increasing in volume like an approaching plane hurtling along the runway. In an instant, Gerald withdrew, knowing that there was nothing more he could do to help. He went to wait in the front garden for the doctor to arrive and soon saw the man's car struggling to get up the slope to the cottage, followed by a silent ambulance.

The doctor got out of his car, slammed the door, and walked over to Gerald to shake his hand.

"I decided ter call t' ambulance immediately after what tha told me, Gerald. It sounds like Florrie's probably had a bit of a nervous breakdown."

Gerald nodded and led the concerned doctor into the cottage where Florrie had not moved from her position at the far end of the settee.

"Go away. Leave me alone. You're not taking my baby, so don't even try," Florrie growled.

"Nobody is going to take t' babby, Florrie Dear. Daisy can stay with yer," calmed the doctor. "I think thee and t' bairn need to spend a few weeks away from here in a nice peaceful atmosphere where both of yer can relax and get back to yer old selves."

Florrie's tense shoulders noticeably lowered, and the fire disappeared from her eyes. Her voice sounded almost, but not quite, back to normal.

"Yes, I just need some rest, Doctor. Everything is so tense here with Gerald around all the time and Georgie looking so sullen. Why can't they understand I just need some peace and quiet? Why are they being so selfish?"

Gerald flinched as he heard Florrie's uncharacteristically unkind words. The doctor glanced over at him as if to plead with him not to retaliate. At that moment the ambulance crew, a young man and woman, came through the front door dressed in their uniforms. Florrie looked surprised.

"It's okay, my love," soothed the young woman, "We're going to give you and the baby a ride to a very peaceful hospital where you can relax and start to feel better."

Florrie's eyes started to widen and look nervous as she turned towards the doctor. He nodded encouragingly, and she once again relaxed. The young woman gently took Florrie's tense elbow, not attempting to loosen her patient's firm hold on the now sleeping baby and led her like a submissive child out to the waiting ambulance. The doctor put a comforting hand on Gerald's shoulder as they stood in the doorway, watching the vehicle turn around and disappear down the lane.

"Will Georgie and I be able to visit?" asked Gerald as he closed the front door.

"It's probably best if yer don't visit fer now. It could delay Florrie's recovery, and it's not really a suitable environment for young Georgie ter see her mam in."

Gerald nodded.

The doctor tried to reassure Gerald by telling him that the hospital would contact the surgery with information about his wife's progress, and he would be sure to pass that on.

"Now can I give yer a lift back t' village store? You'll be wanting ter pick up that wee bairn of yours. She'll need lots of reassurance from yer while her mammy's away."

"Thanks, Doctor, I'd appreciate that."

When the doctor dropped him off at the bottom of Half Mile Lane, Gerald thanked him, and turning towards the shop entrance, took a deep breath. As he moved forward, he wondered what sort of emotional state he'd find Georgie in. This wasn't how he had thought his new family life would end up. However, he determined there and then to make the most of the month or so he would spend alone with Georgie before she started school in September. Who knows, Florrie might only need to spend a couple of weeks in hospital before she and the baby return home. Maybe then their real married life could begin. Maybe he could finally consummate their union.

As Gerald entered, Georgie looked up from her stool behind the post office counter. She and Pattie were busy placing new postage stamps into their relevant pages in a big book. Pattie smiled as Georgie jumped down from the stool and ran round the counter straight into her daddy's waiting arms.

"Is my mummy alright?" were her first and only words.

"She will be, Darling. She just has to have some peace and quiet for a few weeks in a special hospital, and then she'll be as good as new."

This seemed to satisfy the little girl, who climbed down from Daddy's arms and proceeded to look behind him, before opening the shop door and looking outside. Gerald and Pattie exchanged a bemused look.

"Where's Daisy, Daddy?"

"She's gone with Mummy, Georgie. Mummy must feed Daisy, so that was the only way she could do it. But don't worry, they'll be back in no time at all."

Georgie looked thoughtful as she processed her daddy's words. "Who will look after me?"

"Well, I will of course," he responded

"But who will look after me when you're at work?"

That was Pattie's cue to join in.

"Do yer mean to say tha've already forgotten that you're me post office helper, Georgie?"

Georgie let out a little giggle for the first time that day.

"Oh yes. Sorry, Pattie, I forgot. I will be working with you when Daddy's at work."

Gerald felt a little uncomfortable.

"No need, Pattie. I can take a few more weeks off work to be with Georgie."

"Ey Gerald, I wouldn't hear of it. I need my little helper, and yer've been off work long enough. Yer don't want ter chance losing t' job, Lad. Then where would yer be?"

Gerald was on the spot, and he knew it. Far better to agree with Pattie and spend the time looking for a job – maybe a little further afield this time – somewhere that hadn't heard Alfie's nasty rumours. He smiled and thanked Pattie, took George's hand, and they walked together up to the cottage. Once inside, Gerald turned to the little girl and with a big smile on his face said,

"What about a game of chase?"

Georgie screeched and immediately ran away from her daddy.

"You can't catch me," she shouted as she disappeared out into the back garden.

"Oh yes I can, and when I do, you're in for the tickling of your life."

Georgie shrieked with laughter as Daddy pursued her round and round the garden.

"I'm getting closer, Little Girl."

More shrieks from Georgie as her daddy caught up with her and began to tickle her under her arms until his daughter could take no more and shouted for him to stop. He moved away from her wriggling body, leaving her to lay on the grass and recover for a few moments. Then he moved closer and said in a mock threatening voice,

"Aha, that means I'm the winner. That means I can do whatever I like."

Georgie instantly jumped up and ran toward the open kitchen door.

"Only if you can catch me."

So, Gerald chased her again, this time around the living room, up the stairs and into Georgie's bedroom, where he grabbed the squealing child and threw her onto the bed. Before she had bounced back up, he restarted the tickling until she begged him to stop, and both ended up on the bed in fits of laughter.

"Right young woman, if I'm to go back to work tomorrow, we're going to have to get an early start. Time for tea and then bed."

"Can I have beans on toast, Daddy? I already had a big meal at Pattie and Robert's earlier."

So, both sat at the kitchen table enjoying their tea, Georgie chatting in her old exuberant way, while a relieved Gerald felt glad that just a bit of fun had been all that was needed to bring back the happy child that he knew and loved.

The next couple of weeks passed quickly for Gerald. Each morning he would rise early, wake Georgie and leave her washing and dressing herself in the bathroom, a task her mummy had encouraged her to do herself for several months now, while he prepared their porridge for breakfast. He would then drive his car down to the village store with his daughter sitting beside him, to find either Robert or Pattie waiting for them in the shop doorway. Georgie would jump out of the car and run into waiting arms for a morning hug. Then, holding hands, they would wave Gerald off.

Gerald only spent the first two days driving from one building site to another before he found a building company that was happy to take him on immediately. His relief at no longer having to deceive his friends and his daughter was evident in his manner. He could see that Pattie and Robert had noticed the difference in him but thought they had probably put it down to him having got used to the idea of being apart from Florrie and the new baby and having returned to the normality of work. Often Pattie would hand a casserole dish to Gerald on his return from work in the evening. It meant that he only had to warm up the food in the oven rather than spend time on food preparation, which allowed him more time to give Georgie the attention she needed in the absence of her mummy and little sister. It was easier at the weekends when there was more time to relax, and the foursome soon got back into the habit of having tea together on Saturday evenings. The fun and laughter returned to the lives of Gerald and Georgie. Only in quiet moments at nights did Gerald have time to think about Florrie and Daisy, missing them and wondering if his wife's mental state was improving.

Three weeks passed by until one Friday evening after Georgie had gone to bed, there was a tap at the door. Gerald opened it to find the doctor standing on the doorstep with a sombre expression on his face. Gerald's heart missed a beat as he invited the man in.

"Come in, Doctor, can I get you a cup of tea?"

"Thanks, Gerald, but I've just had one, so no thanks."

Gerald led the doctor into the living room where they both sat down.

"I assume young Georgie is in bed?"

"Yes, she is, Doctor."

"Good. That's t' reason I left me visit till late. I don't want ter upset her more than she already has been."

Gerald's heart was beating faster as he looked questioningly at the man on the settee.

"Hospital rang me terday. Not good news I'm afraid. Florrie hasn't reacted well ter psychiatric input she's been getting. In fact, she's got worse. She's even showing signs of rejecting t' babby – but don't worry,

the nurses have taken on Daisy's care, and she is doing fine. They hope that keeping Daisy with her will eventually help in tha wife's recovery."

Gerald could only stare at the doctor, unable to find any words to express his shock and dismay.

"To cut ter chase, Gerald, it's likely to be some months before Florrie is well enough ter return home. The hospital will try a little longer with t' psychiatrist, but if it doesn't work, they will have to try E.C.T."

"E.C.T?"

"Electroconvulsive therapy. It's a medical treatment used in patients like Florrie with severe depression that hasn't responded to other treatments. It involves a brief electrical stimulation of t' brain while t' patient is under anaesthesia. Don't worry, she won't feel a thing, and there's lots of evidence ter show that this has an immediate positive effect."

Gerald looked confused.

"But Florrie has baby blues. What do you mean severe depression? What's going on. She went into hospital to get better, not worse."

The doctor's sympathetic face made Gerald remember that this man had not caused the problem but was only trying to help. He listened calmly to what the caring man had to say.

"Try not to distress tha self, Gerald. I know it all seems like negative news right now, but given time, I feel sure Florrie will make a good recovery and return home to yer both as if nought has happened."

"I hope you're right, Doctor. I apologise for my harsh attitude. It's just that everything is getting on top of me."

The doctor stood and shook Gerald's hand warmly.

"No need to apologise to me, Lad. I hope yer can help young Georgie ter cope with t' news that she won't be seeing her mummy and sister for a while yet. Just call me if yer need anything."

Gerald showed the doctor out and returned to the living room where he sat down heavily on the couch. Head in hands, he vented his feelings with quiet tears, praying that he'd find a way of breaking the news to his beloved Georgie without causing her too much pain. He couldn't keep the thought out of his mind that he might have lost the real Florrie forever, never having consummated their union. Oh, why did he not do so on their wedding night? Why did he act like the overconcerned person that he really wasn't? Just for once, why couldn't he just be himself - the real him that he'd kept hidden for so long?

Gerald slept restlessly that night, pictures flashing through his mind of his life before moving up to Ousby. The next morning, he felt weary, wondering how he was going to break the bad news to Georgie without upsetting her too much. He concluded that this was an impossible task, but it did occur to him that there was a way of cheering her up afterwards. So as soon as his little girl woke up, he sat her on his knee and told her as gently as he could that it would be a while longer than expected before she would see Mummy and Daisy again. Georgie's first reaction was to burst into tears and ask why.

Georgie tried to take in what Daddy was saying to her.

"The treatment to make Mummy better hasn't worked as well as the doctors and nurses expected, Darling. But don't worry, there are other treatments they can try. One of them is bound to make her better. But meanwhile, we need to remember that you'll be starting school in just a couple of weeks, and I thought we might drive into Penrith today to buy your school uniform."

Georgie jumped off Daddy's knee and bounced up and down clapping her hands.

"Yes please, Daddy. I can't wait to go to school. I want to look like all the other boys and girls in their uniforms. Mummy showed me a picture of the uniform before Daisy was born. She was going to make the pale blue dress and the games skirt herself to save money. She even thought she'd be able to manage the grey winter skirt and pale blue blouse herself. In fact, I know she started knitting the maroon pullover. I wonder where she keeps her knitting."

Daddy laughed and gave Georgie a hug, which she 'lapped up hungrily' before listening to Daddy's words.

"I don't think Mummy got around to making anything, but that's not a problem, we can buy the dress, skirt, blouse and everything else you need in the school uniform shop in Penrith. We could even go into a café for our dinner if you like. What do you say?"

Georgie started bouncing again, encouraged by the look of relief on her Daddy's face. She needed no persuasion to wash and dress herself, and breakfast was a chatty affair as Georgie swallowed mouthfuls of porridge between her excited words. Soon father and daughter were on their way to Penrith to enjoy their day's uniform shopping, and their sausage, egg and chips in the café followed by chocolate ice cream.

When Robert and Pattie arrived for their weekly social evening, Georgie was still full intermittently bouncing up and down.

"I'm going to be a model in a fashion show for you, Pattie and Robert, so you can see my new school clothes."

"Ooh what excitement Our Lass. A proper Saturday evening treat," gushed Pattie.

Georgie disappeared upstairs to her bedroom, returning within five minutes wearing her new pale blue dress. Walking up and down the length of the living room with her hands on her hips and turning around with an exaggerated wiggle and what she imagined was a model's stare, she had the small audience in fits of laughter and loud applause, which encouraged her to repeat her act several times, repeatedly running back to her bedroom and returning wearing another part of her school uniform.

"When I grow up and become a dancer, the audience will clap me just like you are," the wide-eyed little girl declared seriously.

"I dare say yer reight there, Bairn," replied Robert as his wife and Georgie's daddy nodded vigorously.

"And I'll be clapping the loudest, Darling Girl," said Daddy.

Georgie felt six feet tall but very tired by the time she climbed into her bed after the guests had left. When Daddy came to tuck her in, she suddenly felt sad.

"What's up, My Darling?" he asked her gently.

"I miss my mummy and Daisy, Daddy. I want them to come home 'cos I feel lonely without them. I want Mummy to take me to school with Daisy in her pram on my first day like all the other mummies will. Why can't you go and get her from the hospital and bring her and my baby sister home? Why can't things be like they used to be before Daisy was born?"

Georgie let the tears stream down her face as Daddy lifted her gently out of her bed and into a cuddle.

"It's okay to be sad, Georgie. I am too. I wish Mummy and Daisy could come home, but we must be patient. I'll tell you what, you can sleep in my and Mummy's big bed with me tonight if you would like to. Maybe you'll feel less lonely that way."

"Yes please, Daddy. I'll feel less lonely with you cuddling me all night."

So, she allowed Daddy to carry her into the other bedroom and tuck her up under the covers on the side nearest to the window – Mummy's side. Georgie felt reassured as he kissed her goodnight and told her that he'd be coming to bed very soon. Georgie turned on her side and snuggled down as her eyes began to close involuntarily. The last thing she knew was Daddy stroking her blonde hai

CHAPTER 8

Late August – Mid September 1951

A new challenge

Gerald's mind was in a turmoil as he sat at the kitchen table sipping his hot bedtime drink. A battle was raging inside his head. His sense of responsibility fought against his personal desire. His love for his four-year-old daughter brawled with his own secret needs. His loneliness wrestled with his knowledge of what was right and what was wrong, what was decent and what was indecent. He was aware that he needed help, and for the first time since moving up to Ousby, he missed the support he'd been given when he'd lived in London.

'Why can't I be like other normal men?' he asked himself, whilst knowing deep down that this thing was too embedded in his personality to change it.

His thoughts continued as he slowly climbed the stairs.

'I must control it. I must control me. I must be strong. Oh, Florrie, why can't you be here. Everything would have been fine if you hadn't got ill. It's not my fault. I've tried so hard. I need you here now. I need your comfort, the soothing comfort of your warm body wrapped in my

embrace. I'd have been fine if it wasn't for you. Oh God, help me, please, please help me.'

Gerald turned right at the top of the stairs and walked into the bedroom that had been his and Florrie's sanctuary since they married. He silently changed into his pyjamas and slipped under the covers. Turning onto his left side, he expected to see the blonde hair of little Georgie shining golden in the moonlight. Instead, there was nothing. He lifted the covers where he had left her earlier and yes, nothing.

"Georgie. Where are you, Georgie?" he whispered loudly.

Silence. The man sat bolt upright as panic rose from his stomach. He leapt out of bed, moving swiftly around the end towards the window. No, his little girl had not fallen out of the bed in her sleep and slid onto the rug. Initially paralysed for the split second it took for his common sense to take over; it occurred to Gerald that his daughter had probably decided to play a game with him. After all, fun and games were their favourite pastimes together. He moved back to the other side of the room and opened the large oak cupboard that he and Florrie hung their clothes in. He slid the hangers apart and peered into the back thinking that any second, he would find a giggling Georgie crouching in one of the dark corners and they'd laugh together. No, not there. At that moment he heard a tiny snort – the sort that his daughter often made in her sleep. A river of relief flowed through his tense body, knowing that this small sound meant that she was at least in the cottage somewhere. Then a light switched on his mind. How could he be so stupid? He crept out of the bedroom, along the short landing, and into the bedroom next door. There he found his precious child, huddled up under her covers with only a fan of golden hair on the pillow as proof of her presence. Gerald moved to the side of the sleeping child's bed and gently tidied some strands of hair away from her face. Her eyelids fluttered and half opened.

"Shhh. Go back to sleep now, Sweetheart. Daddy's here."

A smile flickered across the little face as Georgie turned over and snuggled back into her deep sleep.

Back in his own bed, Gerald offered up a silent prayer of thanks to the One he'd pleaded with on his way upstairs. Saved from himself, a sense of peace pervaded his tense body and he relaxed as he fell fast asleep.

A serious-faced Georgie sat beside her Daddy in his car. They were parked in the road opposite Ousby School gates. The temperature had dropped quite significantly over the weekend, so Daddy had advised her to wear her grey skirt and pale blue blouse, rather than just her pale blue cotton dress beneath her school blazer. Georgie sat beside her daddy silently watching other serious faced children holding tightly on to the hand of their equally serious faced mummies. It was clear to Georgie who were new starters. Those arriving on their own, running or skipping confidently through the gates, were happily greeting their friends after the long summer holiday. Some boys were already kicking a football around the playground, shouting commands to persuade whoever had the ball to kick it to them. A group of girls were playing 'It', screeching whenever they were near to capture, whilst a few more were practising handstands against the brick wall of the school building. Georgie looked up at Daddy as he turned his head towards her and spoke.

"Well, this is it, My Love. Your big day. How're you feeling?"

Georgie let out a quiet sob.

"Hey now. Why the sobs? This is a happy day – one you've been looking forward to for a long time. There's nothing to be worried or frightened about, Darling. You'll make lots of friends and learn lots of new things. It will be exciting."

"It's not that, Daddy," Georgie said between sobs. "It's just that nearly everyone has their mummy with them, and I don't. And I miss my mummy so much."

Daddy leaned over to comfort Georgie.

"Now look here, My Big Girl, you are the luckiest child of everyone. You have your daddy here. That's pretty special 'cos most daddies are at work this time of the day. So, let's wipe the tears away, get out of the car together, and stand tall as we hold hands and walk over to the school gate. I'm telling you you'll be the envy of every one of those new children. They'll all be wishing they were you."

86

Georgie removed her clean handkerchief from up her left sleeve, wiped her eyes, blew her nose, replaced the handkerchief and then without a second glance opened the car door and got out onto the pavement. She stood and waited for Daddy to emerge too, before she grinned up at him, took his hand and walked proudly beside him to the school gate.

Soon a jolly-looking middle-aged teacher appeared at the gate, coughed a few times to get everyone's attention, and proceeded to greet the new children.

"Well, what a smart-looking bunch of new pupils we have here! I'm Miss Longmore and I am your teacher."

Georgie couldn't take her eyes off her new teacher. She watched Miss Longmore survey the silent group, her smile broadening on her rosy, round face as she did so. Georgie was even more transfixed when she lifted her arms in welcome, causing her halo of tight mousy curls to quiver and bounce, providing a dazzling effect against her pinafore dress of bright patchwork squares over a shocking pink polo shirt, and her flat-heeled, yellow shoes with T strap and buckle to hold them in place. Georgie was mesmerised. Different parts of the woman's ample body vibrated as she spoke. The louder she spoke, the more animated she became, and the more vibrations were set up. Georgie sneaked a look up at her daddy's face. She could see his muscles working to stop his grin escaping. She moved a little closer to him and gave him a gentle nudge. Then she realised she had missed part of what Miss Longmore was saying.

"So, now then children, give your mummies … and daddy," she added as an afterthought, "a nice hug and kiss goodbye and let's start our adventure."

Georgie obeyed, as did all the other children and then she moved to stand in a straight line along the school fence facing towards her rainbow teacher. She felt like a soldier in her crisp new uniform.

"Well done, Children. Now just a quick word with your … er… parents before they leave. Mums and Dad, you may collect your little darlings at three-fifteen sharp here at the gate. We try to discourage parents entering the playground so that our children are clear where their boundaries lay. From tomorrow morning, if you accompany your children to school, you may leave them at this gate to enter the playground by

themselves. Any children finding their own way to school should come straight into the playground to wait for the morning bell to sound. So, off you go mums and dad, enjoy your day – the time is yours, so use it wisely."

The parents grinned and moved away from the school gate, giving their children a last, quick wave as they left. Daddy did the same and exchanged that suppressed grin with Georgie as he crossed the road, got into his car, and drove off to work. He'd told Georgie he'd been given special permission to arrive at the building site late and leave early for her first day at school. Thereafter, Pattie and Robert would take over school duties.

Georgie felt a frisson of nerves as Miss Longmore turned to her 'crocodile' and smiled.

"Right, Children. You are now Class 1, so follow me into the first day of the biggest adventure of your life. Georgie smiled as did the other eleven children, and none of them looked back.

Two weeks passed and Georgie felt happy and settled at her new school. She didn't mind at all that her daddy couldn't take her and collect her each day. She had learned to love Pattie and Robert as a second mum and dad, and they seemed to be enjoying their new role. Pattie told Georgie that she and Robert had always been sad not to have had children of their own, but now they were loving having Georgie to look after and felt like she was almost like their own daughter. Pattie had hugged Georgie and told her that they just wanted to make her happy. Georgie knew how much they cared about her and Daddy and was touched by the practical support they freely gave to make life much easier for him.

Another month went by with no further news about Florrie, and Gerald was feeling increasingly concerned for her wellbeing. Also, he was fearful that the bond between Georgie and baby Daisy would be damaged if the two were separated for much longer. In the evenings after Georgie had gone to bed, Gerald tried to distract himself with a good

book, or the daily newspaper that one of his mates on the building site had passed on to him. Sometimes he found himself not taking in the words on the page, but instead trying to picture little Daisy's face. He was scared that his memories were fading and feared that such a little baby wouldn't know him at all when she returned home. He found it less difficult to picture Florrie, although he had to try hard to visualise her happy face rather than the distraught one that she'd displayed the last time he saw her. It was now the middle of October. Florrie and Daisy had been gone since late July – two and a half months. Gerald began to descend into a mild depression, and continually scolded himself.

'Remember your daughter, Man,' he would say to himself, 'She needs you to remain happy for her. Just stop this feeling sorry for yourself. Pull your socks up and get on with it. There are many others in a worse position than you!'

Then just a couple of days later, he received another visit from the local GP. The knock came in the evening again, so it came as no surprise that the news was not what he wanted to hear.

"I'm so sorry to be the bearer of bad news again, Gerald. I wish it could be different, but it is what it is. Florrie has, not unexpectedly, rejected little Daisy completely. The decision has been made to try the ECT, but there's a problem. The nursing staff no longer have the capacity to take care of the baby. The medical staff have discussed it and feel that Daisy's wellbeing is now paramount and must take priority over everything else that's happening. They think the baby should come home. The question is, are you able to look after her? I know you work, so I realise that you may well not be in a position to have her."

"But what will happen to Daisy if I can't have her, Doctor?"

"The hospital will have to find her a temporary foster home."

Gerald knew immediately that he couldn't let that happen to Daisy. After all, what would Florrie think of him if she came home only to discover he'd let her down so badly.

"No. I could never let that happen, Doctor. I'll find a way. When do I need to fetch her from the hospital?"

A look of visible relief showed on the doctor's face. He clearly cared about his patients – even one as tiny as Daisy.

"No need to collect her Gerald. I'll arrange for an ambulance to bring her home. One of the nurses who's been closely involved with the baby's care will want to officially hand her over to you safe and well."

So, it was agreed that the ambulance would bring Daisy home during the evening of the following day after Gerald had got home from work and picked up Georgie from Pattie and Robert. The doctor rose to take his leave, shaking hands with Gerald when he reached the door.

"Florrie is a very lucky lady to have a husband like you, Gerald. It will mean a lot to her when she's better to know you kept the family together."

Gerald watched as the caring man walked down the garden path, closed the wooden gate behind him, and raised his hand in a casual salute as he got into his old car. It wasn't until Gerald returned to the living room and sat back on the settee that panic set in. How on earth was he going to manage this? He couldn't ask Pattie and Robert to look after a three-month-old baby all day whilst running the village store. It was one thing to take care of Georgie before and after school, but quite another to add this extra burden to their already very busy life. No, he'd have to think of some other way, and he'd have to think fast. He could maybe get a few days off work to get the baby settled and Georgie used to her little sister being around again, but he had to think of a more long-term arrangement. Maybe Pattie and Robert would have an idea. He'd speak to them first thing in the morning when he dropped Georgie off.

Surprisingly he slept well that night. The thought of having the baby back again seemed to counteract the concern about how he was going to manage. He awoke the next morning bright and early with a spark of excitement in the pit of his stomach. He was looking forward to seeing Georgie's reaction when he told her the news. He waited until they were both sitting at the kitchen table eating their porridge.

As Georgie was happily enjoying her breakfast, she noticed that Daddy seemed to be a bit fidgety. She looked over at him just as he began to speak.

"I've got some news for you, Georgie," he said.

"Is Mummy coming home, Daddy? Is that what the news is? Will we all be together again at last?"

Daddy seemed taken aback and paused for a second before responding.

"Sorry, Georgie, not Mummy ... but the next best thing."

Georgie felt perplexed. What could be the next best thing after Mummy? Daddy had raised and dashed her hopes within a few short seconds. Didn't he know that it was Mummy she wanted – Mummy that she missed so badly? How could he be so mean? Georgie couldn't stop the tears from appearing in the corner of her eyes.

Daddy saw the tears too and tried to rescue the situation quickly.

"Don't be upset, Darling. Come with me and I'll show you a clue."

He offered his hand to Georgie who scraped her chair back from the table and willingly took hold of it. He squeezed her small hand and led her upstairs into her bedroom. Then he pulled open the drawer with Daisy's clothes still neatly stacked inside. Georgie caught on immediately and let out a squeal of delight.

"My sister's coming home, isn't she? I'm going to see Daisy again aren't I, Daddy?"

Georgie pulled her daddy to his feet, held both of his hands, and danced him around in a circle whilst laughing with pure joy. He then held his arms wide, and she jumped into his hug whilst he continued his dance, both laughing and hugging each other until Daddy was out of breath. He gently placed his daughter back on the floor in front of him.

"When is she coming home, Daddy. How are we going to take care of her? Will Pattie and Robert help us?"

"In answer to your first question, she's coming home this evening."

"Hooray!"

"As for how we are going to take care of her, I don't yet know. I think it will be too much for Pattie and Robert to take care of her as well as running the village store and looking after you before and after school, but I'm hoping they'll have some bright ideas as to what we can do. I'll ask them when I drop you off ... and talking of that, look at the time! Quick, get your blazer on, we've got to get going."

Georgie could see Daddy felt nervous as he stopped the car outside the village store. Robert was waiting in the doorway and looked surprised when Daddy got out of the car as well as Georgie.

"Ey up, Gerald. We're not used to seeing you get out t' car this time of t' morning. Come on in, Lad."

Robert took Georgie's hand and led Daddy inside where Pattie was sorting out the tills ready for the start of the day. She looked up with a welcoming smile as she saw Georgie coming through the door holding Robert's hand, and then her smile turned to surprise as Daddy appeared.

"Gerald! I wasn't expecting to see thee this morning. Is sommat up?"

Daddy explained his dilemma to the attentive pair.

"... and so, you see, I need to sort something out pretty quickly. I just wondered if you had any bright ideas. I know it would be impossible for you to have her as well as Georgie, so please don't feel there's any pressure on you to do so. I just need help to find an answer to my problem 'cos there's no way I'd let Daisy go into a foster home – even on a temporary basis."

"Hmmm, that's a difficult one, Gerald," said Pattie. "You're right o' course. As much as we'd like ter; there's no way we could manage t' bairn. But I think I might have t' answer. My sister's girl, Molly, has just finished at college. She's seventeen now and told me when I last saw her that she wants ter be a Children's Nanny. She's been doing a child-care course, so she knows what she's doing."

"Molly sounds perfect, Pattie. I knew you'd have the answer. Will you be able to contact her to see if she's interested in the job? I'm sure my boss will give me the next few days off to get Daisy settled back in, so that'll get us to the weekend. If Molly could start on Monday, that would be perfect. Meanwhile, it would be good if she could pop round before

the weekend to meet and get to know Daisy before she's left alone with her."

"No worries, Lad. I'll call in ter see her and her mam after I've dropped Georgie off ter school. I reckon she'll be thrilled ter bits. Now you go off ter work and leave it ter me."

By the time Daddy arrived to pick up Georgie that evening, it was all sorted out. Molly was more than happy to take the job, as Pattie had suspected she would be, and Daddy's boss had agreed to him taking the rest of the week off. So, it was an excited pair who arrived home at the cottage that evening

CHAPTER 9

Mid-September – Mid October 1951

A new normal

Light suddenly filled the room. Gerald and Georgie had been sitting in the living room by the light of the open fire, Georgie happily recounting her day's activities at school with the colourful Miss Longmore. On seeing the light, she immediately jumped up from the settee.

"They're here, Daddy."

Daddy didn't have to look outside to check. There were no streetlights in Half Mile Lane, and it was already dusk at eight o'clock on a mid-September evening. He, too, jumped up and rushed with Georgie to open the front door, turning on the electric light as he went. There they found a nurse walking down the garden path towards them, cuddling a well wrapped up, sleeping Daisy in her arms, and followed by a uniformed ambulance driver carrying a large holdall.

"Come in, come in," said Daddy as the bouncing Georgie by his side moved backwards to make room.

"Yer must be Georgie," said the nurse to the excited little girl, "Tha mammy has told me all about yer."

Georgie was a bit thrown. She'd forgotten Mummy in the excitement of Daisy coming home. This made her feel momentarily guilty and sad before the excitement of the event took over.

"Yes, I am, and you're holding my little sister, aren't you?"

The young nurse laughed and nodded as she continued into the living room still followed by the uniformed, bag man, but with Georgie in close pursuit.

"Do sit down. Can I offer you both a cup of tea?" said the ever-polite Daddy.

As the nurse loosened Daisy's wrapping, she thanked Daddy but declined, explaining that they needed to return to the hospital as soon as possible. Georgie and her daddy let out a small gasp as they caught first sight of the baby.

"Wow, she's so big," exclaimed Georgie.

"She's certainly grown since the last time we saw her," agreed Daddy.

"May I please cuddle my little sister, nurse?" said Georgie jumping from one foot to the other.

"Please call me Nurse Sandra," said the nurse looking up at Daddy to get his consent for Georgie to hold the baby.

"Reight, Georgie, sit beside me here on t' settee."

Georgie obeyed, fidgeting about until she was resting against the back with her arms out ready to accept the precious load. By now, baby Daisy's eyes were wide open and surveying the scene around her. As soon as she saw Georgie's smiling face, she too beamed.

"She remembers me, Daddy. Look, she remembers me."

The nurse smiled at the happy reunion, and the look of wonderment on Daisy's daddy's face as he moved over towards the baby and stroked

her soft brown hair. Daisy didn't seem to be at all worried about her new environment and these two strangers who were chatting and cooing to her. She had clearly got used to seeing lots of different faces in the hospital as nurses came and went. At that point Nurse Sandra brought the little group back to the practicalities of the occasion.

"I've put a couple of full baby bottles in the holdall, so you don't have to worry about mixing feeds tonight. You just need to place t' bottle in a jug of hot water till t' milk is at skin temperature. Sprinkle a little on t' back of yer hand to test it."

Georgie was fascinated but Daddy looked shocked.

"I never even thought about getting any dried milk in for Daisy," he confessed.

"It's okay, I've also included a tin of dried baby milk," said the nurse.

Daddy looked relieved and heaved a sigh of relief.

"I know Florrie was feeding Daisy herself, so this might all be a bit strange for yer, but don't worry," continued the nurse. "There are instructions on tin and it's really quite simple. After Daisy has drunk what she wants of her bottle; empty t' rest out and wash it with hot soapy water, checking that teat's not blocked. Then rinse it under running water ter remove t' soap suds, and place both in a large saucepan of water. Bring it ter boil and leave for a couple of minutes ter sterilise bottles."

"Thank you, Nurse Sandra. I'm sure I can manage that, and I've already been taught how to change a nappy," said Daddy. "As you can see, I also have a very able helper in young Georgie here."

Georgie, who had been occupied chatting to Daisy and making her laugh, looked up and grinned at the sound of her name.

"Mummy and Mattie taught me lots about looking after babies."

Nurse Sandra looked questioningly at Daddy.

"Mattie is the local midwife who looked after Florrie during late pregnancy and also attended Daisy's birth," he clarified.

With a nod, the nurse stood up and signalled to the ambulance driver that it was time to go.

"Well, goodbye Georgie and little Daisy. I'm sure your daddy will manage fine with such a good helper to assist him."

Georgie waved goodbye and took Daisy's hand, guiding it to wave too as Daddy showed their visitors out. Within fifteen minutes of them leaving, one of the bottles was warming in a jug of hot water on the kitchen table, and Daddy had tested it several times on the back of his hand.

"We must be sure we don't burn Daisy's mouth," he called from the kitchen.

As Daddy returned to the living room, Georgie was feeling a little uncomfortable.

"Phew, Daddy, Daisy is so heavy that my arm is really aching. Please will you hold her now?"

Daddy carefully balanced the bottle of milk on the arm of the settee and reached out to take Daisy from Georgie's arms. He then sat down, rested Daisy against his left arm and offered the milk up to her pretty lips. Daisy didn't hesitate for one second. She immediately latched on to the teat and was soon sucking away happily as she snuggled up. Daddy looked entranced as he held Daisy. Georgie sensed that his heart was melting in the same way as hers had. Love shone from his eyes as he watched his baby daughter drinking. Georgie snuggled closer to him and felt certain that her daddy loved her little sister as much as he loved her. At that moment Daddy was her's and Daisy's knight in shining armour, and she felt sure that he would protect them both forever.

"Please may I hold the bottle, Daddy?"

He nodded and, without disturbing Daisy, allowed Georgie to take over the feeding until the bottle was half empty. He then instructed his eldest daughter to gently withdraw the teat from Daisy's mouth before he sat the baby up, only to discover that was all she needed to make her burp loudly. Georgie and Daddy laughed, and Daisy joined in with a smile, happy then to lay back and continue with her meal. However, after just a little more of the warm liquid, her sucking began to falter spasmodically

as she dropped off to sleep and immediately woke up again when the milk stopped flowing. Soon, however, she fell fast asleep, allowing the teat to drop from her slack lips. Both Daddy and Georgie had been transfixed throughout the feeding process, but now Georgie removed the bottle and took it out into the kitchen, placing it on the draining board ready to be washed. By the time she returned to the living room, Daddy had laid Daisy on the settee and was in the process of changing her nappy, which took him a short while to master, but he finally managed it and pulled her long nightdress back down over her chubby little legs. As he lifted the sleeping baby off the settee and on to his shoulder, she gave another contented burp, which again elicited a grin from Georgie.

Earlier that evening, Georgie had pleaded with Daddy to move the Moses basket into her bedroom, which he had done, placing it on the floor next to her bed. He'd said he wasn't sure how much the baby would be moving around at this stage, so he'd decided to discard the chairs that had previously supported the basket.

"Right, Young Georgie, let's get this sleeping bundle up to bed, and while I'm getting her settled, you can clean your teeth and get into your nightdress. I think we can miss your wash for one night."

So, Georgie followed Daddy as he carefully climbed the stairs with Daisy asleep in his arms, and soon both she and her little sister were settled in their beds. It was a late night for Georgie, so sleep came quickly.

Gerald had a few chores to do before he could get to bed so he quietly made his way back downstairs and into the kitchen. He was still feeling elated from the evening's events, so was happy to reflect on them as he washed up his and Georgie's dinner things, and Daisy's bottle. He had no idea what time the baby would wake up in the morning, so he decided to go straight to bed after the washing up was finished. As he fell asleep, he hoped that Daisy would continue to be as contented in the future.

It was the bright morning light shining in through the bedroom window that woke him the next morning. He lay relaxed and half asleep until he suddenly remembered Daisy. Oh no, had he slept through her waking cries? He was immediately alert, leapt out of bed, and rushed next door where he found both of his little girls lying side by side in Georgie's bed.

Georgie was holding up her favourite picture book about the little girl who had become a dancer and describing the pictures to her little sister in detail. Daisy, however, was not looking at the pictures but seemed more fascinated with Georgie's face and voice.

"Hello, Daddy."

"Good morning, my two beautiful daughters. What's happening here?"

"Well, when I woke up it was hardly light, but I looked down at Daisy and she was just quietly laying there with her eyes open. So, I decided to pick her up and bring her into bed with me. I've been showing her pictures ever since."

"I see. Well, it's way past the time we usually get you up for school, but as you've been such a good girl entertaining your sister, I think we'll give school a miss today. One day won't hurt, and I can give you a letter to take into Miss Longmore tomorrow explaining your absence. I'm sure she'll understand. You can run down the road to tell Pattie and Robert while I sort Daisy out. I'm not at work for the rest of the week and Molly, Pattie's niece, is dropping by to get to know Daisy before she starts looking after her while you and I are at school and work."

Daddy leant across Daisy's Moses Basket and lifted her gently out of Georgie's bed while Georgie scrambled out from under the covers, shuffling to the end of her bed and getting out onto the floor. Daddy looked pleased that Daisy smiled contentedly as he carried her downstairs. Georgie followed closely behind, keen to keep her little sister happy.

"This little girl is so placid, Georgie. If she continues like this, she'll be easy to look after," said Daddy.

"What's placid, Daddy?"

"Contented, Darling. She's very easy-going for a three-month-old."

"Oh. You mean she's a good girl like me?"

Daddy laughed and agreed, which brought a wide grin to Georgie's face, instantly replicated by her little sister.

When Georgie got back from the village store, Daddy was halfway through feeding Daisy.

"Right, Love. If you take Daisy from me and finish feeding her, I'll get our breakfast sorted out, then I want to get up into the loft to find your old cot. I think Daisy has grown out of the Moses Basket."

Georgie was more than happy to agree and finished feeding her sister, passing her over to Daddy to change her nappy while their breakfast sizzled away in the kitchen. Soon Daisy was lying happily in her pram in the hallway, wearing a pretty, long-sleeved, vyella dress, and enjoying kicking and trying to catch her own toes. Daddy and Georgie sat at the kitchen table eating their breakfast together, and by the time they'd finished, Daisy had settled into a snooze. Georgie gently covered her sister with a small, knitted blanket while her daddy carried on with the washing up and sterilising of the two empty bottles. Just as he was finishing, there was a gentle knock at the front door. Georgie, as usual, rushed to answer it.

"Hello. You must be Georgie. Me aunt told me all about yer," said the friendly, smiley faced girl standing on the doorstep pushing a stray dark curl behind one ear as she spoke.

Georgie nodded.

"I'm Molly. I've come about t' job of tekking care of t' babby from next week."

"Please come in. I'll get my daddy."

Daddy had heard Molly arrive and came out of the kitchen drying his hands on the damp tea towel. He shook Molly's hand and led her over to the pram where Daisy was still sleeping peacefully.

"Meet my youngest daughter, Daisy. Sorry she's sleeping at present but if you'd like to give Georgie your coat, she'll hang it on the stair post for

you while I make us a nice cuppa. I'll show you around the kitchen while the kettle's boiling if you like?"

"That'd be grand, thank yer. I'll need ter get to know my way around if I'm ter be taking care of t' bairn."

"You say, 'if'. Does that mean you're not sure if you want the job, Molly?"

"Nay. I'd love ter tek t' job. It's more about if yer happy ter have me. I've brought a reference from t' college, and I'd be more than happy ter demonstrate me skills."

Gerald looked a little taken aback as if he hadn't expected this situation, but then he quickly thought on his feet.

"Well, I was just about to make up Daisy's next bottle. It's already sterilised so perhaps you can show me how you would do that, please."

Georgie grinned in the background and saw Daddy notice. She knew that he didn't know how to do this task without closely reading and following the directions on the tin, but she wasn't going to let on and embarrass him.

"Course I will. Where do yer keep t' dried milk?" responded the confident Molly.

"It's right here on the kitchen table."

"Can I watch you, please, Molly?" piped up Georgie.

"Course yer can, Flower. Come and pull out t' chair here beside me so yer can see what I'm doing. We can use some o' that water yer daddy's boiling for a brew."

Two pairs of eyes followed Molly's every move as she poured in the boiling water up to the top mark on the bottle, opened the tin of dried milk and proceeded to count out the required number of scoops, levelling each one off with the blade of a knife. Having manipulated the teat onto the bottle rim, being careful not to touch the part that would go into Daisy's mouth, she gave the bottle a gentle shake until all the powder had dissolved. Georgie spontaneously clapped and Daddy smiled and nodded.

"Well done, Molly. Perfectly executed," said Daddy in a formal voice that made Georgie grin again. "We've now just to see how Daisy reacts to you."

"Thanks. Meanwhile it might be a good idea ter place t' bottle in a jug o' cold water so it's cool enough for t' babby when she's hungry."

"Right, yes. Er ... I'll find the jug now."

As Daddy rummaged around in the kitchen cupboards, Molly looked over at Georgie and gave her a co-conspiratorial wink. Georgie tried to wink back, not quite managing it. However, she knew at that moment that she really liked Molly.

"Here it is," said Gerald as he half-filled it from the cold tap and placed the bottle gently into the water to cool.

As if on cue, Daisy started to make a gurgling sound from the pram and all three moved to her side.

"Ey up, Little Lass. I'm Molly, and you must be t' lovely Daisy."

Daisy looked straight into Molly's eyes and smiled broadly as she let out a couple more gurgles as if to say hello.

"May I pick yer little sister up, please, Georgie?" asked Molly with a side glance at Daddy for affirmation.

"Yes. That will be fine, Molly. Daisy says she's happy with that."

After that, there was no looking back. Molly carried Daisy to the settee and patted the space beside her for Georgie to sit down. They immediately started to play with Daisy together as if they'd been lifelong friends.

"I'll finish making the tea, then," said Gerald and disappeared into the kitchen. He soon returned with a tray on which were two cups of tea, a glass of juice for Georgie, and a tea plate of malted milk biscuits. The rest of the morning was spent getting to know each other better over the tea and biscuits.

"I reckon t' milk will have cooled by now, Gerald. Would yer like me ter feed Daisy before I go?"

"No thank you, Molly, we've kept you far too long already. I think it goes without saying that you've got the job and we'll see you at half past seven on Monday morning."

He lifted Daisy from his new Nanny's capable arms, and after she'd slipped on her coat, he and Georgie stood at the door and waved her off.

"Can I feed Daisy, Daddy?"

"Oh, but I wanted to do that."

"But it's my turn."

"No, it's definitely my turn and I'm the daddy so I get to decide."

Daisy looked from one to the other and back again until her big sister and daddy burst into laughter and agreed to share the task as they'd done on the previous evening. Daisy let out a tiny giggle, which made them laugh even more.

The rest of the day went just as smoothly. Daddy found the pieces of cot in the loft and fitted them together, helped by Georgie while Daisy was snoozing. They washed and dried it thoroughly, and Georgie found some clean sheets in the baby drawer in her bedroom. Between them they decided where the best spot was to locate the cot, and it ended up against the wall opposite Georgie's bed.

Georgie awoke to the sound of Daddy's alarm clock the next morning, and by eight-fifteen they were walking together down Half Mile Lane on their way to school with Daisy in her pram and Georgie in her uniform. Soon it was Monday and Daddy had to return to work. Molly turned up on time, and Daddy dropped Georgie off at the village store where Pattie was waiting.

"Please will you get me in some powdered milk for Daisy?" he called out from the open car door.

"Course I will, Gerald, Lad," was the response as Pattie took Georgie's hand and led her inside.

"So how did yer get on with our Molly, Young Georgie? She's a lovely girl, isn't she, and she'll tek great care of yer little sister."

"I like her lots, Pattie, and so does Daisy."

"She does, does she? How d' yer know that, Lass?"

"Daisy told me. Do you know she remembered me after all that time, and gave me a big smile as soon as she saw me?"

"Well, Lass, I'd never have believed that if I hadn't heard it from yer own mouth."

So, life got back to a new normal. Georgie was happy at school, Daddy seemed happy at work, and Daisy thrived in the care of the lovely Molly. The Saturday evening meals with Pattie and Robert continued, be it always at the cottage and with them bringing the food every alternate week. The only sadness that hung over the little group was the absence of Mumm

CHAPTER 10

Mid November 1951

The slippery slope

Guy Fawkes night had come and gone, and Georgie had celebrated her 5th birthday, with Pattie arranging a surprise birthday party after school. Molly took Daisy along, and several children from Georgie's class attended with their mummies. Daddy had to miss it because he couldn't get the time off work, but nevertheless Georgie had a whale of a time. She loved opening all the presents and birthday cards, especially the card from her mummy that Pattie told Georgie Mummy had asked her to write.

Another month passed by before the doctor visited again. It was one evening in the middle of November after Georgie and Daisy had settled down to sleep for the night.

"Evening, Gerald Lad," said the doctor as Gerald invited him into the living room, "I hope yer don't mind that I've left it so late, but I wanted to make sure t' bairns would be in bed so that I could talk wi' yer in private."

"Thank you, Doctor. No, I don't mind at all. It's very considerate of you to think about the children's wellbeing."

"I'll get straight t' point. Florrie had her ECT two weeks ago but sadly, it's not done t' trick. She hasn't responded as the doctors had hoped. She's no worse, mind, so it's not all bad news. The plan is to let her recuperate from that round o' treatment and then try again in mebbe a week from now. Fingers crossed it'll work better next time."

"But what if it doesn't work better. What will happen then?"

Gerald was biting his nails. He hadn't done that for a long time.

"I reckon we're best to take one step at a time, Lad. I know it's not easy for yer, but no sense in getting yer sen in a state about something that might not 'appen."

Tears came into the corner of Gerald's eyes, and didn't go unnoticed by the kind man before him, who stood up from the settee and put one hand on Gerald's shoulder.

"Let me go mix a brew for thee, Lad. Nothing like it to calm t' anxiety."

Gerald didn't object but sat staring into space until the doctor returned with two steaming cups and handed one to the distraught man, before sitting back down again.

"Are yer not coping, Lad? Are t' bairns too much for yer?"

"It's not that, Doctor. It's just that I'm worried about being here alone with them so often. I want to protect them but I'm not sure I'm capable of that."

"But yer clearly doing a fine job, Lad. Daisy's been home for two months now and she's thriving. I saw her recently when young Molly was pushing her in her pram down to t' village store. And Pattie tells me Georgie is happy as a sandboy at school, and never stops talking about Daisy. Is it t' work, Lad? Is that causing t' problem?"

"No, Doctor, you don't understand. The children are fine and work's fine. It's just me that's the problem. I'm not sure I can protect them from me."

"Nay Lad. I can see yer love 'em to bits and they love yer back. No worries there."

106

Gerald gave up trying to explain – in fact he lost his nerve. His courage left him. He forced a smile as he thanked the doctor and took the man's empty teacup from him.

"You are very kind to give up your good time to listen to my ramblings. I'll not keep you from your home a minute longer. Thank you kindly for coming to update me. Please let me know if and when there's any change. I know Georgie misses her mum badly although she tries to keep a brave face on it for the sake of me and Daisy. She's such a grownup little girl and only just five years old. I'm so proud of her."

"And so tha should be, Gerald Lad. And so tha should be," said the man as he shook Gerald's hand and left. "I'll be in touch," and he was gone.

Gerald returned to the settee and sat with head in hands for several minutes before he spoke out loud to the empty room.

"I can't do this any longer. God help me but my strength has gone. Anyway, I'll be doing Georgie a favour in the long run. It will awaken sensations she doesn't even know exist for her to enjoy. It will help her to grow up quicker. That's got to be good for her."

At that, he stood up decisively and made his way upstairs.

At the top of the stairs, he looked into the girls' bedroom. He knew what he was going to do as he walked quietly over to Georgie's bed. He stroked the sleeping child's hair before he slipped his hand beneath her cover.

The next morning, Georgie felt a little confused and was quieter than usual. Daddy seemed not to notice and just treated her the same as always. Molly arrived at her normal time and Georgie left with Daddy as usual. When they arrived at the village store, Robert was waiting for Georgie and she jumped out of the car as normal, waving to her daddy as she took the hand Robert offered and walked with him into the store. Georgie knew immediately that Pattie would pick up on her mood and was ready for her questions.

"Morning Georgie Lass. What's up wi' yer?"

"Oh, nothing, Pattie. I'm okay."

"Now Lass, I can't accept words that don't match yer face, and okay is not how yer look. Come here and we can have a little chat before it's time to tek yer to school."

Georgie approached Pattie warily at first but as soon as Pattie opened her arms, the child fell into them sobbing. Pattie held her close until the sobbing subsided and then lifted her up, carried her into the living room at the back of the shop where she sat down on a soft armchair with Georgie on her knee.

"It's all reight, Lass. There's nought we can't deal with so just tell us what's mekking thee so sad."

"I had a bad dream, Pattie. I didn't know what was happening and I didn't understand. I just know it didn't feel right."

"Can yer tell me more about it, Lass?"

"No. All I know is that it felt wrong, and I didn't understand."

"All reight, Me Darlin. Don't worry yer sen. Dreams can't hurt yer. Just try to forget t' dream and concentrate on t' day ahead. How's that lovely babby o' yours?"

Georgie immediately perked up and a smile returned to her face as she told Pattie about all the new little things that Daisy was starting to do.

"Oh, she's so clever, Pattie. Yesterday Daddy sat her on the floor propped up with cushions from the settee. She balanced for ages but when I made her laugh, she toppled over onto her back, but do you know what she did next?"

"No, Georgie, but I can't wait for yer to tell me."

"She rolled over onto her tummy! I've never seen her do that before. But that's not all. When I picked her up and held her with her little feet touching the floor, she tried to stand. She kept putting her feet down and pushing herself upwards. How clever is that, Pattie? I really love my little sister, you know."

"Ey Lass, I know yer do, and what's more Daisy loves yer back. Yer can see it a mile off."

Pattie was glad she'd refocussed Georgie's thoughts away from her dream, but she still felt a little concerned. 'How can a bairn of not even six-years-old have dreams that she can't understand but that don't feel reight?' She'd talk it over with Robert while Georgie was at school. She dropped a happy Georgie at the school gate that morning, and when she returned the store was full. She quickly removed her coat and got behind the post office counter to serve her customers. Things didn't ease off all morning, and by the time they closed for lunch, her concerns for Georgie had slipped her mind. Nothing else was said, as an excited Georgie came out of school that afternoon, accompanied by Miss Longmore looking as colourful as ever.

Georgie introduced her teacher to Pattie.

"So nice to meet yer, Pattie. Georgie often talks about thee in t' warmest terms. She is clearly very fond of yer."

"Thank yer, Miss Longmore. The feeling is mutual, I can assure yer."

"I'd like ter ask yer if yer mind passing on a message to Georgie's daddy, please? We've started to plan our Christmas nativity play, and we think that Georgie would make a really good Mary, especially as she's so good at helping to look after her baby sister. We'd supply t' costume but we wondered if Georgie might be able to bring t' babby along?"

"Yer mean yer want her ter bring one of her dolls?"

Georgie giggled as she realised Pattie had not quite understood her teacher's request but continued to listen, bouncing up and down as she did so.

"Nay. We were thinking more along t' lines of her bringing her baby sister so we can have a real live Jesus."

Pattie looked taken aback.

"Oh, I see, Lass. I'll ask her daddy for yer and let yer know what he says."

As the two walked away from the school gates, Pattie looked down at the bouncy Georgie.

"So that's why yer bouncing up and down so much, Lass,"

"Yes. Not only will I be Mary – and that's the lead role, you know – but Daisy could be Baby Jesus. Do you think Daddy will let me take Daisy to school to be Jesus, Pattie? Also, if Mummy is home by then, it would be such a surprise for her to see both of us in the school nativity play."

"Let's just wait and see what Daddy has ter say. He has ter make t' final decision and yer mustn't be upset if he decides against it, Lass."

Georgie quietened down at the prospect of the answer possibly being 'No', but when Pattie started talking about Christmas and asking Georgie what she was hoping to receive from Santa, her bounciness returned, and the conversation flowed happily for the rest of the way back to the village store.

Most nights after that first time, Daddy appeared in Georgie's bedroom and had taken to sliding into the bed beside her, which invariably woke her up to a feeling of confusion and apprehension deep in her stomach. Daddy whispered reassurances in her ear, telling her he would not hurt her, but it would be nice and would be their little secret. He didn't hurt her, but she instinctively knew that what he was doing was wrong. She felt unsettled and anxious, and her enthusiasm seemed to drain out of her. No matter how often Pattie asked her if she was alright, she always said that she was fine because she didn't even have the words to describe what Daddy was doing to her, and anyway he would be angry with her if she gave away the secret. She had tried telling her daddy that she didn't want him to do it, but he became very persuasive and bribed her with the promise of sweets or a new toy. When she said she didn't want sweets or toys, he used veiled threats of punishment, which frightened Georgie. She'd never been punished in her life and was frightened that her daddy might hurt her.

Georgie's only respite from the emotional turmoil she was feeling was Daisy. She spent many hours amusing her little sister and encouraging her to crawl and repeat simple words after her. By the time the nativity play came around, the five-month-old was able to pronounce the soft 'g' sound, so everything that started with a g was referred to as 'ger'.

Daddy gave his permission for Daisy to be baby Jesus in the nativity play at school, so Molly brought her along to a few rehearsals, so she'd get used to laying in the manger. The other children in the class were entranced by her, which made Georgie even more popular amongst them, gaining her several new friends. On the day of the nativity play, as Georgie peaked through the curtains, she spied Molly, Pattie, and Robert in the audience. She knew Robert had planned to shut up shop and put a notice on the door saying, 'Sorry for the inconvenience. At an important event. Back in one hour'. Then, with only minutes to spare, Georgie saw Daddy rush in and heard him telling Pattie that he'd been given permission at the last minute to take the time off work.

As the curtains opened and all the children filed onto the stage, the audience clapped. Georgie was dressed in a white headscarf and a long blue robe underneath which a cushion had been placed. She glanced at her guests and gave them a tiny wave. Miss Longmore was last on the stage, looking her usual colourful self in bright red dungarees and a green jumper with red and green horizontal striped sleeves. She was carrying a wide-eyed Daisy, who was wrapped in a large white towel and looking around at the audience inquisitively. The sight of her evoked a loud 'Awww' from the audience, and a huge grin from Georgie and her guests. The pianist played the introduction to 'Once in Royal David's City', which signalled the start of the nativity play and prompted the audience to stand up and sing with the children and their teachers. Georgie could see that everyone was transfixed as the performance commenced, with all her classmates playing their parts perfectly after having rehearsed for so long. Then Georgie walked onstage with Joseph, knocking at the scenery doors but finding no room. Georgie held her cushion tummy as if she was in pain and looked so relieved when one of the inn keepers offered her and Joseph a space in his stable. Joseph supported Mary as she made her way painfully over to the wooden manger full of straw and the narrator explained that she would give birth to a son, who would be called Jesus. At this point Miss Longmore appeared and placed Daisy in the manger in front of Mary to a few quiet giggles from the audience. Daisy looked up and as soon as she saw her sister, waved her arms in the air saying 'Ger – Ger'. For a

split second, Georgie was horror-struck, looking over at her teacher for direction. Miss Longmore had her hand over her mouth trying to stifle her giggles, so Georgie decided that the only thing to do was to lift Daisy out of the manger and onto her lap. This was not easy for Georgie because Daisy had gained a lot of weight over the past three months, and she couldn't manage to lift her quite high enough, which prompted Miss Longmore to rush to her aid. This made Daisy giggle, which started Mary and Joseph off, followed by the donkey, the lamb, and the cow. It wasn't long till it spread to the other children and the audience. Soon the whole room was giggling, and Georgie wondered what her teacher would do. She saw that as much as Miss Longmore tried to stop herself and bring things to order, she couldn't because every time she tried to say something, only giggles would come out of her mouth. In the end, only the quick-thinking pianist was able to save the day by playing the opening line of 'We three Kings of Orient Are'. This prompted the three small boys dressed in their finery and carrying their gifts for the baby Jesus to appear stage right as the choir of small children stood to sing the carol. At once everyone quietened down so that the performance could proceed to its conclusion. The whole audience then stood and clapped and cheered so loud that Georgie thought the ceiling would lift off. It immediately triggered her thoughts and longings to become a dancer when she grew up like the little girl in her dancer book. After a minute or two, Georgie saw Pattie rush towards her to retrieve Daisy from her lap, for which Georgie was more than grateful because her little sister was so heavy. As Pattie bent down, she whispered into Georgie's ear.

"Yer done good, Lass. Real good."

The happy group made their way home that afternoon, talking and laughing about Daisy's behaviour as they went. Robert dropped off to reopen the village store, but the others continued up Half Mile Lane to the cottage where they agreed that an impromptu celebration was the order of the day. Pattie brewed the tea while Molly and Georgie amused Daisy. Daddy went into the kitchen to find a packet of biscuits and stood chatting with Pattie while the kettle boiled.

"What a fantastic afternoon that was," said Gerald.

"Aye Lad, it was better than a dose of medicine. I've not laughed that much for a long time."

As Pattie set out the cups and saucers on a tray on the kitchen table, she looked up at Gerald thoughtfully.

"I'm glad I've got yer on yer own for a minute, Lad. I've been wanting to talk to yer about Georgie for some time now."

Gerald stiffened, sensing what was to come.

"Have yer noticed how t' bairn has changed over the last couple o' months?"

"No, Pattie, I can't say that I have."

"She seems to have gone inside of herself. T' enthusiasm seems to have disappeared and she dunt smile so much anymore. I've not seen the bouncing Georgie for so long. Surely yer've noticed?"

"Perhaps she's missing her mummy more, especially as she wasn't around on her birthday and seems unlikely to be back home for Christmas."

"Mebbe. But I sense there's something more that t' bairn is not letting on about."

"It's probably just her nervousness leading up to the nativity play today. She'll probably be her old self again by tomorrow."

At that point, Gerald picked up the tray of teas that Pattie had made and moved out of the kitchen and into the living room where Molly and Georgie were chatting away animatedly, and Daisy joining in here and there with her unrecognisable gurgle.

As Pattie returned to the sitting room, her mind eased a little. After all, Georgie appeared to be fine right now, and surely Gerald would have been first to notice if there had really been something wrong. Pattie put it out of her mind and handed the teas and biscuits around to Molly, Gerald and Georgie, who had taken to drinking tea rather than orange squash of late. Molly sat Daisy on her knee, bobbing her up and down happily.

"Georgie me darlin," she said, "will yer fetch me Daisy's bib and her bottle of water from t' kitchen, please?"

Georgie jumped up and ran out to the kitchen, appearing to have regained her bounce. As she put the bib around Daisy's neck, the tiny girl piped up with "Ger - Ger." This triggered everyone to start laughing again as they recalled the events of the afternoon, and it was this scene that Robert walked into, having shut up the shop.

"There's no way I'm missing t' celebrations," he said as Pattie handed him a cuppa and the little party continued for another hour before Molly announced that it was time for her to go home. This prompted Pattie and Robert to stand up and say their goodbyes too, leaving Georgie and her daddy to feed and bath Daisy and get her to bed. With both working as a team, Daddy organised Daisy's pureed apple, and Georgie fed it to her whilst Daddy made and cooled her bottle of milk and handed it to Georgie to give to Daisy. The sleepy little girl drank every drop before Georgie undressed her, wrapped her in the towel provided by Daddy, and carried her into the kitchen where the sink of water was full and ready for her bath time. For some reason this evening, blowing soap bubbles for Daisy reminded Georgie of her real daddy, Alfie. She recalled what fun they'd had when Mummy and Alfie had blown bubbles for her only a few years ago. It occurred to her that her old daddy had never done things to her like her new daddy did. Suddenly she was brought out of her revelry by Daisy saying a new word. "Bo - Bo."

"Oh, my goodness, Daisy. Daddy, did you hear what Daisy just said. She was telling me to blow the bubbles."

"Yes, she got fed up waiting for you to come out of your daydream."

Georgie felt the heat rising in her face and hoped that Daddy didn't see her going pink with guilt over what she had been daydreaming. She quickly started to blow more bubbles for her sister until Daddy said it was time to get Daisy dried and ready for bed. Ten minutes later, Daisy was snuggled up in her cot drifting off to sleep. Georgie stood looking lovingly at her little sister.

'Being a celebrity for the day has really tired her out,' she thought.

Back downstairs Georgie and Daddy decided they weren't very hungry after all the biscuits they'd consumed earlier, so they settled for a can of tomato soup and slices of thick bread and margarine for their tea.

114

CHAPTER 11

Early January 1952

The Monster Rears its Ugly Head

Christmas had been spent with Pattie and Robert. Georgie had gone back to the introverted little girl that Pattie had been so worried about. Daddy kept making excuses for her quietness, telling her off at one point for acting so rudely in company. His words slid over her head without effect. She knew she was slowly disappearing into a parallel world where she felt safe, and nobody could follow. Her daddy's night-time activities intensified. He was now making her perform oral sex on him. Each time she pleaded with him to stop but he persisted, and each time she vomited into a bucket that he'd placed beside her bed for that purpose. Daisy never stirred from her deep baby sleep. Georgie silently cried herself to sleep when he left the bedroom.

The doctor came with more news in early January. This time he came during the early evening when Molly had gone, Daisy was asleep in her cot, but Georgie was still up. He was grinning from ear to ear. Georgie's heart leapt in anticipation.

"I'm so happy to bring you good news, Gerald and Georgie, for t' first time since Florrie went into hospital over six months ago. I'm pleased ter

say that she responded positively to t' last round of treatment and is almost back ter her old self. She is constantly asking about you all and wanting ter come home. What d' yer think? Are yer ready to have her back?"

The doctor's words seemed to bring Georgie out of herself, and she immediately smiled – both with relief and anticipation.

"Oh yes, Doctor, please bring my mummy home. Can she come home tomorrow? Does she really remember me and Daisy?"

"She certainly does, Georgie, Lass. She talks about yer both non-stop. As to coming home tomorrow, that's up to yer daddy ter decide."

Gerald had sat in silence up till now. The news had shocked him, and he was wondering if he could get used to having his wife back in bed beside him again? He preferred his present habits, which satisfied his needs perfectly well, but he knew that couldn't continue with Florrie back home. He was tempted to say that he wasn't ready yet, but he thought that would raise suspicions, especially with Pattie who was questioning him more often nowadays.

"Er… yes, yes of course she must come home tomorrow. We've all missed her so much that we don't want to wait even one more day to have her back."

Georgie glanced at Daddy and wondered if he was telling the truth. She had discovered the real him over the past months, and she was worried that Mummy might find out what he was really like too.

"That's agreed then. T' ambulance will bring her home late afternoon tomorrow. She'll need a little peace and quiet at first until she settles down, but I'm sure it will make all t' difference to her continuing recovery being back home with her loved ones. Now I'll bid yer both goodnight and hope that I won't have to visit again fer a very long time."

The doctor grinned as he stood up and looked surprised as Georgie rushed over to give him a long hug.

"Well how nice is that, Lass? Thank you."

Gerald shook his hand heartily trying to feign the enthusiasm that he didn't really feel.

Georgie went to bed that night hoping that her daddy would keep out of her bedroom, but that didn't happen. She couldn't believe what was happening as Daddy got on top of her. She was terrified and did a silent scream with the pain as he penetrated her. She felt she was in a never-ending nightmare, especially when he rolled off her and she felt his breath next to her perspiration covered face. The look in his eyes shocked and terrified Georgie even more than she already was. As he spoke in a strange deep and threatening voice, droplets of spittle sprayed Georgie's face.

"If you ever say one word to your mummy or anyone else about what you've been letting me do, I'll not only hurt you more than you can imagine, but I'll also hurt that little b*****d sister of yours."

Georgie had no idea what that word meant as she lay paralysed, white faced and wide-eyed in her bed. Not until he left her bedroom, did she dare breath. While she lay there in shock, she knew he'd be drifting off to sleep in the next room, feeling satisfied with himself. Georgie lay still for what seemed like hours until she heard her stepfather's tell-tale snores coming from next door. Only then did she find the courage to lift her covers to see the extent of the injury he'd inflicted upon her. She gasped as she saw the patch of blood on her bottom sheet, and automatically placed her fingers on the centre of her pain only to find them smeared with a mixture of slime and blood when she withdrew them. She reached for the bucket that was still in its usual place beside her bed and vomited as quietly as she could into it. Having emptied the contents of her stomach, she sat exhausted on the edge of her bed, the beads of perspiration on her forehead glinting in the moonlight from the window. She felt empty and numb. As young as she was, she knew that something inside of her had died.

'I must wash. I must get that stuff off me. I need to get it off my sheet. What if Molly sees it when she brings Daisy up for her snooze tomorrow.

If she says something to Daddy – no, not 'daddy' anymore, but that monster – he'll think I told her, and he'll hurt me and Daisy really badly."

Georgie crept out to the bathroom carrying the bucket of vomit with her and closed the bathroom door quietly behind her. Having emptied the vomit down the toilet, heaving because of the smell, she flushed it away, rinsed out the bucket and put it under the sink. She then spent the next fifteen minutes with a face flannel and cold water and soap from the bathroom sink, cleaning herself up as best she could. When the bleeding stopped, she rinsed the face flannel over and over, trying to flush away the filth left behind by that monster. She then carried the flannel into her bedroom and scrubbed away at the blood stain as if her life depended upon it. The blood wouldn't go no matter how hard she scrubbed – it just spread out and out, becoming bigger and bigger. Georgie felt as if she was the stain – her guilt spreading uncontrollably, until she collapsed on the floor in a flood of tears. She was tired and exhausted. She just wanted to sleep forever and forget what had happened. She crawled to the far side of her bed, lay down pulling the covers over herself as she did so, and drifted into a restless and troubled sleep.

The next thing Georgie knew, she was being woken up by someone gently shaking her. She opened her eyes, and it was all she could not to scream when she saw the monster's face looking down at her.

"Time to get up young lady. Me and Daisy have been downstairs for ages and eaten our breakfast already. Molly will be here soon so get dressed quickly and come down for your porridge."

Georgie was stunned that he was behaving as if nothing had happened, and she looked over to Daisy's empty cot as the monster left the room. Had it all been a bad dream? She lifted her covers and found the offending patch of dried blood. No, it was not a dream. If that hadn't confirmed it, the soreness between her legs as she tried to get out of bed did. She dressed as quickly as her pain would allow her and went slowly down to the kitchen. The monster lifted off the tea plate that was keeping her breakfast warm, and then disappeared upstairs. She heard him moving about in her bedroom. She hoped he was removing the offending sheet so Molly wouldn't see it. Daisy was happily gurgling away in her highchair trying to get Georgie's attention.

"Ger – Ger."

119

Georgie looked over at her little sister and couldn't help but smile in response to the adoring love that shone out of Daisy's eyes. Then a sudden stab of fear pierced her heart and mind. She knew that her mission in life from now on would be to protect her little sister, no matter how much she herself would have to suffer. As far as today was concerned, she'd get through it by focusing on her mummy's homecoming that evening. She would allow the excitement to swell in her chest every time she thought about Mummy, her saviour, coming back through that door to make life bearable – maybe even happy – again.

Pattie and Robert looked shocked when Georgie slid out of the car that morning. The little girl saw their faces change when they saw her pale, drawn face and the careful way she was walking.

Robert led Georgie out the back and sat down on the easy chair in the living room, holding both of her hands as she stood before him.

"Ey, Lass, won't yer tell Robert what it is that's ailing yer?"

Georgie couldn't bring herself to lie anymore to this man who she loved unconditionally, so she just bowed her head and let her tears trickle down her face as Robert pulled her onto his lap and hugged her close. She flinched with pain as he sat her down. Pattie came into the room then, and Georgie saw Robert look up at his wife with worry etched across his face. At that moment, she knew that her very best friends had guessed what had been going on and she felt a huge weight lift from her small shoulders. Pattie approached and knelt beside the chair, taking Georgie's trembling hand in hers. Georgie was glad that Pattie said nothing as she felt the warmth from her friend's hand permeate her whole being, bringing with it the comfort Georgie so badly needed. After a few minutes Pattie spoke up.

"Ey up Georgie Lass, have yer forgotten what today is?"

Georgie wiped her tears away with the back of her other hand and sniffed a few times before she could look into Pattie's eyes.

"My mummy's coming home," she replied with a watery smile.

"Ey, Lass. She is that. It's a day ter be excited and ter celebrate, so guess what I've done? I've baked a cake and it's on t' kitchen table waiting for you and me ter decorate it."

Georgie's heart swelled with excitement as she carefully slid off Robert's lap and walked hand-in-hand with Pattie into the kitchen.

The monster got home early from work that evening and picked up Georgie and Pattie, who was carefully carrying the celebration cake. All four were now waiting in the living room in anticipation. Pattie had changed Daisy into a pretty dress while Georgie changed into her best party dress. Then Pattie brushed Georgie's hair while Georgie brushed Daisy's. Georgie felt nervous and sensed that Pattie did too, so Daisy's constant chatting in her baby language interspersed with her big sister's name, brought a sense of relief. Now all four were silent – Daisy because it was near to her bedtime and she was tired, the others because there seemed nothing appropriate to say. The monster walked up and down, up and down, seemingly unable to settle. Georgie periodically walked over to the window, searching for signs of the ambulance coming up Half Mile Lane. Pattie cuddled little Daisy, stroking the child's hair as if to release her own tension.

"They're coming, they're coming. I can see the ambulance coming up the lane," shouted Georgie, initially jumping up and down but then thinking better of it.

The monster was first to the door this time, joined quickly by the others. Georgie took Pattie's free hand and grasped it tightly. As the Ambulance slowed down and stopped in front of the cottage gate, dusk was just settling in. Georgie stood back with Pattie and Daisy as she watched the monster walk down the path and out of the gate before the ambulance driver had even turned off the engine. Georgie felt Pattie's reassuring hand on her shoulder and continued to watch as the driver jumped out and walked to the back of the vehicle. He turned the door handle anticlockwise, opened the door and pulled down the steps. Then, as Georgie thought her heartbeat might break through her ribs, she saw her smiling but pale-faced mummy accept the hand that the driver offered and descend the few steps slowly and deliberately. Georgie continued to watch as the monster moved around the ambulance until he stood face to face with Mummy. He seemed to force a smile. Mummy's smile broadened. He leaned forward and gave her a peck on the cheek. Mummy moved forward, placed her arms around his neck and pulled him

121

in. Georgie felt physically sick as his arms encircled Mummy's waist and an expression of relief covered his face, followed by tears. As they stood back from each other, Georgie saw tears in her mummy's eyes too. The nausea disappeared and was replaced with hope that now Mummy was home, life might return to the way it was before she went away.

Then Mummy turned to face Georgie, Pattie and Daisy, and Georgie felt her tummy leap up into her chest, as her legs took off of their own accord up the garden path into Mummy's open arms. The two held each other for a full minute before Georgie would loosen her grip and move her head back to look into the eyes of the mummy she'd missed so profoundly for so long. They were both laughing with pure joy as Georgie took Mummy's hand and lead her through the gate and down the garden path where Pattie still held little Daisy. The beaming Pattie immediately held Daisy out towards Mummy, and Daisy, in her usual easy-going way, smiled broadly and lifted her arms toward the woman in front of her, gurgling between attempts to say unrecognisable words. Unbeknown to any of the adults, Georgie had been trying to teach her baby sister to say 'Mumma'. She tapped Daisy's arm.

"Ger - Ger."

Mummy laughed and squeezed her youngest daughter.

"What a clever little girl you are, Daisy," she said looking lovingly into the smiling child's eyes.

This time Georgie tapped Daisy's arm and pointed towards Mummy.

"Daisy, this is Mumma. Say Mumma for Ger."

"Ger - Ger."

"Never mind, Lass, they'll be plenty of time for t' babby to learn her words later," said Pattie as she took Daisy from Mummy and placed her other arm around her friend's shoulder, leading her into the cottage.

Georgie watched as her mummy stood and looked around her, then walked into the kitchen as if to make sure nothing had changed. Mummy breathed in a deep sigh before she turned back and slipped off her coat, which she hung over the stair post before she made her way into the living room. Again, she looked around the room as if taking in every detail

before she nodded. Another sigh and a smile before she sat down on the settee. Pattie placed Daisy on Mummy's knee and Georgie pushed up close beside them. The monster had disappeared upstairs with Mummy's holdall.

"I'll get t' kettle on t' boil, our Florrie. Yer must need a brew after all t' excitement."

Mummy smiled at Pattie before returning her attention to her waiting children.

"My word, Georgie, your baby sister has grown so big. Has she been good?"

"She's amazing, Mummy, always so happy and smiling. Molly has been looking after her during the weekdays. I go to school now. I was Mary in the Nativity Play."

"Molly? Wow, so many things have happened while I've been away. You've grown for a start. You look a little pale though, Baby."

"I'm fine, Mummy, especially now you're home. I really, really missed you."

"I missed you, too, Baby. Have you been helping Daddy?"

"Yes."

Just at that moment, Daisy looked at Georgie and then at Mummy.

"Mumma."

Mummy and Georgie laughed with surprise and each hugged Daisy in turn just as the monster and Pattie arrived back in the room, Pattie carrying a tray of tea, complete with celebration cake. Once they'd finished their tea and cake, Daisy started to yawn and happily went into the arms of her stepfather, who took her upstairs to get her ready for bed. Pattie hugged Georgie, then Mummy and said her goodbyes.

"You're tired now, Our Florrie, so I'll see yer tomorrow for a catch-up. I'll see yer in t' morning bright and early, Georgie. Is that okay with you

123

Florrie? I thought that if I continued ter drop our Georgie at school for t' rest of t' week, it would give yer a chance to settle down."

Mummy stood up, walked over to Pattie and hugged her.

"Thank you, Pattie, I do feel tired. I'm so grateful for the way you've been supporting my family."

Mummy escorted her friend to the door, with Georgie hanging on to Pattie's hand. After another round of hugs, Georgie stood in the doorway next to her mummy, waving goodbye to Pattie as she disappeared into the darkness of the Lane. Mummy then closed the door and turned to Georgie.

"How about we both go upstairs to say goodnight to Daisy?"

Georgie nodded her agreement, and they ascended the stairs hand in hand. When they stepped on the creaky step, Mummy giggled and turned to Georgie.

"Now I really do feel at home," she said.

Daisy was already in her cot as Georgie and Mummy entered, passing the monster as he disappeared into the bathroom to clean up after Daisy's bath. A small stab of fear pierced Georgie's mind. She made a mental note never again to leave the monster alone when he bathed her sister. Daisy was half asleep as she looked up at Mummy and Georgie with a drowsy smile. Mummy slid the side of the cot down so she could lean over and kiss her baby daughter's cheek, which was warm and rosy from the heat of the bathroom. Georgie did the same. As Mummy slid the side of the cot back up, Daisy's eyes started to close.

"Ger, Mumma," she said as she drifted into her deep baby sleep.

"Would you like me to help you get ready for bed now, Baby?" asked Mummy.

Georgie would dearly have loved to accept the offer but knew she couldn't take the risk of Mummy noticing her soreness.

"No need, Mummy, thank you. I'm grown up now that I go to school, and anyway the doctor told us that you have to rest until you're used to being home again."

Georgie regretted having turned down her mummy's offer as she saw a faint look of disappointment pass across her face, but she stepped forward and hugged her tightly, which made Mummy smile before she made her way back downstairs. Georgie felt momentarily sad but then remembered her mummy was home for good, and hopefully her own soreness would soon heal and she could accept Mummy's offers of help again. She proceeded to wash herself, put on a clean nightdress from her chest of drawers, and get into bed. She heaved a sigh of relief to see no sign of the blood stain that had so distressed her the night before.

"Mummy, I'm in bed," she shouted, keeping her fingers crossed under the cover that only her mummy would come up to tuck her in and kiss her goodnight.

Her wish was granted, and she felt safe once more as Mummy tucked in her covers, kissed her cheek, and told her how much she loved her. As Georgie heard Mummy leaving her room and descending the stairs, creak and all, she turned onto her side and quickly slid into a secure and peaceful sleep.

Downstairs in the living room, Florrie and Gerald sat chatting for a while but soon made their way up to bed. It had been a big day for both, but as they snuggled together in bed that night, they finally consummated their marriage. It was fortunate that Florrie didn't know what was going on in her husband's imagination during that act.

CHAPTER 12

Early February 1952

Disclosure

Life had become almost normal for Georgie once Mummy was back home. The five-year-old felt at peace, but somehow couldn't quite find the old bouncing Georgie that she once was. Neither could she bring herself to call the monster Daddy anymore. Georgie knew that Mummy had put it down to her having grown up a lot while she was away. Pattie and Robert had appeared to be less worried about her too, which Georgie thought was because they knew her mummy was now there to monitor the situation.

A month passed by until one Sunday morning early in February Mummy announced that she was popping down to see Pattie for a couple of hours for a catchup.

"Would you mind keeping an eye on the girls for me, please, Gerald? It would be lovely to have a bit of girlie time with Pattie on our own. Daisy's just gone down for a nap, so she shouldn't be a problem."

Georgie had overheard what Mummy had said as she sat on the settee in the living room quietly reading her book about the girl who became a

dancer and dreaming of her longed-for future. When Mummy popped her head around the door to say goodbye, she asked Mummy if she could go with her.

"Not this time, Baby, you'd be bored anyway. It will just be me and Pattie chattering away as usual. You and Daddy could play your chasing game like you used to. I haven't seen you two laughing together once since I came out of hospital. Daisy's fast asleep in her cot so you don't have to amuse her. Have some fun."

Then Mummy disappeared, leaving Georgie sitting on the edge of the settee, holding tightly on to her book. Should she stay where she was and keep quiet, hoping not to attract the monster's attention? Tingling fear crept its way up her tense body, switching her mind on to red alert. Maybe she could creep outside to the front garden and play five-stones in the lane. Somehow, she would feel safer outside. She would still hear Daisy if she woke up, so at least she'd know her little sister was safe. Yes, that's what she would do. She crept into the hallway and slipped her coat off the stair post. She would put it on once she was outside. She walked quietly over to the front door, holding her breath, but as she lifted her hand to turn the knob, she jumped at the sound of the monster's voice.

"Where d'you think you're going?"

It took all Georgie's control to stop her voice quaking as she turned to him.

"Just going out to play five-stones in the lane."

He approached her, took her coat, and put it back over the stair post.

"Upstairs now."

Georgie immediately obeyed. She remembered his threat and knew that she had to protect her little sister. He followed closely behind. At the top of the stairs, he guided her into the bathroom and locked the door behind him.

"Kneel down in front of the toilet."

She obeyed.

"Open the lid."

She obeyed. He loosened his trousers, and she immediately knew what she had to do. He approached her.

Afterwards, he left the bathroom, leaving Georgie vomiting down the toilet. When she'd finished, she flushed away the proof of her action, rinsed her mouth out with water from the washbasin, and quietly exited into her bedroom to check that Daisy was safe. Pale-faced and trembling, she knelt on her bed to look out of the window and down the lane where she knew her mummy was. She didn't notice the monster return quietly to her room, so his loud whisper made her jump.

"Get back downstairs to your book, now."

Georgie was paralysed to the spot for a long moment. Was he going to touch Daisy? Then she felt the harsh grip of his hand on her arm, pulling her off the bed and guiding her out of her bedroom and down each step, including the creaky one, until she found herself shoved back onto the settee. He picked up her precious dancer book and for a painful moment she held her breath, fearing that he was going to destroy it. Instead, he pushed it into her hands before turning away and returning to the kitchen. Georgie was numb. She sat there for several minutes, clinging on to the book, knowing that she didn't have the option of crying, because her mummy would notice her red face and swollen eyes. Suddenly she heard the front door open and saw Mummy enter.

"Don't tell me you're still reading that same old book of yours, Baby?"

Georgie used every bit of her willpower to force a smile onto her face as Mummy took off her coat and placed it on the stair post over Georgie's coat. As she did so, there was a small cry from Daisy, and Mummy tripped upstairs to retrieve her baby. As she came back downstairs holding Daisy, Georgie jumped up from the settee to meet them, immediately responding to her little sister's open arms and taking her from Mummy.

"Ger, Ger," the child gurgled as Mummy smiled and headed towards the kitchen, leaving Daisy with her big sister.

Georgie was happy to be distracted from what had happened by amusing Daisy for the rest of the day and avoiding the monster in the

process. It wasn't until she got into bed that night, and endured Mummy and the monster coming up together to tuck her in, that she gave way to the silent tears that she had been swallowing since the incident. As sleep eventually overtook her, she decided that she would disclose her secret to Mummy and beg her not to tell. She knew she couldn't continue the way things were.

As it happened, Mummy broached the subject herself. Georgie came out of school on the Monday afternoon to find Mummy, with Daisy in her pram, waiting for her as usual. As they were walking home, Georgie holding on to the side of the pram handle and making Daisy laugh by repeatedly leaning towards her little sister and pretending that she was about to tickle her, Mummy spoke.

"Georgie, Babe, what's wrong? Won't you tell me why you always look so serious these days? What's happened to your bounce? I really miss it."

Georgie knew that this was her opportunity, so she took a deep breath and keeping her eyes on the ground, she opened up to Mummy, who she knew loved her more than life itself.

"He's been doing things to me, Mummy, and I don't like it. He said he would really hurt me and Daisy if I told anyone."

It was such a relief to get the words out that Georgie allowed the tears to trickle down her cheeks and plop to the ground.

"What do you mean, Baby? Who has been doing things to you and what has he been doing?"

"Gerald. When you were in hospital, he did things to me in my bed, and made me do things that made me sick."

"What are you talking about? Why are you calling your daddy Gerald? What things did he do to you?"

"He touched me between my legs, he put his thing in my mouth, and one time he put his thing inside me, and it hurt me so bad, Mummy, that it made me bleed."

"Georgie, daddies don't do things like that to their little girls. These are terrible things to say about your daddy. Where on earth have you heard such things in the first place? Have you been listening to the bad kids in the school playground?"

Georgie gulped. She was shocked into silence. Her own mummy didn't believe her.

"Georgie, I never want to hear you say such outrageous things again. Do you hear me?"

Georgie's eyes didn't leave the ground. She knew it was pointless arguing. She just nodded. The rest of the way home was spent in silence. Even little Daisy went quiet as if she sensed that something was wrong.

CHAPTER 13

March 1952 – July 1953

A glimmer of hope

Life got no better for five-and-a-half-year-old Georgie. The abuse continued as the monster encouraged Mummy to leave the children with him more and more.

"Florrie, my love, why don't you find yourself an interest outside the house? You need more time to yourself, a bit of freedom to make sure you don't get depressed again. I'll look after the children."

Mummy told the monster how lovely it was of him to care, and promptly joined a women's group in the village, to which she and Pattie went at least once a week. Georgie didn't think it was lovely at all, but she didn't say another word to anyone about what the monster was doing to her, knowing for sure that if her mummy didn't believe her, then nobody else would. As much as Mummy flourished because of her new lifestyle, Georgie gradually disappeared within herself again – the only way she knew how to cope with the pain and humiliation that her stepfather inflicted upon her. Her only motivation for going on was to protect Daisy. Her sixth birthday came and went as did Christmas. Daisy, now eighteen months old was calling Georgie, 'Gorgy', and toddling around getting up

to mischief and talking, sometimes quite clearly and other times in her own baby language. She was Georgie's reason for living - together with the Saturday evenings spent with Pattie and Robert. At least she felt able to relax in their presence. Were it not for these three people, she knew she would have run away.

Georgie was growing taller, but she was also losing weight and knew that her face looked pale and sallow with dark lines beneath her eyes. Mummy told her it was probably because she'd had a growth spurt and tried to tempt Georgie with, what she told her, were protein-rich foods to build her up. Georgie didn't feel hungry but did her best to eat at least some of the food that Mummy put in front of her. Then Georgie's teacher, the colourful Miss Longmore, who'd moved up to Class 2 with the children, had expressed her concern at the annual parents' evening that Mummy had attended on her own. When she'd got home, Georgie, who was in the bathroom with the door open cleaning her teeth before bed, heard Mummy telling the monster what Miss Longmore had said.

"She asked me if Georgie is alright. She said she's not the same as when she first started school when she always looked healthy and never kept still. She's right, you know, Gerald, she was always bouncing up and down every time she got excited, and she doesn't do that anymore. Maybe it's because she's growing so fast, but she seems to be losing weight too and is always tired."

"I haven't noticed a change in her, Florrie," the monster said in a casual tone. "As you say, it's probably a growth spurt and nothing to worry about."

At that moment Georgie hated the monster even more.

'He's just scared of being found out.' She thought. But then she heaved a sigh of relief when she heard Mummy's next words.

"Perhaps I'll pop her round to see the doctor just to check that there's no medical reason for the change in her."

'Maybe the doctor will be able to guess what's happening when he discovers I'm still sore,' thought the unhappy little girl. 'Mummy would have to believe me then.'

The doctor looked pleased to see Mummy looking so healthy when she walked into his surgery with Daisy in her pushchair and Georgie by her side.

"Ey up, Florrie, yer look really well. And who's t' bairn? It's surely not wee Daisy."

The kind man chatted for a few seconds to Daisy who obliged him with a huge smile and a couple of words from her baby-talk vocabulary. He finally turned his attention to Georgie, who was sitting on Mummy's knee, feeling dazed and in a world of her own.

"Ey up, Georgie Lass. Yer sitting there in a world o' yer own. Are yer not feeling well, Lass?"

"I'm alright thank you, Doctor."

"Well, I'm glad ter hear it, Lass, but just let's check thee out ter make quite sure."

The doctor felt Georgie's glands in her neck, took her temperature and counted her pulse rate. He then sat her on the side of his examination couch and tapped her knees with a little wooden hammer. Georgie couldn't help but be fascinated by this.

"Why did you bang my knees with that hammer, Doctor?"

"Just ter see if yer legs would flick out like that cos it makes me smile," he joked.

Georgie relaxed a little as he lifted her legs onto the couch and laid her down. After pressing and prodding for a while to check if anything was tender and discovering that the only time Georgie took in a sharp breath was when he pressed her lower abdomen, he lifted her down and returned her to Mummy's knee.

"I'd like ter refer Georgie ter specialist at t' hospital in Penrith, Florrie. Her abdomen appears ter be a little tender, so I'd like ter check if that's got any connection ter weight loss. I'll write a letter today, so yer should hear back with an appointment within a couple of weeks."

Mummy's eyebrows rose questioningly as she looked anxiously at the doctor, but he had nothing else to add, so she took Georgie's hand and bade him farewell as she wheeled the pushchair out of the surgery. The three continued in silence until they reached the corner of Half Mile Lane.

"Shall we pop in to see Pattie and Robert, Georgie? We could have a nice cuppa with them, and maybe Pattie would let you be her assistant for a while like you used to."
Georgie nodded unenthusiastically.

"What about you, Daisy? Would you like to see Pattie and Robert for a while?"

"Attie, Attie," bubbled Daisy, bouncing up and down in her pushchair.

Pattie and Robert were as pleased as punch to see the little group. The store wasn't busy, so Pattie took Mummy and the two children out the back to mix a brew. Daisy toddled around happily chewing the biscuit that Pattie gave her, whilst Georgie sat quietly looking after her sister, having refused the offer of a biscuit for herself. After a while, Georgie asked Pattie if she might go and help Robert behind the counter.

Pattie was happy to agree to the request, as she sensed that Florrie needed to get something off her chest. She was right. As soon as Georgie left the room, Florrie told her friend about the visit to the doctor and how worried she was that there might be something medically wrong with Georgie. She felt ashamed of her failure to pick up the problem sooner.

"It was only because Miss Longmore mentioned it that I took Georgie to the doctor."

"Has the lass said anything ter you about feeling unwell?"

"No."

"Is she worried about something? She looks so haunted these days?"

"She's not mentioned anything."

"Has Gerald upset her, do yer think? I've noticed she doesn't call him daddy these days."

"Not as far as I know – although she did say something very strange to me quite a while back. I reckoned at the time that she must have got in with a bad bunch at school, 'cos she said some quite outrageous things about poor Gerald. I had to tell her off quite severely at the time."

"What things did t' bairn say?"

"I can't remember her exact words, but it was something to the effect that Gerald had been doing things to her in her bed."

Pattie went quiet as the old suspicions shot to the surface of her mind.

"What?" asked Florrie. "Why are you looking like that?"

"Mmmm. Well … It's probably nought, but while yer was in t' hospital, one or two things happened ter make us start ter worry about t' lass."

"What things?"

Pattie felt embarrassed and a little reticent to say what was on her mind but decided to continue for Georgie's sake.

"Georgie became quite introverted – much like she is nowadays. We kept asking t' lass what were wrong, but she'd never let on. One day when Gerald dropped her off on his way ter work, she was clearly in discomfort and was walking very carefully. Robert asked her again to tell him what was troubling her. She just quietly cried, and when he sat t' bairn on his lap, she flinched as if it hurt to sit."

"Pattie, what on earth are you insinuating? I know Gerald better than anyone and I know he loves my girls and me dearly. He'd never do anything to hurt any of us – especially anything like you're suggesting. How could you? I thought you were my friend."

At that, Florrie rose from her chair, picked up Daisy and walked out to the store.

"Come on, Georgie. We're leaving right now."

Georgie felt confused and turned to Robert, who looked equally as confused.

"It's okay, Lass. Do what yer mammy says, and I'll see yer at t' weekend.

"I wouldn't count on that," said Mummy, flicking her hair back and lifting her chin defiantly as she left, followed by Georgie. Having strapped Daisy into her pushchair, Mummy grabbed Georgie's hand and walked quickly away from the store, continuing at the same fast pace up Half Mile Lane.

"Mummy, you're hurting my hand. I can't keep up with you."

"Well, I'm sorry about that, Georgie, but you're the cause of this, so just walk faster."

Georgie was even more confused and felt hurt at her mummy's harsh voice that prompted her to increase her pace until she felt that her legs could go no faster. But she dared not complain. She just quietly wondered what had happened to make mummy so angry. She was sure that she hadn't been the cause because she'd been in the shop with Robert. And why did Mummy behave so rudely towards Robert too? He had been with Georgie so couldn't have offended her.

Georgie felt uneasy for the rest of the day. Suppose Mummy and Pattie had been talking about what she'd said to Mummy about the monster. Georgie had guessed long ago that Pattie and Robert had suspected what was going on.

Mummy remained cross with Georgie for the rest of the day and was clearly still angry when the monster got home from work. They both came up to tuck her in as usual but as they went downstairs, Georgie determined she was going to eavesdrop on their usual evening conversation. She crept out of bed and sat behind the bannister rail at the top of the stairs. Mummy and the monster were in the living room with the door open, so Georgie listened hard to catch what they were saying.

"Pattie made insinuations about you, Gerald. I couldn't believe what she was saying."

"Insinuations about what?" came the response in a slightly raised voice. "Shh. Keep your voice down or the children might hear you."

Georgie couldn't catch the next couple of sentences until Gerald suddenly forgot himself and shouted.

"WHAT? She insinuated I was doing what?"

She heard Mummy shushing Gerald again and continuing in a lowered voice, which again she couldn't catch, until Gerald raised his voice once more.

"Georgie said I did THAT?"

Georgie had heard enough and was just about to creep back into bed when she heard Mummy say something else.

"On top of all that, I'm pregnant again."

Georgie crept carefully back into her bedroom and under the covers. She lay there reflecting on her present situation. She knew that she was in danger from her monster stepfather, and that Mummy was clearly not on her side, so she could no longer count on her protection. She knew that she really needed to get away from this place, but she remembered Gerald's threat of hurting both her and Daisy if she ever told anyone. Now he knew that she had told Mummy, and maybe even thought she had told Pattie. Georgie desperately wanted to run away for her own safety. But how could she leave Daisy at risk – maybe even greater risk than before? Would that monster turn his attentions towards Daisy if Georgie was no longer around to vent his twisted needs on? Georgie couldn't take that risk, especially now that Mummy was expecting another baby. Supposing Mummy got ill again. Who would look after her now that she was no longer friends with Pattie? No, Georgie was stuck. She had no choice but to stay and hope that Gerald wouldn't hurt her and Daisy while Mummy was around. Maybe Mummy would stop going to the women's group if she no longer had Pattie to go with. If so, Georgie wouldn't be left alone with Gerald. Georgie eventually fell asleep hoping upon hope that this would be the case.

To Georgie's surprise, the monster behaved like his old self the next morning when she went downstairs for breakfast. It was Saturday so he didn't have to leave early for work. Georgie noticed that he was being very loving towards Mummy, kissing her hair as he passed her by. He was also very attentive towards Daisy who was enjoying the extra attention. When they had finished eating, the monster tapped a spoon on the table.

"Attention everyone, I've a very special announcement to make. Georgie, Daisy, you are going to have another baby brother or sister. Georgie tried her best to feign excitement, scraping her chair back from the table and going over to Mummy to give her a big hug. Mummy pulled Georgie close to her and whispered into her ear.

"Are you okay, Baby? You know Mummy loves you, don't you? I'm sorry about the way I behaved on the way back from Pattie's yesterday."

Georgie felt a certain level of relief hearing her mummy apologise and knowing that things would improve between them.

"I love you too, Mummy," she whispered back.

Maybe things wouldn't turn out to be as bleak as Georgie had imagined. Maybe they could all get back to a better normal now that the monster seemed to be behaving differently. The prospect of another sibling in the family was quite exciting for Georgie, and she found herself smiling for the first time in ages.

"When will the new baby be born, Mummy?" she asked.

"Probably around July or August time, Baby - another summer baby."
"Mumma bubba," chimed in Daisy.

All three laughed together and Georgie's hopes for the future increased.

"How about we all go out for the day next weekend," suggested the monster, "I know it's still only the end of March, but Easter is early this year so we could pack a picnic and visit the Lakes. Do you remember when I drove you there, Georgie, when you were only about four? We laughed so much on that journey, didn't we?"

Georgie remembered and smiled as she recalled the laughter. The she realised that her real daddy had been with her on that day, and her smile faded. The monster didn't seem to notice and carried on in the same vein.

"In fact, the sun is shining today, if we all wrap up to protect us from the chilly breeze that's blowing across the fells, we could go for a walk to the park and give Daisy a ride on the roundabout and baby swings. What do you think, Georgie?"

Georgie turned to Daisy.

"Do you want to go to the Park with Gorgy and Mummy and Daddy, Daisy? You can have a go on the swings. Gorgy can push you higher and higher till you reach the clouds?"

"Wing Gorgy?"

"Yes swing, Daisy," Georgie replied proudly.

So, after the breakfast things had been washed up and Mummy had changed Daisy's nappy, they all left for the park wearing warm coats and scarves and enjoying the fresh air and sunshine. Georgie taught Daisy to roll down the hills, which ended up with both girls in a tangle at the bottom, giggling together. Then the monster ran towards them with a broad grin on his face.

"I'm coming to tickle you both," he shouted.

Georgie instinctively and without thinking, jumped to her feet and ran away screeching, leaving Daisy to enjoy her daddy's tickles. The next minute, he'd picked up Daisy and with her under one arm he ran towards Georgie, who getting lost in the excitement of the moment, screamed "No. No." and turned to run away again, laughing out loud. But it was too late and within a few seconds, he had caught up with her and pounced, still holding Daisy.

"Come on Daisy. Let's tickle Gorgy," he gasped.

Daisy copied her daddy, attempting to tickle her big sister like he was. All three ended up in a laughing, gasping heap, too worn out to continue.

Georgie noticed Mummy silently smiling in the background with a look of contented pleasure on her face.

As the little group made their way home, Georgie started to wonder if a miracle had happened.

'Maybe I just dreamed that I heard Mummy telling Daddy about what I'd said to her. Maybe I'm not in danger after all.'

That thought brought Georgie a huge sense of relief, and by the time they reached the cottage, she was convinced that all would now be well.

'The news about the new baby must have changed the monster back to the daddy he used to be,' Georgie told herself. She couldn't quite bring herself to call him Daddy again, she decided to at least refer to him as Gerald rather than the monster.

Later that afternoon, Mummy popped down to see Pattie and Robert. Georgie knew they must have made up because the couple arrived at teatime and all seemed back to normal.

Georgie slept well that night and for several weeks to follow. She started to gain weight and her complexion returned to its former radiance. Life was good again – until one day in the middle of July.

CHAPTER 14

July 1953

A cry for help

"I'm bleeding. I'm bleeding. Oh no! Please God no."

Georgie was fixed to the spot. Her stepfather hadn't yet arrived home from work, and she had been playing with two-year-old Daisy on the floor in the living room building towers out of bricks when she heard the scream.

"Georgie, Georgie, I need you now," shouted Mummy, having calmed down slightly.

"Daisy, you stay where you are and play with your bricks while Gorgy runs upstairs to Mummy. Can you do that, Sweety?"

Daisy, wide-eyed from the scream, nodded vigorously.

Georgie ran up to the bathroom faster than she'd ever done before to find her ashen-faced Mummy sitting on the bucket from under the sink.

"Baby, I'm going to have to ask you to be a very grown-up girl. Do you think you can do that?"

"Yes, Mummy, what do you want me to do?"

"Run down the lane to Pattie and ask her to ring for an ambulance and tell them the new baby is on its way but I'm bleeding badly. Do you understand, Baby?"

"Yes, Mummy."

With that, Georgie turned tail, almost flew down the stairs and out of the door, remembering to put the latch on before she dashed down to the village store. Pattie was on the telephone as soon as she was able to decipher what the gasping six and a half-year-old was telling her. Having made the emergency call, the two rushed up to the cottage, arriving at the same time as the ambulance. Georgie couldn't help but remember the last time that an ambulance had to be called – the time her mummy had a breakdown a few weeks after Daisy was born. That time she didn't see Mummy again until six months later. Was it all going to happen again?

The ambulance men spoke to Pattie and then rushed into the cottage and upstairs to Mummy. Georgie and Pattie rushed into the living room to check on Daisy who was still sitting on the floor where Georgie had left her playing with her bricks.

"What a good girl you are," said Georgie to her sister, before she turned back to Pattie, to find her standing at the living room door, repeatedly glancing up the stairs and looking worried. Just then, one of the ambulance men came rushing down the stairs and out to the ambulance, returning immediately with a stretcher.

"What will happen, Pattie? Will Mummy be alright?"

Pattie put her arm around Georgie's shoulders and pulled her closer.

"T' ambulance men will look after yer mammy, Lass. They know best."

Ten minutes went by with seemingly nothing happening, until suddenly came the sound of a new-born baby's cry. Pattie and Georgie, both open-

mouthed, looked at each other. As they did so, Daisy toddled over and cuddled up to Georgie.

"Bubba cry," she announced perfectly clearly.

Daisy's words brought smiles to the faces of all three and soon they were all giggling together. They stood in the hallway looking up the stairs, waiting to see what would happen next. As they looked, one of the ambulance men appeared with the crying baby wrapped in a towel, and made his way carefully downstairs, before he plonked the warm bundle into Pattie's arms.

"Can you take care of the baby for a few minutes while we bring Florrie downstairs, please?" said the ambulance man. "She's okay but has lost quite a lot of blood, so we'll pop her and the baby to the hospital to check them out. We think that the placenta was blocking the baby's way out, and that's what caused the bleeding."

Pattie just stood there looking stunned, jiggling the tiny baby in her arms.

"Is it a brother or sister, Pattie?" asked Georgie just before the ambulance men appeared at the top of the stairs, one at each end of the stretcher carrying Georgie's mummy. They expertly negotiated the stairs without their smiling patient sliding even a few inches down the stretcher.

"Don't worry, Baby," Mummy said to Georgie, "Mummy's fine and I'm sure I'll be back home with your baby brother in no time at all."

Pattie, Georgie, and Daisy were all grinning as the stretcher carrying Mummy disappeared out of the front door, and a few minutes later one of the ambulance men returned to take the now quieter baby from Pattie.

Five minutes after the ambulance drove away, Georgie's stepfather pulled up to the kerb, jumping out of his car and running indoors.

"I saw an ambulance turn out of Half Mile Lane as I turned in. What's happened?"

Pattie calmly explained to the agitated man what had taken place and finished off by giving him the good news that he had a new son.

"What? Did you say I'm the father of a little boy?"

"That's right, Lad, and now I'm going ter mix yer a brew before yer get right back in that car and drive to t' hospital to see yer wife and new babby. And don't worry about yer two beautiful lasses here, cos I'll stay wi 'em until yer get back."

Daddy nodded, thanked Pattie, and ran upstairs to wash and change out of his work clothes. Within ten minutes, he was back in the kitchen drinking his tea as quickly as its temperature would allow. After a quick hug of his two daughters, he disappeared out of the front door shouting out another thank you to Pattie as he went.

"Reight, Lasses, I don't suppose you've had yer tea yet?"

The two little girls shook their heads.

"Let's take a walk down ter shop where I've got a big stew bubbling on t' stove. Also, as there's a telephone there, we'll be ready in case yer daddy decides ter ring us ter let us know how Mummy and t' new babby are doing."

"Ooh yes please, Pattie. I love your stews," said Georgie, clapping her hands with glee, and laughing and jumping up and down just as she used to. When Daisy decided to copy her big sister, all three found themselves giggling again. Seeing both girls bouncing down the lane hand-in-hand beside her, gave Pattie a real sense of relief and peace that all must be well again in her beloved Georgie's life.

Robert looked pleased to see his wife return with his two favourite little girls in tow. While Pattie updated him on the afternoon's happenings, she gave Georgie the plates and Daisy the cutlery to lay out on the red-checked kitchen tablecloth. They all chatted happily as they ate their stew, and it wasn't until they'd nearly finished that the telephone rang. Pattie quickly made her way into the post office section of the store, leaving the door open behind her so that everyone could hear.

"Hello, who is that please?"

"Oh, Gerald, I'm so glad yer rang. How's Florrie and t' babby?"

"Oh, that's reight good news, Lad."

"Okay. Well, I've saved yer some stew, so when yer get here ter pick up t' girls, I'll have it ready for yer."

"Not a problem, Lad. Give that bonny babby a kiss from me, and we'll see yer shortly."

Pattie put down the 'phone and returned to the kitchen to find three faces looking at her.

"Yer mammy is fine, but t' doctors decided to keep her and t' new babby in hospital overnight just ter make sure. Yer daddy will come in for his tea and then tek yer both back home so yer can sleep in yer own beds tonight."

"Mummy really will come home tomorrow, won't she, Pattie?" asked Georgie.

"Ey, she really will, Lass. No need ter worry yersen about that."

Pattie collected the dirty plates and crockery and took them over to the draining board before she opened the oven door and removed a steaming hot apple crumble, which she put on a placemat on the table.

"Now Daisy Lass, don't you touch t' dish or it'll burn you. We'll leave t' crumble to cool a little while I make t' custard and Robert gets t' pudding bowls."

Two small mouths were watering as Pattie and Robert completed their tasks. Then as they all ate their delicious pudding, they discussed what their new brother's name might be. Georgie reminded everyone proudly that she had chosen Daisy's name, at which Daisy happily said her own name over and over, spitting small crumble and custard missiles over everyone as she did so. They were still laughing at the cheeky little girl as they heard a loud rap on the shop door.

"Yer daddy's here, Lasses, so yer can ask him for yerselves if t' babby has a name yet."

The two girls jumped down from their seats around the table and ran towards their stepfather, who crouched down and opened his arms to receive them.

145

"He has no name as yet, girls, but Mummy and I decided that as Georgie chose such a pretty name for Daisy, you could decide on your brother's name together, and tell us what it is when Mummy and the baby return home tomorrow."

"Hooray," shouted Georgie.

"Hooway," mimicked Daisy.

Then the whole room resounded with laughter all over again.

"Congratulations, Lad," said Robert as he shook his friend's hand. "It'll be interesting to see if t' babby ends up with a flock of red hair like his daddy."

Pattie put the plate of hot stew on the kitchen table for their visitor to enjoy. With one small girl sitting either side of their stepfather, he answered everyone's questions about the health and wellbeing of his wife and new baby son as best he could. He explained that the placenta had, indeed, been slightly blocking the baby's birth canal, which was the cause of Mummy's bleeding, but fortunately, the remainder had then come away complete, and the only reason to keep her and the baby in hospital overnight was to double check that the baby hadn't been starved of oxygen, and Mummy didn't need a blood transfusion. Pattie, Robert, and the girls nodded knowingly but, in truth, Georgie only half understood what Daddy had said and Daisy hadn't got a clue.

As Georgie got herself ready for bed that night, Daddy helped Daisy, who was only lately getting the hang of how to remove her clothes and put her nightdress on. He then tucked both girls in and kissed them goodnight. Sleep came quickly.

The next thing Georgie knew, she turned over and opened her eyes, to find herself in Mummy and Daddy's bed looking directly into Daddy's face.

"It's okay, Love, you had a dream and were talking in your sleep, so I lifted you into my bed so's not to wake Daisy."

Georgie, who was still half asleep, started to snuggle back down when a danger light suddenly flashed into her mind. She instantly sat up and

tried to slide out of bed to return to her own room. Gerald held her back and pulled the cover back over her.

"It's okay, Georgie, you're safe here with me. Just go back to sleep."
Georgie's whole body tensed as she lay stiffly on her side facing away from the man she feared and waiting for what was to come. Nothing happened, and her tiredness began to overtake her until she could keep her eyes open no longer, and involuntarily drifted back into a deep sleep. She didn't know how long she'd been asleep before she slowly drifted back into a dazed consciousness and found the monster's hand between her legs. Suddenly she was wide awake. She knew what this was a prelude to and wasn't about to stay where she was to prove herself right. She leapt out of bed so suddenly that the monster didn't have a chance to grab her, but his reactions were quick enough to enable him to be out of his side of the bed and reach the bedroom door in time to block Georgie's escape. He picked her up as she battered his chest with all the strength she could muster. He carried her back to the bed and lay on top of her to pin her down. She continued to fight but had no hope of pushing him off. As he repeated the act that had caused her so much pain before, she bit her bottom lip to stop herself screaming and waking up Daisy. When he'd finished, he rolled off her and as he did so, whispered a reminder in her ear about what he'd do to her and Daisy if she told anyone at all about what she'd let him do to her for the second time.

Georgie immediately got out of his bed and walked quietly and painfully into the bathroom. She ran cold water into the sink and first wiped away the tears from her face with a wet flannel, and then dealt with the part of her body that had been injured. She wished she could wipe away the emotional hurt so easily. The next morning when she woke up, she knew what she had to do. It was too early for Daisy and the monster to be awake, so she crept out of bed and quietly removed all the items from her school duffle bag and pushed them under her bed, ensuring they were out of sight. She then replaced them with clean underwear, socks, and tee shirts before putting the duffle bag in its usual place. She got back into bed, and with a sense of relief that her decision was made, she turned on her side and went back to sleep. When she woke up, she could hear the monster downstairs chatting to Daisy. She went into the bathroom, cleaned her teeth, dried her toothbrush, and placed it in the front pocket of her duffle bag. She was about to zip up the pocket when she suddenly realised that she'd forgotten to include her two most precious possessions – her dancer book and her bible that she'd had

since her christening. She quickly reached up and took them down from the shelf, placed them in with her toothbrush and did up the zip. Next, she dressed in her school clothes and crept into the next bedroom where she knew she'd find the monster's wallet in the bedside cabinet. She opened it and removed a pound note, which she slipped into the pocket of her pale blue school dress. She was just about to close the drawer when she noticed the corner of a photograph protruding from under some papers. She slid it out and looked to see whose photo it was. To her surprise, it was her real daddy, Alfie, dressed in an army uniform and looking very handsome. Tears came to her eyes as she recalled the happy times she'd had before he left them. She took the photograph and returned to her bedroom where she opened the front pocket of her duffle bag and slid it between the pages of her bible. She then picked up the duffle bag and made her way downstairs.

"Hey, Georgie, you don't have to go to school today. Mummy will be coming home with the baby, and you haven't even thought of a name for him yet."

Georgie thought on her feet, saying the first thing that came into her mind.

"Yes, we have, haven't we Daisy? His name will be John, like in my Janet and John reading books at school."

"Oh, okay. John is a good strong name. I like it and I'm sure Mummy will too, but you can still have today off school so you're here when Mummy and baby John arrive home later. I'm sure Miss Longmore will understand."

"No. I need to go to school today. It's our special projects lesson and I have to be there to help my team. It's a competition and I can't let them down or they'll have no chance of winning. Please take me. I'll see Mummy and the baby later when I get home."

"Gorgy go school?" chirped Daisy, looking at the monster.

"Oh, alright then. We'll take Gorgy to school, Daisy. How can I resist the pressure from both of my little girls? Finish up your porridge, Georgie, and then we'll be off."

Ten minutes later, he was pushing Daisy in her pushchair with Georgie, duffle bag securely in place on her back, walking beside him.

"I'll just quickly run in to ask Pattie to pick you up from school later, so I don't have to leave Mummy on her own," he said, leaving Georgie holding on to the pushchair as he popped his head round the shop door to ask Pattie if she was free to do him the favour. She was happy and willing to help, so without much delay, they continued on their way to school. As soon as they got to the gate, Georgie gave Daisy a quick hug and kiss on her cheek and disappeared into the school playground without looking back. The lines of children were just filing in through the school entrance, so the monster turned Daisy's pushchair around and made his way back home. Meanwhile, Georgie disappeared around the side of the building where she planned to hide until the playground was empty and all the mummies and daddies had gone home.

As soon as the coast was clear, Georgie walked as swiftly as her injury would allow her out of the school gates. She made her way back towards the village store, hoping that she wouldn't be seen, and turned left along the road that she knew led to Penrith. She had seen a police station there when visiting on shopping trips and wanted to report the monster's actions. She hoped the police would believe her and help her, and not just take her back home. She knew she had to take that chance, even though it meant she had a nine-mile walk in front of her. But Georgie was a determined child, so she walked and walked, all the time reflecting on what had happened. She thought about how upset her mummy would be when she got home from the hospital with baby John and discovered Georgie had run away.

'Well, it's her own fault for not believing me.'

Georgie thought about how much she would miss Daisy, and tears came to her eyes as she continued to trudge along the road.

'But Mummy will be there and it's her job to protect Daisy now.'

She thought about the new baby who she'd only had a glimpse of.

'I won't worry about him or miss him if I don't even know him.'

The morning became afternoon and still Georgie walked. Her legs were aching, and her soreness was getting worse, but she tried to ignore both.

It was a warm July afternoon, and the sun was beating down on her making her hot and thirsty, but her determination and the thought of getting away from that monster kept her going. She had no idea of the time when she finally arrived in Penrith. Evenings were still light so giving her no clue. Her feet were sore, so she decided to sit down on a bench and check them out. She placed her duffle bag beside her, removed both of her sandals and socks and was shocked to see large blisters on the soul of each foot. She'd just have a short rest on the bench to air her feet and revive her energy.

The next thing she knew, she was awoken by a gentle nudge to her shoulder. She opened her eyes to find that it was dark and standing over her was a large policeman.

"Hello, Lass. What's a little girl like you doing sleeping on a bench this time of night?"

Georgie immediately sat up and saw that the policeman, though a large man, had a kind face and a jovial glint in his eyes.
"I must have fallen asleep after walking so far. I was hot and thirsty, and my feet had blisters on the bottom."

"Yes, I can see that, Lass. But what are you doing here?"

"I've run away from home cos my daddy – not my real daddy – has been hurting me for a long time and I was coming to the police station to report it so that he would stop."

"How has your 'not real' daddy been hurting you, Lass?"

"He's been putting his thing inside me, and it hurts a lot. He's also been putting it in my mouth, and it nearly chokes me, and the stuff makes me sick."

"He has, has he? Well, I'll tell you what, we'll put your socks and sandals back on and I'll carry you to the police station to save you walking any further on those sore feet."

"Thank you, Mister Policeman," said the relieved Georgie.

"The name's Sergeant Carter, Lass," he said as he crouched down and gently put Georgie's socks and sandals back on, trying his best not to touch the painful blisters as he did so.

"Thank you, Sergeant Carter," said Georgie as the policeman lifted her off the bench and into his arms as if she was as light as a feather.

CHAPTER 15

July 1953

Safe and found

Sergeant Carter carried Georgie up the small slope leading to the entrance of Penrith Police Station. The old red brick building looked quite foreboding, but once inside, the atmosphere was warm and inviting. Georgie looked at the big clock on the wall as they entered and saw that it was now, eleven o'clock. The sergeant sat Georgie on the high desk, behind which stood another policeman. This policeman was slimmer and looked younger than Sergeant Carter, but also displayed a twinkle in his eyes when he saw Georgie.

"Hello little girl. My names Sergeant Greenhill. What's yours?"

"I'm Georgie."

"Ah, Georgie. That's one of my favourite names. So, what can we do for you Georgie?"

Georgie was reticent to repeat her story, so she looked at Sergeant Carter who gave her an understanding nod.

"Young Georgie here has had a very long walk today. I found her asleep on a wooden bench with her duffel bag, shoes, and socks beside her. She had bad blisters on the soles of her feet, which is why I carried her here. She came all this way to report her father – not her real father (nodding at Georgie) – for doing things to her that have caused her a great deal of pain. I'd describe these things as sexual assault, but I'm sure Georgie will explain more to the lovely PC Sandy, our police lady, once she's had something to eat and drink."

A timely rumble from Georgie's tummy confirmed that food was her primary need right now, and as she held her tummy in an attempt to stop the rumbling, all three grinned at each other.

"I'd say you're quite right Sergeant Carter. I'll organise that right now," agreed Sergeant Greenhill, who then disappeared into another room for a few minutes and returned with the police lady.

"Georgie, this is PC Sandy Bell. She is going to look after you and make sure we deal with that rumbling tum. She's going to take you into one of our rooms – and don't worry, Sergeant Carter will come too – then after you've eaten, you can tell PC Sandy all about your problem."

Georgie nodded as Sergeant Carter lifted her down from her high perch and took her through a little wooden gate next to the high desk where PC Sandy Bell was standing with a broad smile on her face. She had sandy coloured hair tied back in a high ponytail and she was nearly as broad as she was tall. Georgie fleetingly wondered how the police managed to find her the black uniform skirt and white shirt that she was wearing, but she knew that was a rude question, so she kept her mouth closed.

"Hello, Georgie. Pleased to meet you," said PC Sandy Bell, holding out her hand to shake Georgie's. Georgie, feeling very grown up, accepted the handshake with a smile.

"I'm pleased to meet you, too, PC Sandy Bell."

"Please follow me," said the PC as she turned left into a corridor with doors either side. She stopped at the last door on the left to wait for Georgie who was holding on to Sergeant Carter and hobbling along slowly. Then she opened the door and stood back for Georgie and the sergeant to enter. Georgie looked around the small room. There was a

brown wooden desk in front of her with two chairs in front of it and one behind it. The desk stood in front of a tall window that reached almost to the high ceiling, and on the pale green walls were a couple of randomly placed police posters. The chair behind the desk was the same brown wood as the desk, as was one of the chairs in front. The other chair was a green padded swivel chair with padded arms and wings. Georgie was attracted to that chair. She felt she could sink into it and feel safe. She saw Sergeant Carter watching her as she took in her surroundings – especially the chair. PC Sandy Bell walked around the desk and sat on the wooden chair in front of the window.

"Sit down then you two, and Georgie, please just call me PC Sandy," she said.

Sergeant Carter led Georgie to the comfy chair and grinned as she smiled her thanks to him. He then sat himself down on the wooden chair beside her, watching as Georgie hoisted herself up onto the padded seat and wiggled back until she was comfortable. As she did so, she felt the soreness that Gerald had caused, and flinched slightly. PC Sandy looked at Georgie sympathetically.

"I'll get you some food, Darling, then perhaps we'll ask the doctor to come and see you. He might be able to make you more comfortable. Is that alright?"

Georgie felt instantly horrified at the thought of another man looking at her private parts. She saw the look of realisation on PC Sandy's face, before she immediately apologised.

"Oh, I'm so sorry, Darling. I'll make sure it's a lady doctor. Will that be alright?"

Georgie relaxed a little and nodded.

"Good. Now maybe Sergeant Carter wouldn't mind fetching the food while you and I get to know each other a little?"

"Happy to do that, PC Sandy. Can I get you anything too?"

"Thanks, Sarge. Just a cuppa will be fine for me. Will a sandwich and orange squash be okay for you, Georgie?"

154

Georgie nodded and watched Sergeant Carter leave the room. She liked and trusted him and now felt a little nervous without him by her side.

"Have you got any brothers and sisters at home, Georgie?"

"I have a sister called Daisy. She's two now and is very funny. She tries to say lots of words but sometimes they come out wrong."

"Well, there's a coincidence. I have a little girl the same age as Daisy. She's called Eleanor, but we call her Ella most of the time. She makes us laugh too."

Georgie relaxed a little and happily continued to chat with PC Sandy about Daisy's antics.

"I've got a baby brother, too," she continued, "His name is John. He was only born yesterday but Mummy had to go into hospital for the night – just to check she and John were okay after he was born in the bathroom in our house."

"My word. How exciting. So, you haven't really met him properly yet?"

"No."

Just at that moment, the door opened, and Sergeant Carter came back in carrying a tray on which were balanced two mugs of tea, a glass of orange squash, and a plate of little square sandwiches. Georgie's mouth watered as he placed the plate and glass in front of her, handed one mug to PC Sandy, and took the other one himself before sitting back down next to Georgie. She was already preoccupied eating her sandwiches, feeling like she'd had no food for a fortnight. She only stopped to take a gulp of orange squash now and again until both her plate and glass were empty. As she wiped her mouth with the back of her hand, she looked up to see two faces grinning at her. Suddenly she felt embarrassed.

"I'm glad you enjoyed that, Georgie," said Sergeant Carter with a smile that made Georgie smile too.

"I was very hungry." Her cheeks turned pink.

"And thirsty, too, by the look of it," said PC Sandy. "Would you like another glass of orange?"

"Yes please. When I was walking, the sun was really hot and made me really dry."

"So where did you walk from, Darling?"

"Ousby," answered Georgie realising at once she'd let slip a piece of information that she had intended to keep to herself.

Would the police make her go back home now she'd told them where she lived? Her whole body tensed as she waited to hear what PC Sandy would say next.

"That's a very long walk indeed. No wonder you were so hungry and thirsty. So, what happened to make you decide to walk so far on such a warm day?"

"Daddy hurt me in the night when Mummy was still in hospital."

Gradually, the PC coaxed all the information she needed out of Georgie, including her address in Ousby, leaving the child tired but feeling a huge sense of relief at having offloaded the secret she'd kept for so long.

"Please don't send me home," Georgie suddenly blurted out before breaking down into floods of tears.

PC Sandy came around to the front of the desk and crouched down until she was eye to eye with the sobbing child. She took both of Georgie's hands in hers.

"Georgie, Darling, don't be frightened. We're going to let the lady doctor check you out and make you more comfortable – and don't worry 'cos I'll stay with you the whole time. Meanwhile, Sergeant Carter here is going to make a few phone calls to find you a family to stay with for the night."

Georgie calmed down a little and allowed PC Sandy to lead her into another room along the corridor where a lady doctor was waiting. Half an hour later, the personal examination to see what the monster had done to Georgie was complete, and Georgie was feeling a lot more comfortable after the doctor had applied some soothing ointment. PC Sandy led her out of the doctor's room and along the corridor to the entrance hall where Sergeant Carter was waiting with Georgie's duffle

bag hanging from one arm and a glass of orange squash in his hand. He gave his female colleague a nod as he passed the orange squash to Georgie, which she drank down in one go. He then took her hand and led her out of the police station, followed by PC Sandy to a waiting police car. Georgie got into the back seat with PC. Sandy, whilst Sergeant Carter got into the driver's seat.

"Where are we going?" asked Georgie with a slight quiver in her voice.

"Don't worry, Love. You know I said we'd find you a family to stay with for the night, well, while we were in with the doctor, Sergeant Carter here was arranging it. He found a lovely family and we're taking you there now."

Georgie nodded at PC Sandy apprehensively as they set off.

"Wake up, Darling. We're here."

Georgie opened her eyes and found she was leaning against PC Sandy's arm. She had no idea how far they'd travelled or how long it had taken.

"Come on, Sweetie. You've been asleep. Let's get you inside."

Meanwhile, earlier in the day back in Ousby, life had suddenly turned upside down. Gerald and Daisy had waited patiently for Florrie and baby John to arrive home from the hospital, and they'd eventually turned up at three o'clock. Gerald was relieved that he'd arranged for Pattie to pick up Georgie from school at three-fifteen. Daisy was pleased to see her mummy after the night's absence and was fascinated with her new little brother.

"Where's Georgie, Gerald?" Florrie asked after she'd settled down on the settee with baby John in one arm and her other arm around Daisy.

"She insisted on going to school this morning – some sort of special project that she couldn't miss – so I arranged for Pattie to pick her up and bring her home for me. They should be here soon."

Right on cue, at three-forty an urgent knocking on the door sent Gerald to open it.

"Oh, Gerald, I'm sorry to bring bad news but Georgie wasn't at school," gabbled a pale-faced Pattie, "I went ter pick her up at three-fifteen and when she didn't come out wi t' others, I went in and spoke ter Miss Longmore. She said Georgie hadn't turned up for school this morning. That's a whole day, Gerald. She's been missing a whole day."

"But I took her to school myself. I saw her go into the playground just as they were all lining up to go in," said Gerald as panic rose within him.

"What's happened?" asked Florrie appearing from the living room with the baby in her arms and Daisy hanging on to her skirt. "Where's Georgie?"

Pattie repeated her story to Florrie, who immediately panicked.

"Oh no. Oh no. What's happened to my Babe? How could she have disappeared out of school before she'd even reached her classroom? Someone must have taken her away. Someone's stolen my Georgie."

Daisy started to cry at that moment having caught the sense of her mummy's panic. Gerald put an arm around his wife as she began to hyperventilate.

"Florrie, just calm down. Come on, take a deep breath and calm down now for the sake of the children," he urged.

He picked Daisy up from beside her mummy and tried to comfort the child. Florrie came to her senses and managed to gain back her self-control. She took a deep breath and looked at Pattie.

"What should we do, Pattie? What do you think we should do?"

"I think we need to call the Police, Florrie. I don't know what else we can do. There's no point in going out to search for her – It's now three-forty-five and she's been gone for so many hours that she could be anywhere right now."

"Are you saying you think she might have run away? Why would she do that? There's no reason at all for her to want to run away."

158

Pattie looked at the ground and Gerald started to feel guilty and scared that Pattie might voice the suspicions that he knew she'd had about him for a long time. She had questioned him on several occasions when Florrie had been in hospital about Georgie's wellbeing. He'd thought at the time that he had managed to allay her concerns. Now he wasn't so sure. Then Pattie suddenly responded to Florrie's question.

"I'm not saying anything, Florrie. It's just that Georgie disappeared several hours ago now, so I think the only thing we can do is call the police - and the sooner the better."

Gerald felt relieved and nodded alongside Florrie as Pattie continued.

"I think you should both stay here with the children in case Georgie turns up. I'll go back home and ring the nearest Police Station in Penrith and report what has happened. Then I'll come back and let you know what they say."

Florrie and Gerald nodded again before Pattie put her hand on Florrie's shoulder reassuringly and then disappeared down the lane to make the call. By now it was four o'clock.

The police officer at Penrith Police Station listened to what Pattie had to say and then asked her to hang on for a moment while he just checked out whether a lost child had been brought into the station. After a short interlude, he came back to the telephone.

"Hello, Madam. I'm afraid that no child has been brought into the station, but if you'll leave your name and telephone number, we will ring you back should we have any news. Meanwhile, please reassure the parents that we'll ask all our beat officers to look out for a little girl of Georgie's age and description."

Pattie thanked the officer and hung up. Robert was standing beside her throughout the call, and immediately asked her what the Police had said.

"Are you thinking what I'm thinking, Pattie? Do you think that Gerald got up to no good while Florrie and the baby were in the hospital overnight, and so Georgie felt she had to run away?"

"It is a bit suspicious, isn't it, Love? Oh, the poor child. Poor little Georgie."

Tears came into Pattie's eyes as she thought about the little girl she had grown to love so much. She realised how desperate Georgie must have felt to have run away at what should have been such a happy time. Why hadn't she and Robert done more? But then Florrie had been so angry with her when she had hinted that something was wrong? She took a deep breath, knowing that she had to go back up to the cottage to let them know what the police had said. At least the evenings stayed light till quite late, so the child wouldn't be out in the dark on her own and the Police might have a better chance of finding her. Pattie took a deep breath before she started on her way back to the cottage.

Florrie and Gerald were in a bad state of anxiety when Pattie returned and reported back her conversation with the police.

"As soon as they find Georgie, they'll ring me, and I'll come straight back up here to tell you - whatever the time of night. Meanwhile, I know it's a stupid thing to suggest, but try to get some rest if you can, Florrie. Remember it's only a day since you had t' babby. I'm sure Gerald will wake you immediately should there be any news."

"Pattie's right, Florrie Darling, you must rest. Thanks so much for your help, Pattie. We both really appreciate it. In years to come I'm sure we'll all look back on this day and laugh because there's bound to be a simple explanation."

Pattie nodded even though she didn't believe that would be the case. It was still light when she made her way thoughtfully back to the village store hoping that they'd get more news soon.

Back in the cottage, Gerald was still feeling decidedly nervous. He had to have a plan in place in case Georgie had run away to report him. He soon knew what he would do.

"Florrie, you don't think Georgie ran away because she's jealous of the new baby, do you?"

"No. Georgie has never been a jealous child. Think how much she loves Daisy."

"But Daisy has the same father as Georgie, so Georgie won't have seen her as competition for my attention. Whereas John is my child. I am his real father. Maybe Georgie thinks I won't pay her attention anymore."

"Do you think so, Gerald? I'd not thought of it in that way. Perhaps you're right."

"Yes. I mean think about those awful things she said about me before. Maybe she's even jealous of the amount of attention you give to me. After all, before we got together, she had your one hundred percent attention most of the time."

Gerald felt pleased with how he'd handled that. The seed was sown and now the doubt was in Florrie's mind. He felt sure that his wife wouldn't want to lose him, so she'd support him even against the words of her not yet seven-year-old daughter.

Even while Gerald was manipulating Florrie's mind, the telephone rang down the lane in the village store. Pattie, who had become increasingly on edge as dusk had come and turned to darkness, jumped up to go and answer it.

"Hello. Is that Pattie?"

"Yes, it is. Is that t' Police?"

"Yes, Madam. My name is Sergeant Greenhill. I have some good news for you. One of our sergeants found young Georgie asleep on a bench in Penrith. He has brought her into the station. She walked all the way here from Ousby, so you can imagine that her feet are quite sore and blistered. She has had something to eat and drink and been checked out by the doctor, and she is currently on her way to a foster home for the night. Meanwhile, I wondered if you'd mind answering a few questions - in confidence of course? We'd like to come over to Ousby in the morning to question her stepfather, but we don't want him to know we're coming, so I need to ask you to keep that information to yourself, please."

"Of course, Officer. What questions would you like me ter answer?"

"Firstly, are you close to Georgie and her family?"

"I am, especially ter Florrie, Georgie's mother, who is my very best friend. I'm also particularly close ter Georgie because I looked after t' bairn very regularly when Florrie was in hospital with very bad depression after she had her second babby, Daisy."

"Good. In that case may I ask you if you've seen any change in Georgie recently?"

"Ey Lad, I have. While Florrie was in t' hospital for six months, Georgie turned very much within herself. She was such a happy, enthusiastic bairn afore that, always jumping up and down with excitement. At first, we put it down to her missing her mammy, but we gradually realised it was more than that. Sometimes Gerald, her stepfather, would drop her off on his way to work, and she was clearly in discomfort."

"Discomfort in what way?"

"The lass seemed to be in pain, couldn't walk easily, flinched when me husband sat her on his lap ter try to find out what was going on. When he asked her, she just collapsed in tears and couldn't tell him. I sensed she was too scared to tell him, but she was also too upset for us to push her for answers. Several months afore that, she'd told me she'd had a bad dream that she didn't understand. She was very tearful, but I thought it best just ter reassure her that dreams couldn't hurt her. Then when Florrie came out of hospital, things seemed to get better for a while until Florrie told me that Gerald had encouraged her to go out more, which of course she did. But it was then that I noticed Georgie started ter withdraw again."

"Thank you for being so candid, Pattie. I do appreciate that. Would you be prepared to make a statement at the police station regarding what you've just told me should we need you to?"

Pattie went silent.

"Are you still there?"

"Ey I'm still here. Yes, I'd be prepared to make a statement at the police station although I wouldn't be particularly comfortable about it. When I tried ter tell Florrie about my suspicions, she took offence, and what wi her being my best friend and all… I suppose I'm worried about upsetting her further."

"I understand how you feel but we need to prioritise Georgie's wellbeing right now, so we'd really appreciate your co-operation as far as not telling the parents that you've heard from us. That way, we can take advantage of the element of surprise when we visit in the morning. Are you able to do that, please, Pattie?"

"Alreight, Officer. I'm not really happy, but if it's just till morning, then I'll go along with it."

Pattie replaced the receiver. She felt like she was betraying her best friend who she loved dearly. But then again, she was also protecting that best friend's little daughter, so perhaps she could justify it in her mind. It was, after all, only for one night.

CHAPTER 16

July 1953

The investigation begins

Rat a tat.

Gerald opened the door and stepped back when he saw a uniformed policeman and policewoman standing there.

"Have you found Georgie? Is she alright?"

"Good morning, Sir. My name is Sergeant Carter, and this is PC Bell. May we come in, please?"

"Oh yes of course. Sorry. It's just that we've been so worried about our daughter that she's all we can think about."

"That's understandable, Sir," said PC Bell as they both followed Gerald into the living room, where Florrie was trying to distract herself by reading a story to Daisy, and baby John was fast asleep in the Moses Basket on the end of the settee.

"If the lady would like to sit on the armchair, I'll fetch a chair from the kitchen for you, Officer," said Gerald.

"No need for that, Sir. If you've no objection, I'll sit on the arm of this chair, and you can just bring a chair for yourself," said Sergeant Carter.

"I'll sit with my wife, thank you."

Gerald walked over to the settee and lifted Daisy up, sitting her on his knee as he sat down.

"Have you found Georgie, Sergeant Carter? Please tell me she's safe. I've been so worried about her," asked Florrie.

"Yes, we've found Georgie and she's quite alright except for some rather sore blisters on the soles of her feet."

"Then where is she? Why isn't she here with you now?"
PC Bell spoke reassuringly to Florrie.

"Please don't worry, Madam. Georgie is being well looked after by a foster family."

"Foster family? What do you mean? We are Georgie's family. She doesn't need a foster family."

Florrie was picking at her fingernails, a habit she'd adopted whenever she felt anxious. Sergeant Carter watched her sympathetically before he addressed both her and Gerald.

"We'd like to speak to each of you separately, Madam, Sir, if you don't mind. Would it be possible for you, Sir, to come into the kitchen with me, whilst PC Bell has a word with your wife in here?"

Florrie and Gerald looked at each other with eyebrows raised before Gerald responded.

"Might I ask why?"

"Nothing to worry about, Sir. This is just the procedure we use to investigate cases such as this one," said Sergeant Carter as he stood up and encouraged Gerald to lead the way to the kitchen.

When they had gone, and with the sitting room door now closed, Florrie looked directly at PC Sandy Bell.

"Your colleague said about investigating cases such as this. What case are you talking about? He made it sound as if a crime had been committed. Are you sure Georgie is alright?"

"As I said before, Florrie – you don't mind me calling you 'Florrie' do you?"

"Please do."

"Well, as I said before, Georgie has blisters on her feet after such a long walk, but she has made some quite disturbing allegations, which is why it's better for her to remain with a foster family for now."

"Allegations? What sort of allegations?"

"What she has told us amounts to an allegation of sexual abuse on her by her stepfather."

Florrie looked almost relieved.

"Oh, that old thing again," she sighed.

"Before we talk any further, I'm wondering if you really want your little girl here to listen to what we are about to discuss?" said the policewoman.

Florrie looked at the clock.
"Come on, Daisy, it's time for your morning nap, Love."

She picked up Daisy, who smiled happily as usual, and left the room to take her upstairs to her cot. As she did so, Florrie glanced towards the kitchen, which was closed. 'Poor Gerald. He doesn't deserve this,' she mused.

On the other side of the kitchen door, Gerald was sitting at the table feeling decidedly uncomfortable under the searching eye of the large policeman sitting opposite him.

"Would you mind if I took notes, Sir? My memory's not always good and I don't want to put anything in my report that isn't completely accurate."

"No that's fine. Go ahead, Sergeant."

Sergeant Carter nodded his thanks and took a notebook out of one of the larger pockets on his uniform jacket, opening it to reveal a blank page. He laid it neatly on the wooden table in front of him before he rummaged for a while in one of his top pockets, eventually removing a ballpoint pen. Gerald started to fidget uncomfortably on his chair as the Sergeant scraped his own chair closer to the table and jiggled around for a few seconds to get comfortable before he looked over at the man opposite him. Just as Gerald thought the Officer was about to speak, Sergeant Carter did a few coughs to clear his throat.

"Would you mind if I get myself a glass of water, Sir?"

"No need, Sergeant. I'll get you one myself."

Gerald scraped back his chair, stood up and walked around the table to the kitchen cupboard where the glasses were stored, took one down and went to the sink. As he held the glass under the cold water, his hand trembled. The Police Officer, who had observed his every move, said nothing. Gerald sensed that Sergeant Carter was watching him, which made his hand tremble more.

"Sorry, Sergeant, I'm afraid the glass is a little wet on the outside," he explained in as confident a voice as he could muster.

"Not a problem, Sir," as he removed a fresh white handkerchief from his right trouser pocket and dried the outside of the glass. "Don't want to get the notebook wet, Sir," he explained as he scraped his chair back again, stood up and placed the damp handkerchief back in his pocket. A few more minutes elapsed before he again scraped his chair nearer to the table and jiggled about until he was comfortable and ready. He then picked up his full glass, held it to his lips and took a slow appreciative mouthful of water. Gerald sat stiffly on the opposite chair, doing his best to appear relaxed. Sergeant Carter looked up, looked straight into Gerald's eyes, and launched straight into the interview.

"Your stepdaughter has told us that you have been – not in her words – sexually abusing her. In fact, from her description of events, we have

concluded that she is alleging that you have raped her. How do you explain her allegations, Sir?"

"Sergeant, she's not even seven years old yet. What would she know of such things? How could she possibly have made an allegation about things that she's just too young to understand?"

"I agree with you, Sir. How could a child of under seven understand such things – unless of course she has experienced them."

Gerald went silent, realising that he had just inadvertently strengthened his stepdaughter's allegations.

"Look, I can easily explain this, Sergeant. It's not what it seems."

"I see, Sir. Then perhaps you'd explain."

Gerald found himself gabbling even though he was doing his best to moderate the speed at which he was speaking.

"Georgie is the eldest of our three children. I am not her real father. He left Florrie high and dry when she was expecting his second child, Daisy. He was married, you see, and said he couldn't provide any more financial support than he was already doing. So, Florrie kicked him out. I offered to marry Florrie and provide the support she needed. Georgie found it quite difficult to accept a new daddy as well as a new sister – you know how children get jealous? She'd had Florrie's total attention for so long and so she missed that. Then of course, when Florrie got pregnant with my child, John, I think that was just too much for Georgie and she made up some cock and bull story about me doing things to her in her bed. Florrie reckoned she might have got in with some of the bad kids at school and learned about sex that way. Anyway, Florrie told her not to make up such an atrocious story because that's not what daddies do to their daughters."

"I see, Sir. That explains it. So basically, what you're saying is, Georgie ran away because she was jealous of her siblings and knew that it was no use making up stories again because her mummy wouldn't believe them?"

"Exactly right, Sergeant. That is what I'm saying."

168

"Thank you, Sir. I've been writing down exactly what you've been saying, so would you be kind enough to read it through just to check that I've got it down correctly?"

Gerald sighed inwardly and his tense shoulders relaxed.

"Of course, Sergeant, I'm glad to have been able to clarify the situation for you."

Sergeant Carter handed Gerald the sheet of paper from his notebook and sat silently observing the man opposite him as he read through the statement slowly and deliberately. When he'd finished, Gerald raised his head and faced the Sergeant.

"Yes, that seems fine, Sergeant. Exactly what I said," as he smiled and handed the page across the table.

"Thank you, Sir," said Sergeant Carter, "I'll be taking that back to the station and writing it out on an official statement form. Then I'll be asking you to come over to the station at Penrith to check through it again and then sign it."

Gerald nodded.

"Thank you for your cooperation, Sir."

"You're welcome, Sergeant," said Gerald as he went to move his chair back from the table.

"Oh, there's just one thing that I don't really understand, Sir."

"What's that, Sergeant?"

"Well, it's just that Georgie was examined by the police doctor when we brought her into the police station, and the doctor confirmed that her injuries were consistent with her allegations. I'm wondering how that could be, Sir."

Gerald's whole body seemed to droop momentarily as he stopped pushing his chair back. He then regained his confidence and looked straight at the Police Officer.

"Hmmm. I'm wondering, too. What has that little girl been up to?"

Meanwhile, back in the living room, Florrie had returned from putting Daisy down for her sleep.

"So, Florrie, perhaps you wouldn't mind explaining what you said before you left the room. I think it was something to the effect of – Oh it's that old thing again."

"Yes, that's what I said, Constable. You see, I was in hospital for six months after I had Daisy, and obviously that unsettled Georgie. She had been used to my total attention all her life until Gerald came on the scene, and she really missed me. Then Daisy came home whilst I was still in hospital, so Gerald could give less attention to Georgie. When I came out of the hospital, Georgie told me Gerald had been doing things to her in her bed. That, of course, is totally untrue and I made it very clear to her that was not what daddies did and it was an outrageous thing to say. Then Pattie said Georgie had become very withdrawn while I wasn't around, so I think it was just the whole situation that got the child down. Georgie never said anything else like that to me again, and she was very good with Daisy. In all honesty, I don't think Georgie was jealous of her, although Gerald thinks differently. Then when I gave birth to John in a bit of a dramatic way, I and the baby had to spend a night in hospital and that's what seems to have prompted her to run away. Gerald thinks that a second baby was just too much for her, and her jealousy made her angry enough to want to get her own back on him. Hence what she has said about him. Honestly Constable I would die for my children to protect them. I'd never let such a thing happen to Georgie – never."

Florrie began to vigorously pick at her fingernails again as she waited for PC Bell to respond.

"I'm sorry to upset you, Florrie. Look I've made a few notes in my notebook, please will you check them through to make sure they are accurate?"

Florrie scanned the notes, but in all honesty, she was far too anxious to take them in, so she just nodded and returned them.

"So, can Georgie come home now?"

"Sergeant Carter and I need to go back to the station now and discuss the situation with our boss. Then we will return – probably tomorrow – and let you know. Meanwhile, try not to worry. Georgie is in safe hands and that's the main thing."

Florrie nodded sadly just as Gerald and Sergeant Carter came back into the living room. PC Bell stood up and moved over to her colleague. They both thanked Florrie and Gerald for their cooperation and reassured them that they'd try to sort things out as quickly as they could. Gerald saw them out and then returned to sit beside his wife. Should he tell her about Georgie's injuries or not? Maybe the policewoman had told her but maybe not, and if he said anything, Florrie might jump to conclusions. No, he'd say nothing about that bit. If Florrie decided to bring it up, then he'd have to think quick. They chatted for a bit, comparing what questions they'd been asked, but Gerald very quickly realised that Florrie still really believed in him and clearly felt no need to discuss their answers. He knew that his wife was convinced that he would never do such a thing to the little girl he loved as if she were his own.

CHAPTER 17

July 1953

The investigation continues

"He's very clearly lying, Sir."

"What makes you so sure, Sergeant Carter?" asked his boss, Police Inspector Grailey.

Sergeant Carter went through his interview notes with the Inspector, then PC Bell did the same.

"The wife has chosen to believe him over her not yet seven-year-old daughter, Sir. She backs up his theory about Georgie being jealous of the other two children so taking it out on her stepfather," she explained.

"What about this woman ... Pattie?" asked Inspector Grailey.

"She has genuine concerns about Georgie, and although she initially shied away from the idea of being a witness against her friend's husband, she agreed to make a statement. I get the feeling she'd agree to be a witness if it came to it. What do you think, Sandy?" asked Sergeant Carter.

PC Bell nodded in agreement. The inspector thought for a short while before he spoke, disappointment etched on his face.

"Hmm. I'm not sure we've got enough evidence to get it through the courts though, and heaven knows we don't want the child to suffer any more than she has already. I'll tell you what, let's have a bit of a dig into his background to see if we can uncover anything to consolidate what we have already. I don't want to take it forward until we're a bit more convinced of our facts."

"Yes, Sir," said both officers in unison as they stood up and turned towards Inspector Grailey's office door. Just as he was about to reach for the door handle, Sergeant Carter turned back towards his boss.

"What shall we do with Georgie, Sir?"

"I suggest you leave her with the foster family for the moment. I don't think we can chance sending her back home just yet."

Sergeant Carter nodded and they both left the office. After a short discussion, they agreed that Sandy would go to see Georgie and her foster family to make sure the arrangements were working well, whilst Sergeant Carter started looking into Gerald's past.

It was a half-hour drive to the foster home, time for Sandy to reflect on the events of the past twenty-four hours. It frustrated her enormously that the courts were unlikely to believe a child over her parents. There needed to be a culture change to focus on the victim and not sweep the issue of child sexual abuse under the carpet. How would she feel if it was her little girl, Ella? She'd kill the perpetrator – even if it was her husband. Sandy suddenly brought herself back to the reality of this case, knowing that she should try to remain neutral but supportive. Easier said than done. She'd seen Georgie's injuries. The child must be feeling so confused right now.

Sandy pulled up in front of the large, Victorian, red brick, terraced house where Georgie was currently being fostered. She made her way along the pathway through the small, slightly untidy front garden and up the two steps to the front door, which was set back inside an arched porch. She knocked and waited for a while until a chubby and rosy-cheeked

woman with naturally curly, mousy hair down to her shoulders, opened it.

"Oh, come in PC Bell, Georgie's playing with my two in t' back garden. It's such a grand day we decided to get t' paddling pool out."

"Thanks, Mrs McDuffy," said Sandy as the woman opened the door wider for her to enter the spacious and bright hallway. Sandy could immediately see down the hallway, through the kitchen and out of the open kitchen door into the garden. She could also hear what sounded to her like bedlam. Mrs McDuffy saw Sandy's eyes open wider and laughed as she led her visitor out into the garden.

"Aye, I know they're a bit noisy, but yer can't resist t' sound of happy children at play, can yer? I can't and nor can my hubby, Cedric, although he's not here just now - he's still at work. By t' way, Lovey, call me Val. We don't stand on ceremony in this house."

"Thanks, Val. Then you must call me Sandy."

"What a lovely name. It right suits yer, Sandy – matches yer hair," grinned Val.

As Sandy arrived in the garden, Georgie looked up. Her cheeks were pink, her eyes were shiny, and her wet blonde hair was held back by a rubber band. She was wearing a pink, spotty swimsuit that had clearly seen better days, but it did the job and Georgie obviously felt comfortable in it.

"It's PC Sandy," Georgie screamed, which brought the other two children to a halt as they looked around, buckets full of water in their hands, ready to soak whoever was their next target. They were twins - a girl and boy a couple of years older than Georgie. Both were chubby and looked a lot like their mum, with natural curls and round smiley faces. Georgie proceeded to jump out of the paddling pool and run towards Sandy, who put her hands in the air and took a step back as she recognised Georgie's intention to give her a hug.

"You're too wet, Georgie," laughed the policewoman. "I'll be in big trouble if I go back to the station wearing a soggy uniform."

Georgie stopped just in time but still proceeded to shake her dripping hands vigorously in front of Sandy's face, spraying her liberally. As soon as the other two saw what Georgie was doing, they came running over to join in, only to be caught in the arms of their laughing mum, who proceeded to tickle them until they were writhing about on the ground shouting their surrenders.

"Well, I don't need to ask if you've settled in, Georgie. I can see with my own eyes that you have. Did you sleep well after you arrived last night, Darling?"

"Yes of course I did," shouted Georgie playfully as she followed the other children back to the paddling pool to continue their game.

"Come and sit over here on t' garden chairs, Lass. Kettle's not long been boiled, so it won't tek a minute ter mek us a cuppa."

Sandy sat back on the comfortable chair that was in the shadow of a large colourful sunshade. She watched the children playing as she thought of her little Ella being looked after by her doting grandma and granddad. She was, no doubt, also playing out in the sunshine at this very minute.

"What are you smiling to yourself about, Lovey? You looked like you were in a little world of yer own as I came out of t' kitchen."

Val was carrying a large tray on which were two mugs of tea and three plastic beakers full almost to the brim with orange squash, plus a plate piled up with a variety of biscuits. She placed the tray on the garden table next to Sandy's chair, and handed over a mug of tea. Then without warning, she yelled over to the children in what Sandy could only describe as a foghorn voice.

"Drinks and biscuits, kids. Come and get 'em."

This resulted in a wet stampede heading straight for the table, prompting Sandy to jump up and stand back just in time to avoid the splashes that came her way. Val didn't seem to mind the spray, which added to the wet patches that she'd gathered on her cotton dress earlier. It took less than three minutes for the children to drink down their orange squash, grab a biscuit in each hand, and stampede back to where they'd

175

come from. Val picked up her mug and sat down in the chair next to Sandy's.

"Right, Lovey, that should give us a few minutes of peace until t' starving hoard comes back for a refill. What can I do for yer, Lass?"
The two women sipped their tea and chatted amiably for a further twenty minutes, having confirmed that Val was perfectly happy to keep Georgie for longer.

"She's a lovely kid, Sandy, and fits in with t' other two - no problem. The only thing is, Lovey, we're off on holiday for ten days in a week's time and we can't take Georgie with us cos we've already booked t' boarding house and I know for a fact they're full up."

"Don't worry, Val. If you can keep Georgie until you go, that will be really helpful and will give us enough time to work with Social Services to sort out something more permanent for her if needed. Would it be okay if I have a quick chat with Georgie on her own before I go, please?"

Val nodded and called Georgie over. She picked up one of the towels that were hanging over the back of an empty garden chair and wrapped it around the child.

"Now, Georgie, Sandy here needs to have a quick chat wi yer, Lovey, so if yer tek her in t' back room, you'll have a bit of privacy. Just wipe yer wet feet on t' mat as yer go in, or you'll be sliding on t' lino."

"Thank you, Auntie Val," replied Georgie as she took Sandy's hand in hers and led her indoors.

"So how are you feeling today, Georgie?" PC Sandy asked as they sat on a couple of wooden dining room chairs.

Georgie thought about it for a few seconds, wanting to give PC Sandy an accurate response.

"I'm still a bit sore but the blisters on my feet are going down, thank you. I think the cold water has made them feel much better."

"Do you like it here with Val, Cedric and the children?"

176

Georgie didn't have to think about her answer to this question as she beamed and nodded vigorously.

"Auntie Val and Uncle Cedric are really, really kind to me, and I love having new friends to play with, too."

"Would you like to stay here for a while longer, then?"

"Oh yes please, Sandy. May I?"

"Yes, Darling, you may, but only till they go on holiday in a week's time, by which time we shall have sorted out what will happen next."

Georgie suddenly felt worried, the look of concern instantly replacing the sparkle in her eyes.

"Please don't send me home, PC Sandy. I don't want to see that monster ever again. He scares me."

Georgie couldn't help the tears of fear forming in the corners of her eyes. She felt comforted when PC Sandy's hands reached out and took hold of hers, giving them a reassuring squeeze.

"Hey, Darling, no tears. They're not allowed in this happy house."

Georgie managed a wan smile before Sandy stood up and led her back out into the garden, where her new friends immediately called out to her to come back and join in.

Meanwhile, back at Penrith Police Station, Sergeant Carter was on the telephone to his mates in the Metropolitan police.

"Yes, I know he comes from somewhere in the South and his accent makes me believe it was probably the London area, so I just wondered if you'd be able to check the files for me. My hunch is that if he is sexually abusing this young girl, then it's likely that he might have a history of this sort of thing."

He listened to the response before he finished the call with, "Thanks, mate. I owe you one. Speak soon."

The Sergeant hung up and sat at his desk wondering what else he could do. This was already a long shot, and he knew how labour intensive it was likely to be for the guys in London. Deep down he'd hoped that one of them would have recognised Gerald's name. He knew that a good memory for names and faces was something that all police officers nurtured. However, all was not lost. The officer he spoke to on the telephone was bound to ask all his colleagues, so they might come up with something helpful yet. He was still deep in thought when PC Bell returned to the office.

"How'd it go, Sandy? Is Georgie doing okay?"

"More than okay, Sarge. She seems very happy and settled already. She's enjoying playing with Val's two kids, and she looked really relaxed. But then, Val is such a lovely woman, and she just adores all children. The only thing that upset Georgie was the worry that we might end up sending her home. She admitted how scared she was. I honestly could have cried for her. Couldn't her own mother see that frightened look in her little girl's eyes?"

"I know. It's hard to believe, isn't it? But I think she's so blinded by her love and gratitude to her husband for stepping in to support her when her boyfriend left and then also while she was in hospital, that her mind just can't entertain the idea that he's not what he's led her to believe. I feel sorry for her really. What woman wants to accept that her husband is a child molester?"

Back in Ousby, Pattie knew that the anxiety about Georgie wasn't helping Florrie's mental health. Her friend appeared edgier each time she saw her. Three days had passed since the police had visited the cottage, so Pattie decided to pop up to Florrie's while Gerald was at work. She was feeling apprehensive as she knocked on the front door and waited for it to be opened. Florrie, with baby John in one arm and Daisy hanging on to her skirt, finally opened the door.

"Good grief, Florrie, yer look terrible. Have yer slept at all over t' last few days, Lass?"

"Not a lot, Pattie. Come in and I'll mix us a brew."
Pattie walked in and closed the front door behind her.

178

"You'll not mix t' brew, Lass. I'll do it. Sit yersen down at table and we'll chat while t' kettle's coming ter boil."

"Oh, Pattie. Why do you think Georgie ran away like she did? And even worse, why won't the police bring her back home?"

Pattie saw the tears slowly make their way down Florrie's cheeks and wished things weren't as they were. Even if her friend wasn't so blinded by love for that husband of hers, she'd still have to be contending with what had happened. It was hard not to feel cross with Florrie for not believing her innocent little daughter, but the fact remained that Florrie was her friend.

'If Georgie was mine, I'd have protected her with my life. But then Robert would never have done what Gerald had,' thought Pattie.

"I wish I could give yer the answer to that, Our Florrie, but I just can't. Yer just gonna have ter hang on in there, Lass."

Florrie took a handkerchief from up the sleeve of her arm that was supporting John and dried her cheeks.

"Mummy cry," said Daisy looking concerned. The past few days had obviously been confusing for the normally happy little girl who was now missing her big sister.

"Mummy's fine, Daisy. Don't you worry. I'm sure you'd love a biscuit while your mummy and I drink our tea?"

Florrie nodded her assent at Pattie, and Daisy cheered up instantly, quickly becoming engrossed in her decision as to which biscuit she was going to choose from the open tin that Pattie had lifted down from the cupboard and placed in front of her. Pattie hesitated for a moment.

"By the way, Florrie, t' school rang. They wanted to know why Georgie has been absent. I said I'd pass t' message on to yer."

"Thanks, Pattie. I haven't got a clue what to tell them. Maybe I can just pretend she's poorly or something. What do you think?"

"Maybe it's best to discuss it with Gerald rather than me, Lass."

179

Pattie busied herself pouring the hot water from the steaming kettle into the teapot. She didn't want to look Florrie in the eye when she mentioned anything about Gerald. She was worried that the guilt she was feeling about opening up to the police might show.

"Pattie, every time you mention Gerald's name you do the same thing. You turn away and won't give me eye contact. What is it about Gerald that makes you do this?"

"You're imagining it, Florrie Lass. The kettle boiled so I needed ter mix t' brew before it stopped."

"Well, you've made it now, so bring it over to the table and let's have this thing out face to face."

Pattie moved to the table, bringing two mugs with her. She went back to pick up the jug of milk before finally sitting facing her friend. She felt intimidated by the thought of what Florrie might be about to say.

"Come on then. What is it you've got against my husband? Let's get it out in the open," said Florrie.

Pattie took in a deep breath before she spoke.

"I've nothing against Gerald, Lass. It's just that I'm concerned about Georgie. I've known her for a long time and she's not a child that tells lies – I think that you know that, too."

Florrie lowered her eyes and seemed to study her mug of tea for a long time before she looked up again.

"Well, she certainly never used to, but don't you think that all she's gone through might have changed her a little? I mean Alfie walked out on us, she's had to get used to having a new daddy, and now there's another baby on the scene. I don't think she'd purposely set out to lie, but don't you think that with everything that's been happening, she could easily have become a little confused?"

Pattie could see that her friend had certainly been taken in by that husband of hers, and she knew she must tread carefully.

"Don't you think we could just as easily say that about thee, Lass? Could yer not be confused enough to be missing the facts too?"

180

Florrie looked thoughtful for a few seconds before she responded.

"Pattie, how could I possibly believe that the man who has been so kind and generous to the whole family could do the unthinkable things that Georgie is suggesting? The child can't possibly know what she's talking about."

"That is kind of my point, Lass. T' bairn is far too young to know what she's talking about – unless of course she's actually experienced it."

Florrie again looked thoughtful for an instant before her expression changed to one of horror. She suddenly shook her head as if to throw the idea out of her mind.

"No Pattie. No. Do you know what you're suggesting? You're suggesting that my Gerald is a child molester and a liar. That's an awful thought to even entertain. Don't you think I'd have noticed some signs if that were true? I love my children. I would protect them with my life. I'd have been the first to know if something like that was going on. No. No. It can't possibly be true."

"Okay, Lass. Don't upset yersen. Have a word with Gerald about what yer will tell t' school and pop down tomorrow morning to use t' phone."

Florrie accompanied Pattie to the door, and Pattie could see that she had planted doubt in Florrie's mind, which she hoped her friend would not easily be able to dismiss.

CHAPTER 18

Late July 1953

Highs and lows

Five days went by before Sergeant Carter received a call from the Met Police.

"Yes. Got him. I just knew there would be something in his past. Can you get a copy of his file up to me asap, please, Mate? Thanks, a courier would be perfect. I know how much work you must have put into this, and I want you to know how much I appreciate it. I'll buy you a drink when you're next up in this neck of the woods. Okay. Bye."

Sergeant Carter replaced the receiver before he lifted his arms up and punched the air with both fists. Sandy walked into the office just in time to see his display of emotion.

"So, what are we celebrating, Sarge? Have you won the pools or something?"

"It certainly feels like it, Sandy. It turns out that our Gerald has got history down in London. Ten years ago, he was prosecuted on three counts of child molestation. He pleaded lack of culpability due to

Paedophilia, a recognised mental illness. He received treatment in a mental institution over several months until they considered him to no longer be a danger and they let him go. He must have moved up here to leave his reputation behind."

"Pity he didn't leave his habit behind, too. Think of the heartbreak he's causing," said Sandy, "I can't stop myself thinking of Ella and how I'd feel if she was the victim like poor little Georgie."

Sergeant Carter nodded before the two officers went to the Inspector's office to bring him up to date.

"Well done, both of you. The thing that concerns me is the fact that the prosecutions were ten years ago, and he received treatment that pronounced him cured. Why hasn't he molested any other children, at least that we know of, in the whole of that time until now?"

The three went silent as each reflected on that question. It was Sandy who finally broke the silence.

"I suppose it's like a seed really. The treatment resulted in that seed within Gerald being rendered dormant for all those years. But like any seed, if you give it the right conditions, it will spring back into life and grow. For Gerald, the right conditions were being with Florrie and young Georgie."

The Inspector considered Sandy's words for a moment before he spoke.

"PC Bell, you really are a very wise young woman, and what you say definitely rings true in this particular case. Either way, I think we have enough now to bring him in. I'll check with the detectives, and if they're happy, I'll leave that bit to you two. Then we can let young Georgie go back home to her mummy and siblings."

"May I follow up once Georgie's home, please, Sir. The whole family will need some support – not least of all the mum?" said Sandy.

"Yes, I agree PC Bell. Do what you can to ease the pain for them."

The two police officers knew that Gerald would be at work on the building site just outside of Penrith, so within the hour they picked him

up and charged him with child molestation. He remained silent throughout the process and during the subsequent interview. Sandy locked the door of the police cell where he would remain until the first court hearing and returned to the office and Sergeant Carter.

"Do you know what, Sarge, I really had the urge to go back into that cell and knee that Gerald right in the crotch. Guys like him deserve to have the offending bit chopped off."

Sergeant Carter raised his eyebrows in mock surprise before he updated Sandy.

"I've just rung Val to let her know we're collecting young Georgie shortly. I've asked her not to say anything so the poor kid won't be worrying that we will be taking her back home with Gerald still there."

"Good idea, Sarge. When we do get her home, you realise we're going to have to inform the wife that her husband won't be coming home for the foreseeable future, so it might be good if you then leave me there with the family for a few hours."

"Good plan, Sandy. You can radio in when you want me to pick you up."

Georgie was surprised to see Sergeant Carter and PC Sandy when Val showed them out to the garden. She had been playing skipping with Val's children, one each end of a long rope and the third one skipping while they chanted a rhyme. Georgie dropped her end of the rope and came running over to hug each officer in turn.

"Do you want to play skipping with us?" asked Georgie while she bounced up and down in her usual excited way.

"Thank you for asking, Georgie, but we've come with some good news, so let's pop into Auntie Val's dining room so we can tell you what it is," said PC Sandy.

"Won't be long," Georgie shouted at the top of her voice to the other two children before she made her way indoors, wondering what the good news was.

PC Sandy was first to speak once they were settled around the dining table.

"Darling, we've arrested your stepfather, which means that he's locked in a police cell at Penrith Police Station. So, it's safe for you to go back home to Mummy, Daisy and John now."

Georgie felt instantly relieved at the thought of being safe from the monster, but then an unhappy thought came into her mind.

"Does that mean I can't live with Auntie Val and Uncle Cedric anymore?"

"That's right, Love, but you will have Mummy again, and you'll be able to play with Daisy and help look after baby John," replied Sandy.

"And you'll be able to sleep safely in your own bedroom with Daisy like you did before," said Sergeant Carter.

Georgie nodded, not quite convinced that that was what she'd prefer.

"So, pop upstairs and get your duffle bag, Darling. Auntie Val will have packed all your things in it already," instructed Sandy as gently as she could.

Georgie ascended and then descended the staircase slower than usual, finding PC Sandy, Sergeant Carter, Auntie Val, and the twins waiting for her in the hallway. Georgie dropped her duffle bag and ran into Auntie Val's arms. Both had tears in their eyes as they said their goodbyes. Even Val's two children looked sad as Georgie hugged each of them in turn.

"Thank you for having me, Auntie Val," said Georgie in the middle of a sob. "Please will you say goodbye to Uncle Cedric for me when he gets home from work."

Val nodded, clearly trying to keep a smile on her face as Sandy took Georgie's hand and led her out of the front door.

"Thanks, Val – and you kids be good for your mummy," said Sergeant Carter with a catch in his voice.

Georgie fidgeted in the back of the police car all the way back to Ousby, looking forward to being home with Daisy and her baby brother but feeling apprehensive about how Mummy might receive her. PC Sandy knocked at the front door and Georgie held her breath. The door opened and there was Mummy and Daisy standing looking shocked. Then Mummy let out a delighted scream and Georgie knew all was well and she could breathe again. Then Mummy bent down and enveloped Georgie in a hug that she thought would go on for ever. Georgie felt her mummy's tears dropping on the top of her head as her own tears soaked into mummy's bosom.

"Gorgy home," screeched Daisy excitedly as she joined in with her mummy.

This woke up baby John who began howling for attention, and prompted the hug to disentangle, leaving everyone laughing.

"Oh, come in, come in," said Mummy amidst her tears of joy, refusing to let go of Georgie's hand as she led them into the living room.

Picking up the howling John, who quietened immediately, Mummy handed him to Georgie.

"Meet your new brother, Babe."

Georgie sat down on the settee and gazed into the blue eyes of her little ginger haired brother. Her first reaction was to recoil as he looked so like Gerald, but as the tiny child gazed up into his sister's eyes, she melted and fell in love with him just as she had done with Daisy. Georgie suddenly felt Daisy tugging at her arm.

"Me too, Gorgy. Me too,"

So, Daisy ended up on Georgie's knee in one arm while John lay cradled in the other. Georgie was overwhelmed by the welcome she had received, and at that moment felt deeply happy to be home again. Mummy suddenly seemed to realise she had forgotten her manners and turned to the two police officers, offering them a cup of tea.

"Yes please. That would be lovely, Florrie," said Sergeant Carter on behalf of them both. "Perhaps I can come into the kitchen for a chat with you while the kettle boils?"

"I'm going nowhere till I've had my turn at cuddling this gorgeous little boy," said Sandy as she walked towards Georgie and Daisy with her arms out ready.

In the kitchen Florrie lit the gas under the kettle and then offered the Sergeant a seat at the wooden table while she busied herself getting the cups and saucers down from the cupboard.

"Florrie, I think you should come and sit down for a moment as I have something to tell you."

Florrie froze, knowing but dreading what Sergeant Carter was going to say. Her doubts about Gerald instantly surfaced and her hands began to shake as she reached out to pull a chair from under the table, dropping heavily onto it.

"I'm sorry to have to tell you that we had to arrest Gerald earlier today. He is currently in a police cell at Penrith Police Station awaiting a hearing. I don't believe he'll be coming home any time soon, Florrie."

"Arrested? On what charge, Sergeant?"

"Child molestation, Florrie. I'm so sorry."

"But we told you that Georgie was lying because she was jealous of the other two children. What's changed?"

"We decided to check Gerald's past and discovered he'd been arrested before when he lived in London. He was charged on three counts of child molestation and pleaded inculpability due to mental illness. He was treated in a mental institution for several months until they thought he was no longer a threat to children. When he was released, he moved up here to Ousby. So, with that background and the injuries that Georgie received, there was enough evidence to charge him."

Florrie's face drained of all its colour.

"Georgie's injuries?"

"Yes, her injuries were those we would have expected from her description of what Gerald did to her."

"Mental illness?"

"Yes, they call it Paedophilia."

There was a split second of silence before Florrie's plaintive scream started from deep down and quickly built up to a loud, heart-wrenching groan. She began to hug herself and rock back and forth on her chair. The sergeant jumped up and went around the table to try to comfort the distressed woman, but she pushed him away with all her might as her groaning grew even louder. At that point Sandy rushed into the kitchen with John in her arms, closely followed by Georgie and Daisy with petrified expressions on their faces.

Georgie knew immediately what was happening. She'd seen this after Daisy was born and Mummy had been taken away in an ambulance, not to be seen again for another six months.

"Mummy's having another breakdown," she managed to say in a flat, monotonal voice, all the time hugging her distressed little sister tightly.

Sergeant Carter radioed into the police station and asked his colleague to ring for an ambulance. It arrived within twenty minutes, and after the children had witnessed an ambulance man escorting their mummy, still groaning, into the ambulance with baby John, it drove off at speed.

Georgie, feeling dazed, cuddled up to PC Sandy on the settee while her sister did the same on the other side. Sergeant Carter told them he would pop down to the village store to ring the Council's Children's Department to find out if there was a foster home that could take Georgie and Daisy together. The time passed slowly before Sergeant Carter returned and sat down opposite Sandy and the two dazed children.

"No foster families available I'm afraid, so they've found a children's home that has available space but it's about twenty-seven miles away in Wetheral Plain. The Home is called Geltsdale and it's not long opened. It's a big old house that was specially converted. The Children's Officer is sending two people to pick up Georgie and Daisy in about half an hour

to drive them there, so we'll need to pack a bag for both girls while we're waiting."

"Georgie's packed duffle bag is still in the hallway so it's just Daisy who needs one," said PC Sandy.

Georgie was still feeling a little dazed when she realised that PC Sandy had turned to her and gently taken hold of her hand.

"Georgie, Darling, did you hear what Sergeant Carter said?"

Georgie looked at PC Sandy and nodded, feeling like the 'helter-skelter ride' of the afternoon was like a bad dream, but knowing in the pit of her stomach that it was shockingly real.

"Will you help me to pack a bag for Daisy, please?"

Georgie nodded again.

"Where will we find her bag, Georgie?"

"She hasn't got one."

"Okay, Sweetie. Do you know where Mummy keeps her shopping bags?"

Georgie nodded for a third time.

"Will you show me, please, Darling?"

Georgie rose from the settee and walked out into the hallway where she opened the door of the cupboard under the stairs. She took a cloth bag from a hook on the inside of the door and handed it to PC Sandy who had followed her, leading a still withdrawn Daisy by the hand. Georgie kept having to remind herself that this was real. This was really happening. Yet again her joy and hopes for the future were dashed.

"Thank you, Darling. Do you know where Daisy's clothes are kept?"

Georgie said nothing but walked towards the front door and turned right up the stairs and straight ahead into her bedroom. PC Sandy and Daisy again followed. Georgie opened the drawer of the chest where Daisy's

underwear, socks and tops were kept, and then moved over to the wardrobe where she opened the door to reveal three little cotton dresses hanging on small hangers. She then took Daisy's hand and sat on the bed, pulling her sister after her. Daisy began to whimper as PC Sandy packed the clothes neatly into the cloth shopping bag. Georgie lifted Daisy on to her lap and held her close.

"Don't cry, Daisy. Gorgy's here. I'll look after you."

Daisy put her thumb in her mouth, a habit she had long grown out of, and cuddled up closer to her big sister. Just as PC Sandy finished the packing, there was a knock at the cottage door, which Sergeant Carter answered.

"Children's Department, Sergeant."

"Come in. My colleague is just upstairs packing some of the children's belongings."

Georgie's stomach lurched as she followed PC Sandy, the packed cloth bag in hand, downstairs still holding her sister's hand tightly. Sergeant Carter introduced PC Sandy, Georgie and Daisy to the man and woman standing inside the front door as he picked up Georgie's duffle bag. The little procession walked up the garden path, Children's Officers first, followed by Georgie and Daisy, and then the two police officers at the rear. Georgie felt like she and her sister were being guarded in front and behind so they could not escape. Her heart was thumping hard against the inside of her chest, filling her ears with a loud throbbing sound. She felt a little light-headed. They reached the open wooden gate and approached the waiting car, at which point Georgie turned around, looked pleadingly into PC Sandy's eyes, and burst into tears. Daisy immediately followed suit. PC Sandy rushed towards the two little girls and pulled them towards her until all three were in a tight huddle and all three were crying. After a few seconds, the policewoman withdrew her arms from around the girls, quickly wiping away her tears with the back of her hand. Georgie could see PC Sandy was trying her best to smile as she spoke.

"Don't cry, Darlings. You are going to a big house where there will be lots of other children to play with, and lots of toys that you'll never have seen before. How exciting is that? The time will fly and before you know

it, Mummy and little John will be back home as right as ninepence, and you'll all be one happy family again."

PC Sandy then removed a clean white hankie from her pocket. Georgie noticed the initials SB embroidered in one corner. After she had gently wiped the tears away from Georgie's and then Daisy's eyes, she held the hankie out to Georgie who put it in her pocket.

"Whenever you feel sad, Georgie, you just look at this hankie and remember that you'll be coming back home soon to return it to me."

Georgie nodded. She felt so touched by the kindly policewoman's action that she reached out to her and gave her and Sergeant Carter a final hug each. Then catching hold of her sister's hand again, she turned towards the open back door of the awaiting car.

CHAPTER 19

Late July 1953

A new environment

The journey seemed endless to Georgie. Daisy had fallen asleep almost immediately, and her head was now snuggled into Georgie's lap. But Georgie, having come out of her shocked daze and relaxed a little, felt wide awake and was too interested in the passing villages and countryside to even consider sleep. Eventually the car turned into a semi-circular driveway in front of a big, red-bricked house and stopped. Georgie roused Daisy and both sat in wide-eyed silence and watched as one of the Children's Officers got out of the car, walked over to the large, dark blue door, and rang the doorbell. A round, cuddly looking lady with a broad smile on her face opened the door, and after a few words were exchanged, the Children's Officer returned to the car and opened the back door.

"Come, Children," she said as she helped Georgie and then Daisy out of the car.

"This is where you'll be living for a while. Come over and meet Matron."

As soon as Daisy got out of the car, Georgie felt her little sister's hand entwine itself into hers and it was as if Daisy was glued to her side as they followed the Children's Officer up the two shallow steps leading to the door. The round, smiling lady crouched down and spoke to them gently.

"Hello, Georgie. Hello, Daisy. My name is Matron Betty. Welcome to Geltsdale. I expect you're both very hungry?"

Both children nodded their heads cautiously.

"Well, that's good. Why don't I take you into the dining room where the other children who live here are having their tea? Would you like that?"

Georgie and Daisy again nodded their heads, and Matron Betty ushered them into the large, high ceilinged hallway where she helped them to remove their coats. She then placed the coats on two spare hooks amongst the several along the wall – most already in use. Georgie looked behind her, expecting to see the Children's Officer but only found the closed front door. At that moment she felt abandoned but was quickly distracted as she and Daisy followed Matron along the hallway. They passed a white door on the right and another, opposite the first, on the left. The walls were plain pale green with framed pictures of children's paintings hung at regular intervals, which reminded Georgie of her school corridor. Just before the end of the hallway, which then turned left, was an open door on the right, from which Georgie caught the sound of happy chatter. As all three entered the room, the chatter died down and all eyes turned towards them. The room was sun-filled and cheerful, with a large table covered in a colourful plastic tablecloth. Five children were sitting along each side of the table, and there were two empty chairs with tea plates in front of them at the far end, behind which were open French doors. Georgie caught a glimpse of the sizeable garden before she turned her attention back to Matron Betty.

"Children, I'd like you all to say hello to Georgie and Daisy."

"Hello, Georgie. Hello, Daisy."

"Georgie and Daisy have come to live here with us for a while, so I hope you will make them both feel very welcome and will look after them until they get used to our routine."

"Yes, Matron Betty," chanted the children.

Matron showed Georgie and Daisy to the two empty chairs, helping Daisy into her chair as Georgie pulled hers out and sat down. It wasn't until she sat down that Georgie noticed another lady sitting at the top of the table with an empty chair next to her. She was younger and slimmer than Matron Betty but had the same broad smile on her face as she gave a small wave to the two newcomers.

"Now, you two," continued Matron, "I'm going to sit at the top of the table with Aunty Bella. She is our cook and general helper around the house. We have another helper, Aunty Joan, who you'll meet tomorrow. You just help yourself to as many sandwiches as you can eat, while I pour you both a drink of milk."

With a mug of milk in front of their plates, Georgie and Daisy watched Matron return to the top of the table where she sat herself down heavily into the spare chair. Georgie was mesmerized by Matron's roundness until she felt a tap on her right arm.

"Would you and Daisy like some sandwiches, Georgie?" said the holder of a large plate, which she held out towards Georgie.

Georgie looked at the girl holding the plate of sandwiches and smiled as she took two of the small triangles, which she placed on Daisy's plate, and two more for herself. After thanking the girl, Georgie started to eat her sandwiches hungrily. They had strawberry jam inside them, and she couldn't help but say a quiet, "Yummy".

"They're my favourites, too," said the girl. "By the way, I'm Helena and this is my little brother, Geoffrey, sitting next to me. "I'm nine and Geoffrey is six. How old are you and your sister?"

"I'm seven in November and Daisy is just two."

Georgie and Helena continued to eat their food in amicable silence, listening to the chat of the other children around the table. Helena, a thin, pale girl, was taller than Georgie with brown eyes, and very dark, straight hair that was cut in a bob with a heavy fringe down to her eyebrows. Geoffrey also had dark hair, cut in the popular short back and sides style, but was remarkable because of his bright blue eyes and cheeky grin. Every time Georgie looked at him, his grin made her smile.

After several more sandwiches had been consumed, large plates of plain sponge cakes appeared on the table, and this time Georgie didn't wait to be offered one. Like all the other children she leant towards the cakes and helped herself to one for Daisy and then a second, which she placed on her own plate. Daisy seemed to be enjoying the scene. Georgie realised that her little sister had never seen so many children around one table and was amused to see Daisy grinning at every child as they spoke to her. Georgie sensed that, like herself, Daisy felt secure and happy in this place. If Mummy had to be in hospital for a long time again, she'd rather be here than at home with the man who had proved himself to be a monster. She would miss her mummy, and Pattie and Robert, but she wouldn't miss that monster – not one bit.

When all the cakes were gone and the mugs of milk drunk, Matron Betty told all the children that they could go to the playroom until bath time. Georgie, holding Daisy by the hand, followed the other children out of the dining room and in through the door opposite that they had passed earlier. As they entered, the scene that greeted them caused both girls' mouths to drop open. They were surrounded by every toy they could conceive of, plus many that they couldn't.

"Toys, Gorgy," said Daisy pointing at the colourful array.

"Yes, Daisy. What would you like to play with?"

Daisy led Georgie over to a small, low table with chairs around it. On the table were lots of books randomly spread out so that the children could select whatever book took their eye.

"Dancer book?" asked Daisy.

Georgie sat on one of the small chairs and pulled Daisy onto her lap.

"I'm not sure if there is a dancer book here, Daisy. Mine is in my duffel bag and I don't know where that is."

Georgie, with the help of Daisy, shuffled through the books but couldn't find anything remotely connected to dancing. She picked up a picture book about baby animals and turned the pages one by one asking Daisy what each animal was and the sound it made. Before long a little boy who looked not much older than Daisy joined them, so Georgie included him in their animal game as they looked through the rest of the book.

After a while, Georgie realised that Daisy and the little boy were getting on famously, so she left them working their way through the book for a second time and walked over to where Helena and Geoffrey were playing with the several dolls.

"Come and join in," invited Helena.

So, Georgie sat with them and became lost in an imaginary adventure played out with the dolls. They were soon roused from their play by the sound of Aunty Bella's voice, announcing that it was bath time for two of the children. Georgie suddenly realised that Aunty Bella had been sitting on a chair just inside the playroom door all the time and she hadn't even noticed. Georgie turned to Helena.

"Do we have a bath every day, Helena?"

"Yes, but it's fun. Aunty Bella is very kind. She will take you up to the bathroom – probably you and Daisy together, where there is a proper big bath. I used to bath with Geoffrey, but I'm too grown up for that now, so he baths with some other boys. Perhaps Aunty Bella will let me go up with you and Daisy so I can show you what to do."

"I hope so. It's all so different here. At home we have a bath, which I'm now big enough to use, but when I was little like Daisy, Mummy and my real daddy used to bath me in the big kitchen sink. They would lift me on to the wooden draining board where I would sit with my feet dangling in the water. Then we'd play bubbles with the soap. Mummy and Daddy would blow the bubbles and I'd have to try to burst them. We always used to end up laughing a lot."

"That sounds like fun," said Helena with a wistful voice. "My mummy and daddy were always fighting, especially when Daddy got home drunk late on a Friday night because he'd been down the pub. Mummy would often throw things at him because he'd spent all his wages so there was no money left for food. So, Geoffrey and I were often hungry. I used to try to look after both of us from when I was quite little. Then the lady next door rang the Welfare and reported my mum and dad. They took me to one foster home and Geoffrey to another. I can remember crying a lot because I missed my little brother, but they told me that they couldn't find a foster home that would take both of us. Then one day, a lady from the Welfare came and told me that Geoffrey had been unhappy too, and that if we wanted to be together, they could put us in a children's home that

had just opened. So, they brought us both here and we love it. Matron Betty, Aunty Bella and Aunty Joan are the kindest people I've ever met."

"Will you live here forever?"

"Yes, I suppose so. My dad is in prison for killing my mum when he was drunk."

Georgie was shocked to the core, and gave Helena a spontaneous hug, which Helena returned.

"Thank you, Georgie. I hope we can be best friends. How long will you and Daisy be staying here?"

"Until my mummy gets better. She's in a special hospital with my baby brother, John. She had a breakdown when the police told her that my stepfather, would be going to prison."

"Why is he going to prison?"

Georgie's cheeks turned pink as she looked at the ground.

"I'm sorry, Helena. I'd rather not talk about it if that's okay with you."

This time, it was Helena who leaned over and hugged Georgie just as Aunty Bella came in and called Georgie and Daisy for a bath. Helena immediately jumped up and approached Aunty Bella, and Georgie watched as she saw the kind lady nod her assent. Having collected Daisy from the book table, she joined Helena and followed Aunty Bella out of the playroom, turning left towards the dining room and left again towards a large wooden staircase, also on the left. As they walked towards the staircase, Georgie could see an open door at the end of the hallway that was clearly the kitchen. The little group followed their leader up the stairs to find another open door directly in front of them. As they entered the room, there was a large roll-top bath opposite, below a tall window with curtains closed. Aunty Bella walked over to the bath while Helena turned left beckoning to Georgie and Daisy to follow. Behind the door were three chairs against the wall, filling the space between the door and a large white cupboard in the corner. The wall at the far end of the bathroom was taken up by three small washbasins, above which was a narrow shelf running the full length of the wall. On the shelf were twelve mugs, each containing a toothbrush and tube of toothpaste. All along the edge of the shelf were hooks, one in front of each mug, with a face flannel hung on

each. Helena nudged Georgie and told her to undress herself and Daisy and put each of their clothes on a chair. Georgie sat Daisy on the end chair nearest the cupboard while she undressed herself. Aunty Bella walked towards them and attempted to help Daisy but the two-year-old would have none of it and grabbed her sister, stubbornly refusing to let go.

"Thank you for trying to help, Aunty Bella, but Daisy wants me to help her if that's alright?" said Georgie.

"That's fine, Georgie. It will probably take little Daisy a while to get used to us, so I'll leave it to you this time."

Georgie, with the help of Helena, to whom Daisy made no objection, assisted the two-year-old together before all three walked over to the bath. Helena managed to climb in herself, choosing the opposite end to the taps, Georgie lifted Daisy into the middle, and she herself, with a hand from Aunty Bella, climbed into the end with the taps behind her. Auntie Bella handed a bar of soap to Helena and one to Georgie and spoke from her chair next to the bath.

"Well now, you two, let's have a race to see which one of you can finish washing yourself first. Daisy sat wide-eyed watching both girls washing as quickly as they could, with Aunty Bella doing a running commentary and all three laughing as Daisy joined in the excitement by kicking her feet and splashing both girls at the same time. Soon Helena raised her hand.

"Finished. I'm finished."

Immediately Georgie copied Helena and shouted the same, while Aunty Bella pretended to look bewildered, declaring that it was too close to call.

"But I'll tell you what, Girls, you both win the prize ... which is ... to wash Daisy."

Daisy shrieked with excitement as both girls covered her liberally with soap, laughing non-stop until they had completed the task.

"Right, you little wet wriggly girl, it's time to get you dried," said Aunty Bella as she lifted Daisy out of the water and enveloped her in a large, warm towel on her lap before the child had even thought to object. She

then held out her hand to Helena and then to Georgie to help them get out of the bath, passing each a towel. Wrapped in their towels, the two older girls made their way back to their chairs while Aunty Bella carried Daisy over to the wooden cupboard next to them and took out three nightdresses, one for each of them. Georgie and Helena dried themselves and put their nightdresses on while Daisy allowed Aunty Bella to dry and dress her. Helena's nightdress came down to just below her knees, Georgie being significantly shorter than Helena found that hers came down to the floor, and Daisy's, though it was much smaller than the other two, covered her legs and feet with some to spare. All three children looked at each other and burst out laughing, as did Aunty Bella.

"I can see I'm going to have to carry young Daisy so that she doesn't trip over the hem," declared the kindly lady. "I'll shorten this for you tomorrow, Little Daisy. Meanwhile you'll have to put up with the scenic view to the wash basins and the bedroom."

Daisy just laughed and wriggled as the two older girls walked and she was carried over to the washbasins. Close up, Georgie could see that above each hook was a sticker with a child's name on, and the same name was on the mug sitting behind it. Helena went straight to her mug that was above the end washbasin, whilst Georgie saw hers and Daisy's above the first washbasin. Georgie and Helena proceeded to clean their teeth while Aunty Bella went over to fetch a chair on which to sit with Daisy on her lap while she helped the child to clean her teeth.

"Right Helena, you show Georgie where the toilets are, while I get the potty for Daisy."

"Daisy doesn't use a potty anymore. I hold her on the toilet," explained Georgie.

Aunty Bella nodded and followed Helena and Georgie to the two toilets located next to the bathroom. After Georgie and Daisy had used the toilet and washed their hands in the miniature washbasins on the wall next to them, Georgie picked up her little sister and followed Helena and Aunty Bella back past the bathroom and along the landing. There was one door at the very end and another half-way along on the left. They went into the room at the very end, where there were seven beds spaced evenly around the four walls and pointing into the middle of the room. There were two tall windows above the beds on the far wall, and one on the

right as you entered the room. The curtains were all closed, and a single light hung from the ceiling in the centre. Helena went straight over to one of the beds opposite the door, and Auntie Bella led Georgie and Daisy to the two beds along the wall to the left behind the door. Two other girls were already in bed at the far end of the room, but the bed next to Helena and the one under the window to the right of the door were still empty. Georgie placed Daisy in the bed furthest from the door and tucked her in securely before she got into the next bed. There was a small bedside cupboard between the two beds, so as soon as Aunty Bella had gone off to do her next round of bathing, Georgie leant over and pulled open the little door that was under a shallow drawer. Inside, she discovered to her delight her duffel bag, still containing the few bits of clothing that she'd packed on the evening before her escape to Penrith Police Station. She closed the door and opened the drawer above it. Her heart leapt as she saw her dancer book and her bible laying side by side. She lifted out the dancer book, slipped out of bed and sat herself on the edge of Daisy's bed. Daisy immediately pulled herself into a sitting position and made room for Georgie to sit beside her.

"Gorgy read dancer book."

"Yes. Georgie will read the dancer book."

Helena had been sitting on the side of her bed reading a comic. When she heard Daisy's request, she looked over at Georgie.

"What's a dancer book, Georgie?"

"Come and see. This is my favourite book that I got from Santa when I was very small. It's all about a girl who became a dancer. That's what I want to be when I grow up. I want to dance on a stage in a theatre in front of hundreds of people."

Helena came over and sat on the edge of Daisy's bed while Georgie read the book to Daisy, showing her sister each picture in turn before she showed the same picture to Helena. Daisy, knowing every picture by heart, pointed out all the different parts of each image. By the time Aunty Bella had returned with two more newly bathed girls, Helena had pushed into Daisy's bed next to Georgie so she could see the pictures more easily.

200

Come on girls, into your own beds now. There's just time for a story before I turn the light off. Helena returned to her bed before she spoke up.

"Aunty Bella, can we have Georgie's dancer story tonight please?"

Aunty Bella gave Helena a questioning look, so Helena pointed towards Georgie who held up her book.

"Read Gorgy's dancer book?" piped up a small voice.

Aunty Bella laughed at Daisy's request as she walked over to Georgie's bed to collect the book. She took it back to the empty bed, sat on the edge, and began to read the story. As she turned the page, Daisy spoke up again.

"Show pictures, pwease"

Aunty Bella smiled as all the children giggled at Daisy's words.

"Pictures tomorrow, Daisy. Just the story tonight because it's nearly bedtime."

Georgie looked over at her sister and put her finger to her lips. Daisy quickly got the message and snuggled down in her bed to listen to the rest of the story. She clearly found the story without pictures to be boring because within just a few minutes her eyes closed, and her thumb found her mouth. When the story was finished, Aunty Bella returned the book to Georgie.

"I'm going to be a dancer when I grow up," said Georgie as she received the precious book from the smiling Aunty Bella.

"Good for you, Georgie."

"Lights out now, Children," said Aunty Bella as she flicked the switch off and, leaving the door slightly open, made her way back down the hallway. The last sound Georgie heard before sleep overtook her, was that of Aunty Bella's footsteps on the stairs.

CHAPTER 20

End of July – Early September 1953

To be or not to be brave

'Where am I?' thought Georgie as she opened her eyes the next morning. Nothing looked familiar except for Daisy who was laying in the next bed still fast asleep. Then it all came flooding back and tears came into her eyes at the memory of Mummy and Baby John going off in an ambulance and then her and Daisy being brought to this place. Georgie pulled herself up to a sitting position and immediately saw her new friend, Helena, in the bed opposite. Helena was already sitting up and gave Georgie a small wave and a smile until she noticed the tears starting to run down Georgie's cheeks. This prompted her to slide out of bed, come straight over to Georgie's bed and put her arms around her new friend.

"Don't cry, Georgie. I know it all seems strange at first and you're missing your mum and brother, but you'll soon settle down, and I'm here to look after you and Daisy."

Georgie wiped away her tears with the sleeve of her nightdress and managed a small, watery smile.

"Thank you, Helena. It's just that I forgot everything while I was asleep, and when I woke up it all came back. I'm worried about my mummy and baby John, and I miss them."

Both were then distracted by the bedroom door being pushed open and a different lady entering.

"It's Aunty Joan," whispered Helena before she returned to her bed.

"Wakey, wakey, My Lovelies," said the lady as she went around opening all the curtains. "It's another lovely sunny day just right for playing in the garden. Who would like us to fill up the paddling pool?"

"Me," came the loud simultaneous shout from all the girls in the bedroom.

"Well, off you all go to the bathroom to wash your hands and face and back here as quickly as you can to get dressed before breakfast."

Georgie and Daisy, Georgie holding up the hem of her sister's long nightdress, followed Helena, with Aunty Joan catching up to take Daisy's hand.

"Hello, you two lovely sisters. Georgie, don't you worry about helping Daisy, I'll do that, or you'll be late for breakfast."

Aunty Joan was older than Matron and Aunty Bella, but the warmth and love radiated from her so much that Daisy immediately took to her and happily allowed herself to be picked up and taken to the bathroom, where a clean set of clothes awaited her.

Washing was a quick affair, with lots of splashing and laughter, and then a race back to the bedroom. Aunty Joan just pretended to be angry at the mess with a grinning, "Tut tut, Me Lovelies" as she proceeded to do a quick mop of the wet patches on the bathroom floor.

Back in the bedroom, Georgie copied the other girls and slipped on a pair of knickers and a cotton dress that were laid out at the bottom of her bed, before she followed the rush downstairs to the dining room. Breakfast was as happy an affair as tea had been the day before, with all twelve children sitting around the table, and Aunty Joan and Aunty

203

Bella sitting at the head with a large, covered cooking pot and a stack of small bowls.

"Let's just say our Grace first," said Aunty Bella, prompting all the children to put their hands together and close their eyes. Georgie and Daisy followed suit and tried to join in as the children and Aunties said a simple prayer together.

Our Heavenly Father, kind and good,
We thank Thee for our daily food.
We thank Thee for Thy love and care.
Be with us Lord and hear our prayer.
Amen.

Then Aunty Bella picked up a large serving spoon and filled each bowl that Aunty Joan held up to her with porridge. Georgie watched the progress of the first bowl as it came towards her end of the table. Soon everyone had one, at which point they all began to eat, and the happy chatter began. Georgie was already beginning to feel at home and noticed that the same seemed to be true of her sister.

The rest of the day was spent in the paddling pool in the garden. All the children stripped off down to their knickers and pants and were not hesitant to jump into the water. Helena's brother, Geoffrey, tripped over the edge as he jumped in, landing flat on his face. Helena and Georgie took an arm each and lifted him up, only to find his usual grinning face with droplets of water dripping down his nose and off his chin. Matron Betty told the children that they would have a picnic in the garden at midday and save their main meal for the evening. At one point, Aunty Joan took off her sandals and stepped into the pool with the children. At once it turned into a water attack on her, and by the time Aunty Bella brought the picnic out into the garden, Aunty Joan was a soggy, laughing mess. Nobody worried about that.

"If we all sit in the sun, we'll be dry by the time we've finished our picnic," laughed Aunty Joan, as all the children joined her in a circle on the grass.

"You're incorrigible, Joanie," giggled Aunty Bella as everyone dug into the picnic that she had spread on a tablecloth in the centre of the circle.

The days drifted happily by. One afternoon a week, the minister from the local Baptist Church, Reverend James, who happened to be Matron

Betty's father, came into the Home to talk to the children and tell them bible stories. Georgie loved those times when all the children would sit on the floor at his feet. Reverend James always seemed interested in whatever she and the other children had to say. One afternoon, he told the children the story of Zacchaeus, a man whose job it was to collect taxes from all the people in his town. The people hated him because he'd always collect too much money and pocket the extra himself. Then one day Jesus came into his town and all the people wanted to see Jesus and listen to his words. But Zacchaeus was a very small man and couldn't see over the heads of the others in the crowd. So, he climbed up into a tree to get a better view. When Jesus saw him, He called Zacchaeus down, and told him that He would like to come to his house to eat. The people in the crowd of onlookers were angry and told Jesus what a nasty person Zacchaeus was. Jesus told them that both He and God loved Zacchaeus as much as all the others. This touched the small man's heart and had such an impact on him that he felt sorry for what he'd done and promised to give half of his possessions to the poor, and to pay back everything he'd stolen four times over.

Georgie listened to Reverend James in amazement. She thought about her stepfather, who she considered to be a really bad person. She didn't see how Jesus could love someone that bad. The monster didn't seem sorry about anything he'd done to Georgie, so as far as she was concerned, he didn't deserve to be loved by Jesus or anyone else. As Georgie was reflecting on this, she didn't notice that all the other children had dispersed to the playroom, and she was suddenly brought out of her reverie by the Reverend James's voice.

"Georgie, you look very deep in thought, and what is that scowl on your face all about?"

Georgie's cheeks went pink. The Reverend's question had disarmed her. He seemed so caring and concerned about her, when not even her mummy had cared enough to believe her. He slid down off his chair and sat beside Georgie on the floor.

"Would you like to tell me what's on your mind, Georgie. It's clearly unsettling you and I may be able to help you. Didn't you understand the bible story?"

Georgie was silent for a moment, and then, avoiding the Reverend's eyes, she took a deep breath and launched into her story. Once she'd

started, she couldn't stop. She told him about everything that Gerald had said and done to her, and by the time she came to her last words, tears were dripping into her lap.

"So, you see, Gerald is much more wicked than Zacchaeus was. He's so wicked that I don't want God or Jesus to love him. I want them to hate him just like I do."

"I can understand why you feel like that, Georgie," said Reverend James, "and I think that if I was you, I'd be feeling the same way. But that story from the Bible tells us that God and Jesus do love Gerald. They just hate the way that Gerald has behaved."

"I don't get it," said Georgie.

"It's very hard to understand when you're only – how old are you, Georgie?"

"I'm six and three quarters."

Reverend James smiled as he continued.

"Yes, well it's very hard to understand when you're only six and three quarters, but I can only tell you that God loves us because His son, Jesus, died so we could be forgiven for the wrong things we do."

"I still don't get it. I'm sorry," said Georgie in a small voice.

"One day when you're old enough to understand, then you'll get it, Georgie. But meanwhile, whilst you're living here, you can ask me any questions you want to whenever I visit. Is that a deal?"

Georgie thought about it and smiled. She was satisfied with Reverend James' answer for now. She looked up into the kind man's eyes as she thanked him, and then jumped to her feet and bounced out of the room to join her sister and the other children in the playroom.

Several weeks passed by and then one Saturday morning while all the children were playing in the garden, Georgie heard her name called. She looked around to see Matron Betty beckoning to her from just outside the French doors leading into the dining room. She ran straight over to her.

"Georgie, do you remember Sergeant Carter and PC Sandy Bell?"

"Yes, Matron Betty."

"Well, they're here to see you. They want to talk to you, so I've taken them into my office. I'll take you to them now."

Georgie felt quite excited to see the two police officers again after what seemed to her such a long time. She followed Matron Betty into the office with a big smile on her face, to be met by two more smiling faces.

"Hello, Georgie," said Sergeant Carter, "How are you?"

"Are you settled in, yet?" added PC Sandy.

"I'm fine thank you. So is Daisy. We are both very happy here and I've got a new best friend called Helena."

"That's so good to hear, Darling," said PC Sandy as Sergeant Carter nodded in agreement.

Matron Betty signalled to Georgie to sit on the chair in front of her desk and pulled a couple more chairs up for the two officers to sit on.

"I'll leave you to it then," said Matron as she left the room, closing the door behind her.

PC Sandy began.

"We wanted to come and let you know what has been happening, and to ask you a question. Is that alright with you, Georgie?"

"Yes. Do you know how Mummy is, please?"

"We only know that Mummy is still in hospital, Darling, but I'm sure she is slowly getting better. We particularly wanted to talk to you about your stepdad," responded PC Sandy.

"He's a monster but Reverend James told me Jesus loves him anyway. I don't. I hate him."

PC Sandy was taken aback by Georgie's words, especially the vehemence with which she expressed her hate. It completely put her off her stroke, and Sergeant Carter, having realised this, took over.

"Okay, Georgie. Well, our news is that it has been decided to put Gerald on trial for what he did to you. That means he will be taken to a courtroom in front of a judge and jury."

"A jury?"

PC Sandy took back over.

"A jury is the name given to twelve ordinary people who have to listen to everything that happened and then decide whether they think Gerald is guilty or innocent."

"If you mean they decide if he did it or not, then that's silly 'cos I can tell them he did it."

PC Sandy grinned.

"You sure can, Georgie, and you may get your chance to tell them that. But some people, not you, Darling, might lie about what has happened, so to be safe, the jury has to listen to what both sides say and decide who is telling the truth."

Georgie nodded as PC Sandy continued.

"That brings us to the question we wanted to ask you. How would you feel if I took you to the courtroom where the jury listens to all the things that happened? That means a man who knows all about the law asks you some questions, and then they ask Gerald some questions too. Then the jury can decide who is telling the truth. We would only need to be in the courtroom while you answer your questions, and I would stay with you the whole time."

"You just want me to tell them about what that monster did to me?"

"Sort of, Darling, but it is more that they would ask you questions, and you would answer them truthfully."

Georgie weighed it up in her mind. It all sounded quite straightforward to her.

"Yes, that's alright."

Sergeant Carter studied Georgie and then spoke up.

"Georgie, you need to know that there will be other people in the courtroom besides the Judge, Jury and Lawyers. One of those people will be Gerald."

The look on Georgie's face suddenly changed. Would the monster hurt her if she told on him? PC Sandy, interrupted Georgie's thoughts.

"Georgie, you don't have to worry because Gerald will have two policemen, one either side of him, and he won't be anywhere near you. You will be safe, and I will be right there with you."

"But what if the jury don't believe me? What if they don't send him to prison after all? He told me he would hurt me and Daisy really badly if I told on him."

PC Sandy walked over to Georgie and knelt on the floor in front of her. She took both of Georgie's shaking hands just as she'd done some months before to reassure her.

"Georgie, do you believe what I tell you?"

Georgie nodded.

"Well, I want you to believe that whatever happens, I promise that we will make sure you and Daisy are safe. Can you believe that, Darling?"

Georgie nodded again.

"So, what do you think? Do you feel brave enough to go to the courtroom with me or would you rather not? Nobody is going to force you."

Georgie considered the question. Could she accept the challenge? Would it be too scary? Could she bear to see the monster again after what he did to her? She hovered between agreeing to go and being too

209

scared by the thought of it. PC Sandy and Sergeant Carter said nothing, but patiently waited for Georgie to answer in her own time.

"I'll do it if you stay with me the whole time."

"Well done," said the two police officers together.

"You're a brave little girl, Georgie," said PC Sandy as the Sergeant nodded in agreement. "We'll let you know as soon as we have a date for the trial, and then we'll make sure we take you to the empty courtroom and show you around before that day so you can ask us as many questions as you wish. Meanwhile, you just try to carry on enjoying life here. And I promise that next time we come we'll make sure we bring more news about Mummy."

Georgie returned to the garden and continued to play happily with the other children, quickly forgetting the conversation with the two police officers.

The next several weeks were happy ones for Georgie. One day, after her visit from Sergeant Carter and PC Bell, Aunty Bella was chatting with Georgie, asking her how she was feeling at Geltsdale and what she wanted to do when she grew up.

"I'm going to be a dancer just like the girl in my book. I will learn to dance so well that I'll be asked to dance on stage in a theatre in front of hundreds of people. They will enjoy my dancing so much that they will stand up and clap and cheer at the end."

"Wow, Georgie. That sounds amazing. Can you dance?"

"Not yet. Well not properly anyway. I used to practice dancing with Daisy when I was at home."

"Would you like to learn to dance properly?"

Georgie's eyes lit up.

"Oh, Aunty Bella, that would be wonderful. It would help to make my dreams come true."

"Do you know what, Georgie, I think I might be able to arrange that for you. I'll have a chat with Matron Betty later today to see if there is a fund that we could use to pay for your dance lessons while you are here."

Without thinking about it, Georgie began to clap her hands and bounce up and down as she used to when she was younger and her life was happier. Aunty Bella began to laugh and clap her hands too.

In truth, Bella loved to see a happy child. That's the only reward she felt she really needed for her work. Later that day, true to her promise, she went to speak to Matron Betty in her office. Matron confirmed that there was a fund from which the lessons could be paid for, and gave Bella her blessing, instructing her to sort out the arrangements, which she did. She couldn't wait to tell Georgie what Matron had said, and she wasn't disappointed at the little girl's response. On the following Saturday morning, a very excited Georgie, holding on to Aunty Bella's hand, bounced her way to the village hall for her first dance lesson. Aunty Bella sat on the wooden chairs that were arranged around the edge of the hall, watching Georgie with as much interest as she would have if the excitable little girl had been her own child.

The dance teachers were a young married couple, Mr and Mrs Trimfit, which Georgie thought was a perfect name for the job they did. They were both tall and slender in their dance outfits, which consisted of a dark suit and shiny black shoes for Mr Trimfit, and white sequined vest and tights plus a pink net skirt and sparkly pink high-heeled shoes for Mrs Trimfit. They began with stretch exercises, and some gymnastic moves on padded mats to loosen up the children's muscles, and then they proceeded to teach the Cha-Cha-Cha. There were girls and boys in the class varying in age from five to ten, and Georgie felt full of confidence, joining in with great exuberance. As she did so, she felt that this was what she was made for as it felt so natural to her. She didn't even feel shy when Mr Trimfit asked all the boys to find girl partners, and a chubby boy with dark hair and a flushed smile approached her. She happily nodded and took the hand he offered without hesitation.

"I'm Henry," the boy offered.

"Georgie," came the confident response.

As Georgie danced with Henry, she tried her very best to copy Mr and Mrs Trimfit's moves, and most of the time was successful. However, the few times she and Henry got it wrong and ended up either in a tangle of arms and legs, or in a bundle sitting on the floor. They both just giggled and tried again. Georgie was enjoying every second of the morning and even did a loud "Yippee" on one occasion when she and Henry got a particularly difficult move right the first time. Georgie noticed that Aunty Bella constantly had a proud smile on her face, which gave the little girl a warm feeling inside. She also noticed that the dance teachers were smiling as they watched her.

On the way back to Geltsdale after the lesson, Georgie bounced even more than she had on the way there. Helena and Daisy were waiting for her as she and Aunty Bella came in the front door. All three rushed into the playroom where Georgie proceeded to pass the lesson on to her best friend and sister. Within a few minutes, two of the other children joined in, and so the activity expanded until every child and Aunty Joan, who was on duty in the playroom, were following Georgie's instructions and copying her dance moves. There was lots of laughter as everyone filed into the dining room for their midday meal, so much so that Matron Betty had a job to quieten them down to say Grace.

Then, one morning in early September, Aunty Joan came into the bedroom to wake up the children a little earlier than usual.

"Up you get, my Lovelies. First day back to school today for you older ones. I'll have your school dresses laid out on your beds by the time you get back from the bathroom."

The mad rush to the bathroom left Daisy with Aunty Joan as usual. This time Georgie stayed behind too.

"Don't you worry now, Pet," said Aunty Joan to Daisy, "You will stay with me and young Raymond today and we'll have lots of fun while the others are at school."

Georgie, satisfied at the arrangements for her sister, left Aunty Joan to get Daisy washed and dressed and downstairs to the dining room. When she returned from the bathroom, she was wondering if she would have a school dress to wear like the others. She was relieved to see a green

gingham dress and dark green school knickers laid out on the end of her bed. She looked at the label which had 'Aged 6' on it, and hoped it wouldn't be too big, knowing that, although she would be seven in two months-time, she was small for her age. It turned out to be just right.

When Georgie entered the dining room with Helena, Aunty Joan was already there, and Daisy was sitting fully clothed in the seat she always occupied with her apron on ready to eat her breakfast. There was a buzz in the room as the children discussed school over their porridge and wondered what teacher they would have this year.

"Right Children, time for school," said Aunty Bella. "All go and get your coats on and line up in the hallway. You little ones, stay where you are until the bigger boys and girls have gone."

Georgie leaned over to Daisy and kissed her goodbye.

"Daisy, you be a good girl while I'm at school, and have fun playing with the toys."

Daisy seemed more interested in little Raymond, than the departing of her big sister, so Georgie just smiled, feeling reassured that her little sister was happy.

Georgie and the older children followed Aunty Bella out of the front door, and down the shallow steps to the gravelled area where the children's officers from the Council had parked their car all those weeks ago. They then arranged themselves in pairs, forming a line behind Aunty Bella for the walk to school. Helena formed a pair with Georgie and spent the time it took to reach the school gates, telling Georgie all about the school day. It seemed to Georgie that the routine was much the same as her school in Ousby, and she wondered if her new teacher would be as colourful as Miss Longmore, which she very much doubted. As it turned out, her teacher was a man called Mr Griffiths who spoke with a very pronounced Welsh accent, which Georgie found attractive and calming to listen to. She noticed that his eyes sparkled with excitement as he taught, and this excitement seemed to rub off on her. The school day flew by, and Georgie knew she would be keen to get back to school the next day. When she and the other children arrived back at Geltsdale, Daisy gave her a welcoming hug and told her that she'd had a good time with Raymond and Aunty Joan.

"We pwayed in the garden, Gorgy, and had some stories."

"Wow that sounds like fun, Daisy. What else did you do?"

"I coloured and had a nap," replied Daisy after thinking about it for a few seconds.

Georgie could see that Daisy had loved every moment of it, and it put her caring mind at rest.

Days passed happily with school each weekday, dancing classes every Saturday morning, and the weekly visit from Reverend James. Georgie almost forgot her former life, including the sexual abuse. Some days she didn't even think of Mummy and Baby John.

CHAPTER 21

November 1953

Happy-sad days

"Happy birthday, Georgie," shouted a chorus of happy voices.

Georgie and Helena had walked downstairs together and made their way into the dining room for their breakfast, where they were hit by the greeting.

In the centre of the breakfast table was a large, iced cake with a little marzipan dancer on the top and seven lit candles spaced evenly around it. Georgie's seventh birthday hadn't entered her mind. She had hardly registered that it was November, her life having been so busy and happy since she and Daisy arrived at Geltsdale nearly three and a half months ago. Georgie had happily participated in birthday celebrations for some of the other children, but it hadn't occurred to her that the same would happen for her. She was overwhelmed as everyone around the table launched into "Happy Birthday to You ..." so much so that tears came to the corners of her eyes and one or two escaped down her cheeks and neck soaking into the collar of her pale green school blouse.

"Come on, Georgie. Blow out the candles," said Aunty Joan.

Georgie's tears turned to giggles as it took her three attempts to get all the candles out before she and Helena could sit down amidst the clapping and cheering – the loudest cheers coming from Daisy.

"We'll save the cake to have with our tea when you get back from school, Georgie."

"Thank you, Aunty Joan. That was such a lovely surprise."

The day went happily with all Georgie's school chums and Mr Griffiths also singing Happy Birthday to her. It wasn't until Georgie arrived back at Geltsdale that things took a turn for the worse. Matron Betty met her at the door.

"Georgie, would you mind popping into my office after you've taken your coat off, please."

Georgie did as she was asked and once in the office and sitting on the chair in front of Matron Betty's desk, she waited to hear what she'd been called in for.

"Georgie, Love, I have good news for you. The best news you could get on your birthday."

Georgie grinned.

"I received a telephone call while you were at school. It was the Children's Officer from the Council. She told me that Mummy is better and is now at home with baby John."

Georgie's first thought was one of relief that her mummy was better. Then another thought entered her mind that made her heart begin to thump. Matron continued.

"So, Georgie, that means you and Daisy can return home tomorrow. A car will come and pick you both up after breakfast."

It was then that Matron Betty noticed a couple of tears trickling down Georgie's face.

"Oh, Georgie. I thought you'd be happy. Why are you crying?"

216

"I don't want to leave here. My best friend is here, and my dance classes are here too. I love living here. I love you and Aunty Bella and Aunty Joan. I'm happy here, Matron Betty, and I haven't yet been to the trial with PC Sandy. Please let me and Daisy stay."

Matron Betty came around the desk and lifted Georgie from her chair, sitting down with the crying little girl on her lap. She hugged Georgie and rocked her to comfort her. She knew how much unhappiness Georgie had already had in her life and had loved watching her blossom into the happy and confident child she had become over the months she'd been living at Geltsdale. She waited for Georgie's tears to stop before she spoke.

"We will miss you, Georgie, but I know you love your mummy and you'll be able to get to know your little brother again. You and Helena can write to each other, so you'll not miss each other quite so much, and Mummy and John will be so glad to have you back home. You know how much Mummy loves you, and you'll soon get used to being home again. And don't worry about the trial. We've let Sergeant Carter and PC Bell know that you're going home, so they can just as easily visit you there. Right now, I need you to be a big girl for Daisy's sake. We don't want her upset, do we? We want that little sister of yours to feel excited about seeing her mummy and brother again, don't we?"

Georgie nodded.

"And right now, we've arranged a birthday party for you in the playroom, so run upstairs and get changed so you can join in the fun."

Georgie's face lit up at the news of a party. She was suddenly filled with excitement and got down from Matron's lap, thanked her, and ran out of the door, straight upstairs. She found a pretty dress on the end of her bed and was dressed and back downstairs within ten minutes. As she opened the playroom door, the first thing she saw were bunches of coloured balloons hanging from the ceiling. She was immediately greeted with a cheer and the other children crowded around her with small birthday gifts that they'd mostly made themselves.

Daisy was first in line with a picture she'd drawn, and was quick to explain that it was Mummy, Georgie, and Daisy with baby John. Georgie gave her a hug.

"That's the best picture you've ever drawn, Daisy. I will always treasure it and when we get home, I'll put it up on our bedroom wall."

When it came to Helena's turn to give Georgie her present, the two girls smiled at each other, but Georgie noticed tears in the corner of her friend's eyes. She guessed at once that Matron Betty had told the other children that this was her and Daisy's last night at Geltsdale. Tears came to the corner of her own eyes too, as Helena handed her a tiny, wrapped gift. When Georgie opened it, she found a bracelet woven from different coloured embroidery threads. She gasped at its colourful prettiness.

"This is beautiful, Helena. Thank you. Did you make this yourself?"

"I did, Georgie, and I hope you will wear it, so you'll always remember me."

The two friends hugged as the other children watched on quietly, until the silence was broken by Aunty Joan.

"Time for Pass the Parcel, Children. All sit on the floor in a circle, and we'll begin."

After that, there was no time to be sad. Game after game followed, accompanied by lots of cheers and laughter. By teatime, which was later than usual, everyone looked quite exhausted and said they felt very hungry. Georgie watched as Matron Betty cut her birthday cake into slices and handed it around. She enjoyed her slice but was more than ready for bed when the time came. When Georgie and Daisy were both in bed, Georgie turned to her little sister.

"Are you excited, Daisy? Tomorrow we'll be going home to Mummy and baby John again."

Daisy nodded, apparently not quite sure whether she was excited or not. Georgie continued.

"We'll be able to sleep in our own little bedroom again and take John for walks in his pram. We'll even be able to see Pattie and Robert again."

Daisy nodded again, this time more confidently. Georgie was relieved as she didn't think she'd have been able to deal with an upset Daisy when she was feeling upset herself.

Aunty Joan came into the bedroom to read a story as usual.

"Can I borrow your dancer book, please Georgie? I thought it would be nice to read that story tonight, and maybe Daisy might be able to help me point out what's in the pictures."

Daisy was out of bed like a shot.

"I help you Aunty Yoan,"

Story time took a little longer than usual, with Daisy insisting on pointing out every element of each picture, but as Aunty Joan read, Georgie lay daydreaming. She could see herself on the stage in a big city, standing in line with lots of other dancers dressed in beautiful costumes. They all danced in exact time with each other as they accompanied a famous singer. She could hear the applause at the end and see everyone in the audience getting to their feet and clapping and clapping – just like they did in her dancer book. As Daisy returned to her bed and Aunty Joan switched off the light, Georgie drifted to sleep and continued her daydream in her sleep.

Morning came all too soon. Aunty Bella helped Georgie to pack her duffle bag and Daisy's cloth bag. Georgie carefully packed each different gift that she'd received for her birthday except for her bracelet, which she placed on her wrist. Breakfast was as chatty as ever with all the children talking about yesterday's party. It wasn't until everyone had finished eating, and the older children were ready to go to school that Matron Betty took Georgie's and Daisy's hands and stood at the front door facing all the other children who were lined up in the hallway.

"Now Children, as you go out of the front door, it's a chance to say your last goodbyes to Georgie and Daisy. They will be off home as soon the car gets here to take them, so it is a really exciting day for them both."

As the children filed out of the door, each in turn hugged Georgie and then Daisy. A few told them how lucky they were to be going back to their family, and how much they wished it was them. Helena was too choked to say anything except that she would write soon. Just as the last one

filed out, the car from the Council drove in. Matron Betty, Aunty Bella and Aunty Joan hugged each of the children in turn, giving them a small gift to open on their way home.

"You take care of Daisy and your baby brother, Georgie," said Aunty Joan, "and I hope you become a dancer one day like you want."

Aunty Bella then spoke.

"I think you're already a really good little dancer, Georgie. Keep practicing and let me know when you do your first big performance so I can be there sitting in the front seats to cheer you on."

Matron Betty seemed to be finding it difficult to speak. Georgie hadn't seen her near to tears before, so she just put her arms around the rounded lady's waist and hugged her.

"Thank you, Matron Betty. I'll always remember you and Aunty Joan and Aunty Bella. I love all of you and I know I'll miss you. And I'm determined to become a dancer, just for you."

Georgie led Daisy down the steps of Geltsdale for the last time, with Matron and the two Aunties following. The two people from the Council opened the back doors of the car and Georgie got in on the far side, while each of the Aunties and Matron Betty hugged Daisy, the third one putting her in the back seat beside Georgie. Both little girls smiled and waved until Geltsdale was out of sight. Georgie then put her arm around her little sister and they both cuddled up together watching the countryside go by. The journey home seemed to take less time than the journey there three and a half months ago. As the car drew up outside the white cottage with the slate roof, Georgie suddenly felt a shot of excitement.

"We're home, Daisy. We're home to Mummy and baby John."

"Home to Mummy," repeated Daisy, her eyes sparkling with anticipation.
As the driver got out of the car and opened the door nearest to the cottage gate, the front door burst open, and Mummy flew down the path with open arms to pick up Daisy and hold her close.

"Mummy, Mummy," said the rapturous little girl as she cuddled close into Mummy's neck. Georgie shuffled across the back seat and stood

looking on, not sure what to expect from the woman, her mother, who hadn't believed her in her days of desperation. Mummy put Daisy down and looked towards Georgie.

"Come here, Baby. Oh, how I've missed my big girl. Georgie felt relief that her Mummy still loved her. Deep down she'd been harbouring the worry that this would not be the case after she'd been instrumental in taking Gerald away from her. Tears started to fall as Mummy came towards her and held her close. Georgie hung on so tight that Mummy had to separate herself from her daughter to acknowledge the presence of the Children's Officers.

"Thank you so much for bringing my babies home," she said as she took Georgie's duffle bag and Daisy's cloth bag from them.

The workers nodded, shook hands with her, said goodbye to the two little girls, got back in their car and drove away. With one daughter clinging on to each hand, Mummy made her way back down the garden path and in through the front door to the cottage. Having put the bags on the floor and removed Georgie's and Daisy's coats, she smiled at them.

"Would you like to see your baby brother?"

"Baby Yon," said Daisy, nodding her head enthusiastically.

Mummy and Georgie laughed at Daisy as she led them through the lounge doorway into the living room where John, now three months old, was laying on his tummy on a blanket on the living room floor. His red hair had grown a little and was sticking up, as he gurgled happily at the flames of the fire burning brightly in the hearth. Georgie broke away from Mummy, took Daisy's hand and led her toward the sturdy little baby. They knelt on the floor and Georgie carefully lifted John into her arms. He looked straight into her eyes, and she fell in love with the little boy all over again. Daisy seemed a little hesitant and clung on to her big sister.

"It's alright, Daisy. You are my most precious sister in the whole world, and John can be our most precious brother."

Mummy came over and lifted John out of Georgie's arms whilst both sisters sat on the settee. She passed John to Georgie while she sat Daisy right at the back of the seat and put a cushion under one arm for support. She then took John from Georgie and carefully placed him on

Daisy's lap with his head resting on her supported arm. Daisy looked mesmerised.

"Baby Yon," she repeated, as she looked into the little boy's blue eyes. "Hawwo, Yon. My name is Daisy. Me and Gorgy are your big sisters and we love you 'cos you are our pweciousest bwother in the whole world."

Mummy and Georgie started to giggle. Daisy looked up wondering why, and decided to join in, at which point baby John did a tiny giggle too. This was enough to take away all the tension from the build-up of anticipation that all three had experienced, and they all ended up in a family hug with John at the centre, the look on his face alternating between amusement and confusion. When they calmed down, Daisy was the first to speak.

"Gorgy wead dancer book to Yon."

"I'll tell you what," responded Mummy. I'll get the book out of your duffle bag, Baby, and you can read it to Daisy and John while I prepare our dinner. It's cheese and potato pie, Georgie, one of your favourites."

The two girls cheered, and Mummy fetched the book.

"What are all those things in your duffle bag, Baby?"

"Oh, they're the presents that all my friends made me for my birthday." Georgie held up her wrist where she wore her bracelet.

"This is one of my favourites. It's a bracelet that my best friend, Helena, made for me. My other favourite was the picture Daisy drew for me of you, me, John and herself. I'll show it to you later. Daisy's really good at drawing, aren't you Dais?"

Daisy's face lit up with pride.

"I dwawed a picture for Gorgy for her birfday pwesent, Mummy."

"What a clever girl you are, Daisy. And, Georgie, what's this all about calling your sister Dais?"

"I only just thought of it, Mummy. At school everyone shortens their friend's names, and Daisy isn't just my sister; she is also my friend."

"Hmmm I'm not sure I like the name Dais, though, Baby."

"It's only like you call me Baby instead of Georgie, Mummy. That's cos you love me, just like I love Daisy."

"Well thank goodness you can't shorten John's name then."

Georgie grinned.

"No but he is a chubby little boy so I could call him Dumpling for a nickname."

"Don't you dare," laughed Mummy and she handed over the dancer book and lifted John from Daisy's sagging arm into Georgie's. Georgie wiggled back into the seat as her sister wiggled closer to her, and soon all three children were engrossed in the story, although John seemed more engrossed in his two sisters than the dancer book.

After tea, Mummy handed Georgie a belated birthday gift wrapped in pretty paper with little dancers all over it. Georgie opened it excitedly to find a box containing a flat cardboard girl and lots of sheets of press-out clothes and accessories to fit onto the girl with little tabs that had to be bent over the cardboard cut-out to the back to keep them in place. One of the sheets of clothes contained dancing outfits – a ballet dress and shoes, a Spanish dancer's dress with little clackers to fit over the wrists, and a beautiful ballroom dancing dress and accessories. Georgie was so happy with the gift that she rushed over to Mummy and gave her a big hug and kiss.

By the time both little girls were tucked up in bed that night, it was as if they'd never left. They'd both bathed together and changed into their own nightdresses while Mummy settled John down. Daisy's cot had been replaced with a small single bed, and the cot had been moved into Mummy's room for John. Daisy had got used to sleeping in a bed at Geltsdale, so happily settled down as Mummy kissed them both goodnight and went downstair

CHAPTER 22

November 1953 – Mid February 1954

Changes ahead

Life settled down for Georgie and Daisy after their return home to Ousby from Geltsdale. Georgie returned to school while Daisy and John stayed at home with their mummy. Now that Georgie was seven, Mummy told her that she was old enough to make her own way to school. Each morning on her way there, Georgie would drop into the village store to see Pattie and Robert and would never come out empty handed.

"Ow do Lass?" Pattie would ask. "Tek a boiled sweet to suck on t' way to school."

"Ey, Georgie. Have this spare copy of t' Girl comic. I'll save yer one each week if yer like it," Robert would add.

Miss Longmore, having continued to stay with her class as they moved up the school, was delighted to have Georgie back, as were her friends who had missed her and wondered where she had been. Georgie didn't go into detail about the monster, but just said she and Daisy had been looked after in a children's home while her mummy was in hospital. Mummy seemed reasonably happy at home and never once mentioned

the monster within Georgie's hearing. She often popped down to see Pattie, where Georgie guessed she offloaded her feelings whenever she was a bit low. Pattie and Robert remained good friends and continued to come up to the cottage every Saturday evening for a social time.

Christmas was spent happily in Pattie and Roberts home at the back of the village store and when they gave Georgie a copy of the Girl annual for Christmas, she was thrilled. She had loved to lose herself in the weekly comic from the moment Robert had started giving it to her, and now the book also provided her with hours of happy distraction. It never took the place of the dancer book, which still came out regularly to be read to Daisy and John, but she often enjoyed losing herself in a book more suited to her age.

All was happy until one Friday morning during the February half-term holiday. There was a knock at the door and Florrie was taken aback to see Sergeant Carter and PC Bell standing there when she opened it. She immediately got butterflies in her stomach and a sense of dread that what she had been forcing herself not to think about since she came out of hospital, was going to penetrate her reasonably contented life.

"Hello Florrie," said Sergeant Carter. "May we come in?"

"Yes, of course. Sorry, I wasn't expecting to see you."

Florrie led the two police officers into the living room where Georgie was happily amusing Daisy and John.

"Hello, Georgie," said the two police officers in turn.

When Georgie turned around and saw who it was, she immediately jumped to her feet and ran over to hug each one in turn. Florrie looked on with a slightly disapproving expression on her face.
"We've come to chat to Georgie, if that's okay with you, Florrie?" said PC Bell.

"Have I got a choice?" asked Florrie curtly.

"No. I'm sorry, Florrie, but we need to chat with Georgie about the court case. You are, of course, entitled to stay while we talk, but if you think it will upset you, then I'm sure we could conduct our chat in another room."

"No, here will be fine. I was just about to put John down in his cot for a nap, and I'm sure Daisy won't mind playing in her bedroom for a while, will you, Darling?"

Daisy, as ever the happy, smiling child, jumped up and made her way upstairs following Mummy as she took John up to his cot. Mummy returned within five minutes and sat on the armchair, pulling Georgie on to her lap as she did so. Sergeant Carter and PC Bell sat on the settee opposite.

Georgie felt apprehensive as Sergeant Carter began.

"We have a date for the court case. It will be towards the end of next month and we'd like to take Georgie over to the court room to help her get accustomed to the surroundings."

Georgie nodded but she felt her mummy tense up and tighten her hold on her.

"Why do you need to get Georgie accustomed to the court room? She's certainly not going to be there for Gerald's trial if that's what you're thinking."

Georgie's face flushed as she realised that her mummy was still angry that the monster had been arrested and had to go to trial.

"I'm sorry, Mummy, but I already agreed to go to the trial to answer the lawyers' questions. I know I just have to tell the truth and PC Sandy will stay with me the whole time."

"No, Georgie. I won't let you go. You could end up getting your daddy locked away for longer than he already has been. I will not give my permission, Sergeant Carter and PC Bell. So, you might as well leave my home right now."

Neither police officer moved. PC Bell spoke after a short silence.

"I'm sorry, Florrie. I know you are Georgie's mother, and you love your husband, but in this case, you can't stop us taking Georgie to the court as a witness. If you tried, you would be seen to be obstructing the course of justice and would end up being prosecuted yourself. I know it's hard for you, but that's how it is. I'm sorry for the stress this will cause both you and Georgie, but we'll do our best to support you both."

"Support us both? You don't think I'm going to be a witness, do you? I won't do anything against my husband, who I know for sure is completely innocent."

Mummy's words hit Georgie straight between the ribs as if she'd been punched. She felt winded and unable to breathe. She pushed herself off her mummy's lap and rushed out of the living room, into the kitchen and straight out of the back door into the garden where she stood trying to get her breath, her face now pale and sweaty. When she felt a gentle touch on her shoulder, she visibly jumped.

"Hey, Darling, it's me, PC Sandy."

Georgie immediately turned around and threw herself into the police officer's arms. The sobs came thick and fast as PC Sandy held her tightly. It wasn't until Georgie calmed down that she started to shiver. The policewoman removed her own jacket and placed it around the shaking little girl.

"Hush, Darling. It will be alright. Sergeant Carter will make Mummy see sense. She loves you really, Georgie, it's just that she loves your stepfather too, so she has a sort of tug of war going on inside her. Now let's go back into the kitchen to warm you up with a nice hot drink."

Georgie allowed PC Sandy to lead her back indoors and sit her on a kitchen chair while the caring policewoman made a cup of tea. Georgie listened as PC Sandy was making the tea and continued to chat to her calmly so that Georgie gradually felt less distraught.

"How are you enjoying being back at your old school, Georgie?"

"It's good thank you."

"Are you still determined to be a dancer when you grow up?"

"Oh yes. I had dance classes when I was at Geltsdale and the teachers said I was a really good dancer."

"That's good. Are you enjoying your new little brother?"

"I love him. He's so cute now I've got used to his ginger hair. Daisy loves him too."

Georgie realising that she was no longer shaking, managed to chat to PC Sandy quite normally until she placed a mug of hot tea in front of her.

"Now you stay here, Georgie, while I take a tray of tea into Mummy and Sergeant Carter. I'll be back in a short while."

As PC Sandy pushed open the living room door, she could hear Florrie weeping. Sergeant Carter was leaning across from the settee with his hand on her shoulder to comfort her.

"Here's a nice cuppa for you both," said PC Sandy as she passed the mugs around and sat on the settee cuddling her own mug.

"How's it going?" she asked.

"I will not go to court. I don't care what you say," said Florrie.

"Not even to support Georgie?" asked PC Sandy.

"No way. She's there to put my husband away in prison for a long time. I won't be seen to have any part of it."

"Calm down, Florrie," said the policewoman. "At the end of the day it's your choice. I will be there with Georgie to support her. I take it that you care enough about her not to want her to be frightened?"

Florrie remained silent. PC Sandy was shocked that a mother could behave so uncaringly. She could not imagine caring more about herself than her little Ella, even if it meant putting her daughter before her husband. The thought of it brought tears to the policewoman's eyes. She physically hurt for the little girl sitting in the kitchen. She realised that Florrie wasn't mentally strong, but for Sandy that was no excuse.

"Right, Florrie. We've got the message loud and clear. We are now going to take Georgie to the courtroom and will bring her back once we've finished," said Sergeant Carter as he stood up and nodded to his colleague.

Georgie saw PC Sandy come out of the living room and remove Georgie's coat from the stair post before she came back into the kitchen.

"Here you are, Darling. Slip your coat on and we'll drive over to the courtroom."

"Did Mummy say that I could go?"

"Yes, Darling, she has accepted that you will be going to court with me," said PC Sandy casually.

Georgie allowed PC Sandy to take her hand and lead her out of the front door, which Sergeant Carter was holding open. As Georgie went past the living room, she shouted, "Bye", receiving only one response from Daisy who was waving from the top stair.

The tour of the courtroom, which was attached to the police station in Penrith, didn't take long, so Georgie was back home in less than two hours. By the time she got back, she felt quite confident about the coming court case but was more than a little anxious about what state her mummy would be in. She was glad that PC Bell escorted her to the front door of the cottage and waited for Mummy to open the door.

"Here she is, safe and sound, Florrie," said PC Bell as Mummy stood at the open door with a sour look on her face.

"Right, come on in then, Georgie. Thank you very much," Mummy said to PC Sandy as she closed the door in her face.
"Take your coat off. We're in the middle of our soup and bread."

Georgie could feel her mummy's anger towards her as she sat down at the kitchen table waiting for her bowl of soup to be put in front of her and helping herself to a chunk of fresh bread.

229

"I've finished mine, so I'm going into the living room to feed John," said Mummy as she left Daisy and Georgie at the kitchen table. It was clear that Daisy also sensed the cool atmosphere because the normally chatty little two-and-a-half-year-old remained silent as she dipped a piece of bread into her soup and popped it into her mouth.

"Are you alright, Dais?" said Georgie in as light a tone as she could muster.

"Mummy's cwoss."

"Don't worry. Let's finish eating, then we can go upstairs, and I'll get my dancer book out to read to you. Would you like that?"

"Ooo, yes pwease Gorgy. Will you read me your comic too?"

"Okay, as long as you eat every scrap of your soup and bread."

Daisy returned to her happy self immediately and within ten minutes both girls had finished their meal, placed the dirty crockery and cutlery on the draining board and raced upstairs to their bedroom. An hour later, having finished reading, they both made their way downstairs and into the living room. There they found John fast asleep laying on one end of the settee, and Mummy also fast asleep sitting on the other end. On the coffee table sat an empty glass tumbler. Georgie turned to face her sister, and with her finger to her lips, whispered,

"Shush, Daisy. We don't want to wake up Mummy and John. I'll bring this empty tumbler and we'll go into the kitchen and wash-up as a surprise for Mummy when she wakes up."

Daisy immediately turned around and crept quietly out of the room followed by Georgie holding the tumbler, the smell from which she immediately recognised as the Christmas sherry. She stood Daisy on a chair next to her and proceeded to fill the sink with hot soapy water, making sure that it was not hot enough to burn her sister's hands. She then rolled up her and Daisy's sleeves and both proceeded to wash up, initially chatting and giggling quietly, but then becoming more boisterous as the washing up turned into a game of flick the soap bubbles. They were laughing at the bubbles that had landed on Daisy's nose when Mummy walked in, and they were both shocked into silence by her shout.

230

"What's going on out here? Georgie, can't I trust you to look after your sister for half an hour without all this noise and Daisy getting soaking wet?"

Daisy started to whimper as Mummy walked over and picked her up for a cuddle.

"Now see what you've done, Georgie. Your sister is upset and the kitchen's covered in soap suds."

"We were just washing up for you, Mummy, so you could stay asleep."

"Stay asleep. Huh! It's your noise that woke me up. Now go up to your bedroom and stay there till I say you can come down."

Georgie had never experienced such harshness from her mummy before. She was shocked and hurt that Mummy hadn't even recognised that she had been trying to help her. She ran out of the kitchen and upstairs to her room where she lay on her bed crying until she finally fell asleep. She was surprised to see that it was almost dark when she opened her eyes, awoken by Mummy's gentle shakes.

"I'm sorry, Baby. Daisy told me that you were both trying to help me by doing the washing up. I shouldn't have shouted at you."

Mummy leaned down and put her arms around Georgie in a hug. Georgie returned the hug with a feeling of great relief that her mummy was no longer cross.

"Come downstairs now, Baby. Tea's ready and John is missing his big sister."

Mother and daughter walked downstairs hand-in-hand.

CHAPTER 23

End March – Early April 1954

Bitter-sweet

After Mummy's anger episode, things started to return to normal. Georgie was a little more on edge, both because she feared triggering her mummy again, and partly in anticipation of the impending court case.

Georgie returned to school after her half-term holiday, enjoying popping into the village store again each morning. After a couple of weeks, she walked into the store and immediately sensed a tension. Pattie and Robert looked serious, and Georgie could see that they were having to make a lot of effort to chat normally. Having become extra sensitive to atmospheres, Georgie couldn't help but speak up.

"Are you upset about something, Pattie?"

"Nought fer thee to worry about, Lass."

Georgie walked over to Pattie and gave her a hug, to which the loving woman spontaneously responded.

"We're fine, Bairn," added Robert as he gave Georgie a boiled sweet. "Yer need to get off ter school now or yer teacher will be standing at t' gate looking for yer."

After Georgie had left, Pattie and Robert let out simultaneous sighs.

"What do we say ter Florrie, Robert? I can't face t' lass wi' out feeling guilty."

"Nought Pattie. Best say nought. Nah then Lass, we can change us minds abart being witnesses if yer that worried."

"Nay, we can't let Georgie down. You heard t' Sergeant. Even wi t' medical evidence from t' Police Doctor, it could still mek t' difference between winning and losing t' case ... and what would 'happen to Georgie if Gerald got off and went home?"

When Sergeant Carter had rung Pattie and Robert the day before and asked them to be witnesses for the prosecution, they had found it hard to make their decision. Pattie knew that more likely than not; Florrie would turn against them if they said yes. She and Florrie had been best friends for so long that Pattie would miss her badly and would also miss seeing the children. But, as Robert had pointed out, if they said no then Georgie would suffer more. So, they tried to put it to the back of their minds until the day of the court case.

The day of the court case arrived, and Sergeant Carter was in already in court being questioned by the lawyers – one for the prosecution and one for the defence. He was aware that Georgie and Sandy were sitting in one waiting room, whilst Pattie and Robert were in another. He had spoken to Georgie earlier and she had appeared confident with Sandy there to support her. Gerald was sitting in the dock with a policeman each side of him, listening intently to the evidence that was being presented. Every now and again, Sergeant Carter saw Gerald glance at the jury, twelve men and women who he'd never have seen before. The Sergeant also noticed the look of quiet confidence on the prisoner's face and was not surprised. He was aware that Gerald's lawyer would almost

certainly have informed him that he had a good chance of getting off unless the prosecution brought in his stepdaughter as a witness, and even then, many judges didn't think a child was a reliable witness, so he was still likely to be acquitted. Sergeant Carter smiled inwardly as he thought of the shock Gerald would have when little Georgie walked into the courtroom with Sandy. He didn't have to wait long and continued to keep his eye on Gerald's face when Georgie's name was called. He wasn't disappointed.

As the seven-and-a-half-year-old Georgie entered the courtroom holding PC Sandy's hand tightly, she held her chin up high. At her tour of the place the previous month, Sergeant Carter and PC Sandy had shown her the witness box where she would need to stand to answer the lawyers' questions, and the dock in which the monster would be sitting. She had decided while sitting in the waiting room that she would try to avoid looking at him unless she was instructed, so she kept her eyes to the front, concentrating on climbing up the few steps to the witness box, and making sure that she could see PC Sandy clearly.

The Judge was the first to speak.

"Hello young lady. I would like you to tell everyone what your name is, please."

Georgie stated her Christian and Surname and then looked back at the Judge.

"Now, Georgie, can you tell me what a lie is?"

"A lie is saying something that is not true."
"Quite right. Now tell me, do you know about God, Georgie?"

"Yes, I do. Matron Betty's daddy was a church minister and when I was staying in the children's home called Geltsdale, he came every week and told us all different stories about Jesus."

"So, you understand that to put your hand on a Bible and say you will tell the truth, and then to tell a lie would make Jesus angry."

"Yes, but Jesus loved Zacchaeus even though he had told lies. Reverend James said that, but Zacchaeus had to show how sorry he was and never do it again."

"So, Georgie, if we ask you to put your hand on the Bible now and say that you will only tell the truth here today; do you understand that we will expect you to stick by that promise to God?"

"Yes. I know that all I have to do is answer questions truthfully."

"Quite so. Quite so."

Georgie was then sworn in and stood waiting for the questions she would be asked. She looked over at PC Sandy, who smiled and gave her a thumbs up for encouragement. She did not once let her eyes stray towards either the monster or the Jury. The prosecution lawyer asked her in a kind voice to describe what had happened. Georgie clearly and fluently told it exactly as she had told Sergeant Carter and PC Bell several months before. All the events were so burned into the little girl's mind that she could remember them as if they happened yesterday. She found tears coming into her eyes in certain places, but she took a deep breath and swallowed hard so that she could carry on. Then the defence lawyer asked her questions, which she answered in the same truthful manner. Many of the questions seemed to be like those she'd already been asked. When this happened, Georgie responded in complete innocence.

"Excuse me, please, Sir. I already answered that question."

A ripple of laughter spread across the courtroom each time she did this, which seemed to disconcert the lawyer, and left Georgie wondering what was funny.

When the questioning was finished, the judge advised that Georgie had no need to remain in the court for the rest of the day's proceedings, so PC Bell took her hand and led her out.

"Well done, Georgie," she said when they emerged from the building. "Let's take you home so you can get some well-earned rest."

"Yes please. I do feel quite tired now."

235

As the policewoman drove Georgie away from the Court, she was grateful that the child would not have to witness Pattie and Robert giving their testimonies. Georgie, in her innocence, believed that because she had told the truth, the Jury would believe her, and the Judge would send Gerald to Prison so that she could feel safe again. It was different for PC Sandy Bell. She knew how difficult it had been over the years for prosecutors to obtain a successful conviction in cases of child molestation, especially if there were no witnesses to corroborate the child's testimony. She hoped that Pattie and Robert's evidence would be enough to convince the Judge and the Jury of Gerald's guilt. She knew that if all else failed, they would have to call Florrie as a prosecution witness, despite her protestations that she would never say anything against her husband. Sandy hoped it wouldn't come to that. However, she was concerned for Georgie. She had seen how Florrie could turn against her daughter if triggered and was worried that if Florrie found out about Pattie and Robert's court appearance, it might provide just that trigger – even more so if she was called to appear at court herself.

"Right Georgie, we're nearly home. I bet Daisy and John will be glad to see you."

"I'm not sure if Mummy will though."

"Don't worry, Darling, I'll take you indoors and stay for a while if that will help."

"Thank you but I think that might make it worse."

"Okay, but if Mummy gets badly upset again, you just run down to Pattie and Robert and ask them to ring me or Sergeant Carter."

They pulled up outside the cottage and Georgie jumped out of the car, waving at PC Sandy before knocking on the door. The policewoman waited until Mummy let her in before turning the car around and driving off.

"Come in, Baby. Give your mummy a nize big hug."

As Florrie bent down to hug her daughter, Georgie screwed up her nose at the strong smell of sherry.

"Z' time for tea, Baby. Johnz azleep on the zettee."

Georgie looked into the living room to find the sleeping John laying very close to the edge of the settee. She gently moved him further back and placed a couple of cushions next to him to prevent him rolling towards the edge, before joining Mummy and Daisy in the kitchen.

"Gorgy you're home."

"Yes Daisy. I'm home. Are you okay?"

"Mummy sleeped, Gorgy. I took care of Yon."

"Well done, Daisy. You are a very clever girl to look after your baby brother."

Daisy grinned with delight at the compliment as Mummy carried a saucepan full of hot baked beans over to the table. She appeared to be a little unsteady on her feet.

"Shall I get the plates out of the cupboard, Mummy?" asked Georgie.

"Oh yez. We need platez don't we," said Mummy before starting to giggle uncontrollably.

Georgie took three plates from the dresser and spread them before her mummy who, still giggling, splatted beans on each plate, liberally splashing the tablecloth with bean juice before going over to the sink and dropping the saucepan into it with a loud clang. Daisy started to giggle along with Mummy. Georgie moved a plate in front of Daisy and pulled one towards herself. She looked over to the stove to see what was coming next. Nothing else was in the oven or on the hob.

"What you looking for, Baby?"

"I just wondered what we are having with our baked beans."

"Zas it, Babe. Nothin elz in the pantry. Have zum bread wiz it."

Georgie nodded and got up from her seat to fetch the bread. The half a loaf in the bread bin felt dry so she also fetched the margarine from the pantry on the way back to the table.

"Whoops, no cutlery," Georgie said

She again got up from the table to fetch cutlery and a breadknife from the drawer. She passed the bread and breadknife to Mummy who proceeded to saw chunks of uneven thickness off the half loaf. Georgie carefully spread the chunks with margarine and handed them around.

"My beans have gone cold, Gorgy."

"No, they're just warm enough, Daisy. They still taste good, and you can dip your bread in too to wipe up all the sauce."

Georgie turned towards Mummy just in time to see her nod off and then jerk her head back upright as she woke up.

"Mummy, you're tired. Why don't you go upstairs and lay down on your bed for a while? I'll look after Daisy and John."

"I think I will, Baby. I'm zo tired."

Georgie and Daisy watched their mummy make her way carefully out of the kitchen and listened for her footfall on the stairs before they relaxed a little and continued to eat their baked beans.

"I still hungry, Gorgy."

"Me too. I'll look to see if there are still some biscuits in the tin."

Georgie discovered three slightly stale Rich Tea biscuits in the tin. She gave two to Daisy and ate one herself. She then looked in the pantry to see what else she might glean for them to eat. She was horrified to see that apart from a half-used bag of flour, an unopened packet of tea and a tin of corned beef there was very little else on the shelves. Then the penny dropped. Georgie remembered that fateful morning when her real daddy left the house, and the words he said to her mummy as he went.

"It'll be the last time tha'll ever see me again. Nor will tha receive another penny from me."

Georgie's face flushed with guilt as she realised that the monster must have been supporting the family after her real daddy left, and now, because she had got him arrested, there were no wages coming into the house. She knew Mummy got family allowance after Daisy was born because she'd often handed the family allowance book over the post office counter to Pattie while Mummy was doing the shopping. Pattie would count out either eight silver shilling pieces, or sometimes two half-crowns and three one shilling pieces. Now little John was around, Georgie presumed that Mummy would be getting two lots of eight shillings – so sixteen shillings. Georgie had always been a forward child, not just in her use of vocabulary, which came from years of only having adults to chat with, but her mathematical abilities. She understood the value of money, having done money sums as part of the arithmetic lessons at school, and having often helped Robert behind the grocery counter and Pattie in the post office. She was aware that sixteen shillings did not buy much. She tried to remember the cost of some of the groceries. She recalled that a pound of brisket of beef, that Mummy often bought to put in her meat pies and puddings, cost around one shilling and sixpence a pound – and they needed more than a pound to feed the whole family. Then there was tea, which cost one shilling and five pence for a quarter of a pound, and baked beans at tenpence a tin. Even plain biscuits cost about eleven pence a packet, and a pound of porridge oats cost over a shilling. She realised that to feed a family of four for a week would cost a lot more than sixteen shillings. Then there were other things that Mummy would have to buy, like toilet rolls, which Georgie remembered cost one shilling and tuppence. Added to that, there was soap and washing powder, which she couldn't remember the cost of. The more she thought, the more depressed she became and the more panic she felt.

'What about money for the electric meter and clothes and shoes? No wonder Mummy is drinking the Christmas Sherry. It probably helps to take away the worry for a while.'

'I wish I'd never reported that monster now. I was just thinking about myself and never once thought about how it would affect Mummy, Daisy and John. I'm just selfish, and now we haven't even got the money to buy enough food.'

After an hour or so, Mummy came back downstairs, her slurry voice and giggles having subsided. Georgie rushed over to her and gave her a hug.

"I love you, Mummy. I'm sorry I've made things harder for you. I'll help you more and I'll ask Pattie and Robert if they can pay me for helping them behind the counter and in the post office."

"I love you, too, Baby. But yes, you have made things worse. You should never have lied about your daddy. I just don't understand why you did that. I've always brought you up to tell the truth."

Yet again, Mummy's words hit Georgie hard, bringing tears to the little girl's eyes.

"I've never told lies, Mummy," she said quietly, trying to swallow her tears, "but I was selfish to report Gerald without thinking about how it would affect the whole family. I'm sorry for that."

Mummy looked aghast.

"See you're still doing it. You're still trying to make out that your daddy did things to you that I know he never, ever would. You'd better just go to bed. I don't even want to see you right now, you bad girl."

Georgie did as she was told.

The next morning Georgie got up early. It was a school day, and she was determined to make amends for her selfishness. Straight after breakfast she said goodbye to Mummy, Daisy and John and walked down Half-Mile Lane towards the village store. She pushed the door open and walked inside as she usually did, to find Pattie and Robert busy behind their counters.

"Ey, Lass, it's good ter see thee," said Robert. Pattie came out from behind the post office counter and gave Georgie her usual hug, a packet of Spangles in hand that she'd picked out earlier as Georgie's treat for the day.

"Yummy. Thanks Pattie. But there's something I need to ask you."
"Fire away, Lass."

240

"Can I have a paid job after school and on Saturdays please?"

Both adults looked astounded. Robert was first to respond.

"What's this about, Georgie, Lass? Why do yer need money?"

"Because Mummy only has her family allowance now that Gerald's gone, and sixteen shillings is not enough. As it's my fault that he's gone, I just want to help Mummy out and stop her drinking the Christmas sherry."

"There's no fault in it, Lass," said Pattie with concern in her eyes. "Gerald's gone cos of what he did. You did the only thing yer could, so yer just stop feeling guilty, do yer hear me?"

"But I didn't think of Mummy, Daisy or John when I went to the police, Pattie. I was only thinking of myself. If I'd thought about the others, I'd never have reported him. I'd have found a way of putting up with it."

"Stop reight there, Lass," said Robert. "We can't employ thee cos t' law prevents us. But we can help thee out. Whenever yer help us, we can reward thee with food. How does that sound?"

Georgie felt a weight lift from her shoulders and found herself unable to speak. She hugged each of her true friends and, as she walked out of the door, managed a quick wave and a 'thank you'.

On her way back home after school, Georgie looked in on Pattie and Robert again.

"I won't stop and help today, or Mummy might be worried. Can I start tomorrow, please?"

Pattie and Robert nodded as Robert said,

"Aye, that's a date then, Lass."

As soon as Mummy opened the door to her knock, Georgie felt the cool atmosphere. She took off her coat, hung it in its usual place, and walked into the living room. There stood Sergeant Carter and PC Bell with broad smiles on their faces. Georgie held back, deciding that to hug the two police officers might trigger Mummy.

"Hello, Georgie. How was your day at school?" said PC Sandy.

"Good thank you."

"We've just come to give you some news about the court case," added Sergeant Carter.

Georgie's heart started to thump. Supposing the monster got off, what would she do? How could she bear to live in the same house as him? But Mummy would be happy, and money would start to come in again to pay for the food. Georgie felt her neck muscles tighten and she realised that the future didn't look rosy for her whatever the outcome. She clenched her fists ready to receive the news - whatever it was. Mummy was sitting stiffly on the edge of the settee, holding on tightly to Daisy who had climbed onto her lap clearly sensing the unease in the room. John lay on the blanket on the floor blissfully unaware of the situation.

"Florrie," said Sergeant Carter, "I'm afraid the news is not good as far as you're concerned. Gerald has been sent down for three years and has been put in a prison quite a way from Ousby. It's too far away for you to be able to visit, unless you know someone with a car who's willing to give you a lift."

Mummy gasped in disbelief. PC Sandy then spoke up.

"Georgie, this means you will be safe now, so you can settle down and enjoy the next few years doing the things that children do. I will pop in from time to time to check that all is well."
Georgie nodded, not knowing quite how to react or even how to feel.

"Thank you, PC Sandy and Sergeant Carter. You have been so kind to me, and I don't know what I would have done without you."

Georgie was aware of the concerned look in PC Sandy's eyes and sensed that this caring policewoman understood how confused she was feeling and what a difficult position she was now in. Mummy just sat on the edge of the settee and said nothing, so Georgie showed the two police officers, who had both become her friends, to the door. When PC Sandy stepped out of the front door, she turned to Georgie and whispered.

"Don't forget what I told you to do if Mummy gets too upset, Darling."

Just as Georgie was about to respond, she remembered something important.

"Oh, I nearly forgot. Would you mind hanging on for just a moment?"

The little girl ran upstairs and returned within a minute. She held out something towards PC Sandy.

"Here is the hanky you lent me on the day we were taken away to Geltsdale, PC Sandy. I promised to give it back to you."

PC Bell accepted the hanky and spontaneously leant forward to hug the little girl. She looked too choked up with tears to speak but gave Georgie a smile and a wave as she walked down the garden path to the wooden gate with the Ceanothus bushes either side.

CHAPTER 24

Early June 1954 – March 1957

Ups and downs

"Get up Georgie. Your sister and brother need some breakfast. My head's killing me. I'm going back to bed."

"But I have to go to school," complained the seven-and-a-half-year-old.

"Don't argue, and don't even think about going to school. It's you that caused me to get ill, so you'll just have to put up with the consequences."

Georgie realised that this was likely to be her life from now on. She dragged herself out of bed, pulled on her shorts and t-shirt and walked downstairs wearily to where Daisy was squeezing one of John's squeaky toys to make the little boy in his highchair laugh. Georgie was pleased that the weather was warm and sunny so that she could hang out the washing that her mummy had managed to do with her help the previous day. When the two children saw Georgie enter the kitchen, they both clapped – a skill that Daisy had been teaching her little brother over the past couple of months.

"We're hungry, Georgie. John keeps crying cos Mummy didn't give him his breakfast."

"Okay, Dais. I'm here now," said Georgie as she tickled John under his chin to make him giggle.

"Come and help me while I make the porridge. Can you find three spoons in the drawer and get three dishes out of the cupboard, please. Then put them on the table."

Daisy did as she was asked while Georgie took the bag of porridge oats and the bottle of milk from the pantry and proceeded to tip the ingredients into a saucepan. She was careful to only use half of the milk in case Mummy wanted a cup of tea when she got up. She topped this up with water from the tap and stood in front of the hob, stirring the thickening mixture over the gas flame while Daisy laid out the dishes and spoons, and continued to prompt John's laughter with the squeaky toy. Georgie daydreamed as she stirred. She remembered her former happy life when her real daddy came to stay each week and all she had to think about was their weekly outings and her treasured dancer book. She remembered her happy schooldays with Miss Longmore and yearned to be able to return to school and her schoolfriends full-time. Daisy's voice brought her back to the present with a jerk.

"The porridge is bubbling, Georgie."

Georgie removed the saucepan from the hob, turned off the gas, and carefully carried the hot saucepan to the wooden table, where she poured the hot porridge evenly between the three dishes. She knew that Daisy's appetite was good, as was John's, so she never gave herself a larger portion than she gave them.

"Blow it, Dais, or you'll burn your mouth."

"Mummy takes the hot away with cold milk," said Daisy.

Georgie realised that she hadn't accounted for milk to cool the porridge, so she put a little in a jug and diluted it with cold water, hoping there was still enough left for Mummy. She shared it between Daisy and John, stirring John's before she touched her lips against a spoonful to test it.

"Here you are, John. Take this spoon and see if you can feed yourself while I'm helping you."

Georgie started to shovel the cooled porridge into John's eager mouth. He reminded her of the baby birds in the garden that offered their ever-open mouths to the mummy birds every time they landed in the nests with a worm. By the time the dish was empty, and John was happily trying to gum the edge of a Farley's rusk to a pulp, Georgie's breakfast was cool enough to eat. She secretly thanked Jesus for Pattie and Robert who had given her the rusks as part of her reward for helping them. These days Georgie seemed to talk to Jesus a lot when she was at home. She felt instinctively that He understood her and that maybe He loved her even though she was the one responsible for getting the family, especially her mummy, into this situation. She remembered how Matron Betty's daddy, Reverend James, had told her that Jesus loved Zacchaeus even though he'd done bad things too.

Georgie had just finished wiping John's face and hands and clearing up the splats of porridge from the tray of his highchair when there was a knock at the door.

"Daisy, watch John for me while I see who's at the door, please."

It turned out to be Pattie.

"Oh, Lass. Is tha mammy bad again?"

They hugged as Pattie came in, walked straight to the kitchen and hugged Daisy before she ruffled John's red hair and put the kettle on.

"Let's mix a brew, Lass. Yer deserve a bit of a break."

"Thank you, Pattie. That would be lovely. I hoped I'd be able to go to school today but Mummy's got another one of her headaches."

"It's not fair, Lass. You'll be tired out at this rate. When was t' last time yer managed ter get ter school?"

"Erm. I think it was last Friday. And I did manage to get in to help you and Robert on Saturday, so not too bad."

"Well, that mammy of yours needs ter buck 'er ideas up," said Pattie in a whisper so that Daisy and John wouldn't hear. "The only time I ever see her is when she comes into t' store ter buy another bottle of sherry, which she's doing more and more often, or on a Saturday evening when she falls asleep before we've even finished one game of Ludo."

"I think she's too sad to buck up, Pattie. Maybe she'll get better when she gets used to Gerald not being here."

Pattie responded with raised eyebrows before she got up to attend to the boiling kettle. Meanwhile, Georgie lifted John out of his highchair and carried him into the living room, where she sat him on the floor surrounded by a variety of his soft toys – all hand-me-downs from Daisy and Georgie. She helped Daisy to sit to the back of the settee and gave her a tray of colouring pencils and a piece of paper that she'd torn out of her school exercise book.

"Daisy, can you draw a picture of Mummy and John for me?"

Daisy nodded and proceeded to draw a variety of circles and lines that, to her, represented her subjects. Pattie soon came into the sitting room with two full mugs of tea, which she placed on the coffee table away from the younger two children.

"Nah then, tek weight off yer feet, Lass and drink yer brew. Then I'll tek t' bairns for a walk ter store ter see Robert. You tek a bit o' time for yersen and then come down when yer ready."

"Thanks, Pattie. I haven't had time to wash myself yet, so that will give me a bit of space to do that and then hang the washing out, if that's okay with you?"

"Course 'tis, Georgie. You tek yer time."

An hour later, having washed herself and looked in on Mummy to check she was still asleep, Georgie took the wet washing into the garden. She breathed in a lungful of clean fresh air before she proceeded to peg out the wet garments with the dolly pegs, remembering how, as a very little girl, she would imagine they were people and chat to them as she handed the pegs to Mummy. She could see herself on the grass, laughing and play fighting with her stepfather before he turned into a monster.

247

"No sense, daydreaming," she said to herself out loud. "Things are how they are, and they aren't going to change anytime soon. At least I don't have to put up with the things he did to me anymore. Jesus, please make my mummy better so we can be happy again."

An hour later, Georgie wandered down Half-Mile Lane taking in the beautiful surroundings and telling herself that she was luckier than lots of other children. By the time she reached the store, her smile had returned, and Robert, who was serving a customer, indicated that she should go through to the back. The warmth of the greeting she received from her two siblings made her feel happy and loved, as did the piece of homemade cake that Pattie handed her.

"Now, Lass, Robert and I have been talking. We've decided ter give thee a bag of shopping each week, whether yer help us or not. We know tha'll have plenty to do at home without doing extra here."

Georgie tried to object.

"That's not all, Lass. I'm gonna come up ter see yer mammy later and tell her I'll have Daisy here every weekday so yer can go ter school. Daisy can enjoy herself behind the counter like tha used to when yer were little, and yer can pick her up on yer way home in t' afternoon."

Georgie's first reaction was to feel a frisson of jealousy. She wanted those happy times with Pattie and Robert to remain exclusively hers, but she pushed her feelings down and hugged Pattie, whispering her thanks as she did so.

"Reight, I'll tek yer all up ter cottage and wake up that mammy of yours. With any luck, she'll be back in her reight mind so I can mek her see sense."

Pattie was right – Mummy was back to herself by the time the small group entered the house with the key Georgie had picked up on her way out earlier.

"Hello, You Lovely Lot, where have you all been?" Mummy asked with a smile on her face. "And Pattie, my lovely friend, how nice to see you."

248

As Pattie hugged her friend, she noticed there was no smell of sherry on Florrie's breath. She was relieved, knowing that a clear-minded Florrie would more readily receive her suggestions for getting Georgie back to school. Florrie mixed a brew and the two sat chatting while the children played. To Pattie's surprise, Florrie, without argument, accepted Pattie's offer of childcare so that Georgie could attend school regularly and she could devote all her time to baby John.

"There's just one condition, Florrie."

"And what's that, Pattie?"

"You've got ter stop drinking t' sherry. It only meks yer more depressed. Yer know that Gerald will be coming home after he's served his sentence, so meanwhile there's no sense in neglecting yersen and yer bairns. He'll want to see yer all, especially little John, safe and well when he returns, and he'll not thank yer if they're not."

"You're right, Pattie. Thank you. You're a good friend and I'll never be able to thank you enough for your help and support. I'm done feeling sorry for myself. From now on, I'll be doing all I can to make life happy for my children."

"Well done, Lass. I knew yer'd see sense."

Pattie touched Florrie on the knee before turning to Georgie.

"So, Georgie, I'll expect to see yer wi' Daisy first thing in t' morning, alreight?"

Georgie nodded with a broad grin across her face.

Bright and early next morning, Georgie was up and dressed. She went downstairs to find Daisy eating her bowl of porridge and Mummy feeding John and laughing at his attempts to find his mouth with his extra spoon.

"Hello, Baby. Your porridge is on the table waiting, and Daisy's dressed and ready to go."

Georgie smiled, feeling relaxed for the first time since the court case. She enjoyed her breakfast as her sister chatted happily about helping Pattie and Robert in the shop. Georgie still felt a little jealous but pushed it to the back of her mind as she left her happy little sister with her two friends.

"Don't forget this, Lass," said Pattie, handing Georgie a boiled sweet for her journey to school.

"And I've got this for yer to pick up on yer way home," added Robert, holding her Girl comic in the air.

Georgie hugged Pattie and Robert before she embraced her little sister.

"Now you be a good girl for Pattie and Robert, Daisy, and I'll be back after school to pick you up."

Daisy gave her sister a big, wet kiss on the mouth, despite Georgie squirming to avoid it, wiping her mouth on her sleeve and laughing as she left.

The arrangement worked well, and things slowly settled into a routine. The next two and a half years were reasonably happy ones for the three children, even though Mummy had her down days. Daisy joined Georgie at school at the beginning of the term leading up to her fifth birthday, and the two girls walked to school together, continuing to pop in to see Pattie and Robert morning and afternoon.

All was happy until March 1957. John was approaching his fourth birthday and still stayed at home with Mummy while the two girls went to school together. Life felt settled to Georgie, and even her mummy seemed to have learned to achieve a reasonable level of contentment. It was late one afternoon after the girls had returned from school that there was a knock at the door. Mummy opened it to Sergeant Carter and PC Sandy, and her welcome was significantly more cordial than it had been on the previous occasions they had visited over the past three years. Georgie knew Mummy was aware that the monster had served his three years and should soon be coming home. She had reminded Georgie and her siblings of this after each of the few times she'd spoken to him on Pattie and Robert's telephone. But Georgie was aware that her mummy

had not once been able to visit him. She could see that Mummy was feeling more and more excited as the time for the monster's release got closer.

Despite Georgie's apprehension, she spontaneously hugged each police officer and offered them a cup of tea.

"That would be lovely, Georgie. Thank you."

Before Georgie disappeared into the kitchen, she saw the officers look over at Daisy and her brother who were sitting on the floor, with Daisy trying to teach John to play Draughts.

"I can't believe how big you two have got," said PC Bell to the two children.

Daisy gave a shy smile and John, who hated it when grown-ups made such comments, kept his eyes on the Draughts board.

"John don't be rude. Say hello to the police officers," Daisy instructed her little brother in her now, clear vocabulary.

John looked up at the two uniformed adults, said a sullen "hello" and returned his eyes to the Draughts board.

"Sorry Sergeant Carter and PC Bell. Please sit down," said Mummy as Georgie disappeared into the kitchen, "I'm hoping you have brought good news today?"

Georgie could hear what was being said from the kitchen as both doors were open.

"Shall we wait for Georgie to bring the tea in, so we don't have to go over things twice?" suggested PC Bell. "In fact, I'll pop out to the kitchen to help her carry the tray in, shall I?"

When Georgie and PC Sandy returned to the living room, Georgie noticed that Mummy was picking her fingernails, something that Georgie knew she did when she felt anxious.

Once everyone had their mug of tea, Sergeant Carter began.

"As you know, Gerald is due to be released this month. He's served his sentence, and we hope he will come home a changed man."

Mummy scowled, clearly as convinced as ever that the monster was innocent of the charges. Georgie felt nauseous at her mummy's reaction and felt sure her face had gone pale.

"For the first three months, Gerald will have to report to us once a fortnight at Penrith Police Station, so we can monitor his behaviour. After that, we very much hope that he will have found a new job and things will have settled down. If he ever re-offends, he will face even more serious charges and an even longer prison sentence. Do you understand, Florrie?"

Mummy nodded without looking at Sergeant Carter. PC Sandy took over.

"Georgie, if your stepfather should ever come near you again, you must run down to the village store and use the telephone to ring us immediately. Do you understand?"

"Yes. Thank you, PC Sandy."

"Right, we'll be leaving you now. Thank you for the cup of tea, Georgie. Gerald should be back home within the next two days. He'll be given his rail fare to Penrith and his bus fare to get back here to Ousby. Good luck and we hope everything works out well for you all."

The two officers saw themselves out, leaving Georgie and Mummy sitting there feeling a little stunned. Even though they had expected the news, they were both a little shell shocked for different reasons. Mummy because, Georgie assumed, she couldn't quite believe that her husband would be coming back home at last, and Georgie because she felt confused about how life would change.

Both were roused from their thoughts by Daisy who had got up from the floor and come over to stand in front of Mummy.

"Is Daddy really coming home, Mummy?"

"Yes, he is, Daisy."

Daisy stood still for a moment taking in the idea that there would be a daddy in the house again. While she did so, John looked up from the Draughts board.

"Who's daddy?"

Mummy went over to the little red-headed boy and took him by the hand.

"Come and sit on Mummy's knee, Darling, and I'll tell you all about your daddy. You were only a tiny baby when he went away."

The whole family was on edge the following day. Georgie and Daisy went off to school as usual, calling in on the way to tell Pattie and Robert their news. Georgie thought that they would say something encouraging, but instead they just looked at each other. Georgie thought she could see a hint of fear in Pattie's eyes, but she dismissed the idea, deciding there was no reason for them to be fearful of the monster, especially as they'd been so supportive whilst he was away. When they arrived home from school in the afternoon, Mummy was rushing around cleaning everything in sight. John had been sent upstairs to play with his toy cars. These days, he shared the girls' bedroom, sleeping on the bottom level of a bunk bed that had replaced Daisy's single bed some time ago.

"Go upstairs and play with John please, Girls. I want to finish down here before we have our tea."

Georgie and Daisy looked at each other with raised eyebrows, but decided it was best to do what Mummy asked. They giggled quietly together as they removed their coats and made their way to their bedroom.

"Hello, John," they said in unison as they entered the bedroom. The sullen faced little boy looked up but said nothing, immediately returning his focus to his cars.

"John don't be rude," said Daisy in her usual way, "Me and Georgie said hello to you. You need to say hello back to us."

John looked up and quickly said a bland 'hello' before returning to his cars. The girls began rummaging through Georgie's shelf to find the dancer book.

"This'll get his attention," whispered Georgie to her sister who nodded in agreement.

They both sat on Georgie's bed leaning against the wall under the window, before Georgie said loudly and distinctly,

"Shall we read the dancer book, Daisy?"

"What a good idea," responded Daisy in the same loud and distinct voice.

Immediately John heard the dancer book mentioned, he abandoned his cars and jumped onto the bed next to Daisy. Both girls laughed as he looked on still with a straight face. An hour later, Mummy shouted up the stairs.

"Tea's ready, Kids. Wash your hands and get down here before it gets cold."

This time it was John who was first down from the bed and into the bathroom to wash his hands. He was always first in line when food was mentioned.

As Mummy and the children sat around the table, Georgie felt a little apprehensive. The monster could arrive at any moment. Then the sound of a key turning in the front door lock. Each person around the table looked up in anticipation, their eyes peering in the same direction towards the front door.

CHAPTER 25

March 1957 – October 1959

Into the unknown

The door opened and the monster stepped into the hallway. He looked pale and drawn. He faced the four pairs of eyes staring at him from the kitchen and stood still, returning their stares, his eyes full of uncertainty. Time seemed to stop still for everyone until a small squeal left Mummy's mouth as she jumped up from the kitchen table and ran down the hall into the monster's waiting arms. The children watched as the two adults embraced, kissed, and cried all at the same time. Daisy was next to leave the table and run down the hall to her daddy and mummy, who lifted her up into their arms to join in the embrace.

Georgie was frozen to her seat. A cold numbness spread through her as she watched the scene unfold. She felt nothing. John stayed where he was with a look of mild surprise and confusion on his sullen face. The scene inside the front door seemed to go on for ever. Eventually, Mummy and the monster put Daisy down and turned towards the kitchen.

"John, are you going to come and say hello to your daddy?" asked Mummy gently.

"No."

The monster touched Mummy on the shoulder.

"Give him space, Darling. I'm a stranger as far as he's concerned. He'll come around in his own time."

But Daisy was ahead of her daddy. She walked into the kitchen straight up to her brother.

"John. Don't be so rude. Your daddy said hello to you. You say hello to him right now."

John shook his head. Daisy grabbed his hand and pulled him off the chair before dragging him along the hall and standing him in front of the ginger haired man.

"Now, say hello to your daddy politely," bossed Daisy.

John burst into tears, prompting Daisy to pull him into her.

"Don't cry," said the tender-hearted little girl. "There's nothing to be worried about. This is your daddy who loves you. I know you don't remember him, but you'll soon get to know him and love him like Daisy does."

Mummy turned to look into the monster's eyes and smiled, which made Georgie, who was still sitting at the kitchen table, feel nauseated. Mummy's eyes then moved to her eldest daughter.

"Say hello to your daddy, Baby," ordered Mummy.

As the monster's eyes met Georgie's, she felt a bolt of electricity. She was scared that if she tried to speak, she would vomit. The monster saved her from that as he was first to speak up.

"Georgie let's put the past behind us. I hold no grudges against you. You are a child, and you did what you had to do. It wasn't you that put me in prison. It was Pattie and Robert. They are entirely to blame for witnessing against me in court."

The monster's words hit Mummy and Georgie like a bombshell. A shocked silence followed.

"You mean to say neither of you knew?"

"No, I did not," came Mummy's raised voice. "Did you know this, Georgie?"

Georgie's shook her head, feeling shocked and surprised. Pattie and Robert's reaction to the news that Gerald was coming home suddenly fell into place, as did the realisation that her two friends had risked everything for her sake, to make sure she would be protected from that monster. Her heart leapt as she thought of all the things that those two amazing people had done to support the whole family and make her life as happy as it could be over the past three years. She realised that they would know for certain they would lose the love of their closest friends as soon as the monster was released, and yet they still did it. Georgie felt physical pain at the certainty that Pattie and Robert would now be banned from their home, and she, Daisy and John would be banned from seeing them. At that moment, Georgie made a resolution. She would not be kept away from the two people who had loved her most throughout her life. At that point Mummy's voice broke into her thoughts.

"I can't believe that my best friend would do such a thing. And what a hypocrite. She kept her betrayal quiet for all three years you were away, Gerald. She gave us food, looked after Daisy while Georgie was at school so I could give more time to John, and supported us in every way she could. And all the time it was only because she felt guilty for doing what she did to you."

Georgie couldn't cope with hearing her mummy bad-mouth her friends after all they'd done for her. She got up from the table, pushed past the group standing in the hall, and walked up the stairs, deliberately stepping hard on each stair and holding her head high as she turned to Mummy and spoke in a bold voice,

"Pattie and Robert are better and more caring people than you will ever be. There is only one hypocrite round here, and it's not Pattie."

Continuing up the stairs, Georgie walked into her bedroom and closed the door quietly.

257

She knew that downstairs, Mummy, and the monster would be feeling furious at her words, but it also comforted her to know for certain that Daisy would love and respect her for what she'd said. Then she heard heightened voices coming from the living room and recognised them to be of the two people for whom, at that moment, she felt only disdain.

After a while Daisy crept into the bedroom to join Georgie and the two girls played together quietly. They heard the front door close and looked out of the window to see their mummy walking determinedly down Half Mile Lane towards the village store, where they knew what would happen. A few minutes later, they heard Gerald and John laughing and presumed John had warmed towards his daddy already because it sounded like they were having a play fight, most likely with the monster tickling his little son.

From then on, Georgie kept out of the way of her parents as much as she could. Being in the same house made her feel physically sick. Her own mummy hadn't believed her when she was younger and was now blaming Pattie and Robert for the monster's imprisonment. Georgie felt so hurt. She couldn't bring herself to speak to what she saw as her excuse for a mother and was certainly not going to break her ties with Pattie and Robert, who she knew loved her more than her mother had ever done.

"I'm calling in to see Pattie and Robert as usual, Daisy," said Georgie as she walked to school with her sister next morning.

"I think you're really brave, Georgie, but I'm frightened to disobey Mummy and Daddy. Do you mind if I don't join you?"

"Don't fret, Daisy, I understand why. It won't stop me loving you just as much as I always have," responded Georgie.

The one positive in Georgie's mind was that her brother, John, seemed to become much happier now his daddy was home. She enjoyed seeing him laughing much more with the extra attention he was receiving. She tried to join in with his laughter but found it increasingly difficult.

When the monster found himself a job on another building site in Penrith, Georgie was pleased for her mummy because as the money started to come in again, the stress disappeared from her life, and she seemed happy again. For Georgie, however, it felt like she was on the outside of her family looking in, and she felt sad, lost, and uncomfortable.

Apart from buying her school uniform, Mummy and the monster showed no interest when Georgie moved up to the all-girls senior school in the September before her eleventh birthday. But school had become Georgie's happy place and she settled quickly, keeping her previous friends, and quickly making new ones.

When Georgie arrived at school each morning, having called in to see Pattie and Robert first, she always received lots of friendly greetings, and she slowly started to feel more confident. She had entered puberty, which Pattie, not her mummy, had explained to her, and was slowly developing a curvier figure. At least Mummy had bought her a bra. Georgie felt she fitted into her class even more now because the favourite class game at break times was to try to ping each other's bra straps.

"Bra pinging time," shouted one of the rowdier girls in her class, and the laughing and screaming would start. Georgie felt sorry for her still-flat-chested friends who couldn't join in and clearly felt inferior as a result.

These happy times at school and the time Georgie spent with Pattie and Robert became the most enjoyable parts of her life, but contrasted significantly with her home life, which didn't improve. Georgie still felt lonely and isolated around her mummy who seemed to ignore her as much as she could. She knew Daisy spent as much time as she could with her, but she still felt like an outsider.

At the end of her first year at senior school, Georgie brought her school report home and handed it to her mummy, who scanned it, nodded, and put it on the kitchen table for the monster to see. Georgie had done well, getting 'A' in every subject, so she felt hurt that her mummy didn't praise her for her achievements. Pattie and Robert tried to make up for this when she showed the report to them.

"Ey, Georgie, that's brilliant. What a clever young lass you are," said Robert as his wife tearfully gave Georgie a hug until she could find her voice.

"I'm so proud of yer, Flower. This calls for a celebration. I reckon it deserves a trip to Penrith and a meal in a posh restaurant for t' three of us."

"Wow. Thank you, Pattie. Thank you both. That would be so special, having a meal out with the two people I love most in the world."

The three had a group hug, laughing with sheer happiness at the thought of Georgie's achievements, after which Robert searched in the telephone directory for the number of a restaurant that they'd noticed on one of the few trips they'd made into Penrith. He booked a table for three for the next evening. Georgie felt excited and sensed that Pattie and Robert realised how emotionally neglected she was at home. She walked into the cottage feeling apprehensive. Would her mummy allow her to go out?

"Please may I go out with some friends tomorrow evening?" Georgie asked Mummy later that day.

"As long as you get home before it's dark," replied Mummy, without any further questioning.

'Well at least I don't have to put up with the monster's unwanted attention these days,' she told herself by way of compensation.

Georgie felt hurt at her mother's apparent lack of interest, but at the same time elated at the thought of going out for the celebration meal with Pattie and Robert. She wasn't disappointed. The happy threesome, each dressed in their best, caught a bus into Penrith, chatting and laughing as they went. When they arrived, Robert steered Georgie and Pattie towards a small candlelit restaurant with a frontage of sparkling leaded light glass. The tables were round with crisp white linen tablecloths and small vases at the centre containing single red roses. The waiters were dressed in black trousers and waistcoats over crisp white shirts complete with black bowties. Georgie was entranced. Everything felt so posh but at the same time so welcoming.

The smiling waiter showed them to their table and asked what they would like to drink. Pattie and Robert chose sparkling white wine whilst Georgie stuck to lemonade. When the drinks had been delivered to their table, Robert held his full glass up and made a toast.

"To Georgie. Well done and we both love yer just like you were ours."

With tears in each of their eyes, they clinked glasses and took long sips. The waiter then broke the emotion by appearing at their table and asking

for their food orders. Robert took the lead. Georgie was relieved as she would have found this process intimidating, not having been in surroundings like these before.

"I reckon prawn cocktail ter begin, then a nice juicy rump steak ter follow. What do you think, Lasses?"

Georgie and Pattie readily agreed as their pink cheeks glowed in the light of the candle on their table. After that, the chatter flowed, and the smiles dominated. Once or twice, Georgie felt she needed to pinch herself to make sure she wasn't dreaming. She'd never experienced a special occasion arranged in her honour. This was such a contrast to her home life where she felt invisible to her mummy. She knew she would remember this evening for the rest of her life.

The homeward journey on the bus was a little quieter as full stomachs and tiredness overruled. Georgie was glad when Pattie and Robert walked with her up Half Mile Lane and stopped a few yards short of the cottage to give her hugs. She felt the love and sincerity as each held her close and told her they loved her before waving goodbye as they left. She knocked on the cottage door, which her mummy opened and disappeared back into the living room before Georgie had even entered. As she called goodnight before walking upstairs to the sanctity of her bedroom, she was pleased that her sister and brother loved her, even if her mummy didn't. Georgie was determined not to let the enjoyment of her special evening be spoiled by the cool reception from her mummy, so she quietly changed into her nightdress and slipped into bed while her mind was still full of the pictures of the restaurant and all its glowing candles.

Over the following weeks, Georgie noticed how seldom her mummy used the village store now. Instead, she chose to take a bus to Penrith with John in tow to do her shopping before she met the monster from work and got a lift home.

"More fool her," Georgie would say out loud every time this happened, wondering who was more of a child – her or her mummy. But life for Georgie continued as before with her experiencing constant emotional neglect and loneliness at home.

She felt happy for her sister and brother on their birthdays. Mummy always threw a party for them, inviting some of their school friends to a

birthday tea complete with home-made birthday cake and candles to blow out. She never gave up hoping that they would do the same for her but was always disappointed when they only gave her one small present of their own choosing, usually socks or underwear, and a card devoid of any personal or loving words.

When Christmas drew closer, Georgie hoped that she would receive the same recognition as her siblings. On Christmas morning, she watched as Daisy and John woke up to discover a pillowcase on the end of each of their beds packed with presents. They were so excited, and Georgie helped them to unpack and open their gifts, catching their excitement and pleasure at what Santa had left them.

When they had finished, John looked at his eldest sister.

"Where's your sack of presents, Georgie?"

Georgie pretended she was too grown up for presents but knew that Daisy saw through her pretence even if John didn't. Daisy hugged her big sister warmly as she saw that just one present sat on the end of Georgie's bed. The psychological impact on Georgie from her mummy's cruelty and neglect wounded her deeply, but she always comforted herself in the knowledge that Pattie and Robert loved her even if her mummy didn't.

Then one Monday morning the unthinkable happened. Georgie was in year three at her secondary school and was looking forward to her thirteenth birthday in a few weeks-time. She called into the village store as usual on her way to school but when she entered, nobody was inside. Presuming her friends to be out the back, she made her way through to the living room, calling as she went.

"Pattie, Robert, it's me,"

As she entered, a sight confronted her that made her stop dead. There, sitting on an armchair was Robert, face in hands, sobbing uncontrollably. Georgie rushed over to him and knelt in front of the armchair.

"Whatever's wrong, Robert? Are you ill? Where's Pattie?"

Robert took his hands from his face, releasing his tears to flow down his cheeks and drip into his ample lap. Georgie was horrified. Her heart seemed to leap out of her chest at the same time as her stomach lurched.

"Pattie's gone, Lass. She's gone. I can't believe it."

"Gone where, Robert? Where's Pattie?"

"She collapsed yesterday morning. She got up right as rain and then complained of a pain in her chest. Next thing I knew, she collapsed on t' floor in front of me. I felt for a pulse but there was nought. She'd gone reight in front of me eyes."

"Gone?" question the dazed Georgie.

"I rang for an ambulance, Lass, and they were here in no time and tried to help her but in t' end, they gave up and pronounced her dead."

Robert's sobs took over and he was unable to continue for what seemed to Georgie like forever. She couldn't absorb what Robert was saying. The words seemed to bounce off the top of her head and disappear into an ever thickening and encircling mist. The last words she heard were,

"My Pattie's gone, Lass, gone."

The next thing Georgie knew was Robert's voice penetrating the swirling mist from above her. She screwed her eyes up and opened them again and again to try to regain her focus. She felt a cool, wet cloth gently brushing across her forehead. She heard Robert berating himself.

"Wake up, Lass. Wake up. Oh, what a selfish, unthinking man I am. I'm sorry, Georgie. Forgive me. Come on, Lass, open those eyes fer Robert. Please."

Things started to look sharper as Georgie tried to push herself up into a sitting position from where she could see that she was on the floor in front of Robert's armchair.

"What happened? What am I doing down here?"

And then she remembered, and the tears started to flow. Robert lifted her to her feet and hugged her, both crying together.

"Why, Robert? Why did Pattie have to leave us? I need her. She loved me so much and I still need her love."

"I know, Lass. So do I. But I can only think that God needs her with Him more than we need her."

"No," shouted Georgie, "No, no, no. We need her here with us. That's cruel of God to take her away. Reverend James told me that God loves us, Robert. If that's true, why would He want to hurt us? I will never forgive Him. Never, never."

"Nay, Lass. Don't say that. Think of Pattie. She's in Heaven and having a wonderful time. I'm sure we'll see her again someday when our turn comes. And you've still got me, Lass. I still love yer just t' same as I always have."

"Yes, I know, and thank you. It's all such a big shock. She wasn't ill was she, Robert?"

"They reckon it was a heart attack, Lass. They said she didn't suffer, so we must be thankful for that much, but aye, it's such a big shock. I didn't even get a chance to say goodbye to her."

"I'll mix us a brew, Robert, and I'll give school a miss today. I couldn't concentrate anyway. I'll stay here and help you in the shop."

"Thank you, Our Georgie. I'll not deny that having company today will be a relief - just to give me t' chance to get used ter living without my Pattie."

At that moment a customer walked into the store, so Robert rapidly wiped his eyes with the large white handkerchief that he pulled from his trouser pocket and made his way stoically out of the sitting room to fulfil his ongoing responsibility as the village shopkeeper.

Georgie watched the kettle heating on the hob and as the steam began to rise and disperse into the air, so the feeling of desolation rose within her and dispersed into her very being. Later that afternoon when Georgie

264

returned to the cottage, Mummy looked at her and spoke with disdain in her voice.

"What's got into you, Young Lady? Talk about come in here and put a damper on things with your miserable face."

Georgie looked at her mummy's complacent face and felt the anger rise from her stomach, through her chest and up to her brain, at which point it exploded. She spoke in as controlled a voice as she could manage.

"Not that you're interested, but as it happens, the person who loved me most in the whole world … the person who meant more to me than anyone else – especially you, Mother, died yesterday. Yes, that's right, the person that cared for our family as if we were her own. The person who risked her own happiness to protect me from your monster of a husband. The person who was such a good friend to you that you brushed her off like she was worthless once you didn't need her anymore. I just hope you have a conscience, Mother, because I believe the hurt you inflicted on her contributed to the heart attack that killed her. I hate you – you and that pervert that you live with. I only hope he keeps his greasy hands off my little sister, 'cause I'm telling you now, if he even harms a hair of her head, I swear I'll kill you both."

Georgie's mother took a step back at the force of Georgie's anger, and Georgie watched as, for a moment, her mother's head seemed to reel from the shock of her nearly thirteen-year-old daughter speaking to her with such hate. After taking a few deep breaths and obviously getting her thoughts together, the woman casually turned away from Georgie and only turned back to utter the words that she knew would hurt her daughter most.

"You are a lying, jealous little bitch. As far as I'm concerned, you are no longer my child. To me you are dead. Now go to your room and I'll expect you to be back down here in twenty minutes with your bags packed. At this moment, I wish I'd never given birth to you."

Georgie couldn't believe what she was hearing. She turned away from her mother and ran upstairs to her bedroom.

'Where can I go? What can I do?'

Georgie remembered that the option of running down to Pattie had been cruelly taken away from her the day before. She also knew she couldn't become a burden to Robert. He had enough to cope with already. For the second time in her short life, she found herself packing her school duffle bag with her belongings. The last time she had walked to Penrith and ended up in the police station with Sergeant Carter and PC Sandy Bell. She couldn't run to them again. The monster hadn't touched her, so she had nothing to complain about. Her bible and her dancer book were the first things to be packed this time. As she put them in her duffle bag, something pricked her memory. She opened the bible at the place where the photograph of her real daddy had been hiding for all this time. She looked at the picture of the man who had brought so much happiness into her life every time he had appeared. She recalled the outings and the special 'Christmas days' they had spent together. She had never once doubted that he loved her. But where was he now? She had no idea where he lived. She knew his name was Alfie. The writing on the back of the photograph confirmed that. Then it came to her. It was a long shot, but maybe Robert would remember Alfie and know where he lives. Georgie would just burden Robert one more time. That was her only option. Suddenly she was ripped out of her planning by the sound of her mother's voice shouting up the stairs.

"You've had fifteen minutes. If you're not down here in five minutes with your stuff packed and ready to leave, then I'll throw you out just as you are."

Georgie stuffed as many clothes as she could into her duffle bag, took a last look at the room she had slept in for as long as she could remember, and made her way downstairs – stepping on the creaky step for one last time. The living room door was shut, and she could hear faint sounds of Daisy crying on the other side. As she walked towards the front door that her mother was holding open, Georgie's already damaged heart broke in two. With eyes to the front, she walked out of the door, which closed behind her, and she made her way along the front path and out of the wooden gate between the ceanothus bushes. As she turned right into Half Mile Lane, she remembered how she would climb onto the bottom rung of that gate when she was a small child, watching for her daddy to appear in the distance before she ran to meet him. She remembered listening to the bees buzzing happily as she waited. On this murky late October afternoon, there were no bees buzzing; just the silence of Georgie's own empty heart as she walked down the slope towards the unknown.

CHAPTER 26

October - November 1959

Desolation

"Ey up Lass. What yer doing back 'ere so soon?" asked Robert as Georgie entered the village store for the second time that day.

Then he noticed the bulging duffle bag, and the desolate look.

"Nay. Don't tell us tha've run away again, Lass?"

"No. Mother kicked me out."

"Mother? Since when did yer call yer mammy mother?"

"Since I got indoors after I left here. The way she spoke to me just pushed me over the edge, Robert. I couldn't help it. I lost my temper and told her what I thought of her. She kicked me out. She wishes I'd never been born. She said that as far as she's concerned, I'm now dead."

"Nay, Lass. She didn't mean that."

"Oh yes she did. She meant every word she said. She's a different person since she's been with that monster."

Robert shook his head in disbelief.

"Yer must stay here, Lass."

"Thank you, Robert, but I can't do that. Nearly everyone in this part of the village uses this store and I don't want to take the chance on people gossiping about my family. Anyway, you've got enough on your plate right now. Besides, I don't think I could cope with living so near to the cottage. It would break my heart whenever I saw my sister and brother, knowing that Mother wouldn't let them speak to me."

"Yer right o' course but I can't bear ter think of yer out there alone in t' world. Where will yer go?"

"I'm going to find my real dad. That's why I came in – to ask you if you know where he lives?"

"All I know is that Alfie lived with his wife, Mavis, and his three children at t' opposite end of Ousby to you and Florrie. I've no idea of the address, Lass, or even if he's still there."

"Don't worry, Robert. It was a long shot and at least you've pointed me in the right direction."

"Georgie, Lass. It's nearly dark outside and yer know how cold t' wind blows across t' fells this time of year. Yer can't go looking fer yer daddy reight now. Yer must stay just fer tonight. Please say yer will."

"You're right of course, Robert. I'll not find my way easily in the dark, so thank you, I'll accept your invitation for tonight, and be up and away bright and early in the morning before too many people are around."

"And with a good hot breakfast inside yer belly ter ward off t' cold, Lass."

"Oh, I do love you, Robert. Thank you for caring so much about me."

"Yer like me own daughter, Lass. Pattie and I have always loved yer like yer were ours."

The older man and the young girl hugged, gaining comfort from each other in their individual hours of need. They ate together and talked until late into the evening, frightened that going to bed would bring their time of separation nearer. Eventually they gave in to their tiredness and retired – Robert to the bed that he had shared with Pattie for so many years but now lay alone; Georgie to the bed in the spare bedroom where she lay thinking of Daisy and John, wondering how long it would be before she would see them again.

The alarm clock next to Robert's bed woke him at six o'clock, just as it had each morning since he and Pattie had taken over the village store. Once he'd washed and dressed, he knocked on Georgie's door and getting no answer, opened it. She was still fast asleep, and in the silence, Robert looked at her face from the doorway, trying to drink in the sight of the blossoming young woman who he would always remember as the bouncing little girl with the blonde wavy hair and the sweet nature. It physically hurt him to think of the suffering that Georgie had gone through, with more likely to come as she set out on the next episode of her life.

'How I'd love to hurt that cruel and perverted excuse for a man with my bare hands,' he thought, before he walked over to the sleeping child-woman and gently awoke her.

"Get yersen washed and dressed, Lass, while I prepare a nice, cooked breakfast for us both."

When it was time for Georgie to go, Robert passed a piece of scrap paper to her with his telephone number on. Then he walked over to the till and took out three one-pound notes, which he passed to Georgie, despite her protestations.

"Nay, tek it, Lass. It's not a lot when you're alone in t' world. You mek sure yer hang on ter telephone number and ring me at any time – night or day – if yer need me."

At seven o'clock Georgie hugged Robert, hanging on to him longer than usual. She then kissed him on his cheek and left the shop, stepping out into the dawn. She placed her three one-pound notes in the front pocket of her duffle bag with the one that was still there from when she ran away to report Gerald to the police. She then felt around until she found her bible, in which she placed the telephone number between the pages with Alfie's photograph. Pulling up her coat collar, she left the village store behind her, turning her back on Half Mile Lane to walk to the other end of the village where she hoped she'd find her father.

It was a cold day when she finally arrived later that morning. Snow had started to fall and was gradually changing the green and brown palette of the Fells into shades of bright white. Even in her devastation, Georgie couldn't help but gasp at the unfolding beauty of the changing scenery around her. After a while, she came across a small butcher's shop and stepped inside. A clock on the wall at the back of the shop showed it to be half-past-nine.

"What can I do fer thee, Lass?" asked the tall, slim, middle-aged man clad in a blood smeared white overall.

"I'm looking for someone and I wondered if you'd be able to help me, please."

"Well, I'll do me best. I know most people living round 'ere. What's t' name of this someone?"

"His name is Alfie. He has a wife called Mavis and he has children too. Oh, and he was a builder on a site in Penrith last time I saw him."

"How long ago was that Lass?"

"When I was four years old."

"And how old are yer now?"

"Almost thirteen."

"So that's nine years ago. Hmmm let me think."

At that moment a petite, dark-haired woman appeared from the back of the shop.

270

"Ey up, Brenda. You remember names better than I. Do the names Alfie and Mavis ring a bell?"

"Course they do, Lad. You know Alfie, tall good-looking man that comes in once-a-week ter get family's meat. He's broad set, with brown hair ... in his thirties."

"Oh aye, that Alfie. In fact, he's due in later this morning - isn't he Bren?"

Brenda nodded then turned to Georgie and smiled broadly.

"Ey up, Flower. I'm Eric's other 'alf. What's tha name?"

"I'm Georgie."

"Well, Georgie, yer look perished. Why don't yer come into t' back for a nice steaming brew ter warm yer up till Alfie comes in?"

"Thank you. That would be lovely. I am cold. I've walked from the other end of Ousby and the wind is really strong today."

Georgie followed Brenda into the back kitchen, where she was led to an armchair beside a roaring fire. She felt the sting of the heat from the fire on her cold cheeks and recognised the smell of fresh baking wafting invitingly across the room.

"You sit there and warm yersen while I get t' kettle on. Best tek off that coat or you'll not feel t' benefit of it when yer go outside again. I just took some fresh baked bread out t' oven, so will yer join me for a nice doorstep spread with me homemade cherry jam?"

Georgie's mouth watered as she realised how hungry she felt after her long cold walk.

"Yes please. That sounds lovely, err?"

"Me name's Brenda, Lass. Call me Brenda."

"Thank you, Brenda. The bread does smell lovely."

Georgie removed her coat and put it over the back of the armchair before she sat down and, while she waited, studied the flames in the

open hearth. Suddenly she was awoken from the sleep she'd just drifted into by Brenda's voice.

"Oh, yer poor lass. You're exhausted. This'll perk yer up."

Brenda passed a large mug of hot tea to Georgie, and then placed a small plate in her lap on which was a thick chunk of fresh white bread, still warm to the touch, and slathered in sweet cherry jam. Georgie smiled gratefully and proceeded to consume every last crumb, which she washed down with the tea, followed by a deep contented sigh.

"Reight, Lass, stay there in front of fire and have a little snooze while I go out ter help in t' shop. I'll come and get yer just as soon as Alfie arrives."

"Thanks, Brenda. I am a bit tired, what with the long walk and not having had the best night's sleep."

Georgie drifted back to sleep almost as soon as Brenda left the room. As she slipped into oblivion, she thought about how kind people were in Ousby – apart from her mother and that monster, Gerald. A few minutes later, she felt a hand on her shoulder gently shaking her and opened her eyes to find Alfie crouched down before her with a look of concern on his face.

"Georgie? Is that really thee? Has my little blonde-haired bairn grown into such a grown-up beauty?"

"Daddy. Oh, Daddy I've missed you so much," throwing herself into Alfie's open arms and clinging on to him as if to stop him disappearing. The soft-hearted Georgie sobbed with the sheer relief of finding her daddy again after so many years of existing only on memories. Alfie, too, had wet eyes as he embraced his daughter. After a while, Alfie gently pulled away and removed a clean handkerchief from his pocket, with which he wiped the tears from Georgie's eyes first, and then his own.

"What's tha doing here, Lass? Have yer walked all t' way from t' cottage?"

"Yes, I have, Dad. I came to find you."

"Does Florrie – I mean yer mammy know yer 'ere?"

"It was Mother who kicked me out. She's really changed since she married that monster, Gerald. She can find no fault in him. I told her what he was doing to me when I was only a little girl and she didn't believe me, Dad, and she still doesn't believe me. I put up with it for as long as I could for the sake of Daisy, so I could make sure he didn't start on her, but in the end, I couldn't cope with it any longer and I ran away."

"When was this, Lass? What age were yer? What did that nasty bit of work do to yer?"

She told him every harrowing detail of what had happened with the monster.

"So that's why I came looking for you, Dad. I came to see if I could live with you 'cos I've got nowhere else to go."

Alfie's face turned from bright red to grey almost instantly. He bowed his head as if trying not to look into Georgie's eyes as he spoke in a faint voice.

"I can't tek yer in, Lass. Mavis and the kids knew nowt about Florrie or you. Then when yer mam kicked me out, I didn't see any point in telling them."

As Alfie's word's sunk in, Georgie's devastation grew. She suddenly saw her father for what he truly was – a coward who thought more about himself than his own daughter. She stood up from the warm armchair, slipped her coat on and picked up her duffle bag. She then turned her back on Alfie and without a word walked out into the shop.

"Thank you, Brenda. Thank you both for your kindness and generosity. I'll be on my way now. Goodbye."

Georgie left the couple, looking questioningly at each other. She now knew exactly what she had to do. She found the nearest bus stop just as the bus to Penrith drew up, and climbed on board to find a seat. The cheery bus conductor soon came her way to collect her fare, which she paid with one of the pound notes.

"Is that t' smallest tha's got, Lass?" he asked.

Georgie realised he had seen the embarrassment on her face as she nodded and apologised.

"Don't you worry, Lass. If yer'd got on t' bus this morning, it'd have been different. As it 'appens I've been unusually busy today so I can change that note fer yer without a problem."

Georgie smiled with relief as he took out a coloured bus ticket from his wooden spring holder, punched a hole in it with the little metal hole punching machine that hung round his neck, and handed it to her with a brown ten-shilling note and some silver coins for her change. Georgie carefully placed her change in her duffle bag pocket and sat back to watch the passing scenery, which was now well-covered in white snow. She noticed how the tree trunks had grown to twice their width with the build-up of snow on the sides exposed to the prevailing wind. She heard the crunch of the snow as the bus wheels compressed it, leaving two patterned furrows in its wake. The sky was grey and heavy, reflecting Georgie's emotions as she travelled towards the unknown.

CHAPTER 27

End of October 1959

St Martin's or the Ambassador

The ride to Penrith seemed to go on forever and the snow was even deeper when Georgie stepped off the bus. She was glad of the thick coat she was wearing, and the gloves that she had discovered in its two patch pockets, but she wished that she'd picked up her woolly hat during the unceremonious forced exit from the cottage the day before. She walked to the railway station, her heart feeling hard and heavy. She fleetingly wished that she was back home in the warmth of the cottage with her sister and brother but immediately forced herself to stop and to focus only on her hopes for the future. She would buy a train ticket to London, get a job, and find a way to continue with her dancing lessons. She could easily pass herself off as fourteen, so she saw no problem with finding employment – maybe even in a theatre. She didn't mind how menial the work was. She would do anything to increase her chances of becoming the dancer she'd always dreamed of being. The thought of this lifted her spirit as she entered Penrith Railway Station and approached the ticket office.

"Ey up, Young Lass. What can I do fer thee?"

275

"How much is a ticket to London please?"

"Is that a return ticket, Lass?"

"No thank you. Just one way. I won't be coming back."

"That's sixty-two shillings fer second-class, Lass."

Georgie took her remaining three one-pound notes and two one-shilling pieces from her duffle bag pocket and handed it over.

"Yer shouldn't have too long ter wait, Lass. The train to London's Euston Station departs at twenty-two minutes past one. That gives yer enough time to warm up with a nice hot cuppa from t' station buffet while yer wait."

"Thank you. I'll do that," said Georgie before placing her ticket in one of her coat pockets and following the sign to the station platform, where she spent the next twenty minutes drinking a cup of hot tea and munching on a Kit Kat. At exactly one-twenty-two the train pulled up at the station platform and Georgie climbed into a carriage and sat down. As the steam locomotive pulled away, she looked out of the window, but by now, the snow was falling so heavily from the slate grey sky that all she could see was her own reflection looking back. She now felt comfortably warm, and with her duffle bag next to her on the seat, she listened to the clackety clack, clackety clack of the wheels on the steel railway track, which soon lulled her to sleep.

Suddenly Georgie felt someone shaking her. She woke up with a start.

"You're 'ere Luv. You're going to 'ave to get off the train nah cos I've got to clean it."

"What's the time? Where are we?" asked Georgie, feeling only confusion as she looked around at the inside of the empty train carriage.

"It's nearly 'alf past seven, Ducks. You arrived 'ere at Euston Station a few minutes ago at seven-twenty-three. You been sleeping all the way 'ere?"

Georgie nodded. She could see it was dark outside and realised that she remembered nothing of the six-hour train journey. Her tummy

276

rumbled, but she tried to ignore it. She only had a ten-shilling note left in her duffle bag pocket and that had to last her until she found a job. She stood up, threw her duffle bag over one shoulder, stepped out of the train carriage and on to the platform. She looked around, trying to get some sort of bearing as to which direction she needed to walk. Above her was the huge metal structure that supported the roof. She looked along the platform. In one direction she saw railway lines disappearing into the infinity of darkness, and in the other she noticed railings with an open gate through which she decided she needed to walk to get out of the station. A uniformed man at the gate held out his hand for her ticket, which she removed from her coat pocket and handed over. As she walked through the gate, she looked around her and gasped. She was in a magnificent high-ceiling hall with a huge white statue in its centre. She stood open-mouthed for a few minutes, unable to take in the magnitude of her surroundings. Behind the statue were wide marble steps, which split into two, part of the way up – one to the left and one to the right, and continued upwards to join together again before leading up to a balcony stretching across the width of the hall. It had giant polished wood doors along it, and four enormous pillars stretching upwards from the front edge to support the high ceiling. Georgie's imagination worked overtime as she wondered if the King and Queen of England had once lived here. She followed other passengers making their way up the stairs to the balcony and splitting to the right or left to make their way to exits at the far ends. Deciding to turn right, Georgie made her way past the pillars and the enormous arched doors, until she turned left out into the open air. The area was illuminated by streetlights, and she found herself walking forwards towards the biggest archway structure she had ever seen. The nearer she got to the archway, the further back she had to tip her head to see the top of it, and the lower her jaw dropped. When she finally brought her eyes back to ground level, she realised that her neck was stiff and a little painful, partly from looking up so much and partly from the position in which she'd slept on the train. She gave it a rub and moved her duffle bag on to her other shoulder. Seeing a couple of cars making their way out of the station forecourt through a narrow road under the arch, she proceeded to follow the pavement to the other side and found herself in a significantly wider road.

'Left, or right?' she asked herself.

Deciding on the latter, Georgie walked along the pavement, finding it hard to take in her surroundings. Penrith had always seemed like a big place to her but wasn't even comparable to the size of this place. She

felt like a tiny, insignificant ant as she proceeded along the pavement with people passing by on either side of her. The whole area seemed to be illuminated by the shopfronts on the opposite side of the road and the lampposts at regular intervals. She remembered the jet-black nights in Ousby where there wasn't a lamppost in sight and was relieved that the light in this city gave her a feeling of security and safety as she walked along not knowing where she was going. Eventually she reached a road junction going off to the left from the other side of the road. She looked up at the road name on the wall above the shops opposite and read it out loud.

"Euston Road."

She crossed over Euston Road to the junction and turned left into it. She discovered that this was Tottenham Court Road so she decided that this would be her direction of travel. As she set off, her tummy rumbled even more loudly than before, so she gave it a rub and carried on walking. People were milling around, and many cars passed by. She kept on walking until she came across a hot chestnut stall on the pavement. She could not resist buying some with her remaining ten-shilling note. After she put her nine shillings change in her coat pocket, Georgie munched on the chestnuts as she walked on. Her eyes were drawn to the bright shop windows, which displayed all manner of clothes, toys, and other wares. She regularly stopped walking just to stare into these windows with amazement, and to put her duffle bag down at her feet to rest her shoulder. Eventually she came to a large crossroads and looked up for the street name.

"Shaftesbury Avenue", she read out loud.

'Shall I turn left or right, or shall I cross over and carry on along Tottenham Court Road?' she wondered.

After a few minutes contemplation she decided to join the crowd crossing Shaftesbury Avenue and continued her walk along Tottenham Court Road. It wasn't long before she came to a turning on the left called Litchfield Street. It was narrower than the previous streets and was lined with houses rather than shops.

"Maybe I'll find somewhere to rest if I go down here," she thought, starting to feel nervous for the first time since her arrival at Euston Station. It was empty and not well lit, but she took a deep breath and

proceeded down it past the rows of three-story white houses that lined each side. Every house had a basement protected by black railings and a gate leading down some steps to a dark passageway. She peaked over the railings of one of the houses but could only see a slight glow from one of the narrow windows. After ten minutes, she reached the end of Litchfield Street where she came to a halt at a slightly wider road running at right angles to where she stood. She looked across the road and her heart leapt as she saw two twinkling theatres on the opposite side of the road separated by a narrow, cobbled lane. She crossed the road quickly and stood in front of St Martin's Theatre. Posters on the walls either side of the entrance displayed pictures of entertainers, including rows of brightly attired dancers on a stage. Georgie was mesmerised by the colours and lights of the building as she wandered along its frontage, passing the wooden and glass entrance doors, through which she could see the red carpeted reception area with stairs leading up to one set of doors and then going up to the right and left to the next level. She remembered the pictures in her dancer book and her heart missed a beat as she thought about the potential future opportunities that she was sure would come her way. She walked further along the pavement and crossed the cobbled lane called Tower Court to reach the second theatre, the Ambassador, where she spent a happy hour looking at all their posters too.

Suddenly people started to spill out of both theatres on to the pavement, several black taxis arriving to transport them away. Ladies were dressed in sparkly long gowns – some with velvet capes, and the sight of them took Georgie's breath away. After half an hour the pavements were empty again and the theatre lights started to go off until the area was almost completely dark. As Georgie was wondering where she was going to sleep, she saw several individuals emerging from Tower Court. She ventured to the corner and looked down it to see that the individuals were coming out of stage doors on opposite sides. After watching until no more people emerged, Georgie saw a uniformed man come out of each, lock up behind them, shout good night to each other and disappear, one coming in her direction and the other turning the other way into the gloom.

Georgie noticed that above the stage door of St Martin's Theatre, there was an illuminated sign, which she walked towards and discovered that beneath the sign, the stage door was recessed into the wall. She decided that this was the perfect place to sleep for the night so that she'd be ready to go into the theatres in the morning to enquire about any jobs

that might be going. She sat down in the door recess, placed her duffle bag in her lap to act as a pillow and quickly drifted into a light sleep, thinking that she was glad it wasn't snowing here in London as it had been in Penrith. The first time she stirred, it was still dark, and she realised how cold and stiff she felt. She moved her duffle bag from her lap to the ground, lay down on her side with her back to the stage door, rested her head on the duffle bag and slipped back into a half-sleep. For the rest of the night, she was aware of the cold rising from the hard ground and seeping deep into her bones, until she forced herself into consciousness only to discover that daylight had arrived. As she was trying to get used to the brightness, she saw a pair of eyes staring down at her from above. They belonged to a young man clad in a navy apron with vertical white stripes, and a white and black peaked cap. Over his shoulder hung a leather satchel from which came the sound of jingling coins as he moved.

"Allo. Who 'ave we 'ere then?"

Georgie, now wide-eyed and frightened, pushed her body upright and sat as far back into the stage door as she could.

"Don't be frightened, Deary. I'm not going to 'urt you. I'm just delivering the milk for them there show people what works 'ere. Me name's William – Bill for short."

Bill held out his hand to Georgie as he introduced himself, and Georgie removed her right glove and shook his hand cautiously.

"Oh, my gawd, Girlie, your 'ands are like ice. Don't tell me you've been 'ere all night?"

Georgie nodded her head.

"Well, we better get you warmed up before you go as solid as an iceberg. I'm just about to go for me break at the café round the corner, will you join me? What's your name by the way?"

"I'm Georgie."

"Pleased to meet you, Georgie," said Bill as he took her right hand and pulled her up into a standing position. As soon as her feet touched the

ground, Georgie discovered they were quite numb, but as she swayed, Bill grabbed her and held her steady.

"Ere, Georgie, 'ang on to me 'arm till the blood starts flowing into them plates of meat again."

Georgie looked confused.

"Plates of meat?"

"Feet, Lovey. Plates of meat – feet. Ain't you ever 'eard of rhyming slang? You don't come from these parts, do you?"

Georgie couldn't help but smile at Bill's twinkle.
"No, this is the first time I've been to London. I came on the train from Penrith last night."

"Penrith? Never 'eard of it."

"It's in Cumberland near the Lake District," explained Georgie.

"No. Never 'eard of that either. Reckon you can walk yet, Lovey?"

Georgie smiled and nodded, feeling the warmth slowly returning to her legs and feet as she hung on to Bill's arm and walked slowly beside him until they reached the café, where he opened the steamed-up glass panelled door and guided her through.

"Lucky for you that the theatre was the last drop off in me delivery round, Ducks, or it would 'ave still been dark and I might 'ave missed you," Bill said as he led Georgie to a table just inside the door and pulled a chair out for her to sit down on.

"Thank you, Bill, but I haven't got much money left. I spent it on my train fare and the Kit Kat and cuppa I had while I was waiting for the train at Penrith, then on the hot chestnuts when I was walking down Tottenham Court Road."

"Don't you worry, Lovey. This is my treat."

Bill sat opposite Georgie as the waitress arrived at the table to collect their order.

"Ello Rosie. How's you this cold and frosty morning?"

"You know me, Bill. Always 'appy to see you. Who's this pretty young lady you've got with you this morning?"

"I'm Georgie."

"Are you now? Ain't from these parts are you, Love?" said the rosy cheeked young waitress.

"No. I'm from Cumberland."

"Bleeding 'ell. Never 'eard of the place," came the response, to which Georgie couldn't help but laugh. Bill quickly joined in and soon the three of them were laughing heartily.

"I like this girl, Bill," said Rosie as she calmed down. "Nothing better than a good laugh first thing in the morning. Now what can I get you both?"

"A nice big fry-up for both of us, Rosie Girl. And don't forget the bread and butter and nice big 'ot cuppa to go with it."

Rosie nodded and made her way to a swing door at the back of the café, which she pushed open and shouted the order at the top of her voice. Georgie started to giggle again.

"That girl 'as got a voice like thunder ain't she? Right then, what's your story, Ducks. Tell Bill all about it."

Georgie proceeded to tell her new friend the outline of her story without going into detail, and by the time she'd finished they'd both cleared their plates of food, wiped up the excess egg and bean juice with their buttered slice, and nearly drained their mugs of tea.

"Well, that's a story and 'alf, Young Georgie. So, what's your plans for today?"

"I'm going to try to get a job in the theatre, Bill. I've always wanted to be a dancer and if I get a job – any old job – in a theatre, I'm one step closer to getting on the stage."

"I wish you luck, Little Georgie. I'll be passing this way tomorrow at the same time, so if you get that job, then you can buy breakfast for me as a celebration."

"That's a deal, Bill. Wish me luck and I'll see you tomorrow."

Bill left the café first while Georgie used the toilet and washed her hands and face before waving goodbye to Rosie and making her way back to the theatres. She noticed that the box office of St Martin's Theatre opened at mid-day, so she sat on the top step with her back resting against the locked theatre doors to wait.

CHAPTER 28

End of October – November 1959

A new life

The top step was as cold as the pavement in the recess of the stage door last night. The wait seemed endless to Georgie. She stood up from time to time, walking back and forth to keep the blood in her feet and legs flowing. At one point she crossed over the road and stood on the corner of Litchfield Street to see how different it looked in the light of day. The white walls of the three-storied houses looked a little grubbier, and some of the wrought iron fences protecting the basements needed some fresh paint. Once or twice, she saw young women appearing at the top of the steps and exiting the gates, but in each case, they turned right, heading away from her in the direction of Tottenham Court Road where, she presumed, they would be going to the shops. She didn't want to wander too far from the theatre in case she missed the arrival of the Booking Office Assistant. Eventually a young woman arrived at the theatre doors accompanied by a smartly dressed gentleman.

"Hello Young Lady. You must be very eager to purchase a theatre ticket," smiled the smartly dressed gentleman.

"No, I'm not waiting to purchase a ticket, Sir. I'm wanting a job."

Georgie found herself trembling in anticipation. Was this going to be the moment she'd longed for ever since she could remember – the start of her career towards becoming a dancer?

The man looked at the woman and both chuckled.

"How old are you, Young Lady?" asked the man, who sported a white moustache that matched the stray lock of hair emerging onto his forehead from beneath his black top hat.

Georgie had never seen anyone in real life wearing a top hat. She remembered having seen them worn in newspaper pictures of special occasions involving royalty, and in history books at school. She fleetingly wondered if this man had royal connections but then decided that it was more likely one of the quirks of show business types.

"I'm fourteen," lied Georgie.

"Well, you're very small for fourteen."

"I've always been small for my age."

The man chuckled again.

"What's your name?"

"I'm Georgie."

"Okay, Georgie, well let's get inside out of the cold."

The woman had already entered and made her way through a door on the right-hand side of the foyer into the box office. Georgie followed the man across the foyer and in through a door on the left, which led into a smallish office with polished wood lining the walls up to waist height, and red and gold velvet-looking wallpaper above that and up to the high ceiling. As the man removed his top hat and placed it on a clothes stand just inside the door, he told Georgie that he was the Theatre Manager.

"The name's Donald Blazenhill – Mr Blazenhill to you, Young Georgie."

Georgie didn't know whether she should curtsy, nod her head, or move forward to shake his hand, but as he made no attempt to turn towards her, she did nothing. He proceeded to remove his outer black coat to reveal a black velvet suit jacket, beneath which was a black, gold and maroon vertically striped waistcoat covering a starched white shirt and gold cravat. His black trousers sported razor sharp vertical creases back and front, with a shiny black silk binding covering the side seams. Having deposited his outer coat on the coat stand next to his top hat, he approached a polished wooden desk, behind which he made himself comfortable on a matching chair with a red velvet seat cushion and back rest.

"Well sit down, Young Lady, we don't stand on ceremony here."

Georgie sat on a matching chair in front of the desk and looked at Mr Blazenhill in as confident a manner as she could muster.

"So, you want a job, do you? What is it you do, Miss Fourteen-year-old?"

"I don't do anything. Well, that's to say, I'm willing to do anything. I mean that I've never had a proper job before, except when I helped Pattie and Robert in the village store, and they paid me with food when my mother didn't have a job and my step-father was in prison."

At that point, Mr Blazenhill's eyebrows lifted so high that they met the lock of silver hair hanging down his forehead.

"Prison! Are you telling me you come from a family of convicts?"

"No, Sir, no! He was only put in prison because I told on him. That's why I needed to get some food for my mother, sister, and brother. I felt responsible and selfish for not having thought of them before I went to the police station in Penrith."

The man behind the polished wooden desk looked confused and was just about to question Georgie further when the lady from the box office came in with two cups of tea, a milk jug, and a sugar bowl on a tray.

"Ere you are, Mr Blazenhill. I thought you and the young lady might need warming up on such a cold November day."

"November?" questioned Georgie spontaneously.

"Yes Ducks. It's the first of November today. Where you been to lose track of the date?"

"Oh, it's not that. It's just that my birthday is in November – on the fourth."

"Thank you, Marjory," interrupted Mr Blazenhill, indicating to the woman to place the tray of tea on the desk in front of him.

"Oh yes. Of course, Sir. I'll be off back to the box office," she said, turning on her heels and exiting the room in as stately a manner as she could manage.

Georgie grinned to herself but was interrupted from her reverie by the clink of the cup and saucer that Mr Blazenhill leaned across his desk and placed in front of her.

"Thank you," said Georgie as she picked up the cup and poured the hot liquid down her throat without taking a breath.

"Were you thirsty, Georgie?"

"More cold than thirsty, Sir, but that tea has warmed me up a treat, thank you."

"You're welcome. Now you were telling me how you reported your stepfather to the police in Penrith. That's in Cumberland if I'm not mistaken? What has brought you all the way to London?"

"Well, my mother didn't believe me when I told her what my stepfather had done to me, and when he came out of prison, she took him back and began to be more and more unkind to me till I lost my temper and told her what I thought of her. Then she kicked me out with only what I could pack in my duffle bag in twenty minutes. So, I went down to Robert, but I couldn't stay with him 'cos Pattie had died suddenly the day before."

The memory unexpectedly sparked Georgie's emotions and she heard her voice crack as she tried to continue. She ran the back of her hand across her eyes, took a deep breath and went on.

"I stayed just one night and then went to look for my real dad who lives at the other end of the village, but he couldn't have me with him because he'd never told Mavis and the children about me. So, I took the bus to Penrith and got on the train to Euston. That was last night."

"I see. Well, not entirely but I think I get the gist. But why do you want a job in the theatre, Georgie?"

"I want to be a dancer – but I also need to find a place to live and pay my rent."

Mr Blazenhill looked confused.

"You didn't say you were a dancer. We always need dancers."

"I'm not a dancer, Sir – Mr Blazenhill. Well, I did have dancing lessons when I was at Geltsdale, and Mr and Mrs Slimfit said I was very good, but I'm not a proper dancer, not yet anyway. That's why I want a job in the theatre, so I can earn money for more dancing lessons and then I'll be in the right place to get on the stage like the girl in my dancer book."

The man looking at Georgie from the other side of the desk didn't appear any less confused than he had before Georgie's attempt to clarify the situation.

"Geltsdale? Mr and Mrs Slimfit? And what on earth is a dancer book?" he questioned.

"Yes, Geltsdale was the children's home that me and my sister, Daisy, lived in while my mother was in the mental hospital. The matron at the Home let Aunty Bella take me to dancing lessons in the village hall run by Mr and Mrs Slimfit. Then I returned home, and the dancing lessons stopped. My mother couldn't afford to pay for dancing lessons in Ousby – not that I know if there were dancing classes there or not. But I still had my dancer book which I'd been given by Santa Claus when I was very small. I often read it to Daisy and John and each time it made my dream of becoming a dancer on the stage even stronger."

Mr Blazenhill began to laugh.

"You know what, Georgie, I don't think I understand any more about you now than I did when I met you at the front of the theatre. But, my

word, you are certainly very entertaining the way you've explained things."

As Mr Blazenhill continued to laugh, Georgie couldn't help but join in – although in truth, she didn't really know what she was laughing at.

"So, you want a job here so that when you've learned to dance properly, you can get on stage as a dancer?" giggled Mr Blazenhill who seemed to be finding the whole idea extremely amusing.

"Yes, but I don't mind what work I do meanwhile, Sir," clarified the mystified Georgie, not knowing whether to join in with Mr Bazenhill's laughter or just wait patiently for him to calm down.

"Okay, Georgie, I'll tell you what," said the man amidst his attempts to stifle his giggles, "I'll give you a job as General Dogsbody, making the tea, helping the wardrobe ladies, sweeping up and that sort of thing, and I'll pay you two pounds, ten shillings and sixpence a week. You start at mid-day every day when I get here to open up, and you finish when the last entertainer has left at the end of the evening performance. Is that clear?"

Georgie had to restrain herself from jumping out of her chair and running around to the other side of the desk to give the kind man a hug. As it was, she jumped up and down on the spot – just as had been her habit when she was small.

"Oh yes, Mr Blazenhill. That's very clear. Thank you, thank you so much. When do I start? Can I start right now? You won't be sorry, Sir. I promise I'll work as hard as I can."

Still chuckling, the man rose from his chair, walked around the desk to Georgie, and shook her hand.

"That's a deal, Young Georgie. Now, let me take you downstairs to meet the Wardrobe Mistress and the Stage Manager who should both have arrived by now. They can show you around the theatre and get you started."

Georgie was about to follow her new boss when something popped into her mind.

"Erm. Before we go, Mr Blazenhill, I know this sounds cheeky, but I haven't let Robert know yet that I'm here and safe. I don't want him to be worrying about me. Would I be able to use your telephone to ring him, please? You can take the cost of the call out of my first week's wages."

"That's fine, Georgie. We don't want Robert to be worrying, and I'm glad to see you have a sense of responsibility. Go ahead."

Georgie found the piece of paper in her bible with Robert's telephone number written on it, picked up the receiver and dialled. He responded almost immediately.

"Hello Robert, it's me, Georgie. I just wanted to let you know that my dad couldn't take me in, so I came to London, and I've got a job in a theatre. I'm sorry I can't chat, but I am using the manager's telephone."

"Ey, Georgie Lass. I'm that relieved ter hear from yer. You make sure yer work hard at t' theatre, won't you?" said Robert, sounding quite emotional.

"I will, Robert. Thank you again for everything."

"Yer welcome, Lass. Look after yersen. Bye."

Georgie replaced the receiver and thanked Mr Blazenhill before they left the office together.

And thus, Georgie's career started – everything according to plan. The rest of the day and evening flew by with Georgie responding to every beck and call of the theatre staff.

"Georgie, make us all a cuppa, Love."

"Georgie, sweep up these scraps of fabric and cotton."

"Georgie, the toilet needs cleaning."

"Georgie, run round to the café and get us all some sarnies, Lovey."

Georgie loved every moment of it. She'd never felt so needed. She sat with the staff and some of the entertainers as they ate their sandwiches and drank tea from thick pottery mugs, sang happily as she washed and

dried the mugs, and even got to stand at the side of the stage during part of the performance, mesmerized by the bright colourful silks and feathers worn by the theatre dancing troupe. Everyone loved her willing eagerness to please and laughed at her blushes when someone told her how well she'd done at a particular task. She cleared, cleaned, and tidied everything in sight until the time came to leave the theatre for the night. She put on her coat and gloves, threw her duffle bag over her shoulder, and left the theatre with the rest of the staff, returning their shouted 'goodnights' as they went their separate ways. But of course, Georgie had nowhere to go. Once everyone was out of sight, she turned right into Tower Court and made her way along to the stage door set back in its recess at the side of the building. This time she sat on her duffle bag and leaned against the door to block the rising coldness from the pavement.

Georgie had worked hard at her new job, filling herself up with sandwiches, including the crusts left by others, and warming her insides with hot cups of tea. Now she felt a contented tiredness as she sat in the stage doorway, sleep soon overcoming her.

Georgie was awoken next morning by the clink of milk bottles against crates. At first, she thought she was in a cloud. All she could see was whiteness as the morning sun shone through whatever was covering her face, head, and whole body. She wiggled and shook her head until the covering cracked and fell away, first from her face and head, and then the rest of her body. Suddenly she felt the icy coldness of the morning air on her wet hair and face and realised that she had been encased in a layer of snow and ice. She tried to stand up, but her limbs were stiff with the cold. She banged her gloved hands together and stamped her feet on the ground to kick start her circulation.

"Well, if it ain't the abominable snowman, 'erself" came a voice that she immediately recognised.

Georgie looked to her left to meet the twinkling eyes of her friendly milkman, Bill. She was aware that globules of thawing snow were beginning to drip from her wet hair, down her red nose, and onto the ground. She realised what a sight she must look as she wiped her nose with the sleeve of her coat, only to deposit a new mound of snowflakes on its end, which in turn melted and doubled the rate of drips.

"Ere Georgie. You look like the Union Jack with your red nose and blue face covered in white snow," bellowed Bill in fits of laughter.

Georgie's shivering increased as she continued to thaw, but she couldn't help but join in Bill's catching laughter.

"Come on, Ducky, we need to get you into the warm again. This is getting to be an 'abit."

The damp heat of the café was even more welcome to Georgie than it had been the day before. Rosie looked up as they came in and her eyes widened to see the state of the young woman she'd met only once before.

"Oh, my gawd, Georgie, you come down 'ere right now. Let's get you out the back and dry you off you poor thing."

Georgie obeyed immediately and allowed Rosie to lead her through a door at the back of the café next to the double kitchen doors. A flight of steep wooden stairs confronted her, which she ascended slowly in Rosie's wake.

"I live up 'ere, Georgie. Stand there while I get you a towel to dry your 'air. Look, I'll switch on the electric 'eater. You stand in front and let it dry your coat and legs. Those blue legs don't look at all 'ealthy."

As Rosie went off to find a towel, the door at the bottom of the stairs opened and a voiced yelled out.

"Rosie. Get down 'ere right now. Café's full of 'ungry customers."

"Coming, Bert," shouted Rosie in return, nearly knocking Georgie backwards with the sheer volume of her voice. Georgie started to laugh as she'd done the previous morning.

"Oops sorry, Lovey. I forget how loud my foghorn sounds close up. You dry and warm yourself while I go back down and serve my 'ungry customers. Give that 'air a good rub to stop it dripping on the rest of you, and then come on down when you're ready."

"Thank you, Rosie," shivered Georgie as she removed her coat, hung it over the back of a dining room chair, and started to dry herself vigorously. She was glad her blonde hair, always dried quickly into its shiny waves, and ten minutes later she was able to go back downstairs to the café feeling only slightly damp. She looked around the tables until

she saw Bill beckoning her to where he was sitting. In front of him was a large full English breakfast with a buttered slice and a mug of steaming tea, identical to yesterday's meal. Bill turned to signal to Rosie, who soon arrived at the table with an identical spread for Georgie.

"Ere you go, Lovey. Get that down you," she said before scooting off to attend to another table of customers.

"But I can't pay yet, Bill," said Georgie in a hushed voice.

"Well, that's as may be but I'm counting on the fact that you will have got that job yesterday and will be able to return the favour this time next week after your first pay packet."

Georgie, faking a sad expression, looked at Bill until the smile faded from his face. Then suddenly she grinned widely and shouted, "I got it, Bill. I got the job."

His face immediately glowed with pleasure. "Knew you would, Doll."

Both laughed happily until Rosie returned to ask why they were laughing.

"She only went and got the job she was after, Rosie."

"Well done, Lovey. That deserves an extra celebration cuppa," as she rushed off to the back of the shop and returned with three full cups on a tin tray.

"Ere's to the future, Georgie. May all your dreams come true," said Rosie lifting her cup.

Bill rose from his chair, lifting his cup high and addressing everyone in the café.

"Ere's to our very own Georgie, London's famous new dancer of the future."

To Georgie's delight and embarrassment, and with the unanimous scraping of chairs on the lino, every customer stood and raised their cup.

"To Georgie," came the toast, followed by the sound of cups being put down on tabletops and spontaneous applause and cheering. Georgie's blue face and red nose were by now as pink as a flamingo under her glowing blonde halo as she shouted her thanks to everyone. She couldn't believe how fortunate she was not only to have got the job she wanted, but to have found such good friends in the process. As Bill left to take his milk cart back to the Dairy, Georgie rose to move to the back of the café where Rosie was sitting at a table eating her own breakfast.

"I left my coat hanging on the back of one of your chairs, Rosie. May I pop back upstairs to get it, please?"

"Course you can, My Friend, but before you go, I want to ask you something. Pull up a chair if you've got time."

"Yes, I've got plenty of time, thanks Rosie. I don't start work until twelve."

"I'm wondering if you're in the position to do me a favour. Well, it's more doing Bert a favour. This café belongs to 'im you see."

"Oh okay. I'll do my best to do Bert a favour, Rosie. What is it?"

"Well, you've seen 'ow busy we get in the morning, and me the only waitress. Bert was wondering if you might consider doing the early morning shift with me?"

Georgie nodded enthusiastically.

"The thing is, the overheads 'ere are enormous, so he couldn't afford to pay you with money. But he could give you a free breakfast every morning, and, if you didn't mind sharing, you could stay with me in the flat upstairs every night. What d'you say?"

Tears were, by now, running freely down Georgie's cheeks.

"I say yes, yes, yes. Thank you so much, Rosie. I can't tell you how cold it is sleeping in the stage doorway at night. Believe me, you and Bert have saved my life."

Georgie and Rosie stood up simultaneously and gave each other a bear-hug. After which, Rosie ran to the double doors, pushed them open and shouted at the top of her voice.

"Bert, she said yes."

Immediately an even louder voice from the kitchen let out a whoop, and a large, jigging, man clad in white, appeared in the gap between the double doors. He was wearing a large, red-faced smile and a white three-cornered scarf tied neatly around his shoulder length black hair. He grabbed Georgie's and Rosie's hands and danced both girls around in a circle of high-spirited joy, before he hugged them both in turn and returned to the kitchen singing at the top of his voice. The few remaining customers simply grinned as if this sort of behaviour was something they encountered daily.

CHAPTER 29

January - March 1960

One step forward, one back

"Wake up, Georgie."

Georgie opened her eyes with a start to see Rosie bending over her.

"Come on, Girlie. It's 'alf past six and you know we open at seven."

Georgie jumped up from the settee on which she'd been sleeping every night since she moved in with Rosie two months ago. She had kept quiet about her thirteenth birthday on the fourth of November, since she'd told Mr Blazenhill she was already fourteen. However, she had celebrated Christmas twice. The first time was with the staff and cast at the theatre after their final evening performance before the big day. Mr Blazenhill had provided finger food and several bottles of beer and wine, and they'd sung and danced into the early hours. The second time was with Rosie and Bert at the café. It turned out that Bert had a wife and three children who arrived at the café with him on Christmas morning. Bert had prepared a delicious Christmas Dinner followed by an afternoon of fun and games with the children. Georgie had enjoyed it tremendously, mainly because of all the laughter, but she had not been able to stop

herself thinking about home as she'd laid in bed on Christmas Eve. She had remembered the happy Christmases that she'd spent with her mum and real dad when she was little. She'd worried about Daisy, hoping that her little sister was safe from the monster, and she'd pictured both Daisy and John opening their presents on Christmas morning. Then she'd made a conscious decision not to let her worries spoil Christmas in her new life.

It was now the middle of January, and Georgie was feeling the strain of holding down two jobs, especially because both were so busy. She'd had little time to think about furthering her longed-for career in dancing until Rosie had asked her at the beginning of the month what her New Year Resolution would be for 1960.

"I'm going to try to find some dance classes, Rosie. It's so long since my last classes when I was living at the children's home that I think I've probably forgotten most of the dance moves by now. Anyway, I've saved my wages from the theatre, so I thought now was a good time to think about my future."

"I ain't ever 'eard of any dance classes round 'ere, Georgie," Rosie had responded, "but we could ask Bert and the customers if they've 'eard of any."

Since Georgie had moved into the flat with Rosie, they'd often chatted into the early hours after she'd returned home from the theatre. Rosie's life had been simple compared to Georgie's. She'd been brought up in a happy but poor family with five siblings in the outskirts of London and had left home at fourteen to take the job in the café, which she'd heard about via a neighbour who was a relative of Bert's. However, the girl seemed keen to hear about every detail of Georgie's past experiences and was a good listener, who had given Georgie the therapeutic outlet she'd needed.

Now Georgie was off the settee and getting washed and dressed as quickly as she could in the small bathroom. As she did so, she reflected on the number of people she had asked about dancing classes over the past month, but nobody had come up with any names other than for one or two ballet schools, which were not what Georgie wanted.

There was one young female customer who often popped into the café for a cuppa halfway through the morning after the breakfast trade had

quietened down, so Georgie and Rosie had got to know her quite well. She usually arrived while the two waitresses were eating their own late breakfasts, so they had had plenty of time to chat with the young woman over their food. They quickly discovered that her name was Theresa, that she preferred to be called Terry, and that she worked locally. Georgie had immediately recognised her as one of the women she'd seen coming out of one of the basement flats in Litchfield Street while she'd been waiting for St Martin's to open on her first full day in London. Knowing that Terry was a local, Georgie had asked her if she knew of any dancing classes in the area, and when Terry had also said that she didn't know of any, Georgie had begun to lose hope that she'd ever be able to further her dancing career. She was starting to realise that, as much as she enjoyed her job at St Martin's Theatre, the type of performances they put on seldom required dancers in their casts. She had often chatted to Mr Blazenhill, who had become somewhat of a father figure towards her, about her aspirations for the future. He had advised her that her best chance of getting into dancing would be to get a job in a theatre showing musicals, where there would be a choreographer who might be willing to give her lessons on the side.

"As much as I love you working here, Georgie, you need to think more about your own future than your loyalty to me and St Martin's. I'll keep my ear to the ground as I know lots of the theatre managers around this area. If I hear of a new musical coming to town, I'll give you the nod."

Georgie had thanked the man who she had grown so fond of over the past few months, but she'd had little time to think any more about it.

Then one day at the beginning of March, Mr Blazenhill called Georgie into his office.

"I've just learned something that may be of interest to you, Georgie. There's a new musical show opening at the Palace theatre on the fourteenth of March. It's called 'The Flower Drum Song' and has lots of dancing in it. I've had a word with the Theatre Manager and he's expecting you to pop in to see him later this afternoon."

Georgie's hopes took off and flew as she absorbed the information that Mr Blazenhill was giving her.

"The Palace Theatre is on the corner of Shaftesbury Avenue and Charing Cross Road. It won't take you long to walk there. Just turn right

out of the theatre, go to the end of West Street, turn left, and continue to the crossroads. You'll see the Palace diagonally opposite you. You can't miss it. It's a red brick building with a concave frontage."

"Thank you, Mr Blazenhill. Thank you so much."

"Mind you, you'll need to give me a week's notice if you get a job there. I've no idea how I'm going to find a replacement as good as you, Young Georgie."

At four o'clock that afternoon, Georgie stood in front of the Palace Theatre, open-mouthed at the size, appearance, and location of the impressive building. Suddenly her young heart began to beat faster as she considered for the first time that this place may be the gateway to her dreams. She took some deep breaths to slow down her breathing, consciously hardened her resolve to appear confident, and stepped forward to push open the door to the Theatre's foyer. Seeing the box office, she approached it and spoke to the lady inside.

"I have an appointment with the Manager, please. My name is Georgie and he's expecting me."

"Ah yes, Georgie, Mr Dewar mentioned that you were coming. Take a seat in the foyer and I'll let him know you're here."

Georgie had hardly sat herself down before a gentleman appeared in the foyer. She stood as he approached her. She hadn't expected to see such a young man in the position of Theatre Manager, and the surprise momentarily took her breath away, although she didn't really understand why. He was tall and slim with blond hair that sat in small curls along the top edge of his shirt collar. His skin was clear, and he was clean shaven, but his eyes were his most striking feature, being emerald green in colour framed by long dark lashes and perfectly shaped eyebrows. Georgie couldn't take her own eyes off them. She was mesmerized by their almost incongruous appearance. The young Mr Dewar held out his right hand to shake Georgie's. She stood unmoving for a moment before she realized he was waiting for her to return the handshake. His eyes developed a twinkle as he looked into hers with subtle amusement.

"Georgie, I presume?"

Another moment passed, both pairs of eyes fixated on each other before Georgie seemed to snap out of her mesmerized state and responded.

"Oh, er, yes. I'm Georgie. I'm er sorry. Yes. Are you Mr Dewar?"
"The very same, but most people call me Derek. Do come into my office so we can talk. Would you like a cup of tea or maybe you'd prefer a glass of water?"

"Er yes. I mean I'd love a glass of water, please."

The office was very similar in appearance to the one at St Martin's, except the accent colour was a rich deep green rather than the red preferred by Mr Blazenhill. Derek Dewar pulled out a chair for Georgie before making himself comfortable in the one behind the desk.

"Well now, Georgie. I understand that you want to gain a position in this theatre because we are about to stage a musical and you have an interest in learning to dance. Is that correct?"

Georgie nodded, still finding herself being drawn to those emerald-green eyes that toned in perfectly with the dark green décor of the office.

Mr Dewar poured water into a glass from a carafe on his desk and pushed it towards Georgie before he spoke.

"Hmm. I see. So, perhaps you'd like to tell me a little about yourself and why you find the idea of a dancing career so attractive."

Georgie noticed that his eyes were still twinkling and wondered why he seemed to find her behaviour so amusing. She also wondered why she felt so drawn to him.

"Oh, yes. Erm okay. Well ..."

Then Georgie launched into her story, suddenly finding her enthusiasm and passion and the words that the Theatre Manager had been trying to prize from her since they'd met in the foyer. When she stopped to take a breath, she noticed that Derek Dewar was no longer twinkling but looked as if he was completely absorbed in what she had been saying.

300

"My, my, Georgie. After such a passionate rendition of your life's experiences, how can I refuse you a position here at the Palace. If you do your job with even half of the energy you've displayed in the past fifteen minutes, I'll be more than happy."

Georgie beamed, the light in her eyes matching those of her interviewer.

"Thank you, Mr Dewar ... Derek. I promise you I will put everything into the work I do for you, especially if I can learn to dance better at the same time."

"Well, I can't expect more than everything, can I Georgie? The job will be the same as you've been doing at St. Martin's but with the option of paying for some private dancing lessons with our choreographer, Raymond, in your own time before you start work at noon every day. I'm willing to pay you three pounds seventeen and sixpence per week. How does that sound?"

"That sounds wonderful. Thank you very much – but I will have to give Mr Blazenhill a week's notice before I can start," said Georgie, hoping that would not be a problem.

"Then we've struck a deal, Pretty Young Lady. Now let us go out for dinner to celebrate."

Georgie was taken aback by Derek's offer and was initially lost for words. Although she didn't understand why, she found herself desperately wanting to accept his invitation.

"Oh, I'm s-sorry," she stuttered, "I can't go out for dinner as I have to get back to work."

"Then we shall postpone that invitation until one week from today, on the first day of your new employment here at The Palace. I shall look forward to it with a great deal of anticipation."

Georgie left The Palace Theatre feeling a little ill at ease, and not quite understanding what had happened regarding her emotions and Derek Dewar's effect on them.

301

'It must be the way things are done in show business,' she told herself as she made her way back to St Martin's where she was soon so busy that she had no time for reflection. That evening she borrowed a piece of notepaper and an envelope from Rosie and wrote her resignation letter to Mr Blazenhill, which she would hand deliver the next morning. Rosie was so excited for her friend that she couldn't stop talking and soon Georgie caught that excitement even though she was very tired. It wasn't until they'd been discussing Georgie's future for a while that Rosie suddenly went silent.

"What's up, Rosie?"

"You say you'll be getting dancing lessons in the mornings before you start work?"

"Yes. Why? Is that a problem?"

"Well, it is if you want to carry on working and living 'ere, yes."

It was now Georgie who went silent. Her friend was right. She wouldn't be able to continue working at the café, which meant she wouldn't be able to continue living with Rosie because Bert would need to find a new waitress to replace her, and the flat came with the job.

Both girls lapsed into a sad silence, which was broken only by Rosie's question.

"Georgie, where you going to live?"

CHAPTER 30

March 1960

Destitution

Georgie held the white envelope containing her resignation letter towards Mr Blazenhill.

"Is this what I think it is Georgie?" he asked with a smile as he slit open the envelope with his silver paper knife, withdrew the letter and scanned its contents.

As he looked up at Georgie, the smile on his face faded.

"Then what's with the troubled face, Young Lady. This is just what you wanted, isn't it?"

"Yes, it is what I wanted, Mr Blazenhill, and I'm actually really excited, especially as it comes with the option of taking dancing lessons before work each morning with the choreographer."

"Then what's the problem?"

"It's just that if I take the dancing lessons, then I'll have to give up my morning job at the café, and if I do that, then I lose my flat share above the café because it goes with the job."

"Ah. I see your dilemma."
Georgie nodded.

"Come on, Georgie. This isn't like you. Where's the optimistic young woman we've all become so fond of? You still have a whole week left to find some lodgings. Why don't you go back and ask Derek Dewar if he knows of anywhere you could live? There may even be a cast member who needs to take in a lodger to help with the rent."

Georgie brightened up immediately. Of course, why hadn't she thought of that? She'd pop back to see her new boss during her break time later that afternoon. She left Mr Blazenhill's office with a bounce in her step and excitement in her heart, ready to tell her work colleagues her good news.

Later in the afternoon, having cleared it with the other staff for whom she'd normally be making their afternoon cuppa, she walked quickly back to the Palace Theatre for the second time in two days. She waved to the lady in the box office, checking with her that Derek Dewar didn't have any visitors before she walked over and knocked on his office door.

"Come in."

When she entered, the Manager had his head bowed over a document, which he seemed to be studying. He looked up casually, and when he saw Georgie, the twinkle immediately reappeared in his eyes.

"Georgie, it's you. How unexpected but lovely to see you so soon."

Then his twinkle was momentarily replaced by a scowl.

"You're not here to tell me you don't want the job after all, are you?"

Georgie giggled as her face flushed a little and she remembered those intoxicating green eyes.

"No, no. Nothing like that Mr Dewar ... Derek. I've come to discuss a problem that I have in the hope that you might be able to help me."

"Phew. Well, that's a relief, anyway. Do sit down and tell me what I can do."

Georgie sat down on the chair in front of Derek Dewar's desk, just as she had the day before at her interview.

"If I'm going to work here," she began, "then I am going to have to find some lodgings."

"But why can't you continue to live where you are? It's not too far to walk here each day, is it?"

Georgie explained her dilemma whilst Derek Dewar listened intently until she'd finished.

"Well, Georgie, I think you should stop worrying right now. I'll make enquiries amongst the cast during this week, and I'll have something sorted out by the time you start work next week. So off you go, stop worrying, and enjoy your last week at St Martin's."

Georgie couldn't believe it was that simple. A weight lifted from her shoulders as she thanked the man profusely and made her way back to St Martin's. She popped her head around Mr Blazenhill's office door when she arrived back, and told him the good news, obtaining a broad smile and a 'thumbs up' in response.

Her final week at St Martin's Theatre flew by and on the last day she was showered with several small gifts from the theatre staff, and a large 'Good Luck' card which they'd all signed. She appeared back at the flat above the café that night with tears in her eyes, only to be greeted by the equally as tearful Rosie, and a large celebration cake provided by Bert. The two girls sat eating cake and chatting well into the night, Rosie declaring that she didn't know how she was going to cope without her friend to work and live with. The café had a new waitress starting the very next morning, because Bert had put a small advert in the café window as soon as Georgie had told him her news. So, Georgie realised that Rosie was apprehensive on two counts; firstly, she had to work with someone she didn't know, and secondly, she'd be getting a new flatmate.

"Don't be upset, Rosie. You'll soon get to know the new girl, and it's not as if I'll be working too far away. I can easily pop round to see you in my

time off," said Georgie trying to reassure both herself and her friend about their new futures.

At eleven fifty-five the next morning, Georgie was outside the Palace Theatre waiting for her new Manager to arrive and let her in. She moved her weight from foot to foot in time with her rapid heartbeat. Had she still been a little girl, she'd have been jumping up and down with the mixture of nerves and excitement that she was feeling. But now she was a young woman pretending to be fourteen, she knew that would not be appropriate.

She spotted the tall, imposing figure of Derek Dewar strolling up Shaftesbury Avenue towards the theatre, his collar length blond hair bouncing in time with each footstep, and his bright emerald-green eyes twinkling in the sunshine. Her heart missed a beat and her stomach flipped at the sight of him. As he got closer, Derek Dewar spotted Georgie and acknowledged her presence with a broad smile that lit up his face and seemed to increase the intensity of his twinkle. Georgie couldn't help but return the smile, even though she felt that her stomach was going to leap right out of her mouth at any moment.

"Good morning, Beautiful Lady," the Manager greeted as he bent low to kiss the startled Georgie on both cheeks.

Georgie tried her hardest not to show her shock at such an intimate greeting, telling herself that this must be acceptable behaviour in Derek Dewar's world. She was aware, however, that she couldn't control the involuntary flush of heat rising from her neck to her cheeks. She was also aware that her new Manager had noticed this and had purposefully kept eye contact with her for just a second or two longer than was necessary.

"Come on in, Georgie. Bright and early, I see."

Georgie followed Derek Dewar into the theatre foyer just as the box office lady came rushing in, red cheeked and out of breath.

"Joanna, rushing as usual?" laughed the manager.

"Ooh. Sorry, Derek. My Pamela just wouldn't move herself this morning. She dawdled all the way to afternoon nursery and then made a scene when I tried to leave her."

"Joanna, dear Joanna, doesn't Pamela always make a scene when you leave her, and don't you always end up rushing in the door at the last moment gasping for breath?"

Joanna giggled, said good morning to Georgie, and slipped off her coat as she made her way into the box office.

"Now Georgie, while we're waiting for everyone to arrive, I'll give you a quick guided tour and then we can have a cuppa in my office so you can ask any questions you might have."

Georgie followed Derek Dewar as he described in detail the use and history of every part of the Palace Theatre as well as introducing her to various members of staff and the cast as they arrived. One of those people was the choreographer, who confirmed that he'd be more than happy to give Georgie dance lessons and promised they could negotiate the cost once she was settled into her job. It was, therefore, a very happy Georgie that sat down in front of the Manager's desk at the end of the tour.

"Now, Georgie, do you have any questions you'd like to ask me?"

"Only one really. I wondered if you'd managed to sort me out some lodgings?"

"Yes, no problem. I'll take you there after we close this evening."

Georgie, with her mind at rest, threw herself into her first day's work. The theatre staff and the cast of the musical show were all friendly towards her, and she was able to get a glimpse of the dance troupe rehearsing their routines. As she watched, Georgie found herself copying the steps and dreaming about her longed-for future. She was so excited that at last she was going to be able to move forward into her dream.

At the end of the evening, she found Derek Dewar waiting for her at the theatre exit. She had brought along her packed duffle bag, which he lifted from her shoulder and carried for her. They walked side by side along Shaftesbury Avenue and turned into a side road, passing several three storey white houses like those Georgie had seen in Litchfield Street opposite the St Martin's theatre. Finally, Derek turned into one of the houses on the left, climbing the three stone steps up to the front door. Georgie followed. Then to her surprise, instead of knocking at the door,

her manager took a bunch of keys out of his jacket pocket, selected one and opened the door himself.

"Come on in, Georgie. The flat is on the top floor."

Derek Dewar began to climb the stairs. Georgie followed. When they reached the third floor, the man used a different key from his bunch to open it, pushed it wide, pressed the light switch on the wall to his left and stood back to allow Georgie to enter. By now, Georgie was feeling a little uneasy.

"Well, here we are, Georgie. Would you like me to show you your room?"

"Who does this flat belong to, Derek?"

"It's mine."

"Do you live here?"

"I do, but don't worry, I have a spare room with a lock on the door, which can be yours. You won't even have to pay rent. I thought that might be difficult for you as you are only on a low wage and you're wanting to pay for dance lessons."

"I see. But won't your neighbours think it strange if you have a young woman living with you?"

"Oh, don't worry about that. Londoners in this area keep themselves to themselves. They probably won't even notice."

Derek opened a door off the lounge and again stood back for Georgie to enter. Her intuition was telling her this was all wrong, but at the same time, the thought of free lodgings was difficult to turn down. Surely this man, the Manager of a large, well known theatre, could be trusted. He seemed to be acting as though this arrangement was quite normal, but Georgie was still hesitant.

"You get yourself settled in while I go and prepare us something to eat," said the upbeat Derek.

Georgie nodded, still feeling uncomfortable.

308

'Stop being stupid,' she told herself as she emptied her belongings on to the single bed that was pushed against one of the walls. The room was clean and pleasant with a large sash window looking out on to the road, and a wash basin in the corner, next to which was a small chest of drawers with a mirror on the wall behind it. Georgie placed her hairbrush and other personal items on the chest and was looking around trying to work out where she could hang her work clothes, when Derek walked into the room without knocking and made Georgie jump.

"Oh, sorry Georgie. I startled you, but the meal's ready if you are."

"Thank you. Yes, I'm ready, but … erm … would you mind knocking next time, so you don't startle me."

"Yes of course. How thoughtless of me."

"Also, do you have the key to my bedroom door, please?"

"Georgie, you've no need to feel nervous, you know. Please be reassured that you're safe with me," Derek blustered in his apparent surprise at this young woman's forthrightness.

"Even so, I'd be happier with the key, if that's alright?"

"That's fine. I'll find it for you after we've eaten. Come on now or the food will be cold."

Georgie sat down with Derek at the small dining table in front of the windows at one end of his lounge. The long curtains remained open allowing the streetlights outside to reflect on both Georgie's and Derek's faces. A lighted candle flickered in the centre of the table, adding a further warming glow. As they ate together, they soon relaxed into easy conversation, Derek asking Georgie about her past life, and Georgie asking Derek how he came to be in the position of Manager of The Palace Theatre while still so young. Georgie skimmed over the details of her life, still not quite trusting the young man in who's flat she was now to reside. She noticed that he was pouring liberal amounts of white wine into his own glass, after offering it to Georgie. She had declined, drinking only water from a jug on the table. When they'd finished eating, Georgie rose and thanked Derek for the meal. As she did so, the light from the flickering candle caught his emerald green-eyes making them twinkle brighter than Georgie had seen them before. This had a disturbing effect

on the young woman, which she couldn't quite explain, especially when he held her gaze, preventing her words of goodnight from escaping her lips. Georgie found herself quivering as Derek stood up and moved in closer to her. She couldn't seem to escape his gaze as he placed his hands gently on her shoulders and leaned in to brush his lips against hers.

"I have t-to g-go to b-bed now," stuttered Georgie, gently pushing Derek away.

Derek seemed not to hear her as his arms enveloped her, drawing her in close to his body. Georgie felt his desire, which in turn increased the strange feeling within her stomach. At first, she attempted to push him away, but as his gentle kiss intensified, she found herself responding and wanting more – even pushing closer into him. Then suddenly, without warning, a picture of Gerald flashed into her mind and the pleasant feelings in her stomach turned to horror. She pushed Derek with all the strength she could muster, noting the shocked look on his face as she turned away and almost ran into her bedroom, closing the door behind her and leaning against it to catch her breath. At that moment, she realised that she hadn't yet obtained the bedroom key, and fear rose in her as she heard Derek's footsteps approaching her room. She heard him turn the doorknob and push against the door to open it. She leaned harder against it, but her weight was no match for his strength, and the soles of her shoes gradually slid across the polished wooden floor as he forced the door open and entered. She ran towards the opposite wall, but he followed, the look of a hunting tiger in his bright green eyes. He grabbed her shoulders and steered her backwards towards the bed, but as she felt the edge of the bed against the back of her knees, she managed to roll sideways out of his grip as he fell forwards on to the bed. She took her chance to run out of the bedroom, out of the flat door, down the three flights of stairs and out of the main door into the street knowing that he was not far behind her. She ran back up the side street and turned right into Shaftesbury Avenue, keeping going until she saw an alleyway next to a shop, cluttered with overflowing rubbish bins. She quickly looked behind her to see Derek appearing round the corner into Shaftesbury Avenue, and without thinking, she dived into the alley, landing in the centre of the dustbins where she crouched down and tried to quieten her laboured breathing. After a couple of minutes, she heard approaching footsteps and held her breath, knowing that Derek would be looking down the alleyway. Then the footsteps quickened again as they continued along Shaftesbury Avenue and disappeared. Georgie dared

not move. She stayed still and silent for what seemed like ages, pleased that the March night was comparatively mild. She eventually heard footsteps walking past in the opposite direction and hoped that it was Derek returning to his flat. She still did not move for fear that it had not been him and he may still be looking for her. As she sat there, it dawned on her that her future had come crashing down around her in Derek's flat that evening. She would not be able to continue working for the man, which meant that she had also lost access to the dancing lessons. Not only that, but she was now homeless and without her money and possessions, which she had left in the flat in her eagerness to escape. Now she had no money so no way of paying for other lodgings. Tears started to drip down her face as her plight became more and more real. She realised that she had lost her Bible with the photograph of her father and Robert's telephone number in it, and also her precious dancer book. Her grief grew heavier as the night moved into early morning and the light of dawn illuminated the dustbins and rubbish in which she sat. What was Georgie to do now?

CHAPTER 31

March 1960

From bad to worse

'I have to think of a plan,' Georgie told herself as she stood up from amongst the bins in the alleyway.

Her joints were stiff and painful as she picked her way through the clutter. It was still very early but she peeked out of the alleyway towards Derek's road to make sure that all was clear before she emerged. A plan was starting to form in her mind. She would go to Bert's café and speak to Rosie about her dilemma. At least she'd be able to sit in the warm rather than wander up and down the streets of London while she considered her future. As she arrived at the café, she saw Bill, the milkman, entering. She felt almost ashamed to follow him in, feeling that he'd be really disappointed at her failure to hold down the job at The Palace after such a short time.

As she walked in, Rosie turned around from where she had just shouted Bill's breakfast order through the double doors at the back of the café. Her eyes brightened until she saw the rumpled state that her friend was in and rushed forward to find out what had happened. At the same time, Bill looked round and saw her too.

"My, my, Georgie. What on earth 'as 'appened? Come and sit down with me and tell Bill all about it."

At that moment Rosie arrived with her arms wide to welcome her friend but at the last minute held back and squeezed the tip of her nose.

"Phew, Georgie, you don't 'alf stink. What you been up to?"

Georgie looked at both of her friends before she spoke to Rosie.

"Please may I use your flat to wash myself, Rosie? I had to hide amongst the rubbish bins all night, which is why my clothes smell."

"Course you can. My new flatmate isn't there at the moment, so you go upstairs an 'elp yourself to some of my clean clothes. You'll frighten off the customers smelling like that."

When Georgie returned from the flat twenty minutes later, she looked and smelled clean and fresh. She'd borrowed Rosie's hairbrush and her long blonde waves were looking neat and shiny again.

"Go sit with Bill, Georgie. I'll bring your breakfast in a sec."

"No thanks, Rosie. I don't have any money to pay for a breakfast, it's all at Derek's flat."

Rosie's eyebrows lifted but she didn't ask any further questions until she'd finished serving a customer and joined Georgie and Bill at the table with a plate of breakfast in her hand, which she slid in front of Georgie.

"And don't object, Georgie. That's my own breakfast so it's already paid for – and don't make no fuss – you look like you need it more than I do."

Georgie explained to her friends what had happened the night before, and how she was homeless, jobless, and penniless.

"Blimey, Georgie. What a nasty git that Derek bloke is," said Bill. "You've 'ad a lucky escape if you ask me. What you going to do now?"

Georgie shook her head. "I don't know what I'm going to do now, Bill. All my stuff is in Derek's flat and I'm certainly not going to chance going back there to retrieve it."

"I wonder 'ow he'll explain your disappearance to the rest of the staff at the Palace," said Rosie.

"No idea. But that's his problem. Mine is deciding what I'm going to do now," said the depressed Georgie.

Rosie put her arm around her friend, giving her a reassuring squeeze as she stood up and removed Georgie's empty breakfast plate.

"Well, you just sit there till we can figure something out. I've got to get on with my job right now, but I'll keep thinking."

"Well, I reckon you ought to go to the police, Georgie," said Bill. "That's real serious - attacking a young lady, especially as he's got all your money and things."

"No. I don't want to do that, Bill, thanks all the same. I've had enough of reporting things to the police for a whole lifetime. I'll just put this one down to lack of experience, but I'll tell you something, I'll never get myself into that position again."

"Okay, Lovey. Well, it's your life. I've got to go now, so you take care."

Georgie nodded as Bill said his goodbyes and went off to finish his round, leaving her sitting and thinking. At one point, Rosie put a cup of tea in front of her friend, smiling encouragingly as she did so. Georgie felt like she wanted to withdraw into herself as all she could see ahead of her was bleakness and despair. A couple of hours later, she was interrupted by the café door opening, and her and Rosie's new friend, Terry, entering.

"Hello, Georgie. What are you doing here? I thought you'd have moved to The Palace by now."

Terry sat in the chair opposite Georgie with a look of concern on her face.

"You alright, Georgie? You look a bit dazed."

"Sorry, Terry, but yes, I am a bit dazed. I'm in a bit of a fix and I don't know what to do about it."

314

Georgie sat and explained the problem to Terry as Rosie put a cup of tea in front of their friend and joined them at the table. Terry looked thoughtful as she listened to Georgie's problem.

"Hmm. I think I might be able to help you, Georgie, as long as you aren't fussy about where you live or what you do," said the girl.

"I'm not fussy, Terry. How can I be in my position?"

"Okay, well, let me finish my cuppa and then I'll introduce you to someone who might be the answer to your problems."

Georgie brightened up immediately. Rosie, however, looked slightly hesitant and when Georgie looked at her questioningly, she just did a slight shake of her head. Georgie didn't quite know how to interpret that, so when Terry had finished her tea and rose from the table with the words, "Come on then, Georgie, let's be off," she turned her attention to Terry without a second thought.

The two girls walked together along West Street, turning right into Litchfield Street, and chatting as they went. Georgie noticed that Terry wore quite heavy make-up and clothes that accentuated her slim but curvy figure. Her new friend was a pretty and vivacious young woman whom Georgie estimated to be older than herself, possibly in her late teens or early twenties. About two thirds of the way along Litchfield Street, Terry crossed the road and turned into one of the houses with the fenced off basements. She opened the iron gate leading to the basement steps and waited for Georgie to follow and close the gate behind her. At the bottom of the steps was a pathway leading to a grubby-looking brown wooden door, which Terry opened with a key and, holding the door back, beckoned to Georgie to enter, before she closed it with a click of the yale lock. Inside to the left was a poorly lit hallway with brown threadbare carpet along its length. The walls were a grubby cream colour, and to the left of the hallway were three cream doors equally spaced along its length. Terry led Georgie past all three doors until they reached an open door at the end leading into a well-lit room. While Terry greeted the four women sitting on the sofas that lined the wall opposite and the one to the right, Georgie took in the environment. To her left there were white plastic-looking kitchen units fitted around the corner and along the wall. They looked old and grubby, with one cupboard door slightly hanging off its hinges. There was a sink and a hob that were clearly used often and not cleaned. A radio was blaring out music from one corner of the room,

but nobody seemed to be listening to it. Georgie noticed that three of the girls were wearing dressing gowns, whilst the fourth one, with whom Terry seemed to be in deep conversation, was smartly dressed in a black skirt and jacket, black patent high heeled shoes, and a white organza blouse with wide ruffles down the front and spilling out of her black jacket sleeves at the wrists.

Georgie was beginning to wonder if any of the girls had noticed she was standing there, when Terry and the smartly dressed girl came over to her.

"Georgie, this is Maxine. She's in charge of the girls working here. I've asked her if there's any chance of you having a room here," said Terry

Georgie smiled at Maxine and said Hello, but as she did so she was wondering what work these girls did. Lounging about in a dressing gown all day didn't seem to Georgie like hard work. As she was thinking, she suddenly realised that Maxine was speaking to her.

"Well, as I say, it's not up to me who has a room here, that's up to my boss. He'll be popping by later so we can have a word with him. Why don't you make yourself comfortable while Terry goes and changes?"

As Terry disappeared out of the door with a small wave, Maxine took Georgie over to the three girls to introduce her.

"Girls, this is Georgie. Georgie this is Sophie, Brenda and Sally," said Maxine, pointing to each in turn.

"Hi Georgie," said the three girls in unison before they carried on chatting between themselves. Georgie sat on the sofa and quietly studied the girls' appearances while she waited for Terry to return. All three girls were heavily made up like Terry, with beautifully coiffured hairstyles. Sophie's hair was long, white-blonde, and very straight and shiny. Brenda and Sally both had dark hair, Brenda's long and curly, whilst Sally's framed her heart-shaped face with a bob, her fringe cut straight across her forehead. Georgie was wondering why Maxine was dressed so smartly and what job the girls did, when Terry returned wearing a dressing gown like the other three girls. She smiled at Georgie as she sat down beside her. Just at that moment, the doorbell rang, and Maxine went to open it, returning with a short, chubby man dressed in a city suit. She clapped her hands to capture the girls' attention.

316

"Now girls, this is Cecil and it's his first visit, so up you jump and get in line."

The girls, including Terry, stood up, removed their dressing gowns, and stood in a row looking provocatively at Cecil, whose face lit up into a lascivious smile. It wasn't until Georgie moved her stare from the man to the row of girls that the shock showed on her face. She couldn't believe what she was seeing. Each girl was wearing a different, scanty, satin costume accentuating their breasts, legs, waists and bottoms, the like of which Georgie had never seen. They were moving from one pose to another while the man looked on. After a few minutes, he moved forward until he was in front of Sophie before he looked round at Maxine and indicated that he'd made his choice. Sophie left the room, opening the first door on the right in the hallway and entering. The other three girls put their dressing gowns back on and returned to the sofa's. Meanwhile, the man removed some notes from his wallet and handed them to Maxine who took the money and placed it in her skirt pocket before escorting him to the room that Sophie had entered.

Georgie turned to Terry and was just about to question her as to what was going on, when a much younger but smartly dressed man entered the room, nodding at all the girls who seemed to recognise him. He and Maxine moved to the kitchen end of the room and were clearly talking about Georgie as the young man kept turning his head to look at her. After a few minutes, Maxine approached Georgie and asked her if she'd join her and the gentleman for a private chat at the other end of the room. By now, Georgie's sense of apprehension was overwhelming her, and with knees feeling like jelly she rose from the sofa and followed Maxine.

"Georgie, may I introduce you to Mr G, my boss."

Mr G looked at Georgie and smiled.

"Well, hello, beautiful little lady, I'm pleased to meet you."

Georgie's insides shrank as his words reminded her of the way Derek had spoken to her at their first meeting. She swallowed hard, and not wishing to appear impolite, smiled and returned Mr G's greeting.

"So, Georgie, I understand you need a room and a job?"

"Yes, that's right but ..."

"Well, I think I may be able to help you, Young Lady. First, tell me, how old are you?"

"I'm fourteen."

"Well, I can't let you have a room here. The girls, and there's twelve of them in total, don't live here, they just use the rooms for their work. That means the rooms are occupied for most of the time."

"Okay. Well never mind," said Georgie with mixed feelings as she started to turn away.

"Wait, Georgie. I haven't finished."

Georgie had a sinking feeling as she turned back, and Mr G carried on talking.

"I have another place just a short drive from here. There's a room there that you could both live and work in. We can go and see it right now if you like?"

Georgie felt cornered. She had no choice but to go along with this, bearing in mind her current situation, but she sensed that she was getting herself into something she didn't understand, and intuitively didn't like.

"Okay, Mr G, but can I first say goodbye to Terry?"

"Oh sorry, Georgie, but Terry is working right now," interrupted Maxine.

Georgie had wanted to ask Terry what this job involved, but she'd have to leave that for now if she was going to go with Mr G to see this room. So, she thanked Maxine and asked her to say goodbye to Terry for her, and then went with Mr G whose car was parked outside in the road. By the time they arrived at the other house, Georgie had become completely disorientated. They had initially turned right out of Litchfield Street into Charing Cross Road, but after a left turn and several other right and left turns, she'd no idea where she was, other than outside another very similar looking three storey house to the one she'd just left.

"Here we are, Georgie. Let's go inside."

318

"They got out of the car and went down the basement steps, along a pathway to another brown wooden door, which Mr G unlocked with a key from his pocket. Inside the layout was almost identical to the one at Litchfield Street but with more doors off the hallway before reaching the room at the end. Even this room looked identical to Litchfield, except there was no cupboard door hanging off and only one dressing gown-clad girl sitting on the sofa. A smartly dressed middle-aged woman stood as Mr G entered.

"Lavinia, how are you?"

"I'm fine thanks, Mr G, we've been really busy. Your money is ready for you," she said as she removed a fat brown envelope from her pocket and handed it to her boss.

Mr G took the money without thanking Lavinia, and then turned to Georgie.

"Come on Georgie, I'll show you your room."

As he took Georgie's arm, he turned back to Lavinia.

"I'll be back in a moment, Lavinia, to explain our arrangement with Georgie."

Lavinia nodded as she returned to the sofa.

Mr G led Georgie out of the room and unlocked the first door on the right, walking straight in. Georgie followed nervously. Was this man going to be like Derek Dewar and attempt to have sex with her. By now, she was beginning to realise what 'work' went on here and in Litchfield Street, but she was determined not to be part of it. She looked around the room. There was a frosted glass window at the far end with the blind pulled half-way down, and a single bed in the far-right corner with a bedside cabinet next to it. An upright chair sat in the opposite corner on the other side of the window. The walls were painted the same grubby cream colour as those in Litchfield, and against the left-hand wall was a curtained off clothes' rail. A large, grubby green rug covered the centre of the floor.

Mr G opened a door to a small bathroom that had been built into the near-right-corner of the room. That too was grubby looking, but Georgie

319

knew that she'd be able to clean up the whole room to make it a lot more comfortable.

"So, what do you think, Georgie?"

Georgie hesitated, her intuition telling her to turn her back on this offer. But then again, she had nowhere to live, and if she could avoid getting involved in what she believed went on in the other rooms, this room would suit her nicely. But she still felt worried, so she decided she'd best make one more attempt to walk away.

"Looks fine, Mr G, except I have no money for rent at the moment, so I'll have to give it a miss I'm afraid."

"Oh, don't worry about that Georgie, we can take the rent out of your earnings."

"About that. What work would I actually be doing?"

Mr G looked incredulous.

"You'll be doing the same as all the other girls, of course, entertaining our male customers. My guess is that you'll be busy because lots of men prefer very young girls like you. You could earn yourself a fortune if you play your cards right."

Georgie's heart started to race as she wondered desperately how she might get out of this.

"But I'm too young, Mr G. I can't do what the other girls do. I could do the cleaning or even cook, but not ... that."

"No, Georgie, you're fourteen. That's old enough," said Mr G sounding frustrated.

"Actually, I'm only thirteen – not fourteen till November."

"Well, I don't care what age you are. If you live in this room, you do the work that goes with it."

"Oh, I see. Then thank you very much, but I have decided not to take the room after all. I'll be off now."

"Oh, you will, will you. I don't take kindly to being messed about, and for your information you're not going anywhere, Miss Hoity Toity."

Before Georgie could reach the door, Mr G let himself out and she could hear him turn the key from the outside. She tried the doorknob to confirm it was locked and then banged on the door as loud as she could.

"Let me out. Let me out ..."

She continued shouting until she heard the door being unlocked from the outside. Mr G entered and closed the door behind him. He pushed Georgie back toward the bed until she fell backward onto it. The next thing she felt was a hard punch to her stomach which winded her so badly that she couldn't get her breath.

"Now shut up, Bitch. You are disturbing my customers and I get very, very, angry when that happens. Learn your lesson now cos I'm telling you, I can punch a lot harder than that, and won't hesitate to do so if you make another sound."

Mr G left Georgie still gasping for breath and with tears running down her face. He shut the door quietly as he left the room, locking it behind him.

CHAPTER 32

March - April 1960

No escape

Georgie woke with a start. It was dark outside, and she wondered how long she'd been asleep. The last thing she remembered was the sharp pain in her stomach and being unable to get her breath. Then it all came back to her, prompting tears and a deep sense of fear to join the now nagging ache in her stomach. As an increasing sense of reality hit her, she started to force herself to think about how she could escape. She realised how hungry and thirsty she felt so she slid her legs over the side of the bed and used her elbows to push herself up into a sitting position. When she tried to stand, the pain in her stomach became so fierce that she was unable to straighten up. Using the edge of the bed for support, she slowly walked towards the bathroom. At the end of the bed, she moved to the wall on her left to gain support until she reached the bathroom door, which she opened and stood for a while holding on to its handle. Continuing forward with the help of the bathroom wall, she finally reached the wash basin and the empty glass that sat behind the taps. She rinsed the grubby glass and having filled it with cold water, she put it to her lips and drank thirstily, after which she wet her hands, using them to cool her now perspiring forehead. Having relieved herself on the toilet, she slowly made her way back to the bed where she lay back down with

a sigh of relief. Just as her head touched the pillow, she heard the lock turn in the door, which induced such fear that it triggered a need to throw up. When Lavinia entered with a tray in her hand, Georgie let out a sigh of relief as the vomit reaction dissipated and she silently thanked God that it wasn't Mr G.

"Right, Georgie, I ain't going to make an 'abit of this but since you're new 'ere, I'm making an exception. I've made you a sandwich and a bowl a soup. Get that down you and you'll feel better."

Lavinia placed the tray on the bedside cabinet and watched Georgie painfully ease herself back into a sitting position.

"Thank you. What's the time please?"

"It's past ten, so I suggest you eat that lot and make yourself presentable for Mr G when he returns. E's got a fierce temper that one, so no sense in giving 'im any reason to start on you again… You can call me Lavinia, by the way."

"Thank you, Lavinia," Georgie responded as the woman left the room and relocked it.

The soup and sandwich did make her feel a lot better, so having finished every drop and crumb, Georgie made her way to the bathroom again, encountering a little less pain than she had before. She rinsed the crockery and cutlery under the washbasin tap and put them back on the bedside cabinet. She washed her face and tried to neaten her hair just in time to hear the door being unlocked again, and she couldn't prevent herself shaking as Mr G entered and approached her.

"I hope you've learned your lesson, Young lady, and that I'll now be able to count on your full cooperation."

Georgie said nothing.

"Now, if you're going to remain here, which you are, I need to explain a few things. Firstly, you need to learn what is expected of you. As I said yesterday, I'm expecting you to be popular with the punters, so I don't want you disappointing them, if you get my drift?"

Georgie remained silent.

"So, I'm going to teach you the various ways you can satisfy a man's ... needs."

Georgie backed off a little.

"For a start, you don't back off like that. You speak nicely to the customers. You ask them politely what their preferences are, then you make sure they get good value for money."

Georgie was paralysed to the spot with fear as Mr G approached her.

"I reckon at thirteen, you're not likely to have much in the way of experience so I've decided to give you a practical demonstration. I'm going to be the customer and you, dear Georgie, are going to follow my every instruction in order to satisfy my preferences. So, go ahead, speak to me politely and ask me what I would like you to do."

As Mr G got closer to her, Georgie's reflex action was to sidestep and run to the door. She tried turning the handle in desperation but very quickly confirmed her suspicion that it was locked. Mr G looked furious as he approached her, and Georgie panicked by running straight towards him and lifting her knee as high as she could, reaching her target with good effect. The man doubled up and let out a loud yelp. Georgie immediately bolted to the bathroom, quickly pushed the door closed and leaned on it with all her might. Within a second, Mr G was shoving at the door with his superior strength causing Georgie's feet to slide backwards on the lino until she was trapped between the door and the wall, at which point he pushed even harder until Georgie couldn't breathe and was begging him to stop. Then, before she knew it, he had grabbed her left arm, almost lifted her from behind the door, and thrown her backwards on to the bedroom rug. She screwed up her eyes, waiting for the next blow to fall, but it didn't come, so she opened them just in time to see Mr G unlocking the door and exiting the room. Georgie let out a loud sigh of relief and, trying to ignore the discomfort in her stomach, pushed herself into a standing position and hobbled to the bed, where she carefully laid back until she was once again horizontal. At this point, her body started to shake uncontrollably as the adrenalin filtered away, and the tears again rose to her eyes. But she had no time to think further as she heard the door unlock again and Mr G approached with a syringe in his hand. She found herself unable to move as, having reached her, he held her down with the weight of his own body before painfully piercing her upper arm with the needle and emptying the contents of the syringe into her.

"Now see what you can do with the big H inside you,"

Georgie just caught Mr G's words before she felt her spirits rise and fly. She ignored her dry mouth, instead focussing on the heat that seemed to come from inside of her, making her feel warm and euphoric. Her hands and feet felt so heavy that she couldn't seem to move, but somehow, she didn't care. She felt the weight of a warm body on top of her and didn't mind when she was roughly undressed. She didn't resist when something warm and firm was pushed into her mouth as far back as it could go. She didn't feel a need to choke, even when she felt a warm spurt of liquid hit the back of her throat. All she continued to feel was euphoria – the rest was arbitrary. When she was lifted from the bed and placed on top of and astride a man's body, she seemed to know what was going on but didn't feel a need to fight it. Hands pulled her hard down until she felt as if she was splitting in two but with no associated pain. Up and down, up and down until she was eventually pushed roughly to the side, landing on the bed, her back slamming against the wall. Again, she felt no pain as a drowsiness enveloped her and she sank into the beckoning darkness.

It seemed like just a moment later that she became aware of the need to vomit. She leapt out of bed to land hard on the floor as her legs buckled beneath her. She knew she needed to get to the bathroom but somehow couldn't work out where it was. She rolled over and pushed with her hands and knees against the floor with all the strength she could muster. She began to crawl in the direction of an open door that she hoped would lead to the toilet where she could allow her body its need to expel her insides. Twice her arms and legs gave way before she finally reached her goal, leaned over the pan, and submitted to her body reflexes. Again and again she tried to catch her breath before the explosive expulsions regained their control. Eventually it stopped as quickly as it had started and Georgie sunk to the floor, perspiration covering her nakedness. She submitted to the exhaustion she felt in every part of her and stayed where she was.

Again, it seemed but a second later that she opened her eyes and immediately felt freezing cold. She tried to move her arms and legs until the stiffness and pain eased enough for her to crawl back to her bed where she collapsed under the covers and fell into unconsciousness.

When Georgie awoke, light was streaming in through the frosted glass window and making shadows on the floor. She judged it to be around

midday. She still felt a little drowsy and disorientated, but her all-consuming urge was to scrub her body clean of the hazy memories of her experiences – memories that were evidenced by her soreness and the blood on her bedsheets. Her mind was fuzzy, and she couldn't quite differentiate between whether she was back at the cottage after Gerald had raped her, or whether this was something new and separate. She looked down at her body to confirm that she was no longer a small child, and this was really happening to her for the second time in her life. The disbelief and shock of that realisation quickly brought on the tears again and she rubbed her sore and swollen eyes with the back of her hand as she looked up to the grubby ceiling.

'Why, God? Why me? If you're there, then please, please help me.'

The silence convinced Georgie that there was no God, but it didn't stop her venting her wrath at Him, as she aimed her silent screams back at the ceiling.

'How could you let this happen to me? What have I done to deserve this? I hate you, hate you!'

As Georgie's mind cleared little by little, she found herself able to get into the bathroom more easily, and eventually managed to run herself a bath. She found a nail brush on the edge of the bath next to an old, half-used bar of soap, and soaped and scrubbed herself until the bath water was cold and she was red and sore all over.

Mr G didn't visit Georgie's room again for another two days, which gave her time to recover and heal a little. Lavinia brought food in from time to time, always reminding Georgie that she wasn't going to make an 'abit of this. However, Georgie sensed that the woman had a kind heart beneath her gruff exterior and didn't doubt that she would continue to look after her youngest 'Girl' for as long as it was needed. By now, Georgie's clothes were becoming grubby and smelly, so she decided to bring up the subject the next time Lavinia came into her room.

"Lavinia, my clothes are in real need of a wash. Is there some way I can get them laundered?"

Lavinia's response was to scream with laughter, as Georgie looked on.

326

"Well, ain't you some sort of Miss Oity Toity?" she choked out between bouts of laughter. "This aint no 'otel, Girl, and I might be the Maid 'ere but I aint no maidservant to you or any of the other girls."

"I'm sorry Lavinia, I didn't mean for you to think I expected you to do it."

Lavinia laughed.

"I know, Girl, I know. Take no notice of my sense of 'umour. I'll tell you what, I'll ask the girls if anyone's got a dress they can borrow you so you can wash yours in the sink or bath and wear the borrowed one while it dries."

"Thank you, Lavinia. That is very kind of you."

"No need to thank me, Girl. Mr G will want to see you looking neat and clean when 'e arrives in the morning."

Lavinia's word's struck horror in Georgie's heart. Was he going to beat her again or inject her with that stuff that made her unable to think straight? She couldn't help but remember again the way the monster had treated her. The apprehension she felt now was even worse than she had felt then. She reflected on the fact that what he had done was not nearly as bad as what Mr G had inflicted upon her. The more she thought about it, the more tense she became.

A little later Lavinia returned to Georgie's room with a short, low necked and very fitted red dress, a black suspender belt and matching G-string, and some black fishnet stockings. She held them up to Georgie who was shocked to the core. Over her other arm was a white, towelling dressing gown.

"Now, Georgie, put this dressing gown on while you wash your clothes and put them over the back of the chair to dry. Then tomorrow morning, make sure you dress in this outfit ready for Mr G."

"But I don't want to wear stuff like that, Lavinia. They're so tarty – and I'm not a tart."

Lavinia's raucous laughter seemed to make the room vibrate, so much so that Georgie grabbed hold of the edge of the bed to steady herself.

327

"Look Miss La-di-da, there's one thing you can be sure of – a tart is definitely what you are."

Still laughing, Lavinia left the room, leaving Georgie to her thoughts. Georgie spent the night considering her options. Was she going to dig her heels in and refuse to cooperate? That would probably mean another beating and another syringe-full of what she had decided must be some sort of drug. She didn't want that, especially if Mr G took the opportunity to rape her again. She was still sore from the previous events. Could she try to escape? With the door locked and, she discovered, the window screwed shut, there was little chance of that option being successful. But what else could she do? After a lot of thought, Georgie decided that her only option was to cooperate with Mr G and to go along with his wishes for her to 'entertain the punters and address their preferences' until he and Lavinia trusted her, at which point she would try to plan her escape.

'I'm going to be a prostitute,' she kept telling herself over and over with disbelief as she washed her clothes and hung them over the chair and the edge of the bath to dry.

Next morning, Georgie dressed in the red tarty outfit, put the dressing gown over the top, and brushed her hair with a hairbrush that Lavinia lent her. When Mr G unlocked the door and came in, he looked pleased.

"Ah I see you've decided to cooperate, Young Georgie. Was the practice run with me more enjoyable than you thought?"

Georgie recoiled at his words but managed to hide her distain and control her facial expression so that, although she didn't respond to his question, she smiled sweetly at the man.

"Right then, come with me and I'll get you started at learning the routine."

Georgie followed Mr G and he led her out of her 'prison cell' and into the lounge next door.

Lavinia and the other girls looked up and smiled as she entered the room. Georgie smiled back using her acting ability to its full.

"Right, Girls," Mr G addressed to the room, "this is Georgie. I know you'll all look after her and show her the ropes."

All the girls nodded warmly.

"Now, Georgie, you do exactly what Lavinia tells you and what I showed you. I know that you are going to be very popular and will earn lots of money, but remember three-quarters of what you earn goes to Lavinia for food and overheads, and you keep the other quarter yourself," said Mr G. "I'll be popping in regularly to check how you're doing."

Georgie thought that at least if she was making money, she could get out of the place sooner. She'd just have to learn to close off her mind whilst doing her 'work.' But her days turned out to be even more harrowing than she'd imagined. No matter how kind or good-looking each customer was, the services they asked for both humiliated and nauseated her. The oral sex caused her to retch, just as it had when the monster had forced her to do it when she was a small child. Now she had to find a way of keeping her reflex actions in control. She tried to focus on the few happy memories she had, but this proved to be impossible, and she discovered that the only thing that helped was for her to zone out of her thoughts and feelings as if she no longer inhabited her body. She did the same when the customers were penetrating her, which still hurt her badly despite the lubricant that Lavinia had supplied, and she'd used liberally. But the worst thing of all was the sweaty aroma from the customers whose hygiene habits were not good. That with the distinctive smell of their bodily fluids was what finally caused Georgie to admit defeat and speak to the other girls.

The girls were supportive and tried to give her advice. One of them, Cassie, showed Georgie some small plastic bags with a white powder inside.

"If you sniff up one of these regular, it'll 'elp you to cope. That's what the rest of us do, don't we girls?"

The other girls nodded, but as Georgie looked into their eyes, they looked blank and dead. Georgie knew that she couldn't allow herself to blank out completely if she was going to plan her escape. Anyway, she didn't think she could cope with sniffing powder up her nose. She'd just have to find some other way of coping.

"Thanks anyway, Cassie, but I really want to avoid taking anything," said Georgie.

"Yeah. Can't blame you. You get so you can't do without it in the end. Trouble is there ain't much else we can get 'old of. Mr G gets this for us but we 'ave to pay for it extra out our earnings."

This made Georgie even more determined to get out of the place quickly, and the only way to do this was to entertain as many punters as possible. She knew she was being watched far too closely to even chance trying to escape, and anyway, the thought of another beating put her completely off the idea. She was in a catch twenty-two situation, and she knew it.

Things got even worse when Lavinia gave Georgie her earnings at the end of two weeks. Georgie had been counting her customers so had been able to calculate a quarter of what they paid Lavinia. When she opened the white envelope that Lavinia gave her, she found substantially less than she'd been expecting.

"Lavinia, you haven't given me enough?"

"How's that then, Georgie?"

"There's only a couple of pounds in here – nowhere near a quarter of my earnings."

"Ah but 'ave you taken into account your rent and your repayments for your outfits?"

"Oh, yes I forgot the rent, but nobody told me about having to buy my own outfits. I'm never going to have any money of my own at this rate."

"Oh, I must 'ave forgot to tell you about the clothes, Girl. Sorry about that."

Georgie was devastated. How would she ever earn enough money to be able to escape this place and find a place of her own so she could get back into the theatre and start working towards her goal of becoming a dancer?

CHAPTER 33

April 1960 – December 1962

A little more trust

Each day for the next two years Georgie woke up exhausted from the couple of hours sleep she'd managed to grab between customers. After so long, she had managed to harden herself into coping with her new alien lifestyle. Mr G had been right. She was the most popular girl in the brothel, which meant she brought in more money than any of the others. But however much she earned each week, most of it disappeared before she even got her hands on it. Lavinia would always find some reason for taking extra from her earnings on top of the rent, new costumes, laundry costs, food, cleaning of her room ... and so on and on it went. Georgie saved every penny but even after two years, the amount was still pitiful – nowhere near sufficient to get far enough away from the place and pay the rent on wherever she would live. She was now exhausted and felt hopeless but resigned to the fact that she was, in effect, a prisoner. At first, she had wondered why Rosie or Terry hadn't tried to find her, but eventually she realised that neither of them knew where she was. She sensed that Rosie had known more about Terry's lifestyle than she had let on. She kept remembering the little shake of Rosie's head when Terry had offered to take her to a place where she might get a room. There hadn't been a chance at the time to question her about it, but Georgie

wished with all her heart that there had been. She'd also wondered why Terry had introduced her to Mr G in the first place when she must have known what he was up to. Georgie concluded that it was maybe to get on his good side, since Terry was clearly a prostitute at the other brothel in Lichfield Road and would have been unable to get out of it for financial reasons, even if she, too, had wanted to.

After the first six months in the brothel, Georgie had accepted the girls' offers to get cocaine to help her through but had managed to keep her intake to a minimum by only taking it when she was desperate. The purchase of the cocaine, however, meant that her savings grew even more slowly, and now she sometimes displayed the same haunted look as the other prostitutes. She had lost weight and her once good figure had all but disappeared, making her almost flat chested. To her surprise, this did not seem to turn off the men that frequented the place. On the contrary it seemed to make her even more popular as if the men preferred to imagine that they were raping a little girl. In fact, although they did not know it, that's exactly what Georgie still was, a child of fifteen being forced to act like a grown woman.

One evening in March 1962, almost exactly two years after Georgie had first been trapped into prostitution, she came out of her room to find two strangers in the lounge, chatting to Lavinia. As Georgie was preparing herself a snack, Lavinia clapped her hands to gain everyone's attention.

"Girls, Girls, quieten down now and listen. These two nice ladies 'ave come from the church to bring us some biscuits and cakes. They're going to be coming regularly so you just make them welcome, you 'ear me? And in case you're wondering, the Rozzers spoke to Mr G about it, an 'e agreed cos they was only wanting to make sure you girls was okay, so it's all above board. The ladies just want to be friendly. They won't be staying very long each time they come, and they'll leave the room when we're doing business, so nothing much will change."

The several girls in the room nodded and moved along the sofa to make room for the lady carrying the large paper bag. The other lady stayed near to Lavinia, chatting away happily with her as if to distract her. Georgie watched warily as she returned to the sofa and took up the space that the girls had made, watching as the woman opened her paper bag and offered cakes around to all the girls. Georgie looked in the bag and saw iced Bakewell Tarts. Her mouth watered. She couldn't remember the last time she'd had a cake, so she dipped her hand in and

helped herself, thanking the lady who handed it to her. The lady perched on the arm of the sofa next to Georgie and held out her free hand.

"Hi, I'm Beverly. Pleased to meet you."

It took Georgie a few seconds to realise that Beverly's outstretched hand was waiting to shake hands with her, a prostitute. Respect wasn't something that Georgie was used to, which made her feel cautious, but after a few seconds, she returned Beverly's handshake and smiled.

"I'm Georgie. Pleased to meet you, Beverly."

"May I sit next to you, Georgie," asked the smiling woman, who Georgie put in her thirties. She was wearing blue jeans and a longish navy jumper under a padded black quilted jacket.

"Oh, yes of course," Georgie replied as she turned to the girls next to her.

"Shove up a bit you lot."

The girls obliged and continued chatting between themselves, while Georgie looked back at Beverly to see what she had to say. At that moment the doorbell rang, and Lavinia rushed to the door, reappearing a few moments later with a customer by her side. She immediately approached Beverly and her colleague and asked them to wait in an empty room down the hall. She clapped to gain the girls' attention again and asked them to get in line in front of the man. Georgie slipped off her dressing gown and moved over to stand in line with her workmates. As was often the case, the man chose her, so she returned to her bedroom. She knew that back in the lounge the man would be passing several ten-pound notes to Lavinia who would quickly pocket them before she accompanied him to Georgie's room. When Lavinia showed him into her room, she informed Georgie that he had paid for more than the usual twenty minutes so, by the time he left, and she returned to the lounge, Beverly and her colleague had gone. Georgie thought nothing more about them until the following week when they both appeared again. Beverly came straight over to the sofa with her bag of cakes. This time she placed the bag on the coffee table just in front of the sofa. Beverly looked at the girls and suggested they help themselves, getting cursory nods in response. She then walked over to Georgie and sat on the arm of the sofa next to her.

"No cake this week, Georgie?"

"Oh, yes. Sorry Beverly, but I'm really tired."

Beverly rose from the sofa, removed a cake from the bag, and brought it over to Georgie, sitting next to her as she held it out. It was an iced Bakewell again, with a bright red glace cherry on the top.

"I believe you like these," she said.

Georgie took the cake and smiled wearily. The gesture had touched her heart and she looked into Beverly's bright eyes and thanked her.

"So, how are you?" whispered Beverly, attempting to provide some privacy in the busy room.

Georgie looked over at where Beverly's friend was sitting deeply engaged in her conversation with Lavinia.

"Oh, I'm coping," returned Georgie also in a whisper.

"Do you like living here?"

"Not really, but I have no choice."

"Well, if you ever need anything, Georgie, you only have to ask."

Georgie studied Beverly's face and saw only warmth and sincerity in her eyes.

"Thank you, Beverly," she replied, her heart warming towards this almost stranger.

Beverly didn't attempt to engage Georgie in conversation after that, but instead spent the next fifteen minutes trying to engage some of the other girls in small talk with little success. Georgie decided to return to her room to try to get some sleep before she was called again. During the time she'd been at the brothel, she had made some regular customers, who in their own way were kind and friendly towards her. These men often asked her what she was doing in a place like this, telling her that prostitution was not a good occupation for such a young woman, and she was worth more than this. Georgie always thanked them but wondered

if they had any perception of her real situation and how difficult it was to escape this 'prison' once you found yourself in it. She thought about the deep psychological fear within her that prevented her even trying to escape – the fear that if caught, she would most likely be punished by Mr G. It made her tremble to remember how he'd behaved towards her when she was first brought to the brothel. Not only that, but she'd grown to despise herself. In her mind she was dirty, disgusting, and worthless. Nobody would want to associate with her even if she got out of here. Nobody would want her to rent a room in their house. She wasn't worthy – not that she had enough money to pay a regular rent anyway, thanks to Lavinia keeping her so short of money. She didn't think she could bear to see people turning their noses up at her when they realised what she was – and they definitely would realise. After all, before this even happened, Georgie herself had noticed something different and not quite respectable about Terry, even though at the time she had not known that the girl was a prostitute. No, she knew for sure she'd not be able to cope in the outside world full of respectable people. Why was she thinking about it anyway? She didn't even know where exactly she was, other than somewhere in London. Then there was Lavinia. Georgie had realised a long time ago that it was Lavinia's job to watch her on behalf of Mr G. As far as he was concerned, Georgie was a goldmine, a very valuable income stream, and if Lavinia was so remiss as to let her escape, then doubtless she'd be in for punishment the Mr G way.

'Hmmm. Maybe a girl like me is too good for a place like this, but there's no way I can think of to change it. There's no two ways about it, I'm stuck here for good.'

So, nothing changed. Georgie continued to be a prostitute, and Beverly and her friend visited every week regularly. The summer passed, and Georgie and Beverly gradually got to know each other better. By the end of September, Georgie was feeling worse than ever. She longed for fresh air and freedom rather than her stuffy room with the window screwed shut, and the almost continuous queue of customers. In her down time, she lay dreaming of her old life in Ousby with her mother, sister, and brother. She missed them so badly, despite her mother's rejection. She often thought of Daisy, hoping and praying that the monster hadn't touched her. Deep down she hung on to the hope that one day there might be a reconciliation. She had no idea how that could happen whilst the monster was still there, but it didn't stop her daydreaming. She had even grown to regret having ever reporting him to the police in the first

place. What she'd had to put up with from him was nothing compared to her current life.

Then one evening an unexpected opportunity presented itself to Georgie. She was sitting chatting with Beverly on one of her regular weekly visits, when Beverly looked over at Lavinia to make sure she was preoccupied, before lowering her voice to even more of a whisper than usual.

"Georgie, would you like to come out for a coffee with me?" she whispered.

"Oh, how I'd love that," Georgie whispered back, "but I'm not allowed out, Beverly."

"Maybe you could convince Lavinia that you are desperate for some fresh air after so long indoors, and couldn't she allow you out for a walk with one of the other girls that doesn't live-in. She seems to have a good heart beneath all of that controlling behaviour."

"Yes, she does," confirmed Georgie. "She was the one who looked after me when I was first brought here."

"Well, why don't you just start working on Lavinia. From what I see, she does seem to like you, so you never know.'

So that's what Georgie did, day after day for three weeks before Lavinia started to relent. Beverly continued her weekly visits, acting normally but just raising her eyebrows questioningly to ask how Georgie's attempts at being allowed out were going.

"I must admit you do look peaky just lately. A bit of fresh air might put the roses back in your cheeks and attract more punters," Lavinia finally admitted. "I'll 'ave a word with Mr G."

At the sound of Mr G's name, Georgie's stomach screwed into a ball.

'That'll be the end of that then,' she thought.

But to Georgie's amazement, she was wrong. A few weeks later, Lavinia called her over.

"I know you're going be pleased with what I'm going to tell you, Georgie. Mr G 'as finally agreed. You're allowed out for 'alf an hour's walk each day with our most long serving girl, Cherry. But if you once betray 'is trust, that'll not only be an end of it, but you'll drop me well in it, too. That means no talking to anyone other than Cherry while you're out, and not going further than this road. Got that?"

Georgie threw her arms around Lavinia's neck and hugged her tightly. When she moved away, Lavinia looked very taken aback and yet Georgie noticed the woman's eyes were wet. Georgie would never want to put Lavinia at risk from that nasty Mr G, so, of course, she would keep to the rules.

"When can we start, Lavinia? Oh, I just can't wait to take in a big breath of fresh air."

Lavinia smiled.

"I've 'ad a word with Cherry. You start this afternoon as long as Cherry ain't busy. But remember, Georgie, Mr G pays me and me alone to monitor what goes on 'ere. E's too busy to concern 'imself with you or any of the other girls. That's my job, an I'll 'ave to take the can back if you let me down."

Georgie nodded compliantly.

After that, the morning seemed to go very slowly, even though Georgie was busy with customers for most of it. Around three, Cherry approached Georgie. She was already wearing a coat.

"Are you ready, Georgie?"

"Yes, I found my old coat in the wardrobe so let's go. And thanks so much for this, Cherry."

Cherry smiled and nodded as they walked down the hallway to the front door, which Cherry opened with her own key before she led Georgie out. The first thing Georgie noticed was the brightness. It took a few minutes of screwing up and rubbing her watering eyes before she got used to it. She followed Cherry up the iron steps and out of the gate. By the time she stepped on to the pavement, Georgie felt a little disorientated and had to hang on to the wrought iron fence while she took a few deep

breaths. She looked to her left and right. The road wasn't a very long one as she could see both ends from where she stood. It was lined with the same off-white three storey houses as the one whose basement she'd been living in for the last two years or more.

"Come on, Georgie. We've only got 'alf an 'our," encouraged Cherry.

So, off the two women went walking side by side and chatting as they walked. Georgie had never really chatted with Cherry before, but she found the woman to be quite open as she told Georgie all about her family. This surprised the younger girl as she couldn't believe how a husband could cope with his wife entertaining other men. But it seemed Cherry's husband was happy with the arrangement as it allowed the family to live in a decent house with a garden for their two children out in the suburbs.

"To tell you the truth, Georgie, it spices up our love-life big time. So, it's win, win all round."

At the end of the road, Georgie and Cherry crossed over and walked back towards the brothel on the opposite pavement. Cherry had a watch on her wrist, which she checked as the brothel came into view.

"I reckon if we walk quick, we can get to the other end of the road and back within the 'alf hour."

So, they both quickened their step and walked the remaining distance in silence, returning to the brothel gate exactly on the half hour. As they entered the lounge, Lavinia looked up and smiled.

"Well done, Girls. 'Ow was your walk?"

"Lovely," exclaimed Georgie. "Thank you so much, Lavinia. The fresh air has made me feel so much better."

"Not sure you could ever call the London air fresh, Girl, but I must admit, you do look better for it."

From then on, most days Georgie got her half hour walk. On occasions, Cherry was chosen by a punter, so it had to be cancelled. Other times it was Georgie that was occupied. Georgie managed to inform Beverly on

338

her weekly visit how things were going, and Beverly kept reassuring Georgie and encouraging her to be patient.

By Christmas time, everyone accepted that whenever possible, the now sixteen-year-old Georgie and Cherry would have their daily walk. Both Lavinia, and presumably Mr G, who Lavinia would report back to on his weekly visit to pick up his money, were beginning to trust her because of her having returned exactly on time every day without abusing the arrangement in any way.

When Beverly turned up for a visit a few days before Christmas, she came laden with minced pies and mulled wine, which Lavinia agreed to warm up in a saucepan on the stove while chatting to Beverly's friend. Even Lavinia had started to look forward to the weekly visit from the church ladies, so everyone felt relaxed as they sipped their warm wine and ate their mince pies. One of the prostitutes had brought in a portable radio from home and found a music station, which she had turned up loud to add to the festive spirit. Amidst all that was going on, Beverly sat down next to Georgie and whispered to her whilst trying to keep a smile on her face as if they were enjoying small talk.

"Georgie, do you reckon Lavinia would trust you enough now to come out with me for a coffee?"

"Well, there's no time like the present to ask her," replied Georgie, "especially as she's looking so relaxed right now."

Georgie rose from her seat and approached Lavinia who was clearly laughing at some sort of joke that one of the other girls had cracked.

"Lavinia, Beverly has just asked me if I would be able to go out for a coffee with her some time. Would that be alright, please?"

"Yeah, why not. You've proved I can trust you. Tell 'er it would 'av to be during the day and then only if you weren't busy."

Georgie couldn't believe her ears. As she thanked Lavinia profusely and returned to tell Beverly the news, her thoughts even dared to wander towards the possibility of escape, although she immediately put that thought aside, knowing that until she had somewhere to escape to, and the money to finance it, she would remain stuck in this place.

339

When Georgie told Beverly what Lavinia had said, Georgie was surprised at the intensity of the girl's reaction. She was so excited for Georgie that she grabbed both of Georgie's hands and squeezed them.

"I reckon 1963 is going to be a good year for you, Georgie."

CHAPTER 34

January – End of July 1963

A Good Plan

"Just off for a coffee with Beverly, Lavinia," called Georgie as she poked her head round the lounge door. It was a week into the new year and Georgie was excited about her first outing without Cherry accompanying her. Lavinia nodded and carried on with what she was doing as Georgie made her way down the dingy hallway, unlocked the front door with the key Lavinia had lent her, and made her way outside, locking the door behind her before she climbed the iron steps to the pavement. Beverly was already there waiting for her, so they made their way down to the end of the road and turned left into the main road, where there was a Lyons Corner House on the opposite side. They crossed over, went inside, and found themselves a table for two. Georgie had never been inside such a smart café. Beverly saw her looking around in amazement and explained that the smartly dressed waitresses wearing black dresses with starched white collars, white caps, and pointed white aprons were affectionately known as Nippies because of the efficient way they nipped around the tables serving the customers. After just a couple of minutes, a Nippy approached their table to take their order, and Beverly asked for two white coffees and two iced bakewells. Five minutes later, they were nibbling their cakes and sipping the delicious

coffee, enjoying the fact that, away from the brothel, they had no need to filter what they talked about.

"So, Georgie, tell me more about yourself. Where do you come from?" asked Beverly

"I come from Cumberland – a little village called Ousby, not far from Penrith."

"Goodness that's a long way away. Whatever brought you down to London at such a young age?"

That was all the opening that Georgie needed. She trusted Beverly and found herself offloading her whole story. Beverly sat listening intently, showing interest but no expression of shock when Georgie explained what the monster had done to her. Georgie just got to the bit where she arrived at Euston Station when Beverly looked at her watch.

"It's time we made our way back to the house. I'll hear about what happened when you arrived in London next week, Georgie. Just to say I think you must be a very strong young lady to have coped as you have, and I feel very honoured that you have trusted me enough to be so open."

Georgie smiled and flushed with embarrassment but followed Beverly out of the café and crossed back over the main road to return to the brothel. As they parted five minutes later, Beverly asked,
"Same time next week?"

Georgie nodded enthusiastically as she waved her friend goodbye.

That was the first of many trips to the Lyons Corner House with Beverly. Most of Georgie's customers were now regulars so she found it easy to arrange her days to ensure she was free at the same time each week for her outing. She no longer had to inform Lavinia of when she was going out or coming back. It seemed she was completely trusted to return – maybe because Lavinia kept her so short of money and knew that she couldn't afford to rent a room anywhere else in London.

Now that Georgie felt free to come and go as she wished, she often just went for a walk in her downtime rather than sitting in the lounge chatting or laying on her bed resting. But she always came back after about half an hour, and always felt better for the fresh air. She realised that, in a

way, she had become institutionalised, but what drove her to always return was the knowledge that if she didn't come back, she would open Lavinia to the wrath of Mr G, and in her own way she had become fond of Lavinia and wouldn't wish her any harm.

Soon the spring came, and Georgie enjoyed seeing the spring flowers growing in the several window boxes along the street, especially when she was meeting Beverly at Lyons Corner House. Georgie had told Beverly all there was to know about her background, and she had also spent lots of time questioning her friend. Then at one of their meetings in early July, Georgie asked Beverly how she started going to church.

"I started going to church when I got married. My husband was already a church goer and had grown up in a Christian family that attended a Baptist Church. Naturally I started attending with him. As time went on, I realised that God gave His only Son, Jesus, to die on a cross to save everyone from their sins. I started to pray and then one day there was a baptismal service at church. One of my girlfriends had decided to be baptised to show she was giving her life to God. When people are baptised in a Baptist Church, the Minister puts them right under the water. When my friend came back up out of the water, she looked like her face was shining and she had such an amazing smile, the like of which I'd never seen. I felt like I could see God's love shining from her and it really touched my heart. As a result of that, I decided I wanted to give my life to God, too. So eventually I was baptised and have been working for God ever since by visiting brothels and trying to make sure the girls recognised that there were people around who accepted them and loved and cared about them, despite what they were doing and how they looked upon themselves."

Beverly's story touched Georgie's heart, and tears began to prick her eyes. Beverly looked at her intently before she spoke.

"Georgie, do you want to get out of the brothel and prostitution?"

The pricking in Georgie's eyes got worse.

"Oh, Beverly, I want to get out more than you could ever know. I have never wanted to be there. It's just that I've got nowhere to go and not enough money to live independently, so I have no choice but to stay."

"Maybe I could help you," said Beverly tentatively.

Georgie's stomach leapt and her excitement began to bubble up.

"Would you? Would you really help me – even though I'm only a cheap and worthless prostitute? Is that the real reason why you visit the brothel to give the girls an escape route, or is it just me?"

"Georgie, never think you're worthless. Jesus died for you as much as he did for me. He loves you. You are his child, and He is your Heavenly Father. And no, helping the girls escape is not my primary role. It's as I told you – so they know they are loved and cared about. But if that is what any one of them said they wanted, then yes, I'd do my best to help them, just as I will help you."

Georgie was taken aback for a second, but then picked up on what Beverly said about God being her Heavenly Father.

"Don't talk to me about fathers. My father walked out on me and my mother when I was a very small child. Then my stepfather abused me. As far as I'm concerned, fathers can't be trusted."

"I can understand why you feel that way, Georgie, but the difference is that nobody's earthly father is perfect, whereas our Heavenly Father is."

"Hmmm," was all Georgie said before she changed the subject back to her possible escape from the brothel.

"Anyway, you were saying you thought you could help me get away. How on earth could you manage that?"

"If I could find a way of getting you back to Penrith, would that be of any help?"

"Sure would, but do you know how expensive train tickets are these days? When I first came down here four years ago my ticket cost three pounds and two shillings and it's bound to have gone up over the last four years. I'll need every penny I've managed to save and more to exist on my own. I just couldn't afford a train ticket on top of that."

"Leave it with me, Georgie," said Beverly. "I'll have a think and we can discuss it again."

Georgie returned to the brothel feeling quite let down. For a minute there she thought that Beverly was going to have some sort of miracle

plan for her escape, but clearly it wasn't to be. For the rest of the week, the thought of freedom kept going round and round in Georgie's mind.

'Oh, why did Beverly have to raise my hopes only to dash them again almost immediately?' Georgie thought.

By the time their next coffee date came around, Georgie was feeling low and was in two minds whether to give their meeting a miss. She finally decided that she couldn't live with herself if she let Beverly down after all the kindness her friend had shown her. The sky was cloudy with a few spots of rain when Georgie pushed the door of Lyons Corner House open. She had dawdled a bit on the way there and so, unusually for her, was a little late. Beverly's face brightened up as soon as she saw Georgie come in, and she waved to catch her attention.

"Hi Georgie. It's unusual for you to be late. I was beginning to wonder if you were okay."

As Georgie sat opposite Beverly at the table, she tried to smile but found it difficult.

"Georgie, what's wrong? You look so serious."

"I'm fine, Beverly, just a little tired," Georgie lied.

"Well, in that case I've got something for you that I think will cheer you up. Close your eyes and hold your hands open under the table."

Georgie was curious so she did as she was asked and felt Beverly place something in her upward turned palms. It felt flat and light.

"Don't lift it above the table, Georgie. Just put it on your lap and look down at it. I don't want anyone to see what I've given you."

With furrowed brow, Georgie looked into her lap and saw that Beverly had handed her a train ticket to Penrith. Her expression immediately turned to one of surprise and amazement.

"No, don't look amazed. Someone might see you. We can't be too careful. If I was ever suspected of helping you in any way, I wouldn't be allowed to continue visiting the brothel," Beverly whispered.

Georgie was lost for words at Beverly's generosity, so much so that she had to take a few sips of coffee before she could say anything.

"I don't know what to say. I'm just so very touched and grateful beyond measure, Beverly. Thank you. Thank you so much. I truly didn't think this would happen. Did you pay for this yourself?"

"With the help of some of my Christian friends."

Georgie's eyes filled up and her voice broke. She realised she had triggered Beverly and watched her friend as she coughed and regained her composure until she could speak.

"You have to use the ticket within the next few weeks, Georgie. Do you think that will be possible? Also, when you've decided on the date, I have a friend with a car who would be willing to bring me to wherever you think would be a safe place to pick you up so that we can take you to Euston Station and see you off."

Georgie was now too choked to say anything coherent, so she just nodded and leaned over to squeeze Beverly's hand.

"So how about we meet once more for coffee next week so we can finalize the date and time?" Beverly suggested.

Again, Georgie nodded, her tears now starting to spill over. Both women sat silently for the next few minutes, finishing their coffee, and regaining their composure. Neither finished their iced bakewell.

Georgie's week of planning was torturous. She couldn't let Lavinia or any of the girls see how preoccupied she was in case they began to wonder what was going on. Entertaining each client felt like she was picking at an open wound, knowing that at last, this would all be coming to an end. She had to try to forward plan to choose the best date and time for her escape so that there would be a reasonable lapse of time between her leaving and Lavinia discovering she was missing. She needed a clear mind, so she tried to keep the cocaine to a minimum even though she felt like she needed more help - not less. When she met Beverly a week later, Georgie was feeling truly exhausted.

"Oh, Georgie, you look all in. Has it been a difficult week?"

"Yes, I must admit that it felt very tense and was made worse, knowing that I was going to escape the continuous sexual activity, so with every customer the experience felt more like rape than a service I was providing. I swear I'll never let another man get near me once I'm away from all this."

Genuine sympathy showed on Beverly's face as she commiserated with Georgie over something she had never experienced. She had told Georgie that her husband was her first sexual partner and he had always been gentle, loving and understanding. She'd said that she couldn't conceive of how it must feel to be continuously sexually abused in whatever guise it happened. After a short while, Georgie changed to a more positive subject.

"I've decided on the date and time. My thinking is that it should be just before your normal visit to the brothel. It would help to take the suspicion off you if, rather than waiting to see me off, you leave me at the station and then go straight to the brothel. The evenings will still be light, so I could pretend to take a walk but meet you and your driver friend instead. That way, by the time Lavinia realises I've not returned, she won't connect you with my escape. What do you think?"

"That's a brilliant plan. But how will you smuggle your belongings out without Lavinia and the girls noticing?"

"Oh, don't worry about that. Everything I own and would want to take with me, I will either be wearing or will fit in my handbag. I definitely won't ever have need of those costumes in my new life, I can tell you. Back to the flannelette underwear for me, Beverly," said Georgie giggling.

"It's good to see you've not lost your sense of humour, Georgie, even though you are feeling so tired," said Beverly also giggling.

"I'll tell you what, Beverly, I'll be pulling my drawers up so high that they'll be under my armpits with shoulder straps to prevent anyone ever pulling them down again."

With this, both girls burst out laughing again, which was an effective therapy to ease the tension of the occasion.

"So, what's your chosen date then, Georgie," asked Beverly, this time in a whisper.

"What is the date of your next visit?"

"This coming Thursday evening at seven o'clock."

"Then that's my chosen date. I'll leave the brothel at six thirty and meet you outside this café by six thirty-five. Will that give you enough time to drop me at the station and get back to the brothel by seven?"

"Yes, I reckon that'll work. I think there's a train to Penrith at around seven, so you won't have to hang about waiting. So, six thirty-five outside here on Thursday evening then. Let's drink to it," said Beverly.

They both raised their coffees and grinned conspiratorially as they clinked their cups.

CHAPTER 35

End of July 1963

The Great Escape

Sixteen-and-a-half-year-old Georgie was trembling as she walked out of the brothel for the last time. She'd left her coat behind because it would have raised suspicion if she had worn it on a warm July evening, but her handbag was carefully filled so that she had the toiletries she needed and a few other small items. She was wearing six pairs of knickers and both bras she owned, plus two dresses and a short jacket that she'd acquired over the past couple of years. Tucked into her handbag was also the precious train ticket that would take her to freedom, and twenty pounds she had managed to save from her earnings. As she walked up the road towards Lyons Corner House, not only did she feel warmer and warmer due to her layers of clothing, but her trembling didn't lessen. It was joined by what felt like a hundred butterflies having a flying contest in her stomach. She increased her pace so she would reach her destination sooner and could cool down a bit while waiting for Beverly and her friend to arrive. In fact, she had less than a minute to cool down before she saw a car stop at the curb and Beverly beckoning her out of the car window. Georgie rushed across the pavement, pulled the back door open and slid into the back seat.

"You look a bit flushed, Georgie, are you okay," said Beverly with concern in her voice.

"I'm fine, thanks, Beverly. It's the layers of clothing I'm wearing and the swift walk up the road on a warm night."

The car moved back out into the traffic as Beverly introduced Georgie to the driver.

"Georgie, meet Peter. Peter this is Georgie."

"Hi Georgie. Pleased to meet you. Forgive me if I don't talk much but I need to concentrate on where I'm going. Euston station, isn't it?"

"Pleased to meet you, too, Peter, and thank you so much for the lift. Yes, it's Euston Station but I haven't got a clue how to get there so can't be of any help to you finding the way."

"Oh, don't worry about that, I've been studying the road map so hopefully I'll get you there as long as I don't miss the road names," replied Peter chirpily.

"How are you feeling?" Beverly enquired of Georgie.

"Nervous but really excited. I only hope that I'm not leaving you at risk of being blamed for my escape. I couldn't live with myself if that happened."

"Oh, don't worry about that. I'm sure it will work out fine. You remembered to bring the train ticket?"

"Yes, it's in my handbag."

"And the money you've saved?"

"Yes, that's in my handbag too, as is my toothbrush and toothpaste and various other bits and pieces I'll need."

Beverly handed Georgie a small piece of paper.

"Here is one more thing to add to your handbag. It's my address. I would really love to hear from you when you reach Penrith."

"Oh, thank you, Beverly. I hope we can keep in touch in the future. I will write as soon as I have an address of my own so you can write back. I owe you so much. Who knows what my life would have been like if I'd had to stay at the brothel any longer? Unbearable, I think. You are definitely my hero and my saviour."

"Well, talking about Saviour, I've written a verse from the Bible on the back. I hope it will help you in the future."

At that point, Peter drove under the archway into Euston Station forecourt and pulled up in front of the station entrance. Beverly jumped out of the car and opened the back door for Georgie. Both girls were in tears as they hugged goodbye before Beverly jumped back in the car and it pulled away and disappeared out of the forecourt and into the traffic. Georgie stood waving even after the car disappeared.

A few minutes later, having put Beverly's piece of paper in her handbag, she was back in the big entrance hall. She immediately recalled the last time she was here almost four years ago and reflected on all the awful things that had happened since she arrived. She looked at the list of departure times for the trains and found the platform for the Penrith train, which was already waiting with many of its doors open. She chose a carriage and heaved herself up the couple of steps into a second-class compartment where she dropped down into an empty seat and let out a huge sigh. 'So far, so good,' she told herself but continued to take a few deep breaths to calm her trembling hands and the hyperactive butterflies. According to the big clock on the platform, she had ten minutes until the departure time, and it felt like the longest ten minutes of her life. When the train finally started to move and increase its speed as it passed the end of the platform, Georgie breathed out. Her whole body began to relax until the reality struck home and a broad smile formed on her previously tense face.

'I've done it. I've escaped. I'm going home to Cumberland.'

Georgie wouldn't allow herself to think of Ousby and the white cottage with the slate roof and wooden gate at the end of Half Mile Lane, or the times she had spent with Robert and Pattie in the village store. She would only think as far as Penrith with its Police Station where Sergeant Carter and PC Sandy Bell had worked, and how they had protected her when she'd first reported the monster. As Georgie fell into a peaceful sleep, she found herself in the sunny garden of her lovely foster carer,

351

Val and Val's family. She was splashing in the paddling pool with the children, laughing and feeling loved and safe. In her dream, she was joined by Daisy and the garden became the one at the children's home, Geltsdale, where she and her sister had been made to feel so welcome and secure.

Georgie didn't know what woke her up or how long she had slept, but when she opened her eyes, it was dark outside. She hoped she hadn't been asleep for so long that she'd missed Penrith Station, so she was relieved when a uniformed young man made his way through the carriage pushing a trolley with drinks and snacks on it. As he paused next to Georgie, she took the opportunity to ask how long it would be before they arrived at Penrith.

"You've got half an hour yet, Miss, plenty of time for a snack. Is there anything I can get you?"

Georgie realised she was starving. She'd not eaten since lunch time, so she chose a cheese sandwich and a cup of tea and paid the man out of her twenty pounds savings. As she sat munching her sandwich and sipping her tea, she realised that she felt light and hopeful for the first time in so long that it sent a frisson of excitement through her, and she found herself wanting to bounce up and down as she had when she was a little girl. The feeling didn't leave her till the train pulled into Penrith Station and she saw the station clock showing that it was one o'clock in the morning. It was then that the severity of her situation suddenly dawned on Georgie. Here she was after three and a half years away, arriving at Penrith in the early hours of the morning with nowhere to stay and nobody to turn to. As she alighted from the train and exited the platform and deserted entrance hall, she was pleased that it was a relatively warm July night, and compared to London and the brothel, she was free and safe. She felt wide awake, having slept for most of the six-hour train journey, so she decided to walk around for a while to get herself re-acclimatised to the place before she thought about her next step. After an hour, Georgie came to a wooden bench. She looked around, getting the feeling of déjà vu, before she realised that it was the very bench on which, as a six-year-old, she had fallen asleep after her long walk from Ousby to report the monster, and where Sergeant Carter had found her and carried her to the Police Station. She sat down, smiling inwardly at the thought of how many years ago that had been, when she was suddenly interrupted from her reverie by a man's voice.

"Now, young lady, what are you doing sitting here alone in the middle of the night?"

Georgie looked up at the uniformed man whose voice slowly dwindled to be replaced by a look of confused surprise.

"Yes, it's me, Georgie, Sergeant Carter."

"Georgie? No, you can't be little Georgie. You're all grown up."

Georgie couldn't help herself. She jumped up from the bench and threw her arms around Sergeant Carter's neck.

"Oh, it's so good to see you. I've never been so pleased to see anyone in my life," she exclaimed.

Sergeant Carter seemed dumbstruck for a few seconds as Georgie freed him and stood back.

"Where have you been? I discovered you had disappeared when I went to visit your mum to check how things were going. She didn't seem to know or care where you were, so I went into the corner shop to speak to Robert and Pattie. It was then that I discovered Pattie had died, and Robert told me you'd gone to find your father. I just hoped you'd found him and were safe."

Georgie sat back down on the bench, slumping a little at the memory of her last meeting with Alfie, whose final rejection had triggered her train journey to London and all that had happened since. She realised that Sergeant Carter had seen the change in her facial expression and was grateful when he changed the subject.

"Well, I can't manage to carry you to the station as I did all those years ago, Georgie," he grinned, "but we could walk there together, and I'll make you a cuppa so we can sit and have a catch-up."

"That would be perfect, Sergeant Carter. I'd be honoured to walk with you to the station."

By the time they entered the station, Georgie had explained to Sergeant Carter what had caused her to run away to London and how she'd managed to get a job in St Martin's Theatre.

"Hang on, Georgie, I've got a surprise for you," said her policeman as he disappeared through the wooden gate next to the high counter. Georgie smiled at the Sergeant behind the counter, who she didn't recognise, and he smiled back. Soon Sergeant Carter reappeared with a woman police constable who had sandy coloured hair.

"Oh, my goodness," gasped PC Sandy Bell, "Georgie, is it really you?"

"Yes, it's really me, PC Sandy," and both women held each other in an affectionate hug as the men looked on with grinning faces.

"Well don't just stand there you two. I've put the kettle on so come through and find a room where we can all catch up, while I make us a brew," said Sergeant Carter.

Two hours and two more cups of tea later, Georgie finally came to the end of her story. Both police officers were wide-eyed with shock throughout most of it, and now the three of them sat in silence as all that Georgie had told them sunk in. Even Georgie felt shocked as she heard her own voice speaking out her experiences and wondered at the miracle of her escape.

Sergeant Carter was the first to speak up.

"Georgie, I really think we need to have a chat with the Metropolitan Police. Firstly, we need to report the young man, Derek Dewar, who tried to sexually assault you, but we also need to talk to them about the brothel and the man, Mr G wasn't it, who beat you up, raped you and in effect imprisoned you and forced you into prostitution."

"Oh, Sergeant Carter, I know you have my best interests at heart, but I just want to leave the episode with Derek Dewar behind me. I couldn't face another court case, not after the one with my stepfather," pleaded Georgie.

"Okay, Georgie, I can't pursue that without your permission, but I think Mr G is a whole other issue. Other young women could be in danger of the same thing. In fact, it sounds to me like he might have had your friend, Terry, looking out for girls on his behalf, and that is just as serious."

"But the Police knew about the brothel. I know that because Lavinia told us that the Police said they would be left alone as long as Beverly and her friend from the church were allowed to come in each week to make sure we were all okay."

"I'm not sure I can let this one go, Georgie. I'm sorry but I feel it's my duty to at least ring the Met to make sure they know what a thug this Mr G is."

Tears started to form in Georgie's eyes.

"But if Mr G finds out where I am, he might come looking for me, Sergeant Carter. I could never feel safe knowing that there is even a slight chance of that happening."

"Don't get upset, Georgie," soothed PC Sandy. "The Sarge here would make sure that the Met understood the risk to you, so they could avoid mentioning your name. It's just important that they have any intelligence concerning what's going on so they can monitor the situation more closely and perhaps avoid another young woman like you being sucked in."

"Okay. I understand that you're obliged to report it, but it's just all so raw still for me."

PC Sandy changed the subject.

"So, what are your plans now, Georgie," she asked.

"Ah. Well, that's something I haven't yet thought out. It was hard to think beyond my escape, not knowing if that would succeed. Believe it or not, it was only when I got off the train here in Penrith that I realised I was homeless, and compared to living in the brothel, that felt like arriving at a holiday destination at the seaside."

"Well, you're going to have to think about it, Georgie," said Sergeant Carter. "You can't just sleep on the streets."

"No," chipped in PC Sandy, "and you must be feeling the effects of not having had any cocaine."

"To tell you the truth, I've been gradually cutting back on the cocaine since Beverly first brought up the idea of escape, so I don't think the withdrawal effects will be quite so intense as they could have been. But I must say I am feeling a little apprehensive, being alone and not knowing what to expect."

Sergeant Carter, who had been looking pensive as Georgie spoke, joined in the conversation.

"I tell you what, Georgie, I think I might have an idea. You and Sandy carry on chatting while I make some enquiries," and he disappeared out of the room.

Fifteen minutes later, the man was back and looking pleased with himself. The women had been discussing the possibility of Georgie returning home to Ousby but had dismissed it as an unwise move, bearing in mind that it had been Florrie who'd kicked Georgie out of the house in the first place.

"So, what have you been up to, Sarge?" asked PC Sandy.

"I know it's still very early in the morning, but I decided to ring a contact and managed to get through. I've got you somewhere to stay, Young Lady, so pick up your handbag, we're going for a ride in the car."

Georgie looked at Sergeant Carter questioningly but he just grinned. She looked at PC Sandy who raised her eyebrows and shrugged. So, Georgie picked up her bag, waved to the policewoman and followed the almost jigging Sergeant out of the police station to his car. Seated in the back seat, Georgie was wondering where he was taking her, until a few minutes before they reached their destination. Her hopes started to rise. Could she possibly be right? She was sure she recognised the area but didn't dare to believe her suspicions until the car pulled up outside the front of the house where a full week of wonderful memories had once been made.

"It's Val's house, isn't it? I can't believe this is happening. Am I going to stay with Val again? Tell me it's true before I burst."

Before Sergeant Carter had a chance to respond, the front door flew open and Val came running down the garden path, her flock of curly hair bouncing in rhythm with her footsteps, and her rosy cheeks shining out

in the early morning light. Georgie pushed open the car door and jumped out just in time to be caught in the open arms of the woman she remembered with such affection despite having only known her for one week so long ago when she was a small girl.

"Auntie Val," she just managed to say before she was smothered by the enthusiastic woman's warm body. After a few minutes, Val stood back from Georgie and held her at arms-length, looking her up and down with disbelief in her eyes.

"Oh, Georgie, you are so grown up and so beautiful. I just can't believe it."

Georgie laughed as Val, one arm around her shoulders, led her up the garden path and in through the front door. At the last minute she seemed to remember that Sergeant Carter was still standing beside his car, so without letting go of Georgie, she turned her head and shouted.

"Come on then, You silly-so-and-so. Don't just stand there looking gormless. I've got your breakfast cooking in the pan."

CHAPTER 36

End of July 1963 – January 1964

Time doesn't stand still

"Uncle Cedric!"

As Georgie walked into Val's dining room for breakfast and saw Val's husband, Cedric, she rushed over to him. He just about managed to stand up from the breakfast table before Georgie landed on him, engulfing him in a big wholehearted hug.

"Ey up, Georgie. Yer nearly knocked us sideways. Lovely to see yer, Lass."

"Oh, Uncle Cedric, it feels like I've come home to my own mum and dad. I'm so, so pleased to be here with you and Auntie Val. It only seems like yesterday that I was here playing with the twins in the garden. Where are they, by the way?"

"Wasn't yesterday, Lass," piped up Val, "It were ten years ago, and twins are eighteen now and away at college. Well, currently they're away working during t' summer holidays, but we miss 'em loads so it's more

than a pleasure ter have you with us for a while. Now sit yersen down –
and you, Sergeant Carter – and I'll fetch t' breakfast."

Over breakfast, Sergeant Carter told Georgie that Val and Cedric would
not be paid by the council this time, so she needed to agree with them
what rent she'd be paying during her stay.

"Well, I know that t' Council rent is fourteen shillings and sixpence a
week for a small flat," piped up Auntie Val, "So, I reckon that twenty
shillings, including yer food, should cover it, Lass. How does that
sound?"

"That sounds more than generous, Auntie Val. Thank you."

So, life was sorted for Georgie for the moment, and she was pleased to
have the support of these two lovely people to help her settle down until
she could get a job and find a place of her own. The next couple of weeks
were not easy for Georgie as she got used to life without cocaine, but
Auntie Val, having been informed of Georgie's experiences in London by
Sergeant Carter, was there for her every step of the way. She
encouraged Georgie when she had difficulty concentrating and felt as if
she couldn't think straight. She brought cups of tea when Georgie felt so
exhausted that she fell asleep sitting on the settee. She sat and calmly
talked to Georgie when she felt so restless that she couldn't settle. Auntie
Val comforted her when she woke in the night screaming after a
particularly unpleasant nightmare and hugged her when she found her
trembling involuntarily without a reason. Then after a couple of weeks,
when the symptoms started to leave Georgie, Auntie Val took her for
walks and shopping trips to cheer her up, helping her to choose some
smart clothes ready for future job interviews.

By the beginning of September, Georgie was feeling stronger and
brighter in spirit even though, alone at nights, it was different. She felt
ashamed of herself, of little value and dirty because of her life as a
prostitute. This sapped her confidence, but she kept it to herself and tried
to put a brave face on it. Then one morning, she decided she must
conquer her low self-esteem. She dressed herself smartly and went
downstairs for breakfast. Auntie Val saw her from the kitchen and looked
surprised.

"My word, Lass, yer certainly brush up well, don't yer?"

"Thank you, Auntie Val. I decided to dress up smart today because I'm going to look for a job."

"Ey, Lass, that's a real positive step forward. I'm that proud of yer after all you've been through. So, what sort of job are yer looking for?"

"I'd like to work in a shop, I think. After all, when I was little, I used to help Pattie and Robert in the village store, so I've sort of got a bit of experience."

"Good fer you. Where yer going ter start looking?"

"Well, to tell you the truth, the one shop I'd love to work in more than any other is Robert's village store in Ousby, but I couldn't face going anywhere near my mum and stepfather yet. But when we were out shopping the other day, I saw a notice in the window of a sweet shop in town advertising a vacancy. I thought I might start there."

"Good idea. You go gerrit darn yer, Lass. Now tek yer breakfast into t' dining room and get it down ya. Always best ter set yersen up with a good breakfast in t' morning."

After Georgie had finished eating and enjoying a cup of tea and a chat with Auntie Val, she set off for town. Georgie felt a little nervous and her mind was still struggling to overcome her low self-esteem, but she made herself walk tall to increase her confidence. She was relieved to see the card advertising the job was still in the window of the sweet shop when she arrived, so she neatened her hair, took a deep breath, and went inside. A little bell sounded as she entered, and immediately a small, upright, neatly dressed elderly woman bustled into the shop from a door at the end of the counter. Her grey hair was cut in a short, modern style and she was wearing bright orange lipstick to match her patterned black and orange dress.

"Morning Lass, what can I get yer, today," she asked Georgie.

"I've come about the vacancy you have advertised in the window."
The woman looked delighted.

"Oh, that's grand you've come in. I was starting to reckon that nobody wanted t' job. I'm Prudence, but everyone calls me Pru. What are you called, love?"

"I'm Georgie. Pleased to meet you."

Prudence spoke quickly with words that seemed to almost fall over each other. Georgie liked her immediately.

"Come out t' back Georgie, so we can have a proper natter. We don't need to fret about t' shop, cos we'll hear t' bell if someone comes in. It'll buck up at lunch time, so you can have a go behind t' counter then - if we get on alright - and I'm sure we will, Lass."

The back of the shop consisted of a room with a kitchen area at one end and sofas and a table at the other. In some ways it reminded Georgie of the layout of the lounge at the brothel, and she shivered as the thought entered her mind.

"Eee Lass, are yer cold? I tell yer, it's hard to keep t' room warm. What with me going in and out and folk coming in and out of t' shop an all. It can get right perishing in t' winter I'll tell yer. Nah then, sit yersen darn whilst I mek yer a nice cup o' tea. Then we can have a proper natter."

Georgie couldn't help but smile at this busy little lady, as she sat down and waited for her tea. Prudence continued to chat throughout the operation until Georgie felt like taking a breath on her behalf, and by the time she handed Georgie a full cup sitting in its matching saucer, Georgie felt quite breathless.

"Right Lass, we settled darn so, tell us a bit about yersen."

Georgie waited for a second, unsure if Prudence had finished speaking, before she responded.

"I'll be seventeen at the beginning of November and I live in lodgings in Penrith. I was born in Ousby – I don't know if you know it. It's a small village about eight miles from here – and when I was a child, I helped a lot in the local village store. I loved serving customers even then, and I was good at arithmetic so was able to take money and give the correct change. I've been working in London for the last few years but decided I prefer life back here in Cumberland."

"Blimey, London! I've nivver been missen, but I've often wondered what it's like. I don't know why I've not been, cos railway station's only down t' road. Ah, but I allus reckoned it's too far to go on me own. I've nivver married yer see, so I've had nobody to tek me. But I'm envious of you,

being able to go there when yer that young. Did yer have a job there, Lass?"

Georgie felt a little sick, thinking of her most recent 'occupation', but pushed the thought away.

"I worked in a theatre. I've always wanted to be a dancer, so I thought a theatre would be a good place to start."

"Aye, that's grand, a dancer on a stage in t' theatre. That sounds reight exciting, lass. Wish I'd had chance to do sommat like that, but I was stuck at home looking after me mam and dad when they got too old to work. What with that and running t' shop, it weren't easy, I can tell yer. No time to go gallivanting to London to enjoy missen."

Georgie recalled how far from enjoying herself London had been, but she wasn't about to go into that with her prospective new employer.

"London is really huge and busy compared to Penrith, Prudence ... Pru," said Georgie, "I'd choose Penrith any day, having experienced the London life."

"But what about yer dancing career then? I wouldn't want to be training yer up in t' shop only for yer to go off."

"No fear of that. I need to save up for dancing lessons before my career in dancing can even get started. No, that's my long-term ambition. For the foreseeable future, I want to be here in Penrith, preferably working in a shop like yours," reassured Georgie.

"Oh, thank goodness. I reckon you'll do well in t' shop, Georgie. In fact, let's go in now, so I can show you where everything is afore t' lunchtime rush. If yer get on alreight, I'd love yer to come and work wi' me."

Georgie's hopes of getting the job grew as both women walked out into the shop, and Prudence began to show her around. It seemed to Georgie that working in a sweet shop would be easier than working in a village store, where sweets were only part of the stock, but she discovered that Prudence also sold packets of crisps and home-made sandwiches that were stacked on a large plate covered by an even larger glass dome. Georgie realised that Prudence was obviously an astute businesswoman, having worked out and addressed the needs of her

customers as a side-line to the sweets. Soon, the customers started to come in thick and fast. Most seemed to be workers on their lunch break, others were children on their way home from school for their lunch. It occurred to Georgie that lunch would be much less enjoyable on top of a stomach full of chocolate or sweets. The time flew as both she and Prudence served the customers, until at the end of an hour, the lunchtime rush subsided as quickly as it had started.

"Blooming eck," remarked Prudence. "Now yer know why I need help. It's all off again come three o'clock, when kiddies come out o' school."

Georgie grinned and nodded, realising how much she had enjoyed that hour. Then she looked at Prudence and waited to hear if she'd got the job.

"When can yer start, Lass? I'd need yer to work Monday to Saturday, eight till six, but we close on Wednesday afternoons, so you'd get that and Sundays off."

"I can start whenever you want, Pru."

"Oh, that's grand. It'll be lovely to have yer help and company. It gets a bit lonely when yer on yer own all day. I can't wait for yer to start. How about, as it's Friday today, yer start on Monday at beginning of a new week. It'll be easier for me to work out yer wages. Eee, I'm daft sometimes, I haven't even told yer how much yer'll get paid yet!! I seem to be getting forgetful in me old age. It's a reight worry sometimes when I get me days mixed up and end up missing doing me weekly order. Yer can't make any brass if yer've got nowt to sell can yer, Lass?"

Georgie laughed along with Prudence, wondering if the woman ever stopped to take a breath between sentences. But, in truth, she had also forgotten to ask about the wages, so she realised that forgetfulness wasn't always down to old age.

"Right, Georgie. Yer'll get paid three pounds ten shillings a week, until yer seventeenth birthday, when it'll go up to four pounds and five shillings. Is that alreight, Love?"

Georgie was more than happy, and left the shop feeling as if she was walking on air.

"See you on Monday, then Pru."

"Aye, tek care, Georgie, and I'll see yer then – eight o'clock sharp mind - ready to serve t' folk going ter work."

As Georgie walked home, she realised that, if she saved hard, it wouldn't take too long to accrue enough money to enable her to find a place of her own to rent so that she could learn to live independently. She loved living with Auntie Val and Uncle Cedric, but knew that was only a temporary measure, and although she would miss Auntie Val's company, she would be able to visit them often, and even invite them to visit her. She started to feel excited about choosing furniture for her own place, even if she could only afford second-hand stuff. By the time she arrived back home, she was itching to share her good news with AuntieVal. She decided to trick her into thinking she hadn't got the job, so it would be much more of a surprise when she told her she had. She walked into the house with a disappointed look on her face.

"Oh, Lass, don't be upset. Another job 'll come along in no time."

But Georgie couldn't hold it in any longer, and she rushed over to Auntie Val, with a 'whoop' and grabbed her into an excited hug.

"I got it, Auntie Val. I got it. I start on Monday. I can't believe it. I actually got the first job I tried for."

Auntie Val joined in with Georgie's 'whooping' as both danced round and round, still in their hug. When they eventually moved apart, both had glistening eyes and rosy smiles, although Georgie's blonde waves couldn't keep up with Auntie Val's wayward curls, which were standing on end and pointing in all directions after their exuberant exercise.

"This calls for a celebration, Lass. Let's get out t' bottle of sherry reight now."

"Auntie Val, you wicked woman. Turning to drink at half past two in the afternoon."

"Oooh I love a bit of wickedness in t' afternoon," giggled Auntie Val as she retrieved the bottle from the sideboard in the dining room, poured two small glasses of the amber liquid, and passed one to Georgie.

"Here's to yer future, Lass. May it be a happy and successful one."

They chinked their glasses together and took long, delicious sips, laughing and dancing as they celebrated. And, in fact, Georgie could only bear to think of the future. She didn't dare reflect on her time in London because she knew it would make her depressed and upset. She even forgot Beverly in her attempt to shut out the past.

Georgie settled quickly at the sweetshop, and before long, Prudence was declaring that she didn't know how she ever managed without her efficient young assistant. At times when they were serving the customers, Prudence would be too busy to chat with Georgie, but the moment they got to a quiet patch, she'd be off, chatting nineteen to the dozen in her tinkling voice. Georgie was only pleased that the quiet times were few and far between, especially after Prudence delegated the preparation of the monthly orders to her.

The months passed quickly, with Georgie celebrating her seventeenth birthday by treating Auntie Val and Uncle Cedric to a meal in one of the local cafés, and they presenting her with a beautiful pink, home knitted cardigan that Auntie Val had made herself. When Christmas came, Georgie selected the largest box of chocolates from Prudence's shop that she could find for Auntie Val and Uncle Cedric's Christmas present, affordable only because Prudence insisted on giving her worker's discount. Val and Cedric's eighteen-year-old twins came home for the celebrations, and although they had little memory of Georgie from the one week they'd spent together over ten years ago, they both had naturally friendly personalities like their mum, so were soon chatting away to Georgie as if she were their sister. They stayed at home to celebrate New Year 1964, before they returned to college, giving Georgie as well as their mum and dad a hug as they left.

The only thing that jaded Georgie's happiness during that time were the thoughts and feelings that came to the surface every time she dreamed about London. Sometimes she'd wake in the early hours crying, still seeing herself as a slut which silently chipped away at the confidence she'd gained from getting a job. Georgie left it until a few days after the twins had gone before she broached the subject of her independence and her need to find a home of her own. It was a Friday evening, and Georgie had booked the next day off work.

"You know how much I love living with you both, don't you?"

They nodded and Auntie Val replied that she and Uncle Cedric loved having Georgie with them too.

"Well, I think it's probably the right time for me to start thinking about becoming a bit more independent. I'm seventeen now and I have a regular job, so I think I'll be able to manage the rent and my own keep. I've been here for almost six months – longer than I expected when I first arrived."

Georgie watched Auntie Val's and Uncle Cedric's faces drop.

"I couldn't have managed without you both, but it was always meant to be a temporary arrangement, and you both deserve to have some time to yourselves now the twins are off your hands."

Auntie Val looked like she was struggling to smile.

"Georgie Lass, you know how we love yer living with us. You've become like our own daughter, and yer really have helped ter fill t' gap left by twins. But we do understand yer need ter stand on yer own two feet, even though we'd love yer to stay. Yer must always see this as yer home, t' place yer visit often and t' place yer come if ever you're in trouble."

Georgie was so touched that she walked over to where Auntie Val and Uncle Cedric were sitting beside each other on the settee and placed her arms around both, drawing them into a three-person hug.

"You'll always be my precious surrogate mum and dad, and I'll be visiting you so much that you'll get sick of the sight of my face," said Georgie, gulping back the threatening tears. "And I hope you'll come and visit me, too, both of you."

"Not only that, Lass. But I'll be there helping yer choose yer furniture if yer'll have me," enthused Auntie Val.

"And helping yer paint t' walls," added Uncle Cedric.

Georgie began to laugh.

"Hang on, I haven't even found a place yet."

"Well, we can both help yer do that, too," responded Auntie Val and Uncle Cedric in unison, then bursting out laughing as they realised that they'd both said the same thing.

So, it was all three of them that set out the next morning to look for somewhere for Georgie to rent.

CHAPTER 37

January 1964

A quick move

"Good morning, Pru. I wanted to introduce you to Val and Cedric whose house I live in."

Georgie had walked into town accompanied by Auntie Val and Uncle Cedric, and Georgie had decided there was no better place to start their search for her new home than with Prudence. She wondered why she hadn't thought of asking her employer in the first place. After all, Pru had lived in her Penrith shop all her life and knew so many people that she was often the first in the town to hear a bit of news like a new birth, someone moving, or someone dying. Also, she often placed cards in her window for her customers advertising something for sale, or a service that was available. Georgie had never taken an interest in these cards since she had found the one advertising her job, but she realised that people wanting to rent their property might also use the service. As she, Auntie Val and Uncle Cedric arrived at the shop, they stood for a while reading the several cards already displayed in the window, but they could see none advertising rentals.

"Let's go inside anyway," suggested Georgie. "I'd love you to meet Prudence, my employer."

So, they entered, and after the introductions, Georgie told Prudence why they were there on her day off.

"I'm looking for somewhere to rent, Pru. Now that I'm in regular employment, I think it's about time I went out on my own and started to get more experience of independent life. That's why we were standing outside reading the cards in the window, but I see there's nothing advertising a place to rent," said Georgie.

"No Lass, there aren't any just now, but we do get some when spring comes on. I reckon folk start looking for pastures new once t' sun starts to shine and t' flowers pop up. Mind you, I've nivver had to look for somewhere to live cos I were born here. But then I have sometimes thought it'd be nice to start again somewhere new. Then again, I reckon to meself, security is worth a lot in life and so I've allus thought, change might not be better than what I've got here...."

Georgie was beginning to fear that Prudence would go on for ever, and she noticed that even Auntie Val was starting to take big breaths on behalf of this little woman. So, Georgie intervened.

"I don't suppose you've heard anything on the grapevine about people intending to move in the near future, have you, Pru?"
"No Georgie Lass, sorry."

Georgie jumped back in quickly.

"Do you know of other shops that have cards in their window like you do?"

"Oh aye, I know t' grocer a few doors down do. Then there's book shop and, oh, post office has a load of advertising cards in a holder."

"Thank yer, Prudence," interrupted Auntie Val in her most polite voice, "I think we should get moving or we'll not have time ter go around all of those places and read t' cards. Lovely ter have met yer."

At that Auntie Val opened the shop door and ushered Uncle Cedric and Georgie through it. Georgie just had time to wave to Prudence on her way out.

"Ey, Lass, fer such a little lady, that one can talk fer England. She's left me all breathless," said Auntie Val as they walked away from the shop.

All three were giggling at the thought of Prudence when they reached the grocer's shop and discovered its plethora of cards stuck in one corner of the window. They began to read, laughing from time to time at some of the things that people were trying to sell.

"How do yer fancy a pet fer yer new home, Lass?" grinned Uncle Cedric. "There's one here with one ear and three legs should yer fancy its company."

Georgie giggled and mockingly chastised Uncle Cedric for being cruel, but all three were giggling as they walked away, picturing the poor little creature. There was nothing in the grocer's, so on they went to find the book shop, keeping their eyes on all the shop windows, just in case Prudence had missed some. There were only a few cards in the book shop, but they read them in hope.

"I think it's time we had a brew, Lass," said Auntie Val looking towards Georgie.

"Well, if we do, it's on me," said Georgie seeing both Auntie Val and Uncle Cedric shaking their heads.

"Nay. I'm buying, Georgie," said Uncle Cedric. "It's not often I get ter come ter town escorted by two beautiful lasses. I'll be getting us each a fancy bun ter go with it, too."

"Come on, Lass. It's not often't man puts his hand in his pocket either," laughed Auntie Val as she led the three towards the café opposite.

Everyone in the café looked towards the door as the laughing trio entered and found a free table among the smiling customers. Almost immediately the waitress came over and took their order, leaving them to wait for their tea and cakes to be delivered to their table. Georgie fleetingly thought of the Nippies in Lyons Corner House in London but

shut the thought out before her unpleasant memories had a chance to follow.

"It doesn't look very hopeful, does it?" said Georgie.

"Don't give up that easy, Lass. We've still got t' post office to look at, and it's not as if there's a rush. Yer know yer can stay with us fer as long as yer like," said Auntie Val.

But Georgie was impatient. Now the idea was in her head, she wanted to make it a reality. The thought of waiting depressed her, even though she knew she was happy where she was and enjoyed the fact that someone was in the house when she had her bad dreams. Soon the waitress returned to the table with the tea and cakes.

"That was quick," said Georgie, "Have you worked here long?"

Georgie judged the young woman to be in her late teens.

"Not really. I came up here a couple of years ago from the south with my family. My dad's a soldier and was stationed here for a while, but he and my mum and sister have moved back to the south again. I've been living in a small, rented cottage not far from here since they left. I was fed up with moving around all the time and I enjoyed this job too much to leave it."

Auntie Val was quick to pick up on what the waitress had said.

"Yer said enjoyed, Lass. Don't yer like it anymore?"

"It's not that. I just miss my family more than I could have imagined. Mum says I should return to live with them in the south, so that's what I'm going to do."

Georgie's ears had pricked up at the mention of the cottage.

"So, what will happen to your cottage when you leave?"

"Well, I rent it from an elderly man who now lives in a care home. He's a lovely man. So sad that he had to leave his cottage because he could no longer care for himself. He's asked me to find someone to take over the rental because he can do nothing about it from where he is."

371

"Have you found anyone?" chipped in Uncle Cedric.

"No, not yet. I work long hours here, so it's been difficult."

Georgie was almost bouncing up and down on her seat as her excitement increased.

"I'm looking for a small place to rent. Do you think your elderly landlord would consider me?"

"He left it up to me. My name's Sally by the way … and you are?"

"I'm Georgie."

The waitress was scribbling something on her order pad, and she handed it to Georgie.

"This is the address. If you want to pop round later, after my shift finishes, I'll show you the place," offered Sally. "I finish at five so give me five or ten minutes to walk home and you're welcome any time after that."

Georgie could hardly eat her cake and drink her tea for excitement, neither could she stop her feet tapping on the floor under the table. She knew that the 'small her' would have been bouncing from one foot to the other. Auntie Val was beaming, as was Uncle Cedric.

"There, Lass, what did I tell yer? Never give up easy. Sommat will allus come along," said Uncle Cedric.

As they left the café, Georgie waved goodbye to Sally and mouthed that she would see her later. The three walked home arm in arm, occasionally bursting into song even though people passing by gave them strange looks.

"Don't be taking any notice of them, Flower," ginned Auntie Val. "When yer happy yer should show it – that's what I say."

Her words immediately triggered a new song from the jolly trio.

If you're happy and yer know it clap yer hands,
If you're happy and yer know it clap yer hands,
If you're happy and yer know it then yer really

want ter show it,
If you're happy and yer know it clap yer hands.

The three joined in with the clapping at the appropriate points in the song, almost collapsing with laughter. A few passers-by even smiled and joined in with the clapping.

"See," said Auntie Val before they did a repeat, "Happiness is catching."

The walk home went quickly and when they got indoors, they all collapsed onto the settee, still giggling.

"Reight, Lass. Show us that bit of paper so I can see if I know t' address," said Uncle Cedric.

"Aye I know where that is," he exclaimed. "Not far from the town centre. It'll be perfect for yer, Georgie – if yer like it that is."

Georgie spent the rest of the afternoon cleaning and tidying her room to use up her nervous energy. At five o'clock Auntie Val shouted up the stairs.

"Are yer ready, Lass? By time we get there, Sally should be home and settled down ready fer us."

Georgie came bounding down the stairs in her usual exuberant manner when she was excited about something.

"Yes, I'm ready. Let's get going."

The January evening was cold and dark so Georgie, Auntie Val and Uncle Cedric couldn't make out the cottage until they arrived at the gate. Georgie shuddered when she first caught sight of it. It had white walls and a slate roof just like the cottage she'd grown up in, but it was smaller. She wondered if she'd be able to live here with all the memories it triggered, but she said nothing, whereas Auntie Val was extolling its virtues before they had even opened the wooden front gate.

"Oh, what a pretty little garden, Lass. Oh, this looks like a really nice little cottage."

Georgie banged the brass knocker and within a minute, Sally opened the door welcoming them with a happy smile.

"Come on in everyone. I'll show you around and see what you think."

The tour of the cottage didn't take more than five minutes. There was one small bedroom upstairs with a tiny bathroom at the back that was obviously added on to the main building in the not-too-distant past, and downstairs there was a small living room and a tiny kitchen with a back door leading out to a sizeable garden. Georgie was glad that the layout was different from the Ousby cottage, and it also had a happier feel about it.

"I love it Sally," said Georgie as they returned to the living room, "and you've made it really cosy with your bits of furniture. This would be perfect for me."

"Well, if you want it, I can leave the furniture, Georgie. I won't be needing it when I move back in with Mum and Dad."

"How much would you be selling it for?" jumped in the ever-astute Auntie Val.

"Oh no, I wouldn't want anything for it," said Sally, "I realise that different people have different tastes, so if you don't want it, I'll try to get rid of it, but if you do – then it's yours. I'd be taking all my nick-nacks of course, but that's all."

"Thanks, Sally. I'd really be grateful for it, but I must pay you something. It means I'll be able to move in as soon as you leave. When will that be, by the way?"

"I'll have to give a week's notice at the café so after that, it's yours when you want it," replied the young woman.

Georgie rushed over to Sally and gave her an excited hug.

"I feel like jumping up and down, I'm so excited," said Georgie as she unlocked Sally from her hug.

"Haven't you forgotten something, Lass?" said Uncle Cedric, grinning.

Georgie looked mystified for a moment until the man laughed and spoke in a whisper.

"T' rent?"

"Oh, I completely forgot that. Thanks Uncle Cedric."

All three turned to Sally.

"The rent is fifteen shillings and sixpence a week. You will have to drop it into the care home every Friday, but that's only five minutes-walk away. I always do it on my way home from work, so you'll probably want to do the same – if you decide to take the cottage at that rent, of course."

"I'll take it – of course I will. It feels such a happy and peaceful place."

"That's settled then. You'll need to pay a week in advance, so if you can give me that now, I'll pop into the care home tomorrow and give it to Mr Pepys, the owner and explain to him what's happening. I expect he'll look forward to meeting you when you take your rent in on Friday week. In fact, I can take you to meet him tomorrow if you like?"

Georgie nodded vigorously.

"Then I'll book my train home to Mum and Dad for next Saturday, so after that it's all yours. I'll give you the rent book after we've seen Mr Pepys tomorrow, and I hope you'll be as happy here as I've been, Georgie."

"I still can't believe this is happening," said Georgie on the way home. "I got a job on my first try and I got a new home on our first day of looking. Life was such a struggle for as long as I can remember until I came back to Cumberland."

Auntie Val put her arm affectionately around Georgie's waist as they continued walking.

"I reckon you've had enough bad experiences in yer past to last yer a lifetime, Lass. Yer due a bit o' good luck."

Auntie Val was right, and the effect of her experiences still hung heavy over Georgie in the quietness of each night when her thoughts and dreams refused to leave her in peace.

The following Sunday, Georgie put her case on the pathway before she placed the key into the lock on the cottage's front door, turned it and opened the door wide. Sally had popped into the shop the previous day to hand over the key before she got her train back to her parents, which increased Georgie's excitement so much that Prudence sent her home early from work to get on with her packing.

"Welcome to my new home, Auntie Val and Uncle Cedric. Do come in," she said as she picked up the case and led the way into her little living room.

"Hip hip, hooray. Hip hip, hooray," chanted Auntie Val, with Uncle Cedric joining in, as they followed Georgie into her new home and put down their heavy bags with a sigh of relief. All three clapped and laughed.

"Now, first things first, Lass," said Auntie Val as she rummaged in one of the bags, bringing out a teapot shaped object wrapped in newspaper. "I've got yer a housewarming present."

Georgie unwrapped the gift while Auntie Val continued to rummage in a second bag, eventually bringing out a packet of tea and handing that over, too.

"Thank you, Auntie Val. That's such a pretty teapot. I've never seen one in the shape of a cottage before," smiled Georgie.

"I know. I thought it was perfect. Every time yer mix a brew, you'll think of yer first day here in t' cottage. So, now's t' perfect time ter christen it, Lass."

"You're not hinting by any chance, Auntie Val?"

"Nay. I don't hint, Lass. So just yer get on with it," joked the woman, pushing Georgie towards the kitchen, their laughter ringing back to Uncle Cedric who picked out a bottle of milk from the bag and followed them.

By the time Georgie had unpacked her case and found places for everything, Auntie Val had emptied the bag of groceries they'd brought with them into the kitchen cupboards and joined Georgie upstairs to help her make up the bed. They'd both had a lovely time picking out the pretty pale pink sheets and pillowcases in one of Georgie's lunch hours during the week, choosing darker pink blankets and a white eiderdown with a pink floral pattern on it to go with them. Once the bed was made up, it blended well with the curtains that Sally had left, which were white with tiny pink and green flowers on them. In one corner of the room was a small white chest of drawers that matched the single white wardrobe standing against the wall opposite the window. Georgie had already placed her dressing table set and bits of make-up on top of the chest of drawers, so the room looked comfortable and lived in.

"There's just one thing I need to get for this room," said Georgie.

"What's that, Lass?"

"A rug. The dark polished floorboards look lovely, but a rug would warm the room up a bit and provide something cosy for my feet when I get out of bed on a cold morning."

"Well, there's no harm in having ter save up fer one, and you'll appreciate it all t' more fer having ter wait."

Georgie agreed as she followed Auntie Val down the stairs to the sitting room, where Uncle Cedric had switched on the two-bar electric fire that was standing proudly in the hearth with its pretend coals glowing and flickering away happily, reflecting its patterns on the cream walls.

"I reckon t' electric fire will heat up t' whole cottage in no time if yer leave t' doors open all through. It doesn't half give out a good heat," said Uncle Cedric as Auntie Val and Georgie entered.

When it was time for Auntie Val and Uncle Cedric to leave, Georgie felt quite emotional. She'd lived with these two, lovely people for six months and would truly miss them. She hugged each of them warmly, unable to say goodbye and as they walked down the short garden path and out of the wooden gate. Auntie Val looked back at Georgie with glinting eyes and a quick wave.

"See yer soon, Lass. Don't be a stranger."

"I won't," said Georgie, waving as they disappeared down the road.

The newly independent seventeen-year-old sat down on the settee opposite the electric fire and stared into its pretend flames, realising that she was living alone for the first time in her life.

CHAPTER 38

April 1964

Towards the light

Georgie paused as she opened the garden gate of the cottage that she had been renting for three months. Daffodils and crocuses had been blossoming in the small front garden, making it look even prettier than it already was. Several trees were starting to display their summer clothing, and the birdsong was loud and continuous. She took in a deep breath of fresh air and sighed with contentment as she exhaled. The lighter evenings added to Georgie's pleasure because there was extra time to be spent in the open air after work, and she used that time to weed the garden and mow the grass with the lawn mower she'd discovered in the small potting shed at the far end. Life was good as spring began its slow journey towards summer, except for Georgie's bad dreams that still continued and resulted in her increasing anxiety that people might find out about her past life and see her as the slut she felt she was.

Georgie would often visit Auntie Val and Uncle Cedric in the evening and sit chatting with them in their garden, sipping a cool drink. The twins came home for their university summer vacations in early July as they'd

managed to get jobs nearby, so Georgie had time to get to know them better.

The problem started when the nights began to draw in and the cooler autumn weather arrived. Georgie continued to visit Auntie Val and Uncle Cedric, but she couldn't do this every evening, so she began to feel a little lonely and her bad dreams were getting worse. Prudence suggested she get herself a pet to keep her company, so Georgie scanned the advertisement cards in the shop windows again until she found one advertising 'Kittens free to good owners'. She went to the address on the card to find the family's cat had given birth to six beautiful black and white kittens, which they were unable to keep. Georgie was besotted with the long-furred, large-eyed little creatures, and as she watched them rushing around the room exploring every corner and trying to climb on the furniture and up the curtains, she couldn't help but laugh. Then she noticed one female kitten that was smaller and shyer than her brothers and sisters. This kitten sat in the corner and watched the others but wasn't adventurous enough to copy them. Georgie picked her up and stroked her, looking into the kitten's wide inquisitive eyes. The moment the furry bundle looked directly at her, snuggling up as Georgie petted her, was the moment she stole Georgie's heart.

"May I have this one, please?" she asked the owners and they readily agreed, fetching a cardboard box from their shed in which Georgie could transport her new pet home, plus a small tin of kitten food to get her started.

'What am I going to call her?' Georgie asked herself as she arrived back at her cottage and let herself in. She went straight into the kitchen and put some of the kitten food in a saucer next to a second saucer containing water before she let the kitten out of the cardboard box where it had been snuggled up in one corner snoozing.

"Come on you little ball of fluff, it's time for you to get to know your new home."

The wide-eyed kitten looked around the small kitchen, and having caught the scent of food, went straight to the saucer, and quickly gobbled down its contents. She was obviously used to competing with her five brothers and sisters and had yet to realise that there was no competition here. Having finished her meal, she looked around the kitchen until she

found a place that suited her needs, and immediately urinated on the linoleum.

"Oh, you poor little thing, I forgot all about that side of things," said Georgie as she wiped up the liquid with a dish cloth and rinsed it out under the tap. "I don't think this cloth is going to be appropriate to wash dishes with now, you little scamp. We'd better keep it to one side especially for you."

Having said this, Georgie decided that Scamp would be a good name for her new furry friend, so her decision was made. She found an old seed tray in the garden shed and placed some gravel in it from a half-used bag that she also found. Scamp quite happily used this from then on, clearly having been accustomed to such an amenity at her previous home. The kitten soon settled in, happily sleeping on a cushion in the corner of the kitchen while Georgie was at work. After a month, Georgie started to let Scamp out into the garden, staying with her at first until she proved that she could find her way home, and then teaching her to scratch on the kitchen door to be let in. Scamp soon became independent so spent less time indoors with Georgie, which meant that Georgie started to feel lonely again. One evening she decided to sort out her handbag to wile away the time. Inside, she found the piece of paper that Beverly had given her on the day of her escape from the brothel in London. Written on it was Beverly's address. Georgie had completely forgotten about it. How could she have done such a thing after all the help that Beverly had given her?

'How selfish I am,' she thought as she looked at Beverly's address. 'I was so nervous about my escape from the brothel that I could think of nothing else at the time. And then I had to get through the withdrawal from the cocaine, then get a job, then find a new home. But none of that is a valid excuse for forgetting the one person who got me out of that place. I must get out my notepad and write to her immediately.'

So that's what Georgie did. When she'd finished, she read through what she had written.

Dear Beverly,
The first thing I must do is to say sorry for not writing sooner. What with the escape and starting a new life here in Penrith I feel like there has been no time to think. I know that is no excuse, but I hope you will forgive me.

I am now settled and have a new job and home and even a new pet kitten. I am still trying to get over the emotional stuff I experienced, but I know I will eventually recover and find lasting happiness here. I hope that you and your husband are well, and I will try to stay in touch from now on.

Love from Georgie.

Having slipped the letter into an envelope, stuck a postage stamp on it and written Beverly's address on the front, Georgie placed it on the windowsill next to her front door to remind her to post it.

Returning to her sitting room, she picked up the piece of paper with Beverley's address on and turned it over to find the Bible text that she'd never read.

"Though my father and mother forsake me, the LORD will receive me" (Psalm 27 v.10)

The words pierced Georgie's heart as she remembered the real reason that she was lonely. Her own mother and father had rejected her when she was only twelve years old. She had often thought about them during her lonely times and had wished that she could contact her mother again, especially to see her sister, Daisy, and half-brother, John. But she knew that she could not go to the cottage in Ousby because her stepfather lived there and she feared that if she encountered him again, the anger and hurt that she'd pushed to the back of her mind, might re-surface. She had lived through those emotions once and did not want to revisit them. She read Beverly's Bible text again and realised it was telling her that God would welcome her even if her family wouldn't.

'But how do I find God?' she thought.

Then it came to her in a flash. She remembered when her mother married the monster in the church in Ousby and the vicar welcomed them to the house of God.

"Yes, that's it - God lives in churches. That's where I will find Him," she said out loud.

The next day, she asked Prudence where the nearest church was, and discovered that there was one within easy walking distance of the cottage, and its Sunday Services started at eleven in the morning. The

following Sunday, Georgie dressed herself in her best dress and jacket and, remembering the instructions that Prudence had given her, set off for church. She arrived at five minutes to eleven and was pleased that the church building was a traditional stone-built Anglican church, complete with spire. She walked through the lychgate and down the pathway to the entrance with its traditional archway leading to a dark wood double door, one of which was open. A friendly man welcomed her at the doorway and handed her a hymn book as he showed her to one of the few empty spaces left in the crowded church. She was sitting in the very back pew and as she looked around her, she thought the interior was beautiful with its cream stone floor, rows of dark polished pews, colourful glass windows along its side walls and at the front, and a fancily carved pulpit with a shiny brass lectern on which sat an open bible. Georgie was surprised to notice that several people were turning around to smile at her. Warmth and friendliness shone out of their faces. The people either side of her greeted her warmly too. Then the Vicar, a smiley man in his thirties with fair Brylcreemed hair combed neatly in place and wearing a dog collar and black vestments stood up in the pulpit and welcomed everyone.

"We would especially like to welcome anyone who has come into our church for the first time. We hope you will be truly blessed by our service today."

His words and the friendly atmosphere between members of the congregation immediately made Georgie feel at ease.

"Our first hymn is a new one. It was only written a year ago so you should all find a copy of the words tucked into your hymn book. Its title is 'Lord of the Dance' and it tells the gospel story as if Jesus, himself, was telling us. I know it's not at all like the hymns you're used to, but I hope you know me enough by now to make allowances for my forward-thinking ways."

People smiled at each other as if sharing a joke and then there was a rustle of paper as everyone found the words and stood as the organ started to play. Georgie followed suit. The singing was loud and enthusiastic, which surprised her a little. She'd expected the dirge-like singing that she'd experienced in the church in Ousby. She concluded that this must be the result of having a trendy young vicar. She looked down at the words but found herself unable to sing. It was as if the breath had been knocked out of her.

I danced in the morning when the world was begun,
And I danced in the moon and the stars and the sun,
And I came down from heaven and I danced on the earth,
At Bethlehem I had my birth.

Dance, then, wherever you may be,
I am the Lord of the Dance, said He,
And I'll lead you all, wherever you may be,
And I'll lead you all in the Dance, said He.

Georgie thought about her childhood dream to become a dancer and wondered what dancing had to do with God. She sensed that the words were speaking directly to her. She felt her emotions coming to the surface, and by the time she reached the last verse, tears were streaming down her face.

They cut me down and I leapt up high;
I am the life that'll never, never die;
I'll live in you if you'll live in me -
I am the Lord of the Dance, said he.

As the congregation sat down, Georgie was trying her best to wipe away her tears with her handkerchief, but her whole body was trembling. She felt a hand touch her gently on her arm and realised it belonged to the middle-aged lady next to her, who had greeted her earlier. The lady's eyes shone, reflecting a love that Georgie had never encountered.

"Are yer okay, Lass?" she whispered.

Georgie nodded and smiled. At that moment she decided she wanted whatever the lady had that caused her to smile with such love and concern. Georgie tried to listen to what the vicar said in his sermon, but his words seemed to bounce off her. She just could not get the words of the first hymn off her mind, and before she knew it, he was pronouncing the benediction. As everyone started to mill around the church, greeting each other with hugs and chatting animatedly, the middle-aged woman turned to Georgie again.

"Ey up, Lass. I'm Marilyn by t' way. Yer got very emotional earlier."

"Hello, Marilyn. I'm Georgie and thank you so much for your concern. It was the words of the first hymn. I felt that they were aimed directly at me

because, since I was a very small child, I've dreamed of becoming a dancer and that hymn was telling me that Jesus is Lord of the Dance."

"Aye He is, Lass."

"But I don't understand, Marilyn. What does it mean? And what has everyone got that makes them sort of shine love out of their eyes?"

"Come with me, Lass, and I'll introduce yer ter Vicar. He'll be able ter answer yer questions better than me."

Both women stood up, and Marilyn led Georgie by her arm towards the door. They worked their way through several groups who were lingering to chat with each other at the back of the church, and waited with the gradually dispersing congregation, many of whom smiled and greeted Georgie and Marilyn, and struck up conversations as they moved slowly towards the door.

"Vicar always stands at t' door to say goodbye ter everyone as they leave," whispered Marilyn between conversations with those around them.

Eventually Georgie and Marilyn reached the door and as they walked outside, the Vicar was ready to greet them.

"Ah, Marilyn, how are you and who's this young lady with you?"

"I'm fine, Vicar, and I'd like yer ter meet Georgie. This is her first time in church, and she has lots of questions for yer."

The Vicar put his hand out to shake Georgie's and she responded to his invitation.

"Hello, Georgie. I'm Reverend Holly. It's nice to meet you. As you can see, I'm pretty tied up right now, but I'd be more than happy to visit you at home if you give me your address," removing a notebook and pen from under his cassock.

"Thank you. I would appreciate that. I'm in most evenings by six, so you're more than welcome to call in after that."

Georgie told Reverend Holly her address and he noted it on his pad, promising to come by one evening in the week.

As Georgie walked home from church, she felt more positive than she had for a long time. Excitement seemed to be bubbling up in her heart, giving her hope for the future. How lovely it would be to feel part of something again.

'I must tell Auntie Val and Uncle Cedric what happened in church,' thought Georgie as she changed direction and made her way towards their home.

"Well, Lass, I've never been a church-goer meself, but yer've clearly found a group of friendly people there so good luck to yer," said Auntie Val followed quickly by an invitation to Georgie to stay for Sunday lunch.

By the time she returned home, Scamp was more than pleased to see Georgie, winding herself around her owner's legs affectionately until Georgie sat down on the settee in the sitting room and allowed her pet to settle on her lap to be stroked.

"Well, Scamp, we're going to have a visit from Reverend Holly sometime this week, so you'll have to be on your best behaviour," said Georgie looking straight into the eyes of her kitten-cat and noticing how much it had grown.

Georgie's feeling of excitement stayed with her even as she fell asleep in bed that evening. She just knew that something significant was about to happen and she couldn't wait for Reverend Holly's visit. She slept well without bad dreams that night for the first time since returning to Cumberland.

A couple of days later there was a knock at her front door. She had been home from work for about an hour and had just finished eating her tea when she heard the knock and jumped up to open the door to the smiling young vicar. He was wearing his dog collar and black top but looked casual in his grey trousers and suit jacket. Georgie invited him in, made them both a cup of tea, and they sat in the living room chatting away as if they'd known each other for years.

"Now, Georgie, Marilyn said you wanted to ask me some questions, so fire away and I'll answer the best I can."

"Well, when we sung that new hymn on Sunday, I felt as if it was aimed straight at me. You see, I've always wanted to be a dancer for as long as I can remember, and it said that Jesus was the Lord of the dance."

"Yes, it did, Georgie, but before I answer your question, why don't you tell me a little more about yourself."

Georgie felt warm inside that someone was that interested in her. For as long as she could remember, she had felt worthless and of no interest to anyone except maybe Auntie Val and Uncle Cedric. Even then she had convinced herself that was only because they'd felt sorry for her. Now here was someone she hardly knew, wanting to know more about her. She felt a little choked and had to cough a few times before she could begin. Reverend Holly noticed and looked concerned.

"Oh, I'm sorry, Georgie. I didn't mean to upset you."

"No that's okay. It's just that life has been a bit up and down for me in the past and I usually try not to think about it."

"You know that whatever you tell me will stay between you and me, don't you?" said the kind man, "but if talking about it will upset you too much, then I will understand."

"No, I think I'm long overdue to talk. The last time was to the police nearly a year ago when I got back to Penrith after almost four years away."

Georgie started to spill out her life story covering the whole seventeen years and five months in an hour and leaving Reverend Holly looking slightly shell-shocked.

"Thank you for trusting me with all that, Georgie. I think that is one of the most amazing stories I've ever heard from one so young."

"The trouble is the memories are forever coming back to me especially at night and when I'm alone. No matter how hard I try to bury them, they come spilling back into my mind at every opportunity and make me feel so sad that I just want to cry. It's as if I'm emerging from a long illness but unable to completely recover. In fact, sometimes I think I must be going mad."

"No, you're not going mad, Georgie, just trying to cope with the effects of what happened to you. Healing will be a long process, but I can tell you about my God who can heal the sick and make sad people dance with happiness because He is the Lord of life itself."

"So that's what the song was about and why so many people in your church on Sunday looked so happy?"

"Yes. Got it in one," beamed the vicar. "Whatever life brings, if you give God control, you can always overcome – even getting over all the traumatic experiences that you have gone through. In fact, the hymn we sung describes how God sacrificed His Son, Jesus, who was cruelly killed so that we could live forever."

"You mean even after we die."

"Yes, Georgie, for eternity."

Georgie sat in silence for a couple of minutes trying to digest what Reverend Holly had just told her before she could explain what she was thinking.

"I'm not sure I want to live for ever. I've only lived just over seventeen years so far, and most of it has been awful."

"That's because you suffered at the hands of people who didn't love Jesus. Those people who abused you so badly were doing wrong, and you'll come across plenty of wrongdoers during the rest of your life. In fact, we all do wrong stuff, Georgie, including me and you. But the good news is that because Jesus died, all these wrongs can be forgiven once and for all. If we give our hearts and lives to God, we can be sure of an eternity where there is no such thing as sin or suffering – only peace, joy and love."

Georgie wasn't finished with her questions. If she was going to give over the control of her life to God, she needed to be sure that God was real. So, she continued asking.

"But some people say that there's no such person as God, and the earth is just the result of an accident in space millions and millions of years ago. What would you say to that?"

Reverend Holly took a small Bible out of his pocket and handed it to Georgie.

"The Bible tells us all about creation. You'll find it right at the beginning in the book of Genesis. Why don't you read it during this week, and I'll pop by to see you at the same time next week to answer your questions. The Bible is yours to keep by the way."

"Thank you. That's so kind," said Georgie before she showed the young Vicar out and reassured him that she'd be in church the next Sunday.

CHAPTER 39

April – End of June 1964

Transformation

Reverend Holly visited Georgie regularly over the next few weeks to answer her questions.

"Did you read the creation story?" he asked Georgie on his second visit.

"Yes, I did but how do you know that it really happened the way the Bible says and not the way scientists say?" asked Georgie almost cheekily.

Reverend Holly smiled.

"Well, Georgie, my answer is I can't prove it to you, but I do know that there are many scholars who believe the Bible account of creation and are pointing us back to the truth of the words 'In the beginning God created the heavens and the earth'. In fact, what we are talking about here is whether the creation was by accident or by design."

Georgie nodded, enjoying the fact that Reverend Holly was speaking to her with respect, acknowledging the fact that she was an intelligent young woman. She listened attentively as he continued.

"As long ago as the nineteenth century, people were arguing about the creation. One man, a well-known theologist at that time called William Paley, argued that if you found a watch and saw how ordered, complex, and purposeful the workings of it were, you would know for sure that it had been made by a watchmaker. Likewise, the universe is just as ordered, complex and purposeful, so how can you doubt that it was created rather than just the result of an accident?"

Georgie thought about this and continued to listen, her fascination growing as Reverend Holly continued.

"What people like William Paley say is that the likelihood of life evolving from all the rocks and matter flying randomly around in space is just not feasible. Therefore it follows that life must have been the product of purposeful intelligence. Have you heard of Albert Einstein, Georgie?"

"No."

"He was a scientist who died in 1955 and was extremely clever. But even with all his scientific knowledge, he concluded that God created the world. So, who am I to argue?"

Georgie was increasingly impressed the more Reverend Holly said. His enthusiasm was contagious, and she was drinking in his every word, but she wasn't about to let him off easily.

"Okay but answer me this. We sung that hymn in church that you said was meant to be Jesus telling his own story, right?"

"Right, you mean 'Lord of the Dance'?"

Georgie nodded.

"So, you're saying that Jesus was a real human person?"

This time it was Reverend Holly's turn to nod.

"But how do you know that?"

Both Georgie and Reverend Holly were enjoying this debate, and both grinned at each other as if to say, 'Try as you may, you won't get the better of me."

Reverend Holly continued to grin as he thought about his response.

"Okay. When I was at Bible College, I learned that there are various snippets of evidence in existence from non-Christian Roman historians, showing that nobody around a hundred years or more after Jesus's crucifixion, had any doubts that Jesus had existed. I remember that one of the snippets came from the writings of a man called Tacitus. He found evidence to show that a man, Jesus Christ, was put to death on a cross by Pontius Pilate, leaving a band of followers called Christians. In fact, Tacitus was known to be disdainful of Christian beliefs so, if anything, was biased towards not believing them, but everything he said corresponded with what the Bible says in the Gospels of Matthew, Mark, Luke, and John. Does that answer your question?" grinned the victorious looking man sitting opposite Georgie.

"Okay. He was a real person who was crucified. So what? What difference does that make to me?"

Georgie was really getting into her stride now and enjoying every moment of it. Clearly Reverend Holly was enjoying it just as much.

"So, Jesus was a real person. That's important because you and I are real people too. Agreed?"

"As far as I know," laughed Georgie, wondering where this was leading.

"Well, as we both know, all people eventually die. Right?"

Georgie nodded.

"Well, how many people do you know that have come back to life, Georgie – risen from the dead like Jesus?"

Georgie sensed defeat.

"Okay. None. So what?"

Reverend Holly's good-hearted enthusiasm was beginning to bubble over at this point.

"So, Jesus, a real man, came alive again, and then was witnessed to ascend up to Heaven to be with his Father, God."

"Yes, and?"

"And Jesus - a real person, died for you - a real person, so that you can go to Heaven to be with Him when you die."

"Really?"

"Yes really, Georgie, those of us that believe in what Jesus did, and give our lives to Him, know for absolute certain that we will live for ever more in Heaven. No need to worry about dying anymore."

Reverend Holly smiled. Georgie was still a bit sceptical. If she was going to consider giving her life to Jesus, she wanted to be sure. Besides that, she was enjoying the discussion too much to let it stop now. She looked straight into the eyes of Reverend Holly and matched his smile.

"So," she paused for effect, "if God loves us so much that He allowed His own son to die for us … why does he let people suffer so much. Why didn't he protect me in London and stop me being tricked into becoming a prostitute?"

As Georgie said this, she felt her emotions rising to the surface, and recognised the increasing anger bubbling up inside her. Reverend Holly reached out to place his hand on her arm.

"Oh, Georgie, we don't have all the answers. I can only say that God gave us all free will, which He won't override because He wants us – you – to choose to love Him – not to be forced into it."

Georgie's tears were close to the surface right then, so she felt the need to deflect the attention onto the man who was still touching her arm.

"When did you choose to love Jesus, Reverend Holly?"

The young vicar sat back in his chair before he answered.

"In the spring of 1954 – ten years ago now when I was nineteen. An American preacher called Billy Graham came to London to conduct a campaign to tell people about Jesus and then to invite anyone who was interested in giving their life to Him, to go forward in front of the thousands of people present. I went forward, and that night I asked Jesus to come into my heart and He did. I felt His presence within me, and to this day I can tell you He has never left me. I know He loves me, Georgie, just like a father loves his child. But unlike an earthly father who can let his child down, God is perfect. He is my perfect Heavenly Father and I know He will never let me down."

Georgie saw the tears in Reverend Holly's eyes and wondered if she should ask the question that was on the tip of her tongue. She found she couldn't hold back.

"Did your earthly father let you down?"

"Yes, he did, Georgie, as did yours."

There was a long silence. It was Reverend Holly who eventually broke that silence.

"I think that's enough for one evening, Young Lady, don't you?"

At this, Georgie's eyes opened wide, and she burst into sobs.

Reverend Holly looked perplexed as he put his hand back on Georgie's arm and waited for her sobs to subside.

"Why are you suddenly so very sad, Georgie. Are you able to tell me?"

Georgie stuttered through her tears.

"You … you called me … you called me a young lady, but I'm not a lady at all. I was a prostitute. That makes me a slut in the eyes of others."

"No. Don't you ever say such a thing. You were made to do some terrible things, but you were never ever a slut. God sees your heart, Georgie, and He loves you more than you know. You are as pure as a sparkling diamond, and even more valuable. You must never forget that. Now, if you'll allow me to use your kitchen, I will go and make you a nice cup of tea to help you relax. Then I really must go."

Georgie allowed him to make her some tea and she sat sipping it as he let himself out of the house, promising that he would answer more questions on his next visit. She sat reflecting on the things he had said for a long time after he left. She reconsidered the description of herself that she had voiced.

'This man is a man of God, and he didn't see me as a slut. Can he be right? Am I not the disgusting and worthless person that I thought?"

That question stayed with Georgie for the next week until Reverend Holly returned. This time, Georgie made him a cup of tea and came straight out with her question.

"With so many millions of people in this world, how come God can possibly know me, just one insignificant person? And if He does know me, then He'll know about all the bad things I've done, so why would He choose me when there are so many other good people to choose from?"

Reverend Holly swallowed down his last mouthful of tea and smiled at Georgie with that caring look in his eyes that she was growing accustomed to.

"When Jesus died, He died for us. He died to take on to his shoulders all the wrong things we ever did and will do in the future. He swept them away from God's sight. God can't see them anymore. In God's eyes we are His perfect children, part of His family. That means that all the other people that love Him become your brothers and sisters."

"What, everyone in the whole world?"

"Yes. When you go to church, all those people there would be your brothers and sisters."

"Wow! So even though my parents didn't want me, I'd have a family again."

"Yes. You know, Georgie, the last time I came, you said you're not good enough to be a Christian. But if God loves you, you must be worth loving, and if He wants you to be part of His family, then you must be worth having. It's true that all of us do wrong things and that makes none of us worthy, but because of what Jesus did, God sees us as worthy. All you must do is accept Him. Simple."

Reverend Holly smiled.

"I need time to think," said Georgie.

"I know you do, Georgie, and that's why I'm not going to come round again for a while, so you have time to think. Just let me know at church when you've had enough time and we'll go from there."

That was the beginning of several weeks of thinking through what the Vicar had said. Georgie found herself talking to the God that she recalled having spoken to before at the most difficult times in her life. She felt comforted doing this, telling Him about her confusions and doubts. She started to read the New Testament in her Bible, a little each day, and sometimes the words would jump out at her as if God was saying 'These are for you, Georgie.' When she got to the part about Jesus's crucifixion she cried, thinking about the pain He must have gone through for her sake. She felt a sense of real joy when she read about Jesus rising from the dead and then returning to Heaven to live with His Father. She was still sad when she thought about how her own father had rejected her, but this was quickly replaced by a mixture of relief, peace, and joy when she remembered that God was her perfect Heavenly Father and He loved her and would never reject her.

Georgie continued to attend church every Sunday, gradually getting to know others in the big congregation. She became close friends with Marilyn despite their age difference and often met up with her for lunch or mid-morning coffee during her breaks at the shop. Then, at the end of June, another friend, Elsa, invited her to attend a baptism in her grown-up daughter's church in Carlisle. Unlike her own church, this one baptised new believers by total immersion, which intrigued Georgie. She readily accepted the invitation and the following Sunday, they set off for Carlisle in her friend's car. The service started at eleven in the morning, so they made sure they arrived with plenty of time to spare and sat in the car, which Elsa had parked in the church car park, until her daughter arrived. After the hugs of greeting, which Georgie was now getting used to and enjoying, they went into the church. It was a Baptist church and she, Elsa and her daughter sat as near to the front as they could so that she would get a good view. Georgie could see what looked like a miniature swimming pool, three quarters full of slightly steaming water, at the front of the church. Elsa informed Georgie that this was called a baptistry. Gradually the pews filled up, until five minutes before the start, the church was already overflowing, and extra chairs were placed at the

end of the pews to cope with the extra numbers. Then three young people dressed in white, each escorted by someone holding a white towel, made their way into the church through a side door and sat in the front row.

The singing was loud and joyful, with people clapping in places, and the sermon was short and about Jesus being baptised by John the Baptist in the River Jordan. Then came the moment everyone had been waiting for. The first white-clad young man stood up and moved to one end of the baptistry where he faced the congregation and explained why he was about to be baptised.

"We call this his testimony," whispered Elsa in Georgie's ear.

When the young person had finished, the minister made his way into the water with the help of another man, and then nodded to the young person, who immediately walked down the steps into the waist-deep water with the help of the person who had been holding his towel. He stood sideways on in front of the minister and placed his hands together in prayer mode. The minister put one hand against the small of the young man's back, and the other one held his prayer hands firmly.

"I now baptize you in the name of the Father, the Son, and the Holy Spirit."

Then, the organ started to play a verse of a hymn while, keeping his hands firmly in place, the Minister guided the young person backwards until he was completely immersed under the water and then brought him back up to standing position. As the young man made his way out of the baptistry to be wrapped in the waiting towel of his attendant, Georgie gasped. His face was radiant – so radiant that the light shining from his eyes seemed to light up the space around him. Georgie saw pure joy and love in that light, and something else that she couldn't quite put her finger on, but that touched the very centre of her being like a bolt of lightning. She was crying and laughing with joy at the same time. She wasn't sure if she was laughing out loud, but she looked around at the congregation, many of whom had made their way forward and they, too, had tears on their smiling faces and were singing, laughing, and clapping. By the time all three young people had gone through the same process, it was as if the whole congregation was in ecstasy. Then, as everyone quietened down and the minister made his way out of the water, he spoke.

"This morning, we have witnessed the baptism of these three young people, who have publicly given control of their lives to the One who created the world and everything in it, including us. If anyone has experienced God for the very first time today, don't just leave it. Tell someone. Get support and guidance so that you can make the public declaration that these youngsters have just made. Above all, remember that God loves you just as you are."

At that, the organ started to play the same hymn, but this time, the words came up on an overhead projector screen on the wall behind the baptistry and everyone joined in.

Just as I am, without one plea
But that Thy blood was shed for me
And that Thou bid'st me come to Thee
O Lamb of God, I come! I come

Just as I am, though tossed about
With many a conflict, many a doubt
Fighting and fears within without
O Lamb of God, I come, I come

Just as I am, and waiting not
to rid my soul of one dark blot
to thee whose blood can cleanse each spot
O Lamb of God, I come, I come

Just as I am, poor, wretched, blind
Sight, riches, healing of the mind
Yea, all I need, in Thee to find
O Lamb of God, I come, I come!

Just as I am, Thou wilt receive
Wilt welcome, pardon, cleanse, relieve
Because Thy promise I believe
O Lamb of God, I come, I come

Georgie was unable to sing out loud because the tears were still sliding down her cheeks. Instead, she prayed the words of the hymn quietly from her heart to her Maker, and her joy overflowed.

'I'm going to live for ever, eternity with God – love, joy and peace just as Reverend Holly told me. It's amazing. It's hard to imagine but I know my Father has saved me and that one day when I die, I'll be with Him for ever.'

As she made her way out of the church and into Elsa's car, Georgie was aware that her friend kept looking at her and smiling.

"What?" Georgie asked.

"Georgie, you look radiant. I can see the light of God's love shining out of you. Did you give your life to Him back there in the church?"

Georgie nodded and Elsa flung her arms around her. They sat side by side in that hug until Elsa pulled away grinning.

"That's wonderful. I'm so happy for you. I'd hug you all over again if it wasn't for the fact that the steering wheel digs into my side when I do it."

Both started to laugh with sheer joy, and this continued spasmodically as Elsa drove the car out of the church car park and all the way home.

CHAPTER 40

End of June – Beginning July 1964

An exciting plan

Georgie couldn't wait for the next Sunday. She was so excited about what had happened the previous Sunday that she had already told Auntie Val and Uncle Cedric, Prudence, and Marilyn at their regular lunch break meeting. Marilyn, of course, had been delighted and hugged Georgie affectionately, while Prudence, for once, had not really known how to respond, and hesitated a little before doing so.

"Well, if it makes yer happy, Georgie, then it makes me happy too," she had said in her melodic little voice.

Then she had reverted to the usual talk about the shop and the day's agenda.

Auntie Val and Unle Cedric had been sincerely happy to see Georgie looking so radiant and had admitted openly that although they didn't have a faith, they'd often envied those who did. They had asked Georgie about how it had happened, and Georgie had recounted in detail the process of the baptism in the church in Carlisle. She'd done so while they'd been

sitting in the garden sipping cool wine, and this had led on to a lengthy discussion.

"Does that mean you'll get baptised like t' lads and lasses did, Flower?"

"I'm not sure, Auntie Val. I haven't even told Reverend Holly yet, but I don't think my church baptises people in the same way. I think they christen babies instead."

"Yes, they do," said Uncle Cedric, "but it's a shame yer can't do it like t' Baptists."

The week seemed endless to Georgie as she waited for Sunday when she'd be able to tell Reverend Holly what had happened. Eventually it arrived and was a sunny and warm July day. As Georgie walked to church, she happily hummed a tune until she suddenly physically bumped into Mariliyn. Georgie hadn't seen her friend just ahead of her until it was too late. Both laughed and walked the rest of the way together, chatting as they followed each other through the lychgate and up the pathway where Elsa was welcoming people and giving them their hymn books.

"I'll show you to your places, but can you save a place for me, please, so that when I've finished my door duty, I can come and join you?" asked Elsa.

All three friends enjoyed the service and when it was over, Georgie made her way straight to the door to speak to Reverend Holly before others started to leave.

"I want to be baptised, Reverend Holly. I've given my heart to Jesus, so I need to do this. The only thing is that I want to do it by going right under the water like Jesus did, and I know you only christen babies, but I'm not a baby so what can I do?"

It was all Georgie could do to stop herself jumping up and down. Reverend Holly laughed and gave Georgie a hug.

"I'm so pleased for you, Georgie. I've been hoping to hear that you wanted to follow Jesus ever since our last discussion, but you are right, we don't have the facilities here to do baptisms by total immersion."

401

"What am I going to do? I don't want to go to the Baptist Church in Carlisle because it is too far for everyone to get to without a car. I've got plans you see. I want to ask all the people I know, including those I haven't seen for a long time, to come to my baptism. I want them to find Jesus too. I just couldn't bear to think of any of them going to hell."

The queue of people wanting to say goodbye to the Vicar was lengthening by the minute, which Reverend Holly couldn't help but notice.

"Leave it with me, Georgie. I'll have a think about it and drop round to your cottage in the week to discuss it further."

Georgie hung about for a little longer so that she could say goodbye to Mariliyn and Elsa before she left, and once they had exchanged hugs, she walked back to the cottage happily. As she opened the front door and entered, Scamp was waiting there to greet her, affectionately entwining her furry little body around Georgie's legs as usual and refusing to stop until she received a stroke and a 'hello'.

That afternoon, Georgie started to make a list of all those she intended to invite to her baptism. As she looked through the names, she realised that many were unlikely to come, especially her family, so she decided she would start praying about it every day. She knew that only God could work the miracle that was needed to make Florrie soften towards her, and Alfie find the courage to acknowledge her as his daughter.

A few days later, Reverend Holly came to visit. As he entered Georgie's sitting room, she could see that he was almost bubbling over with enthusiasm and wondered if he'd come up with a plan for her baptism. She held back her own excitement until she had made a cup of tea, and then she could not keep it under control any longer.

"So, have you come up with a solution, Reverend Holly?"

The Vicar placed his cup on the floor before responding.

"You know what, Georgie, I think I have. It's a bit adventurous so I don't know if you'll like it, but it would make such an impact. It's so different from what people will expect."

Georgie started to fidget in her seat in anticipation.

"Oh, do tell me. I can't stand the suspense."

"How would you feel if we did the baptism in Ullswater Lake?"

"What, in the Lake itself?"

"Yes, in the Lake itself. It's only nine miles from here and easy to get to on the train," said the beaming young Vicar.

Georgie was stunned into silence at first, but the more she thought about it, the more exciting a prospect it became.

"When I was little, while my real dad, Alfie, was still around, we went to a beach at Ullswater Lake. It was one of the happiest days of my childhood and I've never forgotten it. Maybe my dad will remember it too and decide to come to my baptism."

A momentary sadness hung over Georgie, and she knew that Reverend Holly had noticed.

"Georgie, if the idea makes you feel sad, then we don't have to do it. We can think again and come up with something that you're more comfortable with."

Instantly, Georgie's eyes lit up again.

"No, it's a perfect idea. I love it and am so grateful that you thought of it. But might you not get into trouble with the bishop or someone?"

"Don't worry about that. The bishop knows me by now, so I'm sure I can persuade him what a good idea it is. Just think how many people would never walk into a church, but this way we are going out to the people just like Jesus did. And I know that lots of the congregation will love the adventure."

"That's settled then," enthused Georgie. "We just need to sort out a date."

"What about sometime during the first half of September while the weather is still warm? That will give me time to make all the necessary arrangements and will give you time to send out your invitations."

They settled on the second Sunday in September, and Georgie clapped and cheered at the thought of that day less than three months ahead, prompting Reverend Holly to laugh and join in.

"I'm going to invite my mother, sister and brother. I know my mother is unlikely to come without my stepfather, but I'm going to pray about it every day and ask God to work a miracle."

Georgie noticed Reverend Holly had become pensive.

"What's the matter? Have I said something wrong?"

"No, of course not, Georgie. Your self-esteem must be really low for you to immediately think that."

"I know. I try to be more self-confident but it's so hard to change something that's so deeply entrenched in me. But why did you go quiet?"

"You are so direct, Georgie. I love that about you."

Georgie blushed.

"I went quiet because I was wondering if you've ever considered forgiving your stepfather. That way, you could put that episode of your life behind you and move on more easily."

Georgie was shocked at the Vicar's words. As she considered this, she felt anger rise up inside her.

"If you'd ever suffered at the hands of someone like that monster, you wouldn't be asking me to forgive him. He took away my innocence and stole my childhood. He was the cause of my mother kicking me out when I was only twelve. If it wasn't for him, I would never have ended up in a brothel in London. Forgive him? Never. I'd rather see him dead."

"I understand why you feel that way, Georgie, but all the time you're letting him negatively impact your life, you're denying yourself the opportunity of freedom from the hurt of what he did to you."

"Well, to forgive someone, they have to say sorry first, and he will never say sorry. I know that for sure."

"Have you ever thought of asking him?"

Georgie hesitated.

"No. I never want to see him again so why would I ask him anything? And why are you going on about it? Gerald is a wicked, wicked man who deserves to go to Hell when he dies. I don't want to forgive him. I want him to suffer for eternity. He deserves nothing less."

"But Jesus died on the cross for everyone, Georgie, including Gerald. God loves him as much as He loves you."

Reverend Holly's words took Georgie straight back to her time at Geltsdale, the children's home where she and Daisy had spent such a happy time whilst their mother was in hospital recovering from her second breakdown. Georgie pictured herself sitting at the feet of Matron Betty's father, Reverend James, listening with the other children to his Bible story about Zacchaeus. She remembered him telling her that Jesus loved Gerald just the same as He loved Zacchaeus, and she could remember challenging that fact. Now here she was eleven years later, listening to Reverend Holly saying exactly the same thing. Was she going to challenge it again?

"I'm not sure I can cope with that idea, Reverend Holly."

"I know it's hard, but it's not just an idea, Georgie, it's a fact. I'm sorry I've upset you but I'm honestly just thinking of your future wellbeing. Anyway, I'll leave it with you, but you don't need to worry about it. You've got all the positive things about your future baptism to think about."

Georgie smiled. She couldn't feel angry with this man for long. She knew that he was only trying to do his best by her. She'd take his advice and focus on her baptism and the invitation letters she would need to write. If her mother decided to come to her baptism, then she'd think about forgiving Gerald after that.

Within the week, Georgie had written several invitations. She had spent a long time identifying all the positive influences in her life and trying to focus on the good times rather than the bad. She remembered the affection her mother had shown her when she was a small child, even after Alfie had gone when she must have been broken-hearted. Georgie even started to recall the good times she had enjoyed with Gerald and

405

the fun they'd had with their play fights in the garden. The more she thought about it, the more she realised how kind, loving and supportive he had been before and during the time her mother was in hospital after Daisy was born. The picture of them looking after her baby sister together brought a warmth back into her heart that had been completely eroded away by his subsequent actions. What had changed him from a happy, loving, and devoted stepfather, into a rapist? Was it an illness? Had something similar happened to him as a child? Could Georgie ever bring herself to forgive him as Reverend Holly had suggested? She pushed that thought from her mind as her memories moved on to her lovely friends, Pattie and Robert in their shop in Ousby and on those Saturday evenings they'd played boxed games and laughed a lot. She remembered the way they had loved her, supported her, and always believed in her. She wondered how Robert was coping without his beloved Pattie by his side. Her sadness at Pattie's shock death hit her as she remembered the way, despite his loss, Robert had unselfishly provided the support she'd needed when her mother had kicked her out. Then her thoughts moved on to her father. She didn't really want to focus on Alfie's rejection because it still hurt her, so she consciously thought back to when he was still part of her's and her mother's lives and had shown them so much love. She thought about Daisy, the little sister who she still adored. She remembered how much Daisy had loved her to read the dancer book to her, and fleetingly wondered where that precious little book was now. She knew that even without the book, her intention to become a dancer was still as strong as it had ever been, maybe even more so after singing that hymn the first time she had gone to church. She remembered the day her and Daisy had been taken to Geltsdale, both feeling lost and confused, with Georgie taking on her protective big sister role even when she, herself, needed protection. She still felt the joy of that happy place where they were given nothing but real love and support by Matron Betty, Aunty Bella and Auntie Joan, especially Auntie Joan who had taken her to dancing classes to nurture her life's ambition. She smiled to herself as a picture of her dance teachers, Mr and Mrs Trimfit, came into her mind and she realised for the first time how perfectly their name fitted their appearance. Georgie wondered what had become of her best friend at Geltsdale, Helena, and Helena's little brother, Geoffrey, who Daisy got on so well with. She instinctively touched her wrist where the pretty bracelet, a birthday present from Helena, had sat until it got lost with all her other precious possessions. Then there was Sergeant Carter and PC Sandy Bell who had believed her when even her own mother didn't. They had played such an important role in her life by ensuring that a case was built against Gerald

at a time when, she now realised, children in the same position as she, had usually been disbelieved and very seldom protected. The Sergeant and PC had gone that extra mile to ensure Georgie was protected from Gerald by putting her in the care of the lovely Auntie Val and Uncle Cedric, and not just the first time but also when she returned to Penrith after escaping the brothel and the scary Mr G. As she thought about her escape, Beverly entered Georgie's mind. If it hadn't been for Beverly doing the work that God had given her, Georgie would most likely still have been trapped in that awful place. She continued to think about her entire London experience and her life before the brothel when she had almost managed to start on her road to a dancing career. She thought with affection of the fatherly manager of St Martin's Theatre, Mr Blazenhill, who had provided her with her first job, and Bill the milkman who had introduced her to Rosie, the waitress, who got her an extra job in the café that came with a flat share.

Then Georgie's mind turned to the darker part of her life in London, when Derek Dewar, the manager of the Palace Theatre, had tricked her into moving into his flat and then attempted to molest her. Did he still have her dancer book? Then there was Teresa, the girl who'd said she'd get Georgie a job and somewhere to live, but ended up getting her embroiled in the world of prostitution via the frightening Mr G. Did Teresa do that on purpose? Did she get paid for tricking young, naïve women like Georgie? Georgie decided not to continue thinking about that part of her life. Those people certainly had not had a positive influence on her. She forced herself to think about the here-and-now, her funny little manager, Prudence, her good friends, Marilyn and Elsa, and of course the exuberant Reverend Holly.

When all of Georgie's invitations had been written and put in the post, her excitement began to intensify. She tried to imagine what it would be like if everyone she'd invited turned up. Would the staff at Geltsdale manage to contact Helena and her brother? Would the same staff even be working there now? Would her friends from London be able to afford or even want to travel all the way to Ullswater Lake? Would her family just ignore the invitations?

'Suppose none of them come? Will I be able to cope with the disappointment? Will the day be ruined?'

Georgie knew she had two months until the big day in September. She decided she needed to distract herself to stop her constant worrying. Her

mind turned to her longed-for dancing career. She found that she no longer wanted that career to involve theatres. She wanted to keep the stability in her life that she had found in Penrith, and she knew that theatre work would involve lots of travel. She felt certain that she was supposed to be a dancer, especially since singing 'The Lord of the Dance' on her first visit to church, but she had no idea how God might want her to use that skill. She spoke to God about it during her daily prayers and regularly read her Bible looking for guidance. She soon realised that, as she needed to pay her rent, she would have to continue to work. The only way forward that Georgie could see, was to look for evening dance classes. On the very day that she made that decision, she opened her Bible at Psalm 149. When she came to verse 3, she read the words, 'Let them praise his name in the dance...' They seemed to jump out at her from the page. She knew instinctively that God was speaking to her and telling her to pursue her ambition.

On her Wednesday afternoon off, Georgie went to the library to try to discover if there were dance classes in the area. To her amazement, she found that there were classes held in her very own church hall and these were run by an older member of the congregation, a Miss Amy Celeste. So, on the following Sunday after church, she asked Marilyn to point out the lady to her and approached her as she was standing in the queue to say goodbye to Reverend Holly. The dance teacher was tall, slim and in her sixties, with grey hair pulled back into a French pleat.

"Hello. I believe you are Miss Celeste. My name is Georgie."

Miss Celeste put out her hand to shake Georgie's.

"Oh, please call me Amy, Dear. I've seen you in church, but you've always been surrounded by friends, so I've never had the chance to speak to you. I'm so glad to have the opportunity at last."

"I believe you run dance classes here in the church hall and I was wondering if you have an adults' class?" asked Georgie.

"I do indeed, Georgie. Are you a dancer?"

"It's what I've always wanted to do for a career, Amy, but things haven't worked out for me so far, apart from some lessons I had when I was about seven. The dance teachers said that I was a natural but I'm not quite sure what that meant."

"I run my adult classes three evenings a week on Mondays, Wednesdays and Fridays. Why don't you come along and see how you get on?"

"What sort of dancing do you teach?" asked Georgie.

"Some ballet and some modern."

Georgie wasn't quite sure if she was up to learning ballet and didn't really know what modern dancing meant. Was it ballroom dancing or what? She decided to give it a try and arranged to attend her first class the following evening. She felt excited at the prospect of her new adventure and wondered what God had in mind for her in the long-term.

CHAPTER 41

July - August 1964

Karl

Georgie stood inside the doorway of the church hall and surveyed the twenty or so people sitting on chairs in front of Amy Celeste listening intently to what she was saying. Georgie felt a little nervous until Amy caught sight of her and beckoned her over to join in. One of the young men stood up and lifted a chair from the stack in the corner, putting it beside his own for Georgie to sit on. She nodded her thanks as she sat down. Amy continued.

"So, as I was saying, the first half of the lesson will include our loosening up exercises, after which I have a couple of new ballet steps to teach you. Then after the break, we will have a time of free expression, which I hope you will enjoy."

Amy then looked over at the young man next to Georgie.

"Karl, can I ask you to show our new pupil, Georgie, the ropes for the evening, please?"

Karl, a dark-haired slim young man of a similar age to Georgie and with striking blue eyes, nodded and smiled at her as Amy proceeded with her welcome.

"It's Georgie's first time with us so I know you'll all make her feel welcome."

Most of the other people turned and waved or said hello to Georgie, who found herself feeling momentarily shy until Karl touched her arm to gain her attention.

"Do you have any ballet shoes, Georgie?"

"No, I'm afraid I don't. Amy invited me to come along to see if I might enjoy the lessons, so I thought I'd wait and see."

"Very wise, and I see you're wearing plimsoles which will be fine for the warm-up exercises. I believe Amy keeps a cardboard box full of used ballet shoes that people have donated, so you might find a pair your size in there that you can borrow."

Georgie hadn't seen Amy approaching, cardboard box in hand.
"What shoe size are you, Georgie?" she asked, making both her and Karl jump.

Georgie and Karl giggled.
"We didn't realise you were behind us, Amy," explained Karl.

"I thought I'd just keep you on your toes," grinned Amy, joining in with the other two's laughter as they saw the joke.

"I take size five, Amy," said Georgie as the dance teacher searched through the ballet shoes, each pair being held together with an elastic band.

Soon Georgie was standing in her shorts and t-shirt, wearing her borrowed ballet shoes. She was pleased she'd thought of wearing shorts under her miniskirt so she could just take off the skirt to enable her to move more freely. The exercises consisted of lots of stretching, which Georgie found quite demanding and screwed up her eyes and nose as she did her best to get into the positions that Amy was demonstrating. Karl noticed and smiled.

"You're going to feel that tomorrow, Georgie, but it's the price you pay to improve your fitness and flexibility. Give it a couple of weeks and you won't even feel it."

Georgie grimaced at Karl but warmed to him as she continued to attempt a stretching position until she giggled as she lost her balance and almost toppled over. When it came to learning some steps, however, she caught on quickly and managed them almost as well as the other pupils. At break time most of the group crowded around Georgie, and she enjoyed being the centre of attention as they all chatted together, helping her to get to know a few of them and to begin to feel part of the group. The free expression part of the class proved to be really enjoyable. Amy told everyone that she was going to play a piece of classical music, after which she wanted them to get into groups of four and work with their group to produce a free-dance routine that interpreted the music. The portion she played was from the 1812 Overture, and when it was finished Karl took Georgie's hand, which made her stomach flip, and guided her over to a young couple, Susanne, and Brice, who agreed to make up a four with them. Fortunately for Georgie, the other three were full of ideas and soon came up with a routine, agreeing each of their parts and instructing Georgie as to the simple movements that she needed to execute. Amy then called the rehearsals to a halt and told the groups in what order they would perform their routines. Georgie was relieved that her group was first as it meant that she would not have time to forget her moves. Everyone else grabbed a chair and sat down to watch the first routine. Karl squeezed Georgie's hand which gave her a warm feeling inside and increased her confidence. Amy put the music on, and they were off. Everyone in the group managed to perform their parts well and Georgie felt relieved and exhilarated when the rest of the groups spontaneously burst into applause. She realised that it was the applause that she had always yearned for, and it made no difference that they weren't in a theatre. She also realised that she was looking for Karl's approval too, and she was pleased when he patted her on her back and smiled. After having watched the performance of all the groups, Amy gave her critique and then gave each group a mark out of ten. Georgie was delighted when her group was put in second place. She had hoped that her lack of experience wouldn't be a hindrance to Karl, Susanne, and Brice, and they certainly seemed pleased with the outcome. Karl gave her a hug and hung on for a little longer than he needed to. Georgie returned the hug and enjoyed the body contact.

After the class, Karl suggested that all four of them went out for a drink to celebrate, and they all agreed, Georgie feeling a zing of excitement that this attractive and warm young man seemed to want to spend time with her, be it in a group. Karl took Georgie's hand for the five-minute walk to the local public house, and they were all chatting and laughing even before they entered. Karl ordered the drinks, Georgie choosing a lemonade as she'd never drunk alcohol before, and they spent a happy hour enjoying each other's company. When it was time to leave, Karl offered to walk Georgie home, and she readily accepted. It seemed natural to Georgie for him to again take her hand as they strolled along together happily chatting away about all sorts of things. Georgie found herself enjoying the warmth and sharp mind of this attractive young man. Each time that they looked at each other, she noticed how alluring and attractive his blue eyes were and enjoyed the butterflies in her stomach that were set in motion as a result. When they got to Georgie's cottage, Karl leant forward and kissed her cheek. Georgie blushed. Karl grinned and pulled her closer, all the time looking into her clear eyes.

"May I kiss you on the lips, Georgie?" Karl asked hesitantly.

She nodded earnestly and as his lips touched hers, she felt a spark of excitement, which steadily increased as his kiss became deeper. Then it occurred to Georgie that Karl might be expecting more from her than a kiss, and the thought of the brothel jumped uninvited into her mind. She instantly pulled away, leaving Karl looking confused.

"Are you scared of me, Georgie?" he asked quietly.

"No, no it's not that, it's something that happened to me in the past."

"Okay. But I would never hurt you or force you into anything."

Georgie was touched by his gentleness and sensitivity.

"I know. Take no notice of me. Maybe I'll tell you about it sometime but not right now."

Karl hugged Georgie and after a smile and a quick peck on the cheek, told her he hoped she would come to the dance classes the next week.

"Definitely," said Georgie as she waved him goodbye and unlocked her front door to be greeted by Scamp. She felt as if she was walking on air

as she went into the kitchen to make herself some hot chocolate and feed the cat. She also felt a little apprehensive. She'd only felt that spark of excitement once before in her life with Derek Dewar, and that had ended in disaster. It seemed to her that young men were only interested in one thing, and she wasn't interested in that after her experiences in the brothel. Even Gerald had obviously had only that one thing on his mind. Was that how men demonstrated their love for you, even when you were a child? Was that how they expected Georgie to show she was attracted to them? Georgie felt confused. She really didn't know what to think. She knew for certain that the men who'd paid for her services at the brothel were not showing their feelings for her. They were merely wanting to satisfy their needs and using her to do it. Georgie didn't know what to think. This world was very confusing for her. The only thing she knew for sure was that God's love for her was pure, and she could trust Him completely. She didn't know if she could ever really trust any man. She put that thought to one side and concentrated on stroking Scamp, who had settled herself comfortably on her mistress's lap as Georgie sipped the remainder of her bedtime drink. She knew she needed to sleep now if she was to give of her best to Pru and the shop the following day.

July sped by so quickly that Georgie couldn't believe it. It was the middle of August when it came to her that there was only one month to go until her baptism. She had been meeting with Reverend Holly on a weekly basis in the church office and he was teaching her about the meaning of baptism and being an active member of the church. She was soaking it all up thirstily, wanting to show God she meant business and she would be there to do whatever He wanted her to do to bring others to Him so that they, too, would be saved.

She had been going to dance classes regularly each Monday evening and was thoroughly enjoying the new experience, developing her dance and creativity skills rapidly. It had become routine to go out for a drink with Karl, Susanne, and Brice after each lesson, and for Karl to walk her home afterwards. They'd gradually learned more about each other, including that he was nineteen years old and lived on the outskirts of Penrith, and she would be eighteen in November. Their kisses had grown more intense each week, and Georgie knew that she was beginning to care a lot about him, but she had resisted asking Karl in for a coffee or meeting him at any other time, even though he had invited her to go to the cinema with him. She was still unsure about how to behave or how to read Karl's motives. She was scared about the growing

intensity of her own feelings and the increasing demand she felt in Karl's kisses. She knew she was attracted to him sexually and she realised that she instinctively wanted to take their relationship to another level, but she didn't know if that was acceptable or not, and she certainly didn't want to get pregnant. Oh, how she wished she had a mum to turn to for advice. If she gave in to her and Karl's needs, would he see her as cheap? If she didn't, would he see her as frigid? This was just too much of a conundrum for her, and despite her closeness to Auntie Val, she felt too embarrassed to go to her for advice. So, she continued to hold back until after dance classes one evening towards the end of August, Karl brought up the subject.

"Georgie, do you fancy me?"

Georgie was taken aback for a moment. After all, it was usually her who was the more direct one. She flushed and looked at the floor as she spoke.

"Yes, I do fancy you."

"Then why won't you come out on a date with me?"

"For that very reason."

"What do you mean?"

"I mean that I'm not sure I could resist your advances, and I'm not sure I could risk the possible consequences of that."

"But how will we ever get to know each other better? You do want to get to know me better, don't you, Georgie?"

"Yes, I do, but there are things about me that you don't want to know, Karl."

"How do you know what I do and don't want to know? I think I love you, and I want to know everything about you – good or bad."

"No. Believe me, Karl, there are things that you really don't want to know, and that I really don't want to risk telling you. I know that if I do, I will lose you, and I don't want that."

415

"Don't you trust me?"

"I think I do, but to be honest, I'm not sure that I can trust any man fully."

Karl thought about her answer for a minute.

"I see. I think that means that you have been let down or treated wrongly by a man or men in the past. But please believe me when I say that nothing in your past will put me off you, Georgie. What's in the past has gone as far as I'm concerned. I just know that it is you now, in the present, that I've grown very fond of. The past doesn't come into it."

"Oh, believe me it does, Karl. It will definitely turn you off me, I promise."

"How does that work as far as God's concerned, then? You tell me you love Him, and He loves you, and that you are being baptised next month to show that. How come you can accept that God loves you, despite whatever is in your past, but you can't accept that your past doesn't matter to me? I don't get it."

"The reason God loves me is because his Son, Jesus, died on a cross to take away all the wrong things I've done. So, God doesn't see those things. He just sees my heart. You, however, would see those things if I told you about them, and you would definitely find them unacceptable."

"Well okay. Have it your way. But if you are falling in love with me, and I think you are, you're going to have to tell me some time. However, I'm a patient man and I can wait. Time is on our side. You're stuck with me, Georgie."

They both hugged and Karl hung on to Georgie a little longer than usual before he said goodbye. Georgie felt more affection for him at that moment than she'd ever done before. She had to admit that she was frightened, and she didn't know what to do. She was absolutely convinced that if she told him about her having been a prostitute, he would shy away from her in disgust. The thought of it was just too painful to contemplate. She'd put it to the back of her mind and focus on her upcoming baptism.

Over the next two weeks, things continued between Georgie and Karl as if that conversation had never taken place. They enjoyed their dance lessons and their time in the pub with Susanne and Brice. They kissed

and cuddled as usual when Karl walked her home afterwards. On the last Monday evening before Georgie's baptism, she asked Karl if he was going to be there.

"I'm not sure I understand about religious stuff, but yes, I'll be there. I would not miss it because I know for certain now that I love you, Georgie. I want to spend the rest of my life with you, and if I'm going to do that, I need to understand everything about you."

Georgie was touched by Karl's words and at that moment, wished that she didn't have a past that she needed to keep secret. She told Karl the time and location of her baptism and they both held each other close before he turned to go. He had only walked a few steps when Georgie spoke.

"Karl, for what it's worth, I love you, too."

"Woohoo!" Karl exclaimed as he took a leap and punched the air with his fists just like he'd scored a goal.

He turned and leapt back into Georgie's arms, encircling her in his hug and kissing her deeply before she could even take a breath. Then without another word he went running off, leaping into the air and cheering as he went, leaving Georgie standing outside the cottage in fits of laughter. She knew she loved everything about this young man, including his enthusiasm and sense of humour. She also realised that she had learned to trust him. As she let herself in through the front door, it suddenly occurred to her what she'd done.

'Oh dear. He's going to expect me to tell him about my past now. I wonder how that's going to pan out.'

Georgie wondered if the trust she had for Karl would stand the test of her being completely open about her history. She went to bed that night amidst a confusion of feelings. She was both ecstatic and scared, happy and worried all at the same time.

417

CHAPTER 42

September 1964

The baptism

It was Sunday 13th September 1964. Georgie was wearing a long white dress with a weighted hem as she stood beside Reverend Holly who was wearing his black robe, a pair of green wellington boots and his dog collar. They were on the grass slope behind the beach facing the backs of the gathering crowd below them. The warm sun was glinting on the surface of Ullswater Lake and reflecting onto the beach that Georgie had visited many years before with her mum and real dad. All Georgie could see were black silhouettes. She had made the conscious decision not to look at who was present until after she was baptised, lest she be disappointed.

The choir struck up with 'Lord of the dance' which caused Georgie's stomach to flip. Reverend Holly turned towards Georgie.

"You ready?" he asked with an encouraging smile on his face.

Georgie nodded. Reverend Holly took her elbow and led her forward down the grass slope and through the crowd that parted to make way for them. Georgie kept her eyes to the front, trying to swallow the lump in

418

her throat that felt like her thumping heart. When they reached the front of the crowd, Elsa and Marilyn were waiting and took their places either side of Georgie. Reverend Holly continued a few steps closer to the edge of the lake before he turned to face the crowd. As the choir sung the last verse, Marilyn, who was holding a large white towel in one hand, squeezed Georgie's arm with her other hand. Georgie turned to smile at her friend, inclining her head to touch Marilyn's as a gesture of affection. She then repeated the action with Elsa.

The choir finished singing and a few seconds of expectant silence followed before Reverend Holly addressed the crowd.

"I want to give you all a very warm welcome to this very special – and different - baptismal service today."

Again, a few seconds of silence as the smiling vicar looked around, making eye contact where he could.

"We are here because Georgie wants everyone to know she has given her life to the Lord, our Heavenly Father who gave His only son, Jesus to die so we could be saved. When the Man, Jesus was on this earth, He was baptised by total immersion in the River Jordan by his cousin, John the Baptist. Georgie wants to follow the Jesus' example by being baptised in the same way. This, of course, is not the River Jordan, Ladies and Gentlemen, but it's the closest we can get to it here in Cumberland."

A ripple of laughter spread across the crowd as Reverend Holly allowed another few seconds before he continued by explaining what was about to happen.

Georgie had chosen the hymns for the service, which had been printed onto hymn sheets for everyone who attended. As the choir began to sing the hymn, 'Just as I am…' Georgie's heart began to beat rapidly. This was the cue for Reverend Holly to enter the water, followed by Georgie.

By the end of the third verse, they were both in place. Reverend Holly with a deacon beside him, and Georgie standing sideways on to him with her hands in the praying position. The choir stopped singing and the crowd on the beach was silent. Even though they were in the open air, the atmosphere was electric. Georgie was trembling, and Reverend Holly squeezed her hands and whispered a word of encouragement.

"This is it, Georgie, the moment you've been waiting for. Enjoy."

Georgie smiled as Reverend Holly, speaking as loudly as he could so that everyone on the beach could hear him, said,

"I baptise you, Georgie, in the name of God the Father, God the Son and God the Holy Spirit."

The choir started to sing.

Just as I am, poor, wretched, blind
Sight, riches, healing of the mind
Yea, all I need, in Thee to find
O Lamb of God, I come, I come!

Georgie lifted her chin proudly and felt the peace and joy surge into her heart as she went under the water and emerged with that shining smile on her face that had first made her want to have God in her heart. As the choir continued with the last verse, Reverend Holly, helped by his deacon, supported Georgie to walk out of the water and onto the beach where Marilyn was waiting to wrap her in the huge white towel and wipe the drips from Georgie's face. As Georgie turned to thank her, she noticed that just as many drips in the form of tears needed to be wiped from Marilyn's face, and without thinking she wrapped her towel-clad self around her friend in a big hug. She heard some giggles coming from those on the beach who had noticed that she had made poor Marilyn even wetter than she had been before the hug. It was then that Georgie looked up and gasped in shock and surprise. Standing right at the front of the crowd was her mum, her sister, Daisy, and her brother, John. All three had tears trickling down their faces, even the eleven-year-old, red-haired John who was clearly doing his best to appear to be in manly control of himself. It was all Georgie could do to prevent herself running straight over to her beautiful thirteen-year-old sister, Daisy, and pulling her into a loving embrace. But Georgie was aware that this was the moment at which she needed to give her testimony as to why she had been baptised. She took a deep breath, but as she did so, she noticed an old slightly bent over man in the crowd smiling at her broadly and she immediately realised that it was Robert. The deep breath that she'd taken just a second ago, seemed to dissipate and she found herself unable to speak, especially when she realised that a slightly older looking Aunty Joan from the children's home was standing next to Robert, and beside her stood her lovely, long-ago friend Helena, all grown up but

420

unmistakably the giver of that precious hand-made bracelet at her seventh birthday party on the day before she and Daisy had left Geltsdale eleven years ago.

Georgie realised then that the crowd were all standing in an expectant silence, so she decided to stop looking for who was there, but instead lifted her eyes to look at the trees behind the beach and cleared her throat.

"The first few years of my life were the happiest that I can remember thanks to my lovely mum, who devoted her whole energy into loving me. It was during those years that I received a book from Santa Claus about a dancer. I loved that book and from that moment on my one aim in life was to become a dancer. Sadly, things went wrong, and I eventually found myself in London trying to find a way of pursuing my longed-for dancing career. I met some lovely and caring people there who made my life happy and fulfilled for many months but, again things went wrong. Something happened that shattered my life into tiny pieces, and I ended up in the worst place that I could ever have imagined. I was beaten up and abused and spent many months being made to do things that I wouldn't even want to tell you about. I think I was as far away from God as anyone could get. But looking back, I realise that God had never left me. He had plans to get me away to safety through one of his followers, Beverly, who befriended me and organised and funded my escape. For that I shall be forever grateful. Anyway, I got back to Cumberland safely and God continued to care for me even though I didn't know it at the time. He gave me a lovely place to stay, with loving people, Aunty Val and Uncle Cedric, to care for me. He gave me my perfect job in a shop and then led me to my present beautiful little home where I live with my cat, Scamp."

Georgie dared to look back at the crowd in front of her at that point and could see many grins as she mentioned her cat. However, she forced herself not to focus on any one individual, but to look back up at the trees before she continued.

"Then one day, several months after I had returned to Penrith, I was clearing out my handbag when I found a piece of paper that Beverly had given me with her address written on it on the day of my escape. Somehow, I had completely forgotten about it. I had even forgotten to write to Beverly to let her know I was safe. How selfish of me was that? But then I turned over the piece of paper and on the back was written a

Bible text, which I will never forget. It was from Psalm twenty-seven and verse six, and it said,

Though my father and mother forsake me, the LORD will receive me.

At that point, Georgie suddenly realised how insensitive of her it was to relate that text with her mother present. But it was too late, she'd done it and knew she would have to concentrate on the rest of her testimony if she was to get through it. So, she took another breath and continue.

"I'd paid little attention to God during my life, except for at the bad times when I'd instinctively prayed for help. But that text made me search for God, and what better place to look for Him but in a church. So, I went to my nearest church, which happened to be the one where Reverend Holly was the vicar."

As she said this, she looked sideways toward Reverend Holly and gave him a broad smile which he returned.

"The first thing I noticed when I went inside this church was the warmth and friendliness. Lots of smiling people turned to wave and greet me. But it was their smiles that I noticed most. It was as if those smiles were shining with love. I instinctively felt that I wanted whatever they had got. Then we stood to sing the first hymn. It was a new hymn written only a couple of years ago, and Reverend Holly explained that it was written as if Jesus was telling His own story. As I listened to the words, all I heard was 'I am Lord of the dance.' It was as if Jesus was talking directly to me, letting me know that he knew I'd always wanted to be a dancer. I don't mind telling you, it took my breath away, the fact that Jesus knew even that about me. I couldn't sing that hymn, but I was left in no doubt that Jesus knew me, and it left me with plenty of questions that I wanted to get answers to. The person sitting beside me on that day, who is now my very good friend, Marilyn, listened to my questions, and despite having never met me before, she cared enough to introduce me to Reverend Holly, who she knew would be able to answer all of them. And he did. Every week he came to my cottage for his regular grilling, and every week I learned a little more about how God sent his only son, Jesus Christ, to die for me – well, not just me – He died for all of us – you included."

Georgie paused, looked at the crowd and then quickly looked away again.

"Then another good friend, Elsa, invited me to go along to a baptismal service at her daughter's church in Carlisle. I was interested to see a baptism by total immersion, but little did I know about the impact it was to have on me. As I watched each of the three young people emerge from the water after they were baptised, I saw that shining smile again. Only this time, the light from those smiles could only be described as radiant – as if they were full of a love so intense that it glowed. That glowing love entered my heart that day. It was sort of like I'd been struck by lightning. I hope that you have seen that light shining out of my smile today, and if it has struck you like lightning, please know that God loves you despite anything you may have done wrong in the past. Jesus died for you just as He died for me. You can know God's forgiveness and love just as I do. I am standing here as proof that with God anything is possible, and despite a broken past, the shattered pieces of your life can still shine."

Then as Georgie turned away, she remembered one more thing that she wanted to say.

"Oh, by the way, I forgot to say that although my precious childhood book about a dancer got lost while I was in London, my lifelong wish to become a dancer remained and is well on its way to being achieved. Well, that's to say I'm at least back taking dance lessons again, and who knows where that will lead?"

Everyone laughed as she handed over to Reverend Holly, who announced the last hymn, at which point the choir struck up with the first verse of 'Lord of the Dance' again and there was lots of clearing of throats and wiping of eyes as everyone joined in. The singing gradually increased in intensity as everyone got into the swing of it, and by the time it came to an end, it was the loudest that Georgie had ever heard.

"Thank you, every one of you, for coming to support Georgie today. I know she will want to come and greet each of you herself, and while she is doing that, there are some light refreshments for everyone, that some of the ladies of the church have kindly brought with them today. You'll find a table at the back of the beach just behind the choir, so do please help yourselves."

At that, everyone burst into spontaneous applause and then started to mill around chatting with each other.

Georgie walked towards her mother, sister, and brother. Daisy ran to meet her, and the two sisters hung on to each other as if they were scared to let go. They laughed and cried as they looked into each other's smiling eyes and returned to their hug. Eventually they let go and Georgie noticed her little brother standing behind Daisy. He had been so little when she had left Ousby that he could not possibly have recognised her, but he half smiled and put out his hand to shake hers. Georgie laughed but was having none of it. She grabbed him towards her and hugged him affectionately, feeling him stiffen. When she let go, she looked at him and smiled.

"Sorry, John, I know you can't possibly remember me but today of all days, I can't help but hug everyone in sight."

He looked embarrassed but said in a small voice, "That's okay" and turned to walk towards his mother.

Georgie's eyes followed him until she looked straight into the face of her mother. She felt a little awkward, remembering the last time they had seen each other on the day that her mother had kicked her out of the house. It was now Georgie's mum who made the first move by opening her arms and saying to Georgie, "Come here, Babe." No better words could have left her lips. It took Georgie straight back to her three-year-old self when Mummy had always affectionately called her Babe. In a split second they were in each other's arms, deep, healing sobs emanating from them both. It was several minutes before either of them could find their voice.

"Mum, I've missed you so much."

"I've missed you, too, Georgie."
"You came. I didn't really think you would. But where's Gerald?"

Her mum kept her hands on Georgie's arms as she spoke. Georgie could feel them trembling.

"Gerald is in prison, Babe. He did to Daisy what he'd done to you, and this time I caught him. I'm so sorry for not believing you, my darling Georgie. I have felt so bad since I realised that you were telling the truth all the way along, and I didn't believe you."

Mum's voice cracked as she said these words, and Georgie, spontaneously forgiving her, pulled her back into another embrace. As she did so, she turned to Daisy with an empathetic look, and her sister acknowledged the look, conveying to Georgie through her expression that she was okay now.

"It's in the past now, Mum. You're here and that's all that matters. Now I've got to go and say hello to my other guests, so I'll just have a quick chat with Daisy before I do that. Why don't you and John go and get some refreshments and Daisy can join you in a moment. I'll see you a little later."

Mum and John smiled and walked towards the back of the beach, as Georgie turned to her sister.

"Daisy, are you okay? I always hoped that Gerald wouldn't start on you. I feel so guilty for not staying to protect you. I'm so, so sorry."

Daisy said nothing but stepped forward and embraced her big sister.

"Don't feel guilty, Georgie. It wasn't your fault but now's not the time to talk about that. This is your day, and it should be a happy day. We'll have plenty of time to talk about all that in the future. Right now, I want to give you this gift that I found in the bookshop in Penrith. It reminded me of you and the lovely times I remember as a child when you read it to me so often. I'm so glad I decided to buy it for you since you mentioned that you lost the original one in London."

As Daisy handed Georgie the wrapped gift, Georgie couldn't believe what she was hearing. Could it really be what she hoped it was? She tore the wrapping off to find a copy of the same dancer book that she had treasured during her childhood and that had not only given her and her siblings so much pleasure but had been the trigger for her lifelong dream. Her tears were now flowing freely as she looked at Daisy's face to discover tears running down hers, too.

"Let me hang on to it while you say hello to everyone, Georgie. I'll look after it till you've finished."

Georgie nodded. She could find no words to adequately express her feelings at that moment as she stood there watching her sister move away towards her mum and brother.

For the next hour Georgie greeted and chatted with all those who'd responded to her invitation - Robert who despite his apparent frailty, gave her the biggest hug she could have hoped for; Aunty Joan who apologised for Matron Betty's and Aunty Bella's absence.

"Well, someone had to stay and look after the children at Geltsdale, didn't they?" she quipped.

Georgie and Helena then hugged and spent several minutes catching up on each other's news. Helena said she and Geoffrey had been adopted together by a lovely couple who lived in Carlisle, and they still lived at home with their new mum and dad. Helena went on to say that she was engaged to be married to a handsome lad, called Patrick, and the wedding was fixed for spring 1965.

"Ooh, you can be my bridesmaid, Georgie," Helena screeched excitedly.

"Wow, yes please, can I really?" said Georgie grabbing hold of Helena's hands and jumping up and down.

She then moved on to Auntie Val and Uncle Cedric who hugged her affectionately and congratulated her on her testimony. Georgie pointed out her mum who was politely chatting with Reverend Holly.

"Would you mind introducing yourselves to my mum when Reverend Holly has finished, please, Auntie Val. I don't want her to feel left out."

"Course we will, Lass. It'll be a pleasure."

As Auntie Val and Uncle Cedric moved away from her, Georgie saw a young lady out of the corner of her eye. She was standing with Karl, and Georgie immediately recognised her, rushing over as fast as her long white dress and large towel would allow her.

"Beverly!" she shouted as she approached. "Oh, Beverly you came all that way from London," and she leapt towards the young lady pulling her into such a big hug that she nearly knocked Beverly off her feet.

"I wouldn't have missed it for the world, Georgie, came the muffled response from inside the towel-lined hug. "And not just me, guess who I found and brought with me."

426

Georgie looked up from the hug and saw standing just behind Beverly, Rosie from the café. Rosie's face almost cracked open as that same old broad smile spread across her face.

"Lovely to see you, Georgie Girl," she exclaimed in her broad cockney accent, just before Georgie screeched and grabbed her into the hug with Beverly.

"Oh, I'm so happy to see you both," said Georgie breathlessly. "This is just the happiest day of my life."

As Georgie moved out of the hug, it felt like the most natural thing in the world to slip her hand into Karl's as all three stood there chatting and laughing.

"I'm so happy for you Georgie," said Karl as he moved hand in hand with Georgie through the rest of the crowd. Most were members of Georgie's church but also Sergeant Carter and PC Sandy Bell, who she greeted and received hugs and kisses from. As Georgie led Karl towards her family, he asked her a question.

"Did everyone you invited come along, Georgie?"

"Well, they either came themselves or sent their apologies. That is except one. But I suppose that was too much to hope for."

"Who's that?"

"My dad, Alfie. But do you know what, I find that it really doesn't bother me. I have enough love around me right now to keep me going for the rest of life."

"You sure do," said Karl as he placed one arm around Georgie's shoulders and prepared to meet her family.

THE END

MEET THE AUTHOR, GLORIA EVELEIGH

Hello. I hope you enjoyed my book. I'd like to tell you a little about myself: I live on England's south coast but was born in South London just after the second world war. I was the victim of familial child sexual, physical, and psychological abuse until I was fourteen. At that time, child abuse was hidden, not believed, and not acknowledged so it resulted in an emotional life sentence for the victim. However, as an adult, I managed to turn that around, but it was a long journey, which left me with little confidence and no self-esteem. Initially, I opted for a career as a research scientist, which enabled me to hide behind a microscope, but as time went on, my confidence improved and eventually I became a social worker, specialising in safeguarding. I was determined to turn around the negative experiences of my childhood to help other abuse victims and survivors. This inspired me to write my award-winning memoir to reassure other survivors that there is hope of recovery.

The book you have just read is my first fiction novel. I was inspired to write it because of my passion for keeping abuse high on the public agenda. Abuse is often kept hidden by victims because of the stigma that is still attached to it, and in turn, this silence protects the abusers. My aim is to break down that invisible wall of silence so that abuse can be stopped.

I also want victims and survivors to know that, like me, they can find peace through a personal faith in God, who unconditionally understands, accepts, and loves us.

Best Wishes,

Gloria Eveleigh

IF YOU LIKED THIS BOOK, YOU MAY ALSO LIKE

'One Small Word – Surviving childhood abuse' is the first part of my memoir and reveals the lengthy and difficult experience of abuse within the home. It provides a bright glimmer of hope for victims who have not yet started on their road to recovery. Readers share the life of Frankie, a fifty-year-old social work student, and her dramatic memories of physical and sexual abuse at the hand of her father. Frankie journeys from despair to recovery, transforming into a strong woman who is able to turn the negativity of her life into positive help for others. You will experience her emotions at the time of the abuse, gain insight into how this affected her adult behaviour, and share her victory as she learned to overcome.

'No – Sequel to One Small Word' is the second part of my memoir and continues Frankie's story after the age of fifty. During her recovery, Frankie had gained some insight into managing her reactive behaviour by using the one small word, 'No' that she had used to stop the abuse as a fourteen-year-old. As she continues her life's journey, Frankie discovers just how many bullies and abusers there are in the world and finds ways to cope with and overcome the increasingly complex situations that she faces. You will experience Frankie's emotions and determination as she continues to believe in herself, build on her strengths, and celebrate her series of victories as she moves into old age.

All my books are available here:
https://www.amazon.co.uk/s?k=gloria+eveleigh&ref=nb_sb_noss

ACKNOWLEDGEMENTS

I would like to thank the members of my editorial group who supported me, corrected my grammar, and encouraged me throughout this whole journey. Without them this novel would not have been completed, so I owe each one my most sincere gratitude. Thank you, Joanie and John Wood, Lynn Hornsby, Lisa Johnson, Sandra Johnson, Katharine Miller, Janet Hooper, Ann Pither, Tony Johnson, and Alison Law.

I also want to thank Oliver Hambly, who freely shared his knowledge about train journeys, timetables, and ticket costs, bus guides and a whole lot more that helped me to ensure this story was true to its time.

Finally, I want to thank Matt Davis, Lead Pastor of Emmanuel Church in Shoreham, West Sussex. He and his friend, Timothy Jones, provided me with the information that allowed the Reverend Holly in my book to answer Georgie's most difficult questions.

TO FOLLOW ME

I would love to hear from you and send you my free bimonthly newsletter to keep you up to date with my new books. I'd also welcome you with open arms if you would like to join my online editorial group and be first to read a new book as I write it. Just go here https://www.gloriaeveleighauthor.co.uk/439985644 and scroll down to the bottom of the page to leave me a message.

PLEASE REVIEW 'SHATTERED PIECES CAN STILL SHINE – GEORGIE'S STORY

Thank you for reading my book, I hope you enjoyed it as much as I enjoyed writing it. Please will you consider leaving a review? Even just a few words would help others to decide if the book is right for them. It will also help me to improve my writing skills. I've made it super simple. Just copy and paste the link below into your browser, and you'll travel to the Amazon review page for this book where you can leave your review.
Best wishes and thank you in advance.

Gloria.

http://www.Amazon.com/gp/customer-reviews/write-a-review.html?asin=B099X4GH55

Printed in Great Britain
by Amazon